HIGHLAND EMBRACE

Catriona had had enough of Roarke's bullying, enough of his making her keep so close to the castle and his dreaming up all sorts of hobgoblins who were out to get her if she dared go out of his sight! And now the brute was proving himself not only laird of her freedom — but master of her desires as well!

"I hate ye!" she ground out against his marauding lips. "I hate ye, I do . . . !"

"Aye, lass, aye," Roarke murmured, "but nae more than I detest ye, by God —"

Roarke consumed her mouth with savage lips that owed more to fury than fancy; more to a desire to tame and dominate than any pretense at tenderness. Roughly, passionately, he plundered and kissed her inner mouth, wresting a response from her, demanding one, conjuring one, although she still struggled to deny him that victory . . .

Bold Breathless Nights

PENELOPE NERI

ZEBRA BOOKS
KENSINGTON PUBLISHING CORP.

ZEBRA BOOKS

are published by

Kensington Publishing Corp.
475 Park Avenue South
New York, NY 10016

First printing: October, 1989

Printed in the United States of America

St. Agnes's Eve,
And she was waiting
At the twelfth hour,
Anticipating
Magical predictions!

In the mirror
Smoky-swirling,
Came an image,
Silver-purling
Of the man she'd someday wed.

Tall he was,
His black hair curly,
And his eyes were
Loch-mist gray and surly
As he gazed upon her.

"Ye're no' my mon!"
She cried so coldly.
"Ye will never have nor hold me!
Fickle mirror," she vowed boldly,
"I will never be his bride!"

But his reflection
Didna vanish,
And her anger
Couldna banish it
One whit!

Instead, the image
Grew in brightness—
In her breast, a sudden tightness,
In her head, a sudden lightness
Gripped her and held sway!

She didna fear
Her father's anger,
Nor the sudden scent o' danger,
Only that this handsome stranger'd

Steal her heart away . . .

The Prophecy

The old crone and the scrawny lad squatted before the low entrance to their cave. It was a humble abode — even more humble than the crofts up on the moors where the shepherds lived, which were built of sods and wattle. Theirs was a crude shelter that time and weather had hollowed from the rolling moors, one that owed nothing to the touch of mortal hands, save for the crude door the lad had fashioned the winter before from planks of wood and leather strips shaped into hinges.

Morag, the old woman, gazed into the flames of the fire, her eyes of rheumy blue the only indication that she was not asleep, for they were wide open and staring. The soft cooing of a wood-pigeon and the chuckle of a burn repeated endlessly from beyond the blackberry-laden briars that shielded their camp, while the scent of wood-smoke from their fire filled the golden autumn evening with its pungent scent.

"Mother?" he asked. And, "Mother?" again.

There was no answer. Morag had retreated to her dreaming place, the strange place she'd told him of so many times since they brought him to her, the place where the voices of those long gone whispered in her ear and visions of things not yet come to pass moved through her mind in glowing pageants.

She had not heard him, or if she had, she'd declined to

answer. He sighed. Such was her way, when the mood took her, he had learned over the years. He had long since given off questioning her ways or trying to change her. After all, he owed her his very life. One did not question or criticize such a benefactor, especially when that benefactor could commune with the Old Ones from the pagan times before remembering when the gods were dark and bloody and ones such as Morag their priestesses.

With a shrug, the lad turned his attention elsewhere, patiently prodding at the perimeters of the fire with a sharpened stick to determine if the glowing red kindling was hot enough to cook the plump brace of salmon he'd tickled from the burn that afternoon. As he did so, he idly recalled the bonnie sight he'd seen as he lay on his belly along the grassy banks of the stream, waiting.

The hard turf had thrummed beneath his palms, warning him that a rider approached, and was not far off. He'd scrambled up onto his knees and scuttled into the cover of some bushes to hide himself, trembling violently, for 'twas the laird o' Corbin's burn in which he dabbled his paws, and poaching from a nobleman's hunting preserves or fishing in his waters was a crime punishable by death in these harsh times.

Yet he need not have feared. The rider was not one of the Gilchrist's men. In fact, the rider was not male at all, but a slender *maid,* riding acock the creamy palfrey like a man, with her skirts bunched up about her! Black hair billowed out behind her, flying wild in the wind and twining about with the white-green-and-yellow tartan folds of the *arisaid* she wore pinned at her shoulder, as if the pair engaged in some frenzied pagan dance. Her cheeks were tinged bright pink by the swipe of the autumn wind's rough tongue, their bright color lending a rare fire to her green eyes and illumining the delicate loveliness of her face.

The sight of the maid and her horse, etched in vivid colors against the fading amethyst and pink of the autumn skies, had made the breath catch in his throat, had made a peculiar tightness close about his heart like a clenched fist. Holding his breath, he'd watched as she slipped from the mare's back and led the beast to water, pressing her cheek to the rough silk of its creamy mane as it lowered its head to drink. Water had streamed in diamond ropes from the mare's muzzle. Time had seemed to still its endless march. The moment when he'd stood there, watching her for the first time, had been impossibly perfect: the last golden rays of daylight slanting down between the trees, the drowsy murmur of bees filling his ears, the sweet-thundering throb of his heart — all crystal-bright, all sharp as the stab of a dirk, all bittersweet and achingly dear as his own life. And then, just when he'd thought that nothing could ever be more perfect than it had been right there and then, a sweet, mournful singing had reached his ears. For a foolish moment, he'd wondered if 'twas the voices of the wee-folk, the faeries, he was after hearing — if all o' that wondrous moment were not some tricksy spell the faeries had woven about him — before he'd realized belatedly that the sounds were human, and that they came from her:

"For never more
The heathered glens
Will I walk wi'
My true love!" she sang in her lilting, flutelike voice.
"And never more his bonnie
Lips shall kiss.
His heart was mine,
But is nae more —
What bitter draft
Is this — !"

His eyes had filled with tears at the unbearable sweet sadness of her voice. He'd dried them on his knuckles,

9

ashamed of his weakness, but when he looked again, she had vanished, disappeared from sight like a will-o'-the-wisp, leaving only the crushed grass and late wildflowers along the banks of the burn where her horse had watered to mark her presence, the subtle residue of her perfume drifting on the air — and an image of beauty, of sadness, of innocence, burned into his soul forever. The dull ache of his love for her would never leave him, he knew, though she was as removed from him as the stars in the sky are distant from a humble clod of earth . . .

"She's not for you, my bonnie Badger!" hissed Morag sharply, cutting into his reverie. So startled was he by her sudden and startlingly accurate assessment of his thoughts, that his hand jerked. He dropped the sharpened stick, and his thumb was singed by the fire.

"Aye, I ken, Auld Mother," he agreed morosely, ashamed that his thoughts had wandered where they didna belong.

"Nay, lad, she isna, but — aye, she is a beauty, is she no'?" Morag chuckled. "And 'tis little wonder ye dream of her, my puir laddie." Her tired old eyes twinkled momentarily, then darkened with some hurtful memory. They took on their former, faraway look once again as she turned her head once more to gaze into the flames of their fire.

"The time is coming, Badger," she said softly, sadly. "The time I ha'e told ye of before this. 'Tis the year prophesied — and the coming of the long-haired star is at hand. It's dark destiny canna be halted!

"In this year, the lion of England to the south of the Scots will be crushed, brought low by the sons of the lily. Then the white rose of Erskine will rule the Borders of our northern lands no more. And yet, 'tis not the lily the clan McNair should fear, but the evil that threatens them from within our marches! 'Tis this 'twill bring them down and cast them low. An oath carelessly broken, a vengeance never taken, a grief never spilled, will see the sons of the white rose destroyed, and given to feed the worms!"

She rocked back and forth, hugging herself about bony arms as she crooned, "But for her fairest, brightest blossom, the clan McNair will wither and fade. Then will the raven's standard fly high over the Tweed waters, and he that was bastard born be laird above all!" she chanted in the singsong tone in which her voices spoke through her.

"The white rose, Mother?" the lad echoed in a horrified whisper, for the white rose had been the maid's badge.

"Aye," Morag acknowledged with a sigh.

"But then — then if 'tis as ye prophesy, the . . . the maid will also perish!" he cried.

"Och, laddie, I pray not!" Morag said with a shudder. "Is ma wee Cat not the fairest, brightest blossom o' her clan?"

"Aye, that she is," Badger agreed fervently.

"Then if the prophecy holds true, she will triumph over the evil that will destroy her people! She will survive, for she is their only hope. Through her, their clan will live on. Without her, they will vanish from the face of this earth."

"You're certain, Mother?" the lad demanded anxiously, licking his lips with apprehension. "She willna be destroyed wi' her kinsmen?"

Morag hesitated before answering him, but answer him she did, though at some length. "Nay, laddie, I am certain of naught, beyond that the sun will surely rise each morn, and set with the gloaming each even'. Beyond that, what will be, will be. We are but mortals, and can change nothing of our destiny, my son . . ."

Prologue

The keep's somber walls rose from steep black crags that hung over the torrent of the Tweed Waters. Lofty, fairytale turrets soared skyward from either end of the keep, seeming almost to scrape the dark underbelly of the sky with their spired towers.

Skirted by dark-green pine forests that mantled the length and breadth of the Vale o' the Tweed, both river and forests formed a nigh impenetrable border 'twixt southeastern Scotland and Northumbria in winter months. And, secure in her natural defenses, Erskine Keep flung her brooding challenge across the river at the Saxon south, offering mute defiance to all challengers who sought to claim her for their own.

So Erskine had stood silent guardian of the northeast borders, along with her sister-keeps of Glenmuir and Corbin, since the days of Thorwig the Red. The viking *jarl* who'd invaded these lands in the year 865 had found them much to his liking, and had seen the foundations laid for this fortress among fortresses.

Taking a Pictish chieftain's daughter as his bride, he'd begun the proud and fiercely warring line that would one day birth the present chieftain, Angus, laird of the clan McNair, master of Erskine, whose own ruddy beard and fiery locks forever marked him as Thorwig's seed.

On this bitter-cold January night in the Year of Our Lord 1066, Erskine was, for the greater part, shrouded in winter darkness. Naught but glimpses of buttery rushlight escaped the oiled skins that covered the windeyes of her great hall to betray the feasting within. On high, candle-light blazed like a beacon from only one of the two towers, its brightness vying with the radiance of Lady Moon. The light came from the spired turret where the laird of Erskine's wild and willful daughter, the lady Catriona, made her bower, yet she was not soundly slumbering in her bed this winter eve, och, no! Nor yet was she huddled about one of the blazing hearths, toasting her toes by the fire as she sipped mulled wine or warmed mead and enjoyed the yarn-spinning of the graybeards. Rather, in the company of a handful of giggling kitchen wenches and dairy maids, she was hurrying home from an illicit outing that had taken her out into the moonlit night to a snow-covered cornfield, half a league beyond Erskine's walls!

Now, much later, bidding her companions a whispered good night, which they returned with breathless giggles and murmured wishes for the same, she tugged the fringed green-and-white tartan mantle from her shoulders and shook it free of snowflakes. Smoothing down her hair, she drew a deep breath to compose herself, mustered a calm, sleepy expression, and tried to slip unnoticed through the great hall to the stairs that led up to her tower apartments. She knew only too well if her father or brothers discovered she'd been abroad without their permission, some harsh punishment would be forthcoming, And tonight, she didna want anything to stand in the way of what she meant to do!

She almost succeeded in escaping notice, too, but . . . ! Would ye not know it? Tonight, of all nights, her oldest brother, Fergus, who rarely bothered to give her a second thought in the usual course of events, spotted her as she slipped past him!

With a suspicious gleam in his bloodshot eyes, he noted her breathlessness and the rosy flush in her cheeks, and looked her up and down. In an irritable tone that warned her he was already deep in his cups and belligerent, he demanded to know where she'd been.

"T' the privy," she tossed back at him, saucily daring him with her eyes to contradict her.

"T' the privy, is it?" he mimicked, and snorted with disgust. "Och, I'm no fool, sister! A piss doesna bring such a wicked sparkle to yer eyes, nor color yer cheeks wi' fire. What ha'e ye been up to, ye wee slut? Were ye rollin in t' hay o' the stables wi' a lad?"

She bristled, and planted her fists on her hips. "Whist! Rolling in the hay, indeed! Dinna measure others by yer own lewd doings, Fergus McNair!" she retorted. " 'Twas the cold wind pinked my cheeks when I left the keep for t' privy, naught else." Her eyes dared him to contradict her, while she crossed her fingers so the lie wouldna count as a sin.

"Well, ye took yer sweet time, did ye nay? Awa' wi' ye t' the cellars, and draw me a wee dram o' *uise beatha,* ye useless bitch!" he growled.

Catriona had no choice but to obey. Refuse him, and she'd never escape t' her tower! She raced to the cellars for the whisky he'd so rudely demanded, and returned to fill his mug to brimming. She even wished him good health, sweetly murmuring, *"Slainte mhah,* brother dear!" after she'd done so.

But so syrupy-sweet was her tone, when just moments before her eyes had shot daggers at him, it struck home even to such a dullard as Fergus that she wasna happy about his orders, despite appearances, and gave him pause to wonder at her good wishes for his health! Her guileless expression and unusually biddable manner caused Fergus to sniff suspiciously at his whiskey and wonder if his dram might as easily be brimming with poison as the potent water o' life! Accordingly, he made horned fingers beneath the trestle to ward off her "evil-eye," muttering under his breath about a sister who was "nae better than a cursed witch! Better she burn in a barrel o' pitch like her sister witches than linger t' torment a decent mon!" His expression livid, he bade her get out of his sight with a wave of his hand.

Needing no second bidding, Catriona escaped the rowdy great hall and its twin hearths lit with blazing logs, about which congregated her McNair clansmen. She scampered up the steep, winding staircase to her tower chamber—and solitude. There, she didna have to evade the pinches, lewd winks, and indecent propositions of her father's guests, nor run hither and thither to do her brothers' bidding. At last, she could do what she'd been longing to do all day long . . . !

Cheeks flushed, her dark lashes still spiked and wet from melted snowflakes, she took a seat upon the stool set before her looking glass. Her green eyes sparkled with excitement as, drawing a calming breath or two, she reached up behind her and plucked the silver hairpins from her silky black tresses one by one. All pins removed, she unfastened the caul of threads that had neatly confined her hair and shook it loose.

Soot-black ringlets tumbled clear down to her waist. They framed the slender heart of her creamy face like the midnight petals of some rare dark flower. The flames of the many tallow candles the serving wench had lit earlier and placed in holders in every corner of her bedchamber shone in her hair's glossy mass with steely glints of blue and made her eyes shine even greener than was usual.

Dismissing her looks—which were, she'd long since decided with little rancor, too unusual to be considered beautiful in a time which lauded golden hair and eyes of blue—she gazed steadily into the large oval of highly polished tin on the wall before her. Breathlessly taking up a comb of deer horn studded with pearls, she drew it through her hair.

"St. Agnes, hear a young maid's prayer," she murmured to her reflection in the looking glass. "And, when the witching hour is here, reveal to me my husband dear!"

As she chanted the spell, she gazed deeply into the polished oval. But alas, she saw only her own green eyes reflected there, slanted and mysterious as a cat's with the pitchy blackness that surrounded her pricked by the glow of candleflames. An impish smile curved Catriona's full pink mouth, for t' her mischievous mind she looked more witch than woman; more sorceress herself than seeker of the future! *If ye could see me now, brother Fergus, ye wouldna ha'e drunk yer whiskey, sure!* she thought.

Catriona was not alone in her maiden's ritual that night. Even as she sat in her tower chamber waiting, countless other unmarried lassies across the wild and windswept lands of Scotland had likewise ventured out into the darkness — as had she and a handful of giggling wenches from the keep — to visit the nearest cornfield. There, they'd thrown grain stolen from the winter's stores onto the dark field and chanted the proper rhyme for their ritual:

"Agnes sweet and Agnes fair," they'd sung, dancing under the moonlight in a faerie ring, their breath rising from their mouths like plumes of smoke:

"Hither, thither now repair!
Bonnie Agnes, let me see
The bonnie lad who'll marry me!"

Afterward, those same maidens — whether noble or peasant stock — had scurried home through the wintry night to seat themselves before their looking glasses, as had Catriona. Or sped away to peer shyly at reflections of themselves in crystal ponds beneath the frosty full moon, for tonight . . . ! Ah, tonight was the Eve of St. Agnes, the twentieth night of January. And, it was said by the good-wives, if a maiden wished to learn the identity of the man she would wed, she must cast grain onto the cornfield, then hurry home to gaze into her mirror exactly at the twelfth hour when eve passed into day. If she followed the ritual dutifully, she would see the face of her true love, reflected behind her own!

Catriona had, since the day of her third birthday, been betrothed to Alan Mac Quinlann vic Andrew, laird of Rowanlee. It was a match she found most pleasing, and it

17

was her bonnie Alan's face she yearned to see this Agnes's Eve, as much for reassurance as for any other reason.

Angus—her father and the McNair of Erskine—had paid little thought to his only daughter's care since her mother, the Lady Moira, had gone to heaven shortly after birthing her husband a third son to add to his litter. Her rough and battle-hungry half brothers, Fergus, Gil, and even her full brother, thirteen-year-old Bran, the youngest, had paid even less heed to their sister's welfare than their father.

Accordingly, Catriona had been raised by a succession of slatternly serving wenches or doddery old crones who came and went at Erskine. And—since it seemed that the kindest among them had either quickly died or grown too old or infirm to pay her more than a cursory mind— Catriona had been forced to survive by dint of her own sharp mind and keen wits in the harsh world of her father's keep, where women counted for little other than to ease men's lusts and serve their every need. A little girl's, then a young maiden's, wants and needs had been of minor import to anyone when compared to the bloody, seemingly endless, feuds waged between the clan McNair, the clan Gilchrist, the clan Frazier, and other Border clans, or the *enach,* the honor, of the clan itself.

Her life thus far had been devoid of the beauty and happiness, the love, affection, and warmth of companionship, her soul cried out for and her gentle nature needed desperately in order to flourish. Her beloved Alan had been the one bright and constant flame that had illumined her dreary life for these past thirteen years, glowing steadily, constantly, just for her. As a toddling bairn, he'd dandled her on his knee or carried her on his shoulders and played silly baby games that had made her crow with laughter. When she grew older, he taught her the joys to be found in music and song, and the pleasure to be had in the playing of a harp. Aye, though far older than she, his rare visits to Erskine had brought laughter and affection into her life, and the insight that not all men were cast from the same mold as her father and brothers. What was more, Alan loved her, and couldna wait to make her his bride, he'd sworn.

When they were man and wife at last, her whole world would change, Catriona just knew it! She would leave Erskine's dark confines behind her forever, and go with Alan to Rowanlee as its chatelaine and his bride. In that pretty manor with her pretty laird, she would find the pretty fairytale ending to her life she'd always yearned for: happiness, beauty, and contentment—and the love of a good and gentle man. All this would be hers, if *only* Alan did not weary of waiting for her to become a woman! And there, alas, was the rub, the cause for her anxiety . . .

She gnawed at her lower lip and frowned. The oval of polished tin reflected a solemn-faced maid now, one whose green eyes were no longer bright and merry with anticipation but shadowed with dark doubt. Och, what was wrong with her? What ailed her? Had some spiteful wretch cast the evil eye upon her, to keep her always a child?

Morag, the hermit crone who lived in a cave in the woods and was rumored to be a witch, said not. But she was sixteen years, and she'd still not seen her first blood! Sixteen years, and although her breasts had budded nicely and her hips had swelled and taken on the lissome curves of a woman, and although her father's companions cast lecherous eyes in her direction with greater frequency each passing day, there was still no sign of her monthly courses starting. Nothing—when younger serving wenches were already whelping her brothers' bastards like field mice!

Och, it wasna fair! This *life* just wasna fair! Bad enough that Fate had taken her beloved mother from her at so tender an age and left her to the cold comfort of a father who'd no love in his heart for daughters! But if cruel fate had also made her barren and therefore unfitted to be Alan's bride—well, then, she couldna bear it, and that was that! She'd sooner die than spend the remainder of her life here at Erskine, unloved and unwanted by anyone. Or

19

worse, be shut away in a convent while Alan married another . . .

Forcing her thoughts from her worries, Catriona made herself concentrate on what she was about: conjuring up the face of her future husband! In an earnest tone, she finished the spell, repeating it exactly as old Morag the witch-woman had taught it to her that very morning in the wintry woods:

"St. Agnes, hear a young maid's prayer
And, when the witching hour is here,
Reveal to me my husband dear!"

She stared unblinking into the oval mirror, her green eyes wide and expectant.

Moments passed on leaden wings, but still nothing happened. She sighed. A single tear slipped down her creamy cheek. So much! She had hoped for so very much—a face to weave her dreams upon, some reason to go on hoping and praying—but there was nothing!

Her lashes fluttered. She blinked rapidly, then her eyelids dropped with disappointment and weariness. More moments hobbled by on crippled feet and Catriona stifled a yawn. There was no sign of anything happening in the mirror. Perhaps she should seek her bed, she considered drowsily, half rising from the stool . . .

But then, of a sudden, there came a stirring on the air, like the softest flutter of invisible wings. Catriona came instantly awake again as the flames that roared in the hearth to dispel the tower's dampness writhed and danced as if stirred by a draft. A chill trembled through the darkness, making her shiver, for a silvery faerie note seemed to tinkle on the air, a solitary, crystal chime just within the ken of mortal ears!

Her senses wide open now, Catriona stiffened as she heard it, and abruptly resumed her seat. The fine hairs on her nape tingled and crawled as . . . *something* . . . seemed to gather in the mirror behind her own reflection; a smoky

20

swirling she could barely make out, but was there none-theless. Jesu and Mary! A magical reflection was growing from the vapor that owed nothing to the blank tower wall at her back . . .

Blessed Agnes, the spell was working!

She watched, scarce breathing — certainly without blinking! — as a form assembled itself from the smoke behind her. The swimming, silvery murkiness took on shape and substance, until the shadow that towered be-hind her had assumed the unmistakable silhouette of a tall, broad-shouldered . . . man!

Resisting the overwhelming urge to look behind her and by so doing perhaps dispel the image, Catriona man-aged to chant the next part of the spell. She did so with a pounding heart and trembling hands, and in a croaking voice that broke more than a little:

"St. Agnes, by your blessed grace,
Reveal to me my true-love's face!"

A light seemed to fill the mirror of tin, spilling down from its topmost curve to gradually illumine the shadowy outline of the man. Her eyes almost popping from her head now, Catriona sucked in a shaky breath as she saw a fine broad forehead revealed, then the outline of a noble head — a handsome, manly head.

Alan! she thought with a breathless gasp of excitement, *Aye, it must be him, my own true love!*

But the light grew brighter still, revealing all, and her delighted smile vanished; became instead a frown of con-fusion. It wasna Alan she was looking at, nor any man she knew!

She could make out a mane of unruly curls, framing the image's temples then sweeping down about his muscular shoulders, and it was *wrong,* all wrong, for they were black curls — black as the devil's own locks, rather than the wheaten gold she both knew and loved!

There was a slash of raven-dark brows across that no-

21

ble, wind-browned forehead—black brows, yet again, where she'd expected brows of gold! Hooded gray eyes, fringed with lashes that were sooty-dark and thick as cobwebs, appeared. They were sensual eyes, their expression amused, all male, somehow knowing; the kind of male eyes that caused a maiden t' blush and look away, rather than eyes as innocent as harebells and twice as blue, like her Alan's.

Nor was its nose delightfully snubbed and sprinkled with freckles, the chin dimpled, as was her dearling's—och, never! The reflection's nose was slim and aquiline; the strong, arrogant nose of a strong, arrogant man. And his chin and jaw betrayed a will of iron—swarthy, rugged juts of flesh that put her in mind of the chiseled granite found on some windswept tor. Certainly no' a dear little nubbin t' be fondly tweaked! His mouth was wide and firm-lipped, the edges quirked up in a challenging smile as their gazes met and locked in the looking glass of polished tin . . .

She blinked back tears and swallowed, almost choking on her disappointment yet unable to look away! A handsome wretch St. Agnes had shown her, aye, t' be sure; a great dark brute with comely looks t' send the lassies swooning from Inverness t' Edwin's Burgh—but och, he didn'a please *this* lassie, not at all!

"Nay!" she cried indignantly, springing to her feet and tearing her gaze from the reflection's insolent gray eyes. "For shame, Mirror, that ye should lie t' me! This dark-haired lout isna my bonnie Alan, my own betrothed! He isna—he canna be!—my own true love! Whist ye, now, I'll ha'e none o' this roguish black brute, be cursed if I will! Be gone—and him wi' ye!"

With that, a furious Catriona tugged off her green suede boot and hurled it at the mirror, denting it and sending it toppling to the flagstone floor of her chamber with a resounding clang, thus banishing the unwanted image forever.

Or . . . had she?

Chapter One

Erskine Keep, the Tweed Valley.
Yuletide, 1067

"Ye wanted t' see me, Father?" Catriona asked, bobbing her father a dutiful curtsey.

"Aye, lass, I did," the laird acknowledged gruffly, stretching knotted muscles as he rose to his feet.

His distracted expression changed to a scowl as he looked up at his only daughter, for despite her mien, her eyes challenged him as ever.

Catriona. The first child of his second marriage to the Lady Moira. The third born of his loins. And each time he came face-to-face with the girl, he was stunned anew by her resemblance to his dead wife, the only one of his two wives he had truly loved! So, too, he was painfully reminded of Catriona's begetting each time he set eyes upon her, for he and his Moira had loved fiercely and well, and the girl-bairn had been born of that sweet, mad passion.

But now Moira — his wild, willful lassie! — had gone. She'd breathed her last in her efforts t' give him another son, young Bran, now thirteen. And, with Moira's passing, the light and joy had left his life. Sometimes it seemed to Angus she must ha'e taken his heart t' heaven with her, too, for he couldna look upon the lassie wi'out bitterness filling him; couldna gaze into his daughter's lovely face wi'out silently damning Moira for leaving him for Death's cold arms . . .

"Ye ha'e seen your first blood, have ye no', lass?" he demanded bluntly.

Heat and color filled Catriona's cheeks with shame at his question, yet his words also filled her with hope. What was this? Why, surely he was about to tell her he'd decided on a day for her wedding? Aye, surely he was, for why else would he ask her such a thing? Blessed Mary, her prayers had been answered, and mayhap the spring would see her Alan's bride?

"Aye, Father, I have," she acknowledged, crossing her fingers within the folds of her kirtle to ensure good fortune. "I've been a woman since last Candlemas."

The laird nodded and gave a grunt of approval. " 'Tis glad I am t' hear it. I'd almost given up on ye coming t' womanhood, but then, ye were ever a contrary wench!"

"I had no say in that, sir!" she protested, amazed that he would lay even the blame for her tardy courses at her feet.

"Aye, so they say, so they say. Well? What are ye waitin' for? Be gone wi' ye, lass! I have much t' attend to," he dismissed her.

For once obedient, she turned to leave. But as she did so, she caught a glimpse of her expression in the looking glass that hung just within his tower, and was brought up short by her cowed reflection. Her head was bowed submissively, her expression bleak with disappointment as she raised the tapestry curtain to go out. What was she thinking of, t' so meekly scuttle away without asking the question that burned on the tip of her tongue, demanding answer. An answer that might well affect the rest of her life, furthermore!

Straightening her spine, she swung about to face her father, whose head was already bent over some parchment of accounting or other.

"My laird, a word more, by your leave?" she asked

24

quietly, her head held high and proud.

One sandy brow quirked as he looked up at her from beneath pale lashes. "Aye? What is it now?" he growled.

"I would . . . I would know why ye asked me that question, sir?"

"Why? Jesu, your impudence, girl! The 'why' of what I do or ask is none of your concern, lassie! Be gone!"

"Your pardon, sir, but I must disagree. If 'tis plans ye make for my future, then 'tis of certainty my concern. And I willna be gone til ye answer me!"

"Disagree?" he echoed, his blue eyes flinty now. "*Your* concern? Nay, nay, lass, as your laird and father, 'tis all *my* concern, and no other's — no' even yours! 'Tis chattel ye are, Catriona, nothing more, even as the serfs are chattel and my hounds and hawks are chattel. And now that ye're an age t' be bred, 'tis time to put your value t' work for me. I mean t' marry ye off advantageously, Daughter. To wed ye to a man who can earn your *torchia,* your dowry. Someone who'll make me a strong, loyal ally and stand beside me against my enemies! I'll have a rich and landed son-in-law who's lusty enough and mon enough t' breed me a brace or two o' worthy grandbairns on your body," he growled, advancing upon her and waggling his finger in her face. "A mon o' *my* choosing, Daughter, not yours. And so ye see, this doesna concern ye."

His words blanched her cheeks, struck her like a winding blow to the belly. Sucking in an agonized breath, she shook her head slowly from side to side. Surely he was but jesting, a part of her mind insisted — ? Surely this was some cruel joke? Surely she'd misunderstood him!

"Ye canna mean this!" she whispered. "My betrothal was agreed upon some thirteen years past — a match my lady mother begged of ye herself on her deathbed! Ye canna break it, Father! Ye canna break your word to her! Please, please dinna break it, for I love him!"

"Canna? Ye dare t' say I canna?" Angus thundered,

his face thrust so close to hers, she could see the pockmarks that etched his ruddy complexion. "Och, then I bid ye watch me, lassie, for I ride on Rowanlee this verra day t' do the deed! And as for love . . . ! Pah! A plaguey pox on love! Love doesna fill your purse, lassie," he scoffed. "And love doesna fill your belly wi' victuals or bairns. Nor does love gi'e ye a strong sword arm t' protect ye, nor a loyal heart t' honor ye —! Ye're a proud and strong-willed lass, ye are, like your mother before ye. Ye need a mon who can match ye, measure for measure, spirit for spirit. And that mon isna your pretty Alan!" he sneered.

"And what would *ye* know of love, my laird?" Catriona hissed at him, her green eyes blazing, her fists clenched in her fury, all caution tossed to the winds. "You! Ye've never known what it is t' love aught but yersel'—aye, yersel'—and bloodshed! Ye dinna ken the meaning o' the word, sir! I know, for I have lived these seventeen years wi'out receiving a drop o' it from yersel'. Ye may go ahead, my laird father. Do what ye will!" she cried, tossing back her hair defiantly. "Name another as my betrothed, if it please ye—name a dozen others! But I willna wed a one o' them! Ye can ha'e me bound and gagged and carried t' the kirk by force. Ye can stand me upright before a priest, and prick me wi' bodkins like a pagan mannekin—but ye canna make me plight ma troth t' any mon but Alan!"

"Had I three sons wi' one tenth o' your spleen, Daughter, I would yield t' ye and gladly, for I would ha'e no need o' a powerful husband for ye," Angus ground out with the barest hint of regret—an emotion he as swiftly masked. "But I havena, and so in this matter, I willna be disobeyed! 'Tis a willful bitchling ye are, aye, and an impudent one, too! Get ye t' your tower, wench, before I lose patience and ha'e ye whipped! Go from my sight—and dinna show yer face below until ye're ready t' humble yersel' and swear upon your knees t' do my bidding!"

"Then I regret ye must wait till hell freezes o'er, sir," Catriona seethed, her green eyes blazing emerald-fire in the chalky pallor of her complexion. "For I'll stay there till I rot, rather than bend a knee t' your wishes! Hear me, sir, for I mean it! If I canna wed my Alan, I'll marry no mon!"

"Then rot ye must, Daughter," Angus growled with terrible finality. "And remain virgin till your dying breath, for I willna relent! Now, *go!*"

Chapter Two

Angus McNair's hearty bellow of laughter rang out like the clanging of a great copper bell when his reeve had finished speaking. The laird—who was blessed with a ragged mane of wild red hair and an equally fiery beard—brought his gnarled fist down upon the trestle before him in a great thump that set flagons and platters to jiggling about.

"Players at the gates, ye say, Gordie?" he roared. "Well, och, mon, why d' ye tarry? Show them inside! It's been many a winter since we've had players here at Erskine. Bring them into the hall, laddie, an' if they please us, why then we'll give them a wee bite and let them warm their rumps at our fire before we send them on their way!"

With a wink and a grin, stocky Angus lounged back in the carved wooden chair that his position as laird of the clan McNair guaranteed him, tossing aside his green plaid cloak as he settled himself, for he'd no need of warm wrappings this even'. Too much strong drink, the fiery *uisqe beatha,* the "water o' life" he loved so well, had made him warm from the belly out.

As the reeve hastened to heed his command, Angus took a deep draught of whiskey, wiped his mouth on hairy knuckles, and eyed the entrance to his hall expectantly.

Players, eh? he considered with a wheezy chuckle. Why, they'd not enjoyed the players' droll talents at Erskine in nigh . . . what was it? Thirteen years? More? Nay, 'twas thirteen, he confirmed, for there'd been none o' their kind at Erskine since the year his Moira had breathed her last after whelping young Bran, then died and left him alone, curse the woman! He drummed his fingers impatiently, for although battle-seasoned and battle-scarred, the McNair was as excited by the advent of the troupe as any child in his keep!

Moments later, a ripple of excited chatter ran through the McNair clansmen, women and little ones, as the colorfully garbed and masked players entered the hall. They made their bows, then straightaway began skipping among the company, dancing to the foot-tapping beat of tabors and flutes and the melodious strumming of mandolins. Their arrival was greeted by upraised horns and goblets, and rowdy cheers of welcome from the clansmen. The Yuletide revelers fell back behind the avenue of arched oaken pillars to line the smoke-blackened walls of Erskine's hall and make room for the new arrivals.

There were perhaps a dozen players in all. Animal masks and fanciful headresses concealed the features of all but one of the entertainers, Angus noted, observant despite the strong spirits he'd downed. The one who'd remained unmasked wore a rust-colored kirtle and a leaf-green surcoat—and appeared to be delightfully female!

My, my! Angus thought, his eyes narrowing appreciatively as he assessed the buxom wench with her long, silky black hair, *Here's a comely pigeon!* She was a bonnie, snub-nosed morsel if ever he'd seen one, with a pert smile and saucy blue eyes that flirted his way more than once! Why, t' bold lassie was making sheeps' eyes at him, she was . . .

Angus's grin deepened amidst his frizzy red beard. Lust kindled and smoldered in his cold blue eyes in response to her bold and inviting smile, for it had been many a month since he'd taken respite from his feuding and the responsibilities of chieftainship to dally with wenches. Still, he reminded himself cautiously, players being predominantly male, it was far more likely his bonnie wee lass with the beckoning smile was a fresh-faced, beardless lad in a maid's dress than a real woman! He'd have t' find out before he returned her coy looks, 'else risk making a lummox of himsel'!

An enthusiastic roar went up as, their minstrels' ballads done with for the time being, one nimble player cast aside his mandolin and instead turned a half-dozen nimble cartwheels in succession across the rush-strewn floor. Dressed in parti-colored red tunic and yellow breeks, the tumbler performed his tricks with a boneless grace and blurring speed that amazed them all. The spry fellow landed before one gaping serving wench. He came upright again with a spritely bound, and raised his stag's-head mask just long enough to steal a smacking kiss from her parted lips before, with a wicked grin and a courtly bow, he turned handsprings once again and wheeled away, this time circling the hall.

"Och, Shelagh, ye mustna wash yer lips anon!" cried one merry wit. "Happen there'll be no other along t' buss ye!"

The clansmen hooted with merriment at his boldness and teased the homely, red-faced goosegirl, Shelagh, but they soon fell silent again as yet another mummer ran forward to perform.

Withdrawing a half-dozen colored wooden balls from his bag, he juggled them all in the air at once without dropping a single one. Some he caught behind his back, others to either side of him, some between his legs. After a few moments, he tossed the balls aside, and instead drew a trio of sharpened dirks from his belt, demonstrating their sharpness on a lock of young Bran's black hair. He juggled these instead, drawing admiring gasps from the gathering as the finely honed blades caught the flaring torch-light, and came but a hairbreadth away from slicing his palms in two each time he caught them.

Another man joined him, this one twirling wooden hoops about his arms, legs, and neck. In moments, they were passing the hoops between each other with amazing speed, turning somersaults through them just in time to catch the next before it fell. Faggots of kindling, the ends dipped in pitch, replaced the hoops in time. These the juggler lit from the roaring hearths and likewise juggled, while a third fellow performed marvelous sleights of hand as he passed among the clansmen.

The magician's mercurial tricks drew astonished oohs and aahs from the audience as dirks were plucked from some men's belts, slings from others, without their knowledge. Gold coins appeared like magic from scowling Fergus McNair's ears and a silver groat-piece from the nose of his grinning younger brother, thirteen-year-old Bran, while the shaggy brown thatch of the middle McNair brother, Gil, yielded up an indignant brown mouse. The poor beast promptly bit his ear before scampering away to safety — much to the gathering's howling amusement!

"My laird?" came a low voice in Angus's ear.

"Aye, what is it, laddie?" Angus growled, irritated to be disturbed whilst eyeing the saucy jiggle of the player-maid's rump as she passed a cap amongst the gathering.

"The lady Catriona would enjoy the players' clever antics, think ye not?" Gordon, the reeve suggested softly, leaning low over Angus's shoulder to murmur

31

in his chieftain's ear. "Shall I have the wee lassie summoned t' the hall, sir?"

"Nay, Gordon, ye'll not!" Angus snarled, his happy smile curdling like soured cream.

"Nay, sir?" Gordon sputtered.

"Aye, nay's what I said, mon! Let the wee bitchling brood in her tower and ponder her defiance a while longer! It'll do the shrew a deal of good, I fancy."

"But, my laird, surely three days is long enough t' impress upon the lassie that her father is t' be obeyed in all matters?" young Gordon—a kindly man—suggested softly. "Why, sir, she hasna left her chamber once, not in all these days, and 'tis a rare treat we have here at Erskine tonight. Come, sir, come! I know ye for a fond father and a Christian, forgiving mon!" he lied. "Will ye not relent just this once, sir? Mayhap your kindness could achieve what stern words couldna bring about?"

Angus's expression changed, and for a heartstopping moment, Gordon dared to hope that his coaxing had been successful. But alas, it had not. The instant Angus's face hardened, the moment his cold blue eyes grew flinty, the reeve knew the laird would refuse him, and he was right.

"Nay, laddie, nay," McNair growled. "I'll not have my daughter thinking I've grown weak, nor that I've forgiven her defiance, for I havena—nay, not by a bow-shot! Marry that milk-sop Quinlann her mother chose for her on her deathbed? Never! I forbid it! She'll marry the man *I* choose for her, and like it! I intend t' arrange a marriage wi' the one who can do our clan the greatest good in the future, for troubled times are in the offing, mark my words, young Gordie! Within the twelvemonth, those Norman curs will have leeched the Saxons dry. Then King William will come looking elsewhere for rich manors with which t' reward his followers, and rich farms t' feed his armies. Aye, Gordie, ye'll see! The cursed Normans'll

32

threaten our borders, as they conquered Harold t' the south last year. When that day comes, we canna have too many strong allies at our side, methinks."

He scowled and took a swig from his drinking horn, wiping his lips and beard on his fist when he was done. "I'll wed my daughter to a mon who can bring about an alliance between our clan and her husband's—someone who'll prove a loyal friend in case of war for his bride's sake, not some pretty weakling she fancies hersel' enamored of! So ye see, there's an end t' the matter, laddie. Be gone wi' ye now, and bother me nae more wi' yer prattlings!"

Gordon bowed and left as he'd been bidden. But although outwardly resigned, inwardly he seethed with rebellious thoughts and with pity for the young lady, Catriona. Och, that poor wee lass! Denied a mother's care and love from the age of three years, she'd had little of either from her father. And why was that? Well, only Angus knew for certain, but Gordon had long suspected that the reason lay in Catriona's striking resemblance to her lady mother, Moira, whom Angus had loved dearly after his own rough-and-ready fashion, and whom he'd never forgiven for having died and left him. Aye, every time the McNair looked upon his daughter's lovely face, or heard her lilting voice, the knives of grief cut through him anew and hardened his heart to the maid, Gordon suspected, shaking his head. It was grief that drove Angus to such violent, desperate lengths to purge her memory from his heart, he was sure of it.

Without the lady's Moira's gentling beauty and sweetness of temperament to soften him, after his wife's death, Laird Angus had become once again the hard, unbending man he'd been before they were wed, a man who devoted all of his energies to broadening his power along the Scottish borders and to feuding with the rival clans who sought to take powerful Erskine Keep for themselves.

Aye, Erskine was a keep among keeps, Gordon reflected, the flower of the border strongholds. Positioned as she was, straddling the banks of the Tweed, and strongly built to withstand even the most powerful attack or siege, 'twas little wonder less powerful lords coveted her!

At the foot of the staircase leading to Catriona's tower, Gordon paused and turned to look back at the great hall he'd left behind him.

Tall oaken pillars with arched rafters supported the keep's lofty roof, for the manor had been constructed after the norse fashion. The twin towers at either end of the main building housed the laird's bedchamber and that of his daughter respectively, and had been built shortly before the laird's wedding. Originally intended to serve as lookout posts and sleeping quarters for a small garrison of fighting men, they were now used solely as bowers for the chieftain and his family. The remainder of the structure was shored up and planked by stout oaken beams and gray stone, then roofed with slate, and appeared far more Norse than Scottish. Twin hearths blazed at either end of the hall, fed by huge logs. Above them hung the rusty two-headed blood-axes and broadswords with which Thorwig the Red had once claimed these lands by right of victory and bloodshed in the name of his pagan gods of war. Before them sprawled the dozen or so shaggy gray hunting hounds and the smaller yet tenacious terriers with which the McNair chieftain pursued the chase in finer weather.

The hall was, as always, thronged with the McNair clansmen. Each one of them—from the young piper, Robbie, who played the bagpipes like an angel, to Auld Ranulf, blinded in a fire many years hence—had pledged fealty to their chieftain, Angus, and taken his McNair name as their own, after the clan fashion. On this night shortly before the feast of Yule, they were in high spirits and even more deeply in their cups than was usual for the early hour, Gordon noted, though this circumstance didna surprise him a whit. Snow lay thick upon the ground about Erskine. More was falling even now, whipped about by a fierce wind. And, with the advent of winter and bad weather, the McNair clan had eagerly relaxed their customary vigilance, posting neither sentries nor lookouts along the walls surrounding Erskine, nor on the craggy cliffs below, despite Gordon's advice that they do so. Angus—confident that enemy clans and wily Normans alike would forgo further feuding or conquering until the milder months of spring—had shrugged off his reeve's warnings as the prattlings of an overly fearful old woman. He'd bidden him be silent, saying, "Och, laddie, ye may see t' the proper running of my keep and the estates, and t' the collection of my rents, but leave the fighting t' us fighting men—we braw lads o' the claymore who ken what we're aboot!"

As Gordon watched, he saw the player-wench in the rust-red kirtle sidle boldly towards the chieftain's chair. With a coy smile, she twirled a finger in her straight black tresses, and her hips undulated seductively. She—or was it a lad disguised, after all, Gordon pondered, for there was something about the way she moved?—leaned over the laird's shoulder. She must have issued some teasing challenge or other, for with a roar like that of a rutting stag, lumbered to his feet. He made a wild lunge to pinch her buttocks, but missed by a span.

Gordon smothered a chortle of laughter. Well, well! Mistress Russet-Gown must in truth be a female, after all, it would seem—and a teasing wee minx, too, t' so inflame the McNair's long-dormant lust!

Like an eel, the lass twisted sideways, evaded the laird's lecherous paws and skittered away, giggling. Angus, much like an aging dancing-bear, pranced

after her in amorous pursuit, threatening dire consequences and puckering his lips in promise of kisses
by way of forfeits if he should catch her.

Gordon's brown eyes followed the incongruous pair
as they played chase-master in and out of the knots
of people, until they reached the foot of the opposite
staircase. The wench smiled invitingly at Angus over
her shoulder. Skirts raised to reveal a pair of trim
ankles and shapely calves encased in green hose, she
started up the tower steps with her buttocks jiggling
provocatively, and the laird was lost! Angus followed,
bounding after her like a stag in full rut, and Gordon's frown became a delighted smile instead. Och, it
was verra close t' being perfect, the way things had
turned out! he decided, beaming broadly. With the
McNair busy about his bed-sport wi' the seductive
"Mistress Russet", he'd never know if his daughter
Catriona came down t' the hall to watch the troupe
or nay!

But Catriona, much to Gordon's surprise, was far
from readily persuaded to go below. In fact, she
stubbornly declined his invitation with a toss of her
silky black hair! It was not until the reeve — a shrewd
fellow, t' say the least! — slyly remarked that perhaps
it was for the best she stay where she was, since her
father had expressly forbidden her to join the gathering and had himself since retired to his chambers to
sport with a woman, that Catriona suddenly re-
lented.

"What's this ye're saying? The auld fox has *forbidden*
me t' watch the players, an' yet makes his own sport
wi' a player-wench? Whist, mon, then I *must* go
down!" she declared with a wicked little grin that
made her green eyes sparkle so brightly, Gordon's
heart tied itself in lovers' knots. Her expression softened as she saw the one he wore now, and she went

to him and teasingly pinched his cheek. The poor man blushed scarlet.

"Och, Gordie, love, ye should have said how it was at once, rather than blather on! Ye know full well I'll do anything t' outwit my laird father!"

"Ye think I dinna ken that?" Gordon retorted dourly, pursing his lips. "One day, lassie, ye'll go too far, mark my words! So? What will it be? Will ye come below for a wee while t' watch the fun, or nay?"

"Aye, I'll come!"

Catriona gaily whirled about and flung up the lid of a heavy wooden coffer, withdrawing from it an ugly tunic of homespun dyed a rusty hue, one such as those worn by the serving wenches of Erskine.

"I heard the flutes and tabors from up here," she confided as she unfasted the leather girdle about her waist. "They had such a merry sound, I did so long t' see what was happening below! Now. What d' ye think o' this, Master Reeve? Shall I wear this old shift I don each autumn t' gather berries? 'Twill be a while afore my father recognizes me, dressed like one of his serving wenches, will it no'?"

"Ye wee rascal!" Gordie scolded with a grin. "Ye never cry 'quarter', do ye, lass?"

"Never!" she agreed. "Now, oot o' my chamber wi' ye, Gordie! I'll join ye soon enough below!"

Some time had passed before Catriona made her way below. Torches placed in iron sconces along the walls leading down the tower staircase guttered in the draft. Their writhing light distorted shape and depth, and made descending the deep stone steps—slippery with damp—a hazardous task. Accordingly, Catriona kept a sharp eye out and lifted her skirts high to gingerly take each glassy tread with the utmost care. Her attention was fully on the stairs and not on the eerie quiet in the hall below—where all should have been noise, music, and merriment—until she gained the last one.

Frowning, she hastened down the short passageway leading to the silent hall. Och, had she waited too long, then? Were the players, with their singing and dancing, their acrobatics and magical acts, already done wi' their cavorting and gone from Erskine and her clan tumbled into their furs t' sleep? Och, surely not, she thought, hurrying now.

She drew up short at the opening into the hall, and looked about her. And, as the horror before her registered fully on her mind, her eyes widened in shock and disbelief. The expectant smile she'd worn fled. The color drained from her cheeks.

Jesu! Blessed Mary, Mother of God, nay!

In the short while since Gordie had summoned her, her clansmen had been slain to the last man, woman, and bairn without so much as a single scream, a solitary shout, or a clashing of arms carrying to her in her bower!

Teeth chattering with shock, she looked wildly about her. Her brother Fergus sprawled not three tailor's lengths from her toes. His head had been bludgeoned and rested in a pool of his blood. Bran, the youngest, was huddled at his feet, a gaping wound in his chest. She bit back a scream as her eyes found other familiar faces: young Shelagh, the goose-girl, slumped in a corner; blind Auld Ranulf, spitted to the wall by a spear; young Robbie, the piper slumped over his favorite hound, also dead. There was Diarmid. There Ross! There Carlisle, Mistress Gertrude . . . Fat Nan . . . and so many, many others!

So many! Far too many for sanity!

Catriona shook her head slowly from side to side, unable to accept what she was seeing. And yet—*Sweet Jesus*—how could she deny it? There was blood, blood everywhere! On the walls. Pooling on the trestles. Blood splattering the bread and mingling with the mead and whiskey in the goblets, dripping between the wooden planks of the trestles to stain the rushes. Blood and death and the stench of slaughter everywhere — *everywhere!*

She reeled away with an anguished sob, her belly heaving. Bile filled her mouth and she vomited onto the rushes, gagging and retching so violently, her knees threatened to give way beneath her. Dead, every last one of them! But — where was her father? Had he also been slain, and if so, why was his body not among those of their clansmen? And, belatedly, she also began to wonder where their murderers were. Elsewhere in the keep? Looting the storehouses and the granary? Pillaging her father's coffers? Razing the outbuildings? Or, she wondered, trembling, dare she hope that they'd fled into the blizzard with their booty, believing everyone dead?

Somehow, she managed to stand. Gritting her teeth, she forced herself to go among the fallen and perform the gruesome task of examining each of the twisted bodies. The staring, familiar white faces were like melted wax in the guttering torchlight, but nay, her father wasna among the dead!

Perplexed, she didna ken what to do next. Had those butchers taken the McNair hostage for some purpose? Or was her father dead elsewhere in the keep? Sweet Virgin, in her shock, she couldna think!

Her wits shattered, Catriona stumbled away in search of cold, crisp air to sharpen her thoughts. It was then she came face-to-face with Gordie, puir, gentle Gordie. He was dead now, too, of course, but belatedly she remembered what he'd told her. Something about her father, and a — and a wench, was it not? Aye, that's what he'd said! He'd described how Angus had left the hall in pursuit of a player-maid in a russet gown! Then her father, alive or dead, must still be in his tower chamber . . .

Moving like one in a ghastly nightmare from which there was no awakening, her teeth chattering still, her limbs numb and unwieldy, she shuffled her way between the bodies to the tower stairs, keeping her eyes averted from the bloody carnage all about her.

No mountain had ever seemed so steep as did those tower stairs that night! It was an age before she'd crawled to the top. There she stood, sobbing, before the tapestry hanging that curtained the opening to her father's bower. She was afraid to lift it aside, afraid to enter, afraid of what she might find if she did . . .

And then she heard a low, satisfied chuckle from beyond the hanging. A blistering fury filled her of a sudden, ridding her mind of the horror and numbness to which she'd fallen prey. Oh, Blessed Mary, she moaned silently. While her father rutted and chuckled his pleasure over some slattern's plump body, the men, women, and bairns of his keep had been brutally butchered! Mother of God! What manner of chieftain was this? What manner of man?

A curse on ye, ye randy auld bastard! she raged silently, her fists clenched with fury. *While ye lay a-wenching, our keep has fallen t' our enemies! Our clansmen are slain t' the last guid man, woman, and bairn!*

A curse on her lips, she lifted the tapestry hanging. On the wall directly before her hung a looking glass—her mother's own, and the twin to that which hung in her own chamber. The little tableau that was reflected in its shining face from the chamber beyond imprinted itself upon her eyes for all time. The words she heard exchanged robbed her again of speech, froze the curses on her lips. Shaking her head from side to side in disbelief, she was first confused, then horrified by what she saw before her.

"Nay," she whispered hoarsely, too shocked to move. "Nay! It canna be so . . . not this! Dear God,

40

surely my eyes deceive me? Oh, blessed Jesu, *naaay!*"

Her strangled cry betrayed her presence. And too late, Catriona saw the folly of revealing herself. By coming here, by witnessing what she'd witnessed, she had surely placed her own life in peril! Breathless with terror, she let the curtain fall.

"Catriona!" came a harsh voice as she flung about. The voice rose with a mixture of fury and threat as the voice repeated, *"Catriona!* Come ye here, I say!"

But she paid the speaker no heed.

Down the stairs she tripped and stumbled, her mouth working uncontrollably, her legs pumping of their own volition. Her heart was a mighty thundering in her breast; her blood a roaring, savage sea in her ears. Across the hall she fled, wild as a mad thing, her glazed eyes blind t' the bodies of her clansmen, sprawled hither and thither; blind even to puir Gordie, the reeve, who lay at a ghastly angle with his throat cut.

Out she fled, into the swirling snow, careening through the gates of Erskine Keep and escaping into the furious blizzard that swept the moors beyond her like one gone mad.

Moments later, a brace of riders whipped their mounts into a furious gallop and clattered through Erskine's gates in her wake. Hurling curses into the raging snowstorm, they thundered along the banks of the Tweed after the fleeing girl—with murder in their hearts!

He stood in the center of Erskine's hall, looking groggily about him. His hands were held out before him, and they were stained to the elbows with blood. 'Twas McNair blood. The blood of his enemies. The blood of vengeance. All dead, he thought drunkenly, and threw back his head and laughed uproariously. All dead—save one! Like a child with a platter of

41

sweetmeats, he had savored each one, but spared the best 'till last . . .

Lurching forward, he stumbled between the broken bodies, the trestles and overturned settles, to the staircase, ignoring the shouts of his comrades to join them in finishing the remains of a cask of *uisque beatha*. God rot the lot of them! He needed no water o' life, not this night, this long awaited night. He had drunk from the cup o' vengeance, and had found its liquor sweet indeed; intoxicating beyond aught they had to offer!

At the head of the stairs, the other stood waiting, dirk in hand. He pulled up short. He stared and he knew. Thrusting past, a low keening began deep in his throat as he flung himself into the chamber beyond, where Angus McNair lay dead. Dead at another's hand.

"Damn ye t' hell!" he howled, swinging about with eyes that blazed with fury. "Ye've cheated me, ye treacherous dog! He was mine, ye swore it! *Mine!*"

"Come, come, laddie," the other soothed in syrupy, cajoling tones. "He is dead, and that is all that really matters, is it no'? Ye have done what ye set out t' do so long ago, have ye no'?"

"Ye tricked me," he said sullenly.

"No tricks. I did what I felt best."

"Ye lied!"

"Mayhap a little. But . . . I did it for you. I feared it was too much for ye, ye ken, t' bear such pain all yer life, and then endure this, too. Ride home now, laddie. Ride home, before ye're discovered here," the coaxing voice continued. "Leave before your part in this be made known and held against ye."

"Aye, ye're right. I must. I should go home," he mumbled. His eyes filled with tears. "They mustna find out!" Yet as he looked about, his eyes were those of one who walked in his sleep, glazed and unseeing.

The other stepped down a tread or two, took him

by the shoulder and shook him gently before turning him around. "Enough, my bonnie lad. Enough! Turn about. Go down the stairs, and seek out the cold air t' revive ye. Ye'll find your mount awaiting ye below. Go now!"

Obediently, he turned about and started down the stairs, stumbling out into the blizzard and to his waiting horse like a drunkard. The hooves of the brace of horses that galloped furiously past him narrowly avoiding mowing him down, went unheard and unseen, as did their riders and their quarry.

Chapter Three

It was the fifteenth day of the twelfth month of the year of Our Lord 1067. The wild and desolate moors of the Northumbrian Marches were hidden under the fury of a blizzard—the third to blast them in as many days.

November had ushered in a terrible winter, one worse than even the bitterest the graybeards still living could recall—and they remembered many harsh winters, here in the north on the borders of Scotland and northern England.

The beginning of December had held little promise of kinder weather to come, for entire flocks of sheep had been buried under the snows that had fallen in the last fourteennight, leaving only the airholes the silly animals made visible above the snow so that the frantic shepherds who braved the bitter cold could find their missing flocks. Icicles hung in sharp fringes under the eaves of the crofters' cottages, the milk froze in the buckets, and birds fell stiff and dead from their roosts to the iron-hard earth.

So, too, did the snow swirl in blinding furies about a hunter and his three wolfhounds as they staggered homeward through the deep drifts heaped upon Strathmuir to Corbin Keep. The hunter's shoulders were bowed under the weight of a small red doe slung across his back and beneath his heavy spear, lodged in its leather carrying sling. The hunter's beard and hair and the massive hounds' shaggy gray pelts were strung with beads of ice, as was the cloak of wolf-skins in which the man was wrapped. The wind howled and raged. It hurled the snow hither and yon like a fierce, ravening beast that had a fleecy sheep held fast in its cruel maw. The hunter shuddered and cursed and wished himself home and warming his rump by the hearths of his hall, a roaring fire before him and a horn of mead in his fist, instead of fighting the blizzard to his door.

"Halloo, Castor, my laddie, what ha'e ye there?" the hunter growled some while later. His deep voice sounded loud on the snow-hushed air, for the blizzard had abated for the moment, her fury spent, and the uncannily still world around him was mantled in white.

Scowling, he saw that one of his hounds had strayed from their forward path across the knee-high drifts to worry at something dark half-hidden beneath the snow.

"Och, ye auld cur, leave be, and get on wi' ye, laddie! Home t' Corbin, ye great brutes, before dusk falls and the blizzard returns t' find us far from shelter!"

The warm breath poured like streamers of dragon-smoke from his mouth as he spoke, and the hunter, already exhausted by a long morning spent stalking his quarry, the weight of his kill and the difficult trek against the blizzard, was panting heavily when he again fell silent.

But for once the hounds ignored their master's curses and command. Now, all three worried and yelped and whined at the thing they'd found. Castor—the oldest of the three and the sire of the two younger wolfhounds—began scratching and clawing at the snow. He made worried little whining sounds deep in his throat and lifted his shaggy head from time to time to howl when his master, ignoring the sound the canny hunting hound made, continued onward.

"Curse ye, ye hairy beasts! Have done!" the hunter roared, turning back at last and letting the doe slither heavily from his shoulders to the snow, spattering it with ruby drops of blood.

In three long strides that sent snow flying up about him, he'd reached the hounds. Looming over them, he was about to grab their scruffs and set them firmly back on their path with a stern cuffing when he saw what it was they'd found. The hounds—tails wagging now—were forgotten as the hunter dropped to one knee, his jaw agape with astonishment.

Like a fairy-tale princess asleep in a glittering, crystal casket, a beautiful maiden lay before Roarke. Her skin was nigh as fair and translucent as the snow that veiled it with virginal flakes. Her hair—as thick and ebony-black as his own—fell in twin swathes on either side of her heart-shaped face, streamed down over slender shoulders to rest in great dark arabesques across the gentle mounds of her bosom. Upon it, her hands—graceful with long, tapering fingers—were folded. 'Twas as if two pale, lovely lilies had been pinned there! Her eyes were closed—what color they were, he could but guess!—the lashes sooty crescents where they rested against her ivory cheeks. Her lashes and her delicately arched dark brows were the only color in her lovely face, for in the light of the wintry moon, her lips were such a pale, pale pink, they appeared quite bloodless . . .

To Roarke's seasoned eyes, the little lassie appeared quite dead, entombed in a casket of snow. But . . . was she truly gone? he wondered belatedly, or had she merely fallen into the profound sleep that is engendered by bitter cold, and often but a prelude to the endless sleep of death itself? Dead, he decided, and his eyes narrowed as he shook his head in regret. She couldna have survived! The puir lass wore neither mantle nor heavy woolen tartan, despite the bitter weather! Her only garment was an ugly shift of stained brown homespun that couldna keep out the cold.

But to his surprise, on pressing his ear to her breast, he could hear a feeble throb. The wench was yet alive, though unless he was mistaken, the life was fast fleeing her body! He'd have to act swiftly, or not at all . . .

A look of grim determination crossed his swarthy, handsome face as he cuffed the frolicking hounds aside. He stooped and hefted the girl over his shoulder as he had the doe earlier. With a regretful glance for the fine kill he perforce must leave behind him, he started on his way once more, laboring through the deep drifts north towards Corbin, and whistling up his hounds to follow him.

Roarke had hoped and prayed that the blizzard had blown itself out, but as he staggered homeward, reeling now under the maid's small but persistent weight, the wail and shriek of the wind resumed. The dash of icy pellets against his cheeks scorned his hopes.

Rather than abating, the blizzard had now increased in ferocity. With every step he took, Roarke was forcefully made aware that he was too exhausted to go much farther. If he battled on and obstinately tried to carry on in his weakened state, he might well fall and be too feeble to rise again. And then—och, both he and the lassie would succumb to the deep, cold sleep of death! Corbin still lay over a league yonder, he judged, thinking wistfully and with fondness of his distant keep. But he would never make it there, not with the lassie slowing him down . . .

Deciding quickly, Roarke veered from his northward trek and headed northwest instead, his three faithful hounds floundering through the deep drifts at his heels. An abandoned crofter's hut lay yonder, if he could only find it amidst the driving sleet that distorted shapes and distance and obscured familiar landmarks from view. *If?* Och, there was nae "if" about it, he *must* find it, 'else the lassie would die! Peasant or nay, no bonnie little lass deserved t' perish alone on the freezing moors with no loved ones at hand—and nor would she, not if he could help it! Life was hard and rough even at the best o' times here in the north, and therefore most jealously clung to . . .

The crofter's hut appeared suddenly as a small, dark hump looming out of the snowstorm and the gently rolling whiteness of the moors. Roarke swallowed his shout of relief and instead conserved his remaining energy for the struggle to reach its door.

Built of peat sods and slabs of turf, its crevices wattled with mud, its walls half buried now with the snow banked against them, it was a crude, sorry dwelling, but far and away better than no shelter at all! They'd be out of the wind within its crumbling walls, at least . . .

Stooping, Roarke made it through the low opening just as his aching legs finally buckled beneath him. With a grunt, he reeled to his knees and the girl tumbled from his arms and rolled onto the earthen floor, yet she didna so much as stir or utter a single moan of discomfort.

"Your pardon, ma Snow Queen, for this rough and ready welcome t' your bower," Roarke said grimly on the silence when he'd recovered his breath and had managed to rise once more to his knees. "But alas, there wasna a blessed thing I could do about it!"

Unbuckling the black-enameled gold brooch, shaped like a raven, that fastened it, he drew the wolfskin cloak from about his own shoulders and covered the girl to her chin, tucking the edges snugly about her body. Then, squatting on his haunches, he looked about the crude confines of the hut for the makings of a fire, rubbing his hands together.

A broken milking stool and a broom of twigs were all he could find—scant enough kindling, aye, indeed, but fair enough, and beggars couldna be choosers, after all. Teeth chattering, Roarke drew the strike-a-light from

48

his belt with cold-numbed fingers and clumsily set about building them a fire.

It was a puny thing — more smoke than flame, more sizzle that true heat — and yet it comforted, if for no other reason than a fire in the hearth made any dwelling a home, even one as elemental and crude as this.

Rubbing his hands together again, and blowing upon them to warm himself, Roarke turned back to the girl.

His gray eyes were dark and brooding as he grazed his knuckles across her cheek, for it still felt as cold as charity. Growling an oath, he drew down the wolfskin covering he'd wrapped her in, but as he reached to take her hand in his and chafe it, his palm brushed her kirtle.

Blessed Mary, what was he thinking of? Sodden, the lassie's clothing was, aye, and wet and icy now that they were inside, out of the biting wind, for the snow had begun to melt. And, ruefully, he realized that his own tunic and breeks and the woolen *breacan* he'd thrown over them had fared little better. Something would have to be done about that!

Drawing the fur mantle aside, he unfastened the laces to the girl's kirtle and tugged it down over her shoulders, feeding her limp arms through the neck opening to yank the garment down to her knees, then off.

Beneath the scratchy kirtle — which had reeked of wet wool and sheep — she wore an underkirtle of some surprisingly fine, sheer cloth, equally soaked. Through it, glimpsed by the faint flicker of the fire, the mounds of her bosom showed full and firm, the small yet womanly peaks rigid with cold. Yet Roarke — ever a lusty fellow — might have been a celibate monk for the scant thought he gave to either her loveliness or her utter vulnerability to his manhood in that moment.

Without pause, he stripped the clammy garment from her, unlaced her leggings, tugged off her suede boots, then stripped himself of tunic, breeks, and smallcloth. Naked now, as was she, he stretched himself out alongside the girl. Gathering her limp, unprotesting body into his arms and holding it fast against the heat of his own body, he hauled the wolfskin mantle and his clan *breacan* up and over their heads, cocooning them in musty warmth.

The three hounds—who'd followed their master inside—settled down in a cosy heap alongside the fire, and promptly fell asleep.

Against his will, and despite the valiant effort he made to remain awake and chafe some warmth into the maid's icy limbs, an exhausted Roarke quickly did likewise.

Chapter Four

Roarke awoke when it was still full dark. He could hear the moan of the wind about the crofter's hut, and the shrieks and whistles it made as it ferreted out each chink, nook, and cranny. He'd been right all along, he mused, smothering a drowsy yawn. The blizzard had yet to abate.

Struggling up onto his elbows and rubbing his smoke-filled eyes, he saw that the fire he'd lit earlier had burned down to only glowing orange embers and heaps of white ash. Forcing himself to leave the cozy confines of the wolfskin coverlet — and the soft curves of the lass who snuggled heavily against him — for the sooty chill that lay beyond, he crawled out to feed a few more sticks of kindling onto the fire. Then, shivering violently and with his teeth chattering once again, he beat a hasty retreat back to his makeshift bower and pulled the coverings up and over their heads once again.

In the warm, pitch-dark tent he'd made, the fragrance of the lass who slept deeply beside him teased his nose. It was an elusive, female scent that had a subtle floral quality to it he recognized. 'Twas strangely pleasing to his senses, albeit the delicate fragrance of heather was mingled with the less pleasant odor of drying wool and damp wolfskins, and his own salty male scent. Still, sweet-smelling or nay, Roarke realized that the girl was yet chilled to the bone.

Starting with her shoulders, he began to do as he'd intended doing before foolishly falling asleep. Briskly, as he would rub down a fine, blooded horse, he rubbed her bare shoulders, worked his way down her arms, then massaged her wrists and slim hands, trying to chafe some warmth back into her limbs with the friction.

By the Cross, he mused wonderingly as he did so, how very smooth and soft her skin felt beneath his calloused hands! It was as velvety as the petals of a violet or the downy feathers of a wee dark wren.

"Och, ma wee lassie, is it some noble's leman you're after being, then?" he asked her softly in Gaelic, for her skin was certainly far and away more soft than the plump, work-coarsened bodies of the peasant wenches he was familiar with — aye, and a deal more fragrant! "Does that explain why ye feel so soft and smell sae sweet and pretty? And why yer underlinen is sewn wi' such fine cloth?"

He left off massaging her bare arms to coax some warmth into her throat, stroking its slim, graceful column over and over again. He was rewarded to feel the pulse beating there grow stronger. Encouraged, Roarke's palm swept lower, idly grazing the delicate jut of her collarbones before encompassing the full yet chilly curve of one cold-nippled breast with an appreciative male grunt.

"Ah, but 'tis bonnie ye are in every part o' ye, eh, my wee lost lambkin?" Roarke purred. Ever a lusty fellow, and one dearly fond of women, he'd curled his fingers to gently cup the luscious mound and fondle that poor, icy little nipple to rosy tightness before it dawned on him what he was about!

He muttered a disgusted curse at his churlishness, then guiltily shifted his attentions to her belly instead. It was flat, almost concave, and — he discovered in a single, sweeping caress — there was no telltale slackness from child-bearing in the sweet young flesh beneath his hand. She was sae firm and sleek t' his touch, he'd wager a purse that this lassie had never carried a bairn!

Humming a favorite ballad beneath his breath, Roarke continued to rub her belly, circling his palm around and around until the action almost hypnotized him. Mary be praised, it was working, he realized after some time! A rosy flush seemed to be spreading throughout her body now, making it warm with returning life under his fingertips. He also realized with a start that his own breathing had altered in ways that had little to do with exhaustion, but governed parts of his anatomy that had come t' life wi' a vengeance!

Och, Master Longstaff, all shame on ye! She's naught but a helpless bairn! Ye canna have her, ye randy brute! he chided himself, knowing full well in some secret, guilty corner of his mind that his labored breathing owed more to rising lust than flagging strength! Vexed at his weakness, he determinedly left off massaging her belly to devote his attentions to the lassie's chilly thighs and legs instead.

They, he discovered ruefully, were as bonnie as the rest o' her! Her long, slim thighs tapered into slender calves and finely boned ankles and chilly little feet. For all their slenderness of form, they were nontheless legs that were strongly muscled for a woman, especially down the inner thighs. Her wee rump was tight and firm as a bannock, too, he discovered, idly patting her bottom, both indications that the lass was accustomed to riding a-cock a horse like a man, rather than striding across the moors in womanlike fashion. Riding? A peasant wench? "Whist ye, Roarke, mon, what are ye thinkin' of!" he muttered, shaking his head. "Peasant wenches dinna ride!"

To his chagrin, the familiar throbbing and tightness at his loins were not so easily dismissed! Sure enough, he began to tremble as lust streaked through him like lightning. The nearness of her warm, female body made both his hands itch with the unbearable yearning to touch her loveliness more intimately.

"Ye bastard!" he growled. "Ye dishonorable bastard, Roarke Mac Gilchrist, t' consider such a thing!"

With an oath, he drew his hand from her, but somehow found it nestled instead against the soft, fleecy pelt of her woman's mound for a heartbeat—certainly no more—before he snatched his hand away as if burned, and tucked it firmly beneath his opposite armpit, out of harm's way.

"Sweet Jesu!" he growled, for even with so fleeting a caress, his lust had built apace. His groin ached with thwarted need, his mouth felt dry, while his heart had begun to skip and jump like a spring lambkin frisking over a flowery meadow. Awakened to the female loveliness so close and yet so very distant, his manhood had stirred, too. Master Longstaff bucked at his groin, a sleeping dragon rearing its head, growing hard and aching with lust.

"For the love o' God!" he groaned on the darkness. "Am I a beardless lad, that I canna control mysel' for a single night? A stag in full rut, that I must mount each doe that passes? Och, lassie, dinna do this t' me, I beg ye!" Roarke breathed, pulling away from her and returning both his hands firmly to his sides, though they were clenched fists now. "Your savior I might well be, but I'm but a mon, for all that! Aye, and a rogue wi' feet o' clay and scant willpower when it comes t' a pretty wee morsel like yersel'! Go on this way, an' by dawn I'll be your ruin, my bonnie!"

In actuality, of course, Roarke knew full well that the wench—that poor, innocent, sleeping beauty beside him!—had done naught to encourage his caresses nor to stir his male ardor. At least, not of her own free will she hadna, unless the very fact of possessing a faerie loveliness and a body that was decidedly mortal and decidedly female could be considered a guilty act!

And yet, t' cast the blame on her, to talk and reason

54

to take his mind off the pleasant, sinful thoughts he was entertaining, was all Roarke could come up with in that moment by way of diversion!

After all, where could he go in this foul blizzard to put safe distance between himself and the sleeping lass? To where could he run? This close to her, this tantalizingly *next* to her as he was right now, his nostrils filled with her scent, his hands still a-tingle with the feel o' her silkiness, he needed badly to find some means to curb his mounting lust!

"Talk, laddie—and keep on talking!" he cautioned himself grimly. "Talk all night—'else be ready t' face some irate crofter whose daughter ye've ravished, come daybreak."

And so, talk he did, as much to himself as to her.

In his lilting Gaelic, spoken in a deep voice laden with the honeyed, heathery burr of his Border clan, Roarke told the sleeping girl of himself, and of the life he'd lived till now.

And, as he spoke, Roarke remembered the sting of the taunts that had followed him through the years of his childhood, the hurtful singsong jeers and barbed mockery that had made his ears burn with shame, and his eyes smart with tears:

"Where's yer father, Roarke, laddie?"

"Shut yer trap, Harry, else I'll clobber ye wi' ma fists! Ma father's the king, he is!"

"Liar, liar, yer breeks are a-fire!" the urchin had gleefully chanted. *"Yer father's a tinker, he isna the king! Yer mother's a tart who'll do aught for a ring!"*

Another'd chimed in:

"His mother was a whore, 'tis said,
Who took the king into her bed,
She didna care if they were wed
So long he paid his shilling!

"Good wench," our bonnie king did say,

55

"Alas, I have no coin this day
I beg ye, dinna run away!"
"Nay, sire," she vowed, "I'm willing!"

"Ye are my liege," she sweetly vowed,
"T' please my sovereign I'd be proud!"
She spread her thighs and cried aloud
"For Duncan, God, and Scotland!"

The small bard who'd composed those hateful verses had received two black eyes, a bloodied nose, a split lip, and lost three teeth for his cruel wit.

And that day, Roarke had learned the bitter lesson that the only way to silence those taunts and earn respect was with his fists. It was a lesson he'd be forced to put into practice over and over again between boyhood and manhood, for Roarke—although the royal get of the murdered king, Duncan of Scotland—had been bastard-born, and the world did not easily accept those with the taint of illegitimacy.

Duncan's legitimate heir, Malcolm III, ruled now in the treacherous General MacBeth's stead, while Roarke, a true son of the former king tho' sired upon a petty baron's daughter without benefit o' marriage, had been denied both royal name and the princely position that should have been his birthright.

Until his dying breath, Duncan, once high king of Scotland, had churlishly denied seducing or fathering a child upon the young Lady Fionna of Corbin, Roarke's mother. And to his shame, Fionna's father, Kevin Mac Andrew, laird of Corbin Keep, had chosen to believe the lies of his sovereign lord instead of the words of his innocent daughter. Accordingly, Laird Kevin had cruelly disowned the pregnant girl, Roarke continued his tale on the smoky darkness. He had sent Fionna from Corbin with only the garments upon her back to her name.

"Penniless, terrified, and quite alone in harsh times

when a woman must have a man to protect her, else die, my lady mother was forced to throw herself on the mercy of a convent of holy sisters. She found sanctuary with the nuns at an abbey east of here, and in due course gave me birth. Between her birthing pangs, she wept and prayed for death to take her," he recounted. His lady mother had told him this when he was old enough to understand.

But—Fionna was young and strong, and every bit as stubborn in her own female fashion as her lord father. Death had not claimed her. Nor had she truly wanted to die, in her heart of hearts, she'd confessed to Roarke. From the moment she'd held her infant son—lusty and black-haired as his father had been—for the first time she'd known she must live, must be strong to raise her son to manhood. Without her, her poor bairn would have noone in this world—which sneered at bastards, nobly sired or nay—to care for him.

Somehow, with the help of the good sisters, both mother and child had survived. And the lady Fionna had wedded, in due course, a prosperous wool merchant two score years her senior; a widower from the nearby hamlet of Kelso named Master Camden Gilchrist.

Gilchrist had nurtured a great love for the beautiful, auburn-haired Fionna from the moment he'd first set eyes upon her. He'd quickly expressed a genuine fondness for her little son, too, for he'd sired no bairns upon his first wife and had always wanted a son of his own. Gilchrist had had wealth aplenty, too, to support them both in comfort.

For ten years, the three of them had been happy, for Fionna had grown to love her husband dearly, despite him being far older than she. Cam was kind to her, indulgent even, and unusual among his peers in that he cherished and respected her spirit and intelligence, which equaled his own. All might have continued on thus happily had circumstances remained unchanged, but, alas, they did not.

When Roarke was in his fifteenth year, his grandfather, Laird Kevin Mac Andrew vic Quinlann, had died, leaving Corbin Keep and his estates to fall into the hands of a distant cousin Fionna had never once set eyes upon. He'd made no bequest whatsoever for his only child, the daughter he'd disowned, nor for her son, his only true heir.

Fionna had wept for days at the cruel injustice her father had done them. Of course, women were not permitted to own either land or keep in this day and age, and she'd known she could never inherit Corbin. Yet to leave her and his grandbairn without so much as a single farthing, nor a kind word in parting . . . ! Oh, how cruel and unforgiving her laird father had proven to his own flesh and blood, even to his dying breath!

Young Roarke, fierce and hot against injustice in the first flush of righteous manhood, had heard his mother's anguished weeping. He'd hastened straightway to her side.

"Dry your eyes, my lady mother," he'd commanded her in the deep, stern voice of a man, rather than a lad, as he placed a protective hand upon her shoulder. "One day, Corbin shall be yours, and ye shall live there like a Border queen! This I swear t' ye, my lady mother, on my honor as a mon!" he'd vowed, his gray eyes hot as the ashes of a fire with his anger. "If my rightful father would not own me as his royal get, then so be it. Bretwalda Duncan is dead and gone now, and there's naught I can do to change that. But—I willna stand by and see my lady mother disinherited!"

Master Gilchrist had admired the tenacity and resolve of his foster son, of whom he'd grown even fonder over the years, and accordingly had made him a surprising promise.

"Ye're a mon of honor and loyalty, young Roarke. I admire such traits in a mon. When ye have ten and eight winters to your span, I'll provide ye with the gold ye need to purchase fighting men t' aid your cause. And if you're still of the same mind then, laddie, and wish to regain Corbin for your lady mother and yersel'—well, I'll do all in my power t' aid you, as a loving—father— would aid his only son." Cam's hoary brows had raised in inquiry and hope.

"Ah, but you're a guid man, Cam Gilchrist," Roarke had said solemnly, meeting Gilchrist eye-to-eye as one man to another—with respect. He'd clasped hands with his foster father to seal the agreement between them, adding, "My heartfelt thanks, Father."

Alas, Camden Gilchrist had died two years following the pact they'd sealed. Hale and hearty one day, the next he'd fallen mortally ill of a huge quincy in his throat, which had soon burst and spilled its poison through him. Along with his sharp and genuine grief at the fine old man's passing, Roarke had also felt a niggling pang of regret that the merchant had not lived long enough to see his vow kept.

Accordingly, his surprise had been great, his joy enormous, when he learned from Camden Gilchrist's clerk that the old man had, long before his untimely death, left a weighty casket of gold coins in the young cleric's safekeeping, with the instructions that if aught should befall him, they and all he possessed at the time of his death were to be given to Roarke with his blessing, in order that the young man might use them to care for his mother, and to "achieve his heart's desire."

Did Roarke understand what Master Gilchrist had meant, the clerk had asked, frowning in puzzlement? Indeed, Roarke had understood—and very well, too! He'd blessed the old man a thousandfold for his canny insight and the deep and abiding love implicit in his actions.

"Truly, Cam Gilchrist, you were more father t' me than I could ever have wished for!" he'd said solemnly under his breath as he bade his foster father a last farewell. His eyes had been wet with tears as they carried Cam to his final resting place in the kirk yard.

The following summer, Roarke had taken the name Gilchrist as his own and had begun gathering fighting men to his cause. Some rallied to him out of friendship, being lads he'd grown up with and led on numerous pranks and escapades along the borders and deep into England t' raid for Saxon cattle. Others joined him in admiration for his daring and fighting prowess, all too willing to swear fealty to a man they both liked and respected.

Although only seventeen years at that time, Black Roarke's reputation as a "canny fellow" and a "braw mon" wi' a dirk' to have fighting alongside one in battle, was already considerable, as enemy clans had learned to their bitter peril when bloodfeuds flared anew and old enmities were rekindled by some real or imagined slight. Roarke, kilted in the pattern of his adopted clan's red-black-and-gray tartan, a dirk in one fist and a stout claymore in the other, and fury blazing from his smoke-gray eyes as he strode the heathery moors, was a bonnie sight t' see as the skirl of the bagpipes rallied them t' battle!

By late summer of the following year, Roarke the Bastard, as he was also widely known, was ready to march on Corbin, and claim her for his own. By Yule of the same twelvemonth, he was installed there, warming his toes before the vast hearth of Corbin Keep. Beside him sat his lady mother, draped in fur-lined robes as she worked at her loom. His followers — those who'd opted to stay with him after the battle for Corbin, and who'd sworn allegiance to Roarke and vowed to follow him as the laird of his new clan, the clan Gilchrist — were gathered about them in the drafty great hall, drinking the ousted heir's fine wines and mead . . .

Memories teemed in his head as Roarke relived that turbulent yet exciting time in his life. It was several moments before he realized that the girl was no longer lying still and silent beside him but had stirred. She was whimpering softly, and trying with little success to thrust the wolfskin cloak aside and cradle her head. Belatedly, Roarke discovered a lump there the size of a goose egg beneath her hair, though there was no blood that he could feel.

"Dinna touch yer hurt, sweeting," he commanded, drawing her hand away. " 'Twill only make the pain worsen."

Nevertheless, she struggled in his loose embrace, tossing restlessly and mumbling . . . what? A name? A place? He couldn't decipher which!

He leaned over her, his ear close to her mouth to catch her murmurings.

"Nay, please, nay! Och, mon, I trusted ye, ye ken. But now . . . ah, Jesu, now all is lost . . . all of it . . . ruined . . . now!"

Roarke frowned. Despite the lowness of her voice and its rambling quality, the desperation and sorrow to her words was marked.

"Nay, lassie, dinna fret," he soothed. "Tsk! Tsk! All's well now. Aye, it is, ye'll see. By the morrow, God willing, ye'll be mended an'—"

"Love . . . !" she breathed again, and the endearment was a sigh, a prayer, an entreaty, a lovesong when sighed from her lips. "Was it all but a bad dream, then? Are ye here wi' me after all?"

She was not, he knew, speaking to him, but dreaming still, or fevered. Fevered, he decided, touching her brow, which felt burning now. Once again, she threshed about, throwing off his hands and struggling to escape, babbling about death and betrayal. Roarke frowned, disturbed by her frantic movements, her anguished sobbing. The confines of the hovel were pitch black. She could not see him, even had she tried to, and so in an effort to calm her, he murmured, "Aye, lassie, aye, 'tis your own true love, safe here beside ye. Back t' sleep wi' ye, now, dearling. Sleep!"

"I canna sleep, not now!" she murmured, and gave a sighing little sob. "The nightmares—they might return—and I couldna—I couldna bear it that they should!"

Her green eyes were stark with horror in the firelight as she uttered a shuddering sigh. "Oh, my love, I dreamed such terrible, frightening things! But . . . but I can only half remember them!" she babbled. "What's wrong with me, dear heart? Why can I remember naught?"

"Hush, lovie, hush!" Roarke crooned, playing his mummer's part of her sweetheart to the very hilt. "Nae nightmare beasties will dare trouble your slumber anon, not with me t' guard ye. Sleep now, hinnie. Sleep!" he coaxed.

"I will, beloved. Aye, I swear t' ye I will," she promised sleepily. "But first . . . och, first ye must kiss me, hold me, heart o' my heart!"

Chapter Five

Slender arms came at Roarke from the blackness and curled about his neck as the girl struggled to sit up. Little hands pressed hard against the back of his head to bring his mouth down to meet hers.

It all happened so swiftly — so unexpectedly! — that Roarke's lips had parted and crushed down over her sweet mouth before he realized what was happening! His rugged arms encircled her and molded her slender body fiercely against his as he drank the sweet, drowsy nectar of her lips. The warmth of her against him was like flame. Her scent was intoxicating. He nuzzled her throat, her ears, savored the feel of her womanly body beneath his caresses as if he'd been starved of sensation for a score of years!

Still, the throb of his conscience didna relent. 'Twas like the monotonous drum of a tabor in his ears. *Ye shouldna be doin' this, laddie!* it cautioned like a nagging old woman. *She doesna ken who ye are, mon, she's sae fevered and confused! Ye should leave well enough alone!* Yet he blocked his ears and kissed her anew, ignoring the twin demons of Commonsense and Reason who also urged him to come to his senses and put the lassie from him. He heeded only the pulse of desire that throbbed in his blood and wouldna be denied!

"Och, my wee vixen, just the feel o' ye . . . !" he

growled, his voice ragged. He slipped his mouth lower to brand her silken throat, while his warrior's calloused hands twined through the rich cascade of her hair to bind her to him by its glossy tether.

"Love, oh, my love!" she gasped, her voice smoky with wanting. "Too long we've waited for this moment! Make me yours at last, I beg ye!"

Everything felt hazy and golden to her, movement and thought slowed and exaggerated like a strange pagan dance. 'Twas as if she moved through the liquid velvet of a dream. Though darkness cloaked them both, only the man seemed real, his body hard and substantial, his lips salty, hot and sinfully exciting, his caresses gentle and enflaming. The strong arms that held her were her fortress against the vague dangers that threatened her; against the shadowy, faceless enemies she could not name. She clung to him, pressing her body to his, seeking out his warmth and strength as a moth courts the flame of a candle.

Through the fever of his own lust, Roarke forgot the very real fever raging through the girl. He also turned a deaf ear to the endearments she cried so lovingly in his ear. She knew what she was about, did she no'? Why else would she press herself to him and return the pressure of his mouth with her own? And so, with a lusty grunt, he spilled her backward to the wolfskin cloak, rucked up beneath them now, and followed her down to it. He smothered her impassioned pleas with his hungry mouth, and her body with his own.

He kissed her lips, long and fully, and she lifted her mouth and parted her lips most eagerly to accept his tender invasion. She tasted of summer wines, heady and potent, full and rich with promises of passion, and he drank from her thirstily. He kissed the feathery little fans of her lashes, the delicate arches of her brows, and called her his "bonnie wee wren." He kissed her brow itself, so smooth, so blessed hot, and bussed the tip of her narrow little nose, her cheeks, her chin, for 'twas as

64

if he couldna get enough of her taste! Tilting her head, he nibbled and nipped at her earlobes like a playful pup and dipped the very tip of his hot, damp tongue into the shell-like whorls, breathing hard all the while.

Her senses reeled. Through the drowsy haze, she felt the flesh of her arms rise in goosebumps and shivered with pleasure. Her body was trembling beneath his touch as she arched like a cat to rub herself against him and follow the sweep of his hand down her body. Little sighs and gasps broke from her lips, and Roarke smiled knowingly in the shadows. She wanted him, too — aye, and with a fiery passion t' match his own! The lass was hot for a man's lusty loving — and he was the man to give her what she craved.

"Will you no' caress me, too, my lassie?" he asked huskily, and felt her fingertips sear his shoulders as she heeded his command and caressed him.

Down her little hand trailed, grazing over his powerful, satiny shoulders to his massive chest. Slowly, hesitantly, that hand came around to tousle the pelt of rough, springy curls that clung to his torso and furred a dark line down his oak-hard belly. Mother of God, what magic did she own? Her fingers, her nails, sparked tiny lightning bolts wherever they wandered! His own fingers digging deep into her arms, Roarke had to grit his teeth and clench his jaw to still his trembling and curb the fiery lust that rampaged through him.

Dipping his head now to the pallid silk of her throat, he scorched a path of fire down it to her collarbone, and thence his lips found her wee breasts. Cupping them in his large hands, he pressed them up and took the taut buds that crowned them deep into his mouth. He suckled her breasts with heated lips and tongue, all the while fondling her silky thighs and the wee cleft between them or squeezing the curves of her bottom and pressing her hips to the aching hardness that rode at his groin. *Jesu!* he thought, *She feels so rare, so fine!* How he yearned for light to make love to her by; blessed rush-light that would reveal her beauty in all its delicate hues and loveliness of form, the sight of her a garnish to the feast of taste and texture she spread, banquetlike, before him.

"Och, lovie, ye taste that sweet!" Roarke whispered, his voice a husky purr. "Aye, and the feel o' ye, stirrin' to my touch like a wee bird! Why, 'tis enough t' drive a saint t' madness!"

"Mmmm!" she murmured, tangling her fingers in his wealth of springy curls and cradling his fine head between them. "Tell me, dearling, d' ye love me truly?"

"Aye, my lassie, aye . . ." he breathed, and in that moment, it was no lie. He loved her—loved every little curve, every sweetly pliant inch of fresh young flesh and scented hollow that he could taste and feel! Aye, by God, he loved her *everywhere!*

He slipped his hands beneath her hips to cup the swells of her wee rump, fascinated by its boyish yet undeniably female curves. Drawing her hips hard against his flanks so that she must feel the rearing thrust of his manhood, he kneaded her buttocks and demanded hoarsely, "And so? Will ye have me now, my bonnie?"

"Aye, and gladly, sir!" came back her gasping answer on the smoky darkness.

With a low, lusty murmur, Roarke slipped his hands between their bodies, rubbing his palms over her warm belly before reaching lower still to fondle the silky triangle between her thighs.

She stiffened as he explored her secret portals, but her startled gasps quickly became murmurs of pleasure and abandon. She relaxed, grew limp as he teased and pressed and entered her there, plying her with deft, rhythmic strokes of his finger and thumb that made her moan with pleasure and grow moist beneath his touch.

Remaining quite still, she sighed with wonderment as pleasure filled her loins. And, in her confusion and

66

breathless delight, her desire mounted. Her grip in his hair tightened, tugging painfully at his scalp.

Sweet wonder of heaven, Roarke thought, plundering her treasures, she was as blessed tight as a virgin maid — aye, tighter than a Highlander's pursestrings, which were tight indeed! The throbbing weightiness at his groin increased tenfold, becoming nigh unbearable with the hunger t' have her. Nevertheless, he bided his time, as he'd promised himself, summoning all of his lover's arts to bring her to fullest flower before pressing his 'vantage. He combined busy mouth upon her snow-white bosom with busy fingers that pressed and stroked her inner silkiness. Delicately, he played upon the very bud of her passion like a minstrel plucking at the strings of a harp, caressing her honeyed softness until she moaned and swore she would have him tarry no longer, but that he must take her, take her *now*, for the love o' God, and have an end t' his sweet torture!

Roarke needed no second urging. Pressing her down onto her back, he knelt between her thighs. Raising her hips, he drew back, prepared to thrust deep and hard into her heated sheath and exorcise his demon-lust at last —

"Now, my heart, I beg ye, now! Oh, my laird, my husband, I desire thee so!" she cried brokenly from amidst the storm of her passion.

And, in the very moment that Roarke would have thrust forward and claimed her, her words gelded him. Master Longstaff softened, grew shy, as surely as if she'd used a dirk instead of words to cut the manhood from him!

Husband, she'd said. Not sweetheart, nor lover, but *husband*.

Married? he thundered silently as a terrible, thwarted rage filled him. Husband? *Och, nay, it couldna be so!*

"Lass?" he demanded, rolling from atop her to kneel instead at her side. "Speak t' me! Are ye truly wife t' some man, or nay? Who is this man ye call husband, lass? Waken and answer me, damn ye!" he demanded urgently, shaking her.

But she would not . . . could not! . . . answer him.

Exhausted by her ordeal and exposure in the blizzard, drained by her fever and perhaps by his lusty loveplay, she'd drifted off into deep sleep once again. And, he soon discovered, nothing he said nor threatened could rouse her!

Smoldering, Roarke quit the wolfskins' warm confines. Cursing, he drew on his damp clothing. Shivering, he left her to her sleep and huddled moodily over the dwindling fire. Scowling, he gazed into its puny flicker and pondered her words — and the aching discomfort and niggling unease that comes to a man with lust unspent.

The blizzard was done by the following morning when Roarke ducked his head under the hovel's lintel, though the moors stretching about him in every direction bore testimony to its passing.

A mantle of sparkling white covered the world, rounding out familiar hollows and mounding over craggy landmarks, heaping up about fir trunks to render them unrecognizable even to his eyes. A bleary sun had risen and was now trying to shine in the almost white of the sky.

With its efforts, Roarke blinked and covered his eyes, squinting against the blinding glare of sunlight on snow as he staggered from the hut's gloomy interior. He'd best be on his way, and soon, for the sky, though clear, had a pallor that threatened more snow to come later in the day, to one such as he who knew the fickle border weather well.

A short while later found him trudging an arduous path across the moors once again, headed towards his keep on the last leg of the journey. His three boisterous wolfhounds gamboled and frisked ahead of him, barking joyously to be going home as they loped through the deep drifts.

Once again he'd shouldered his slender burden of the afternoon before, but with far greater ease after a good night's rest — though admittedly with far less good grace or enthusiasm, for all that the wintry dawning had brought a pleasant surprise.

Comely enough by the light of the wintry moon, in the full, sharp brilliance of winter daylight — so cruel to many who were passing-fair by twilight! — the girl's faerie loveliness had left Roarke speechless! In truth, that rare marriage of creamy skin, midnight hair, emerald eyes, and rosy cheeks — now flushed from the fever that raged through her in the wake of her exposure — was enough to leave any man comparing all women by the yardstick of her beauty, and having them fall short! And, having such a beauty for his bride, the lucky man would guard her virtue jealously, would he not, Roarke pondered dourly as he headed for home, and challenge any rogue who soiled her honor!

So why, reason demanded in turn, would such a fortunate husband allow his lovely bride to wander the moors unescorted in such treacherous weather? Would a truly loving husband see his beautiful lady go from him with neither mantle nor plaid to keep her warm? Nay! To Roarke's shrewd mind, the answer was obvious. Something had gone awry. Mayhap the girl had been abducted from her escort by robbers, her fine garments stolen, before her captors left her for dead in the snow? Mayhap she'd been held for ransom by one warring clan laird to another? It was common enough in these parts and times. Or else a jealous man, envious of her husband's good fortune, had stolen her from him and their retinue and slain her lord in the process? Either circumstance would explain the knot to her head.

The unanswered questions nagged at Roarke until at last he'd gained the crest of the last hill before home.

He stood upon the rim, looking across the little snow-covered glen below to the keep beyond.

Corbin Keep perched like a dark raven with its wings spread across the rocky jut of dark crags, while below, Loch Tully glittered like a mirror of ebony crystal under lowering skies. *He was home!* The girl weighed heavily in his arms again, for he'd lifted her down from his throbbing shoulder, but he gathered her up and continued on, striding eagerly along now that home was so very near.

He'd taken but a few paces down the hill when to his relief, he saw a horse and rider appear between a stand of deep-green firs, and recognized his steward and friend, Tavish, riding to meet him. The hounds barked a welcome and bounded across the snow towards him.

"Laird Roarke? Graeme? Halloo, who goes? Is that you, mon?" the rider called when he was yet some distance away.

"Aye, Tavish, 'tis I!" Roarke bellowed in answer.

"Our Lady be praised! After last night's foul blizzard, why, we'd given both yersel' and Graeme up for lost, my laird, alone and abroad as ye were!" Tavish cried. "We were afeared if the weather hadna claimed ye, the clan Frazier or the Bloody McNairs must ha'e done so!" he added gloomily, crossing himself.

"Aye, no doubt ye did, mon. But here I am, safe if nae longer sae sound — and no doubt Graeme will return from his wenching likewise! Come, laddie, and bring up your nag — and for the love o' God, make haste! My arms are fair t' breakin'!"

"Well, well! And what is it ye have there?" Tavish queried, squinting against the blinding glare of sunlight on snow as he urged his shaggy mount up the incline towards Roarke. "A doe for the Yule feast, mon?"

"Aye, laddie, a doe it once was, but now . . . ? Why, 'tis become a lassie!" Roarke teased with a grin and a wink. "T' faith, there's a fine riddle fer ye t' puzzle over,

70

eh, friend Tavish!"

"Mmm," Tavish mused, dismounting and already puzzling. "What was once a doe, but is now a lassie . . . ? My silver-banded drinking horn says I can decipher your riddle before Compline!" his sandy-haired steward boasted cockily.

"Och, mon, ye may rhyme and riddle t' your heart's content anon!" Roarke growled. "Fer now, ye porridge head, help me t' get the lassie home!"

Chapter Six

The sevennight prior to the Christ Child's birth dawned bitterly cold yet clear. The blizzards of the past three weeks had abated, and the skies that yawned above Corbin were pavilions of midnight-blue, pricked with dagger-stars that glittered like crystal rowels. The biting wind was a crafty fox that slunk through cloak and mantle both and pawed an entry beneath the oiled skins that covered the apertures in the keep walls. Its panting breath stirred the vivid tapestry hangings, too, so that the huntsmen, stags, and hounds of Scottish legend embroidered upon them seemed not only alive, but galloping madly! The wind also set the flames upon the twin hearths to dancing with a wild pagan joy. Their colors of amber, scarlet, and blue twined about each other like the braided ribands of a Maypole.

The members of the clan Gilchrist had left their manors and crofts to gather within the walls of Corbin and partake of the Twelve Days' feasting together. Now, despite the crackling logs that blazed within each of the twin hearths of the great hall, they shivered and tried to huddle closer to the fires or burrowed deeper into their fur-lined mantles and made themselves warmer from within with draughts of mulled wine, warmed mead, or fiery water o' life and tried to forget their coldness in lively conversation.

Lady Fionna, Roarke's mother, relieved of her duties as nurse to the foundling girl by her serving woman, Flora, sat with her ladies about the fire. She was gently trying to coax her cousin, the lady Elyse, to speak.

Elyse, wife to a Saxon, Edgar, Earl of Thorington, had — in the company of her two small grandchildren, a serving woman, and an old groom — arrived on Corbin's doorstep the evening before, much the same manner that Roarke had returned with the girl. Fionna had discovered that the bedraggled quartet had traveled the several hundred leagues from the south of England to the Scottish Marches unescorted, braving the bitter weather and deep snow in only a horse-drawn sled quite alone. She'd been astonished when Tavish led them into the hall, for it had been many years since she'd last seen her cousin; nor had she expected to see Elyse in the near future, and certainly not in the sorry state in which she had arrived! Her cousin's clothing had been travel-stained and tattered, her eyes swollen and red-rimmed from weeping, her lips bluish with cold and pinched with exhaustion. Moreover, she'd observed that beneath her veil, Elyse's hair — formerly the bonnie McAndrew auburn color so vaunted here in the north — had turned white overnight. Fionna had been convinced that only by voicing her fears could the puir woman put those awful days behind her and had encouraged her to speak of the terrible experiences she'd undergone as she fled England for Scotland,

"Sweet coz, come!" she'd urged gently. "Come here wi' ye, and sit by the fire and warm yersel'! Jesu, ma puir lass, 'tis half frozen ye are! Och, and the puir wee bairns — will ye no' look at the pair o' them, sae blue wi' cold! Whatever was your husband thinking of, t' send ye north sae poorly clothed! Flora, t' the kitchens wi' ye, straightway! Have Cook warm some fresh milk for possets and see if there's porridge made for the wee ones t' sup. Lizzie! I'll thank ye t' fetch furs for these poor, freezing creatures — those in my bower will do, and there's more in the storehouse, if there arena enough there! Drew! Heap another log on the fire, mon—and make haste, mind!" she'd ordered, drawing Elyse down onto a cushioned settle. She'd knelt at her feet and chafed her cousin's icy hands and feet as she'd gently pressed, "Now, tell me, what in the world has happened t' ye, lovie? Where is your Edgar, and what brings ye here t' me sae suddenly?"

Elyse had only wept at first, but then—warmed by the fire, furs, and bracing dram of the water o' life, brought for her by Roarke—and relaxed by Fionna's soothing voice, she'd at last managed to talk. And the tale she'd told had been a disturbing one.

She'd reminded her cousin Fionna of how, in the month of October of the year previous, 1066, Duke William of Normandy and his vast Norman, Breton, and Flemish armies had conquered Kind Harold Godwinson of England, thus fulfilling the gloomy predictions of the Saxon king's astrologers.

"The sages warned us, did they no', Coz?" Elyse had whispered. "Their sky-gazing foretold the coming of the great, long-haired star in that year—one that would appear in the skies and blaze for many nights, d' ye recall? It was an omen, they said. One promising great change and upheaval in our world! Aye, and they spoke truly! Their black prophecies have been fulfilled! The Normans have conquered England, Fionna. Heart, body, and spirit, they have triumphed over her. They've brought her to her knees, beaten and ravaged, and now they will surely bleed her dry!" she'd cried, dabbing at her eyes.

When she'd been able to continue, she'd described in halting tones how her husband, Edgar, Earl of Thorington, had received word that the Normans were advancing on his manor. He'd instructed her to prepare herself and their two small grandchildren for a long and difficult journey north to her Scottish homeland.

"The Normans are marching on Thorington, dear

heart," he'd murmured, tears in his eyes as he took her in his arms. "Within the hour, they will be here, battering at our gates, demanding entry. But ye know full well I could never yield them my sword in surrender, nor bow to our enemies, do ye not, my love? Harold Godwinson was our rightful king, true heir to the throne of England! I swore fealty to him. I fought at his side, as did our son. Gawain and I will bend a knee to no sovereign save Harold's rightful successor. If the Normans would take Thorington Hall and my demesne for themselves, then they perforce must do battle for her!"

"Please, Edgar, nay!" Elyse had implored her husband. "Come with us! Save yersel', and live t' see your grandbairns grow t' manhood! I beg ye, dinna forfeit yer life for a lost cause, when ye canna hope to triumph against sae many! The Normans outnumber ye a thousandfold, my love!"

"Nay, dearest mother," her son, Gawain, had cut in, his voice hoarse with emotion. "My lord father is right. He and I must remain here. It is our duty to stay, for we are men of honor. We've known since King Harold was slain and we retreated from Hastings last year that this day would not be long in coming. Accordingly, we made our decision long since against this moment and have taken oath not to relinquish our demesne without a fight! I implore you, Mother, take my sons north to safety! And, if it is God's will that we should perish beneath a Norman sword, raise them to honor myself and their grandfather in our stead. My blessed Alison is no more. My sons will have need of the mother's love you've shown them since her passing."

Both husband and son had turned a deaf ear to Elyse's pleas, and instead seen to it that she and her grandsons, a casket of jewels, the dead king's charter granting Edgar the demesne of Thorington, and a pitifully meager portion of her belongings hastily loaded aboard a humble if sturdy hay wagon. First Gawain then Edgar had kissed her tenderly in farewell, before, in a stern, choked voice, her husband had instructed the old groom who would accompany them to take his lady north with all possible speed.

They'd fled the Norman's advance but minutes before her Saxon husband's manor had been attacked and taken, his lands razed, his holdings confiscated by the occupying fyrds. Her lord husband had himself been wounded and taken prisoner, then carried off in chains to Normandy, along with her only son and numerous other Saxon noblemen who'd fought beside defeated King Harold, Elyse had ended sadly, close to fresh tears.

"Are ye certain, Coz? How can ye be so sure things are as dismal as ye fear for your Edgar and Gawain?" Fionna had pressed gently, moved to tears herself.

"Because of my abigail," Elyse had indicated wearily, nodding her head towards the exhausted country girl who huddled by the hearth, the two small boys cuddled on her plump lap both soundly asleep now. "Edgar had insisted we travel swiftly and forbidden me the encumbrance of baggage and servants. He said they would slow our journey, and so I was forced t' leave puir Betty behind. But the loyal lass was wet nurse to my grandbairns. She couldna bear t' part wi' them! And so, but a few days after we'd fled Thorington, she stole a carthorse and followed us north. 'Twas from Betty that I learned what sorry plight had befallen my lord Edgar and our son . . ."

Soon after ending her sad tale, Elyse had collapsed from grief, fatigue, and exposure, weeping pitifully. Fionna had seen her cousin carried to a guest bower, one set apart from the main hall, and there made comfortable, not returning to the fireside until Elyse had fallen into a deep, healing sleep, with her grandsons and faithful Betty close by her.

Much as she'd wanted to believe her cousin's story exaggerated by grief, too many of Elyse's descriptions had rung true to be cast off as the doom-filled fears of a distraught woman. As Fionna gazed pensively into the fire, she remembered the alarming news that had reached them the year before.

Late September, it had begun, in the Year of our Lord 1066. The Saxon king, Harold Godwinson, and his armies had been exhausted, having waged several fierce battles against invading Norsemen in the northeast of England, not too far distant from Corbin and the Scottish Marches.

The Viking invasion had been led by yet another king named Harold, this one a Norwegian *jarl* called Harold Hardraada. Later rumors had reported that the English king Harold's own brother, Tosti, had treacherously abetted Hardraada in his attempt to take the city of York, and it was also whispered by some that these battles had in fact been engineered by Tosti as a diversion, one designed to draw Harold Godwinson's attention away from an imminent Norman invasion to the south of England.

Whether the rumors were true, or whether the timing of Hardraada's invasion was but a stroke of good fortune for William, no one knew. Nonetheless, the weary English king and his armies had retired triumphant from one fierce battle only to receive word of a Norman landing at Pevensey led by Duke William, and of his destruction of several forts along the southeast coast of England.

Bravely, King Harold had rallied the remnants of his exhausted troops around him. He'd harried them to march south to Hastings with all possible speed. And there, shortly after dawn but a few days later on October 14 of the same year, while yet weary from the forced march they'd undertaken, Harold's sadly depleted fyrd had immediately been engaged by William and his vast numbers.

A ferocious battle had ensued at Hastings, yet by dusk of the same day, it was over for the Saxon king and his followers. William's far greater numbers had prevailed. Harold's army was vanquished. King Harold himself had been slain and his body horribly mutilated after first receiving a Norman archer's arrow through the eye, a blow which had mortally wounded him.

On Christ's Mass Day of the same year — almost a year to this very day, in fact! — William had been crowned King of England by Archibishop Ealdred of York in the abbey of Westminster, thus fulfilling the astrologers' prophecies of a great change. And, working swiftly and ruthlessly to secure his new kingdom, in the weeks following the battle at Hastings Duke William had distributed the forfeited manors and estates of the Saxon thegns who'd fought against him amongst his own followers, by way of reward for their loyalty in his service.

Next, it had been feared, William would turn his attention to north and west and invade the marches of Scotland and Wales in an effort to add these lands to his kingdom. And having done so, he would then redistribute the Scottish and Welsh thegns' holdings and riches amongst his own men.

Elyse's story had not only confirmed William's ambitions, Fionna thought, biting her lip. It had made the threat of a Norman invasion of Scotland seem terrifyingly close at hand . . .

The lady Elyse's unwelcome news had created a stir among the clan Gilchrist, one that was to last all evening and beyond.

There was heated discussion by the menfolk of the clan over whether the Border chieftains could be persuaded — in the face of this external threat to their lands — to set aside the clan feuds that had already lasted several decades and unite their numbers to keep the northlands free of Norman rule. Some insisted a truce could be accomplished and the Normans driven from Scotland, while others hotly disagreed.

Roarke soon grew restless and impatient with the conversation, for to his mind, the answer was absurdly simple, not even worthy of discussion. He had quizzed the lady Elyse's manservant about the state of affairs in England within moments of their arrival at Corbin. And straightway, he'd realized that he and the other Border lairds *must* unite, must set aside their past differences and fight as one people battling a common foe to repel the Norman fyrds, else the unthinkable would happen; the Borders would be overrun, Scotland would fall to William, and the Scottish thegns' lands would become the property of the bastard Normans instead.

Thus decided, Roarke saw no point in pursuing the matter further in talk. Action was now required, not words! When the weather improved sufficiently to permit easy travel, he intended to send messengers to the keeps of his enemy chieftains at Glenmuir and Erskine, bidding them call a truce to their feuding and hie swiftly to Corbin to discuss the implications of the lady Elyse's news.

Leaving the knot of fiercely arguing men, Roarke was minded to go in search of fresh air and solitude for his thoughts when his *dopifer*, his steward, challenged him to a game of chess. Instead of leaving the hall as he'd first intended, he readily accepted, for the game of strategy was one of which he was fond.

Meanwhile, Graeme, the tall, flaxen-haired fellow who was Roarke's master-of-the horse and one much favored by the wenches for his bonnie face, looked on, adding his witty council from time to time as he peered over the pair's shoulders. The laird's absorbed expression betrayed to all who cared to look that the strategies the red-haired Tavish employed against his chieftain were wily ones, and Graeme's shrewd suggestions not wholly welcome!

" 'Tis fortunate I am ye decided t' cut short your wenching and come home t' us, Graeme, laddie," Roarke observed with a wry grin. " 'Else surely this red-haired popinjay would ha'e trounced me soundly!"

"Checkmate, my laird!" Tavish declared with a smug

79

grin, and Roarke's mouth dropped open in disgust.

"Are ye certain ye didna cheat when I wasna lookin', lad?" the chieftain growled, but his gray eyes twinkled.

"Quite certain, my laird. Besides, there's nae need for me t' cheat. I'm the better player, after all —"

"Braggart!" Roarke had declared. "Set up the playing pieces once more, my friend. I'll show ye who's the better player!"

As they began a new game, a grizzled shepherd began piping his flute at one end of the vast raftered hall. Another took up the rhythm of his song upon a small drum. Soon, a number of the young folks were dancing the much loved Border reels to their music, the lassies lifting their skirts and tossing their heads, tartan shawls flying as they wove their way among the circles and arches the lads made with their arms. The festive spirit of Yule filled everyone, and the Norman threat seemed as distant as the wintry moon.

Meanwhile, far above the hall in the north bower, couched in a small anteroom that led off the bedchamber belonging to the lady Fionna, the foundling girl awakened for the first time in many hours, stretching and yawning drowsily.

Sweat glistened on her brow, for braziers had been placed about her bed, their hot coals warming the frigid air. The thick hangings that surrounded the bed had been tightly drawn, too, and several fur coverlets had been heaped upon her to further keep out the chill and hold at bay the malevolent effects of fresh air. Fresh air — and especially *cold* fresh air — was injurious to both the sick and well, and laden with malevolent vapors, as everyone knew. The girl, however, was of a different opinion in this matter. She felt stifled — closed to suffocating!

"Air! Sweet Jesu, I must have air!" she gasped aloud, and flung the coverings aside.

Swinging her legs over the edge of the bed, she tugged the hangings open. But to her dismay, she discovered that the chamber beyond was little less stifling. Pulling back the draperies yielded no increase of fresh air, either, for the chamber was not only hot but thick with smoke. The reek of camphor and pine balsam made her eyes water!

Standing gingerly—for dear Lady Fionna had forbidden her to leave her bed for aught, although her fever had lessened some two days hence—she dragged one of the fur mantles off the bed, and flung it around her shoulders. Carefully placing one foot before the other like a drunkard in his cups, she tested her legs and found them worthy, if a wee bit trembly.

Moving slowly, for there was a peculiar sensation of unreality about her in the aftermath of her sickness, she glanced at the sleeping serving woman, Flora, lolling in a carved chair. Reassured by her snoring that she would not soon awaken, she left the bower and went out into the short passageway beyond, which was lit with guttering torches of pitch set in metal sconces.

The stone floor felt uneven and icy beneath her feet. The draft that came from somewhere nearby was icy cold and pressed the skirts of her night kirtle close against her legs. The flares from the sconces shifted and danced over the walls and floor, making a giantess of her shadow. Halting, she wetted her lips. A feeling of dread unaccountably filled her as she looked about her, although in the gloom she could see little. There was a heaviness in the pit of her belly, too—a feeling that boded ill. Had she done this before, she wondered? Had she left another sickbed in just such a fashion, with disastrous results—or but dreamed she had? She frowned in confusion, for somehow her actions seemed uncannily familiar . . .

Two flights of stone stairs were revealed by the torches' flickering light; one short flight leading up, the other, longer one, leading down. Casting her forebodings aside, she took the staircase up, in the direction of that welcome blast of fresh air, pausing on each deep tread to catch her breath and rest. She was vaguely amazed that such a little exertion should tire her, for she was certain it never had before.

That, alas, she considered ruefully as she clambered up the steep staircase, was one of the few things she could be reasonably certain of, for not another blessed thing could she recall of her past! Not her name, her age, her family, her home — indeed, nothing that had happened in her life before the moment she'd awakened to see Fionna's blue eyes twinkling down at her remained!

It terrified her, this utter forgetfulness, made her feel much like a small, fragile corracle set adrift upon some vast loch, a tiny craft whipped by wind and current without moorings or oar to hold it fast or steer its course. Still, Lady Fionna had guardedly suggested her memory loss was but a temporary thing — a result, no doubt, of the vicious blow she'd received to her head. She'd taken heart on hearing this explanation, and prayed that Fionna was right.

Her efforts were rewarded as she came out onto the battlements of Corbin. The sky vaulted over the keep, she saw, an ebony pavilion of velvety heavens shot through with pulsing stars that had the fiery glitter of ice in their brilliance. Moreover, she found herself soundly buffeted by the cold, fresh air she'd craved in the stuffy bower. How good its chill felt, how refreshing its bluster, whirling away the cobwebby remnants of her sickness!

Inhaling deeply, she pulled the fur about her and walked cautiously across the slippery, ice-slickened flagstones to an embrasure of rough stone. Leaning against it out of the wind, she gazed down at the snow-stilled world below. A smile of delight curved her red lips.

The glens and moors that swept about the lofty keep on its craggy shelf of black rock slumbered now under a blanket of white. The winding river was a silver-gray riband, and everywhere she looked was drenched in cold, clear moonlight. Stands of firs were nuns in white robes, tall pyramids of purity. The distant mountains made a sleeping giant across the paler horizon, while beyond the walls of Corbin, a loch gleamed under a mirror of black ice.

"Beautiful, beautiful world!" she whispered, hugging herself about the arms. " 'Tis glad I am t' find myself alive — aye, and here t' enjoy your beauty again!"

As if in response to her flattery, the wind stirred her hair. It whipped it about her head and shoulders in wild black streamers. Its cold caress also fired rosy color in the fine pallor of her face, which was haloed by the fur cloak. The deep, silky pile of the mantle riffled in the night wind. The moonlight dusted her fair complexion with a sheen of silver and made the green of her eyes glitter, emerald-bright.

Truly, hers is a rare beauty, Roarke thought, distracted from his ponderings of war by the unexpected sight of her here, when he'd believed her abed. He hardly dared to breathe, let alone speak, for fear the sound would startle her, send her toppling over the embrasure in fright! And yet — he must leave the sheltered nook he'd claimed, quit the shadows and approach her, or risk discovery later and be thought a spying rogue!

Cupping the goblet of mulled wine he'd brought with him from the hall in his hands, he stepped from the alcove and strode across the flagstones towards her.

Light of foot though he was by nature, she heard him before he'd gone more than a half-dozen paces, and swung about to face him. Pushing back the wild mane of hair that flurried across her face the better to see, she stood there in the bright moonlight. And, frowning, he saw her face grow paler and her eyes widen in alarm as she looked him up and down, remarking his considerable height and wiry girth with obvious dismay — and, he fancied, no little terror.

83

"Dinna come any closer, whoever ye are!" she warned. "Though small, I am well armed, and can yet do ye harm!"

Glancing down, too surprised for speech by her words, Roarke saw a bulge beneath her mantle, for all the world as if a dirk were gripped in her fist and concealed beneath its folds.

"Aye, sir, ye have the rights o' it! Another step, a hand placed upon me, and ye willna live t' regret it!"

Chapter Seven

"Well, good even' t' ye, my lady," he greeted her softly and with a teasing glint in his eyes. " 'Tis glad I am t' see ye've recovered your tongue—if not your manners! 'Tis a rare guest who greets her host in such a fashion!"

Her jaw hardened at his flippant response to her threats, and her brow knitted in a puzzled frown. She knew him, she was certain of it. His voice was familiar, his appearance likewise. But from where did her memory of him come? And, more important, was he friend or foe? Foe, she decided, for surely a friend would not hide in the shadows and spy upon her? She fought the urge to rub the aching knot upon her head and instead glared at him, wondering all the while how, once met, she could possibly have forgotten knowing such a darkly handsome brute as he. But her questions remained unanswered, and the niggling unease in her belly suggested that they'd met before. Aye, she was certain, somehow, that they had, and on other than cordial terms.

"Dinna bandy words wi' me, rogue!" she snapped, tossing the inky mane that became her so very well over her slender shoulders. "I would know who ye are, and why ye followed me up here? Why were ye spying on me, curse yer soul?"

Tight-lipped, he responded, "I'll give answer t' your

second question first, if I may, without danger t' ma person?" Heavy sarcasm laced his tone as he gestured towards the bulge in her mantle.

She gave a tight nod in response. "As ye will, rogue, but — stay where ye are, ye ken?"

He inclined his head and began, "You are in error in thinking that I followed ye up here for some dark purpose. I didna. 'Twas *you* who followed *me,* lass, for upon my oath, I came here first! And in answer to your third question, I wasna spying upon ye, as ye feared, I came here t' savor this mulled wine and enjoy the blessings o' crisp, clean air, wi'out the reek o' smoke t' be had below in the hall. And, mistress, in answer to your first question . . . !" Here he smiled confidently and drew himself up to his full height so that he towered above her tiny frame. "I, lassie, am the Gilchrist! Chieftain of my clan. Laird o' Corbin Keep. Accordingly, I go where I will within these walls, and answer t' no one but God and my king for my actions!" His eyes narrowed. "And, my bonnie, I have been known t' devour upstart maids like yoursel' t' break my fast of a morning, so guard that impudent tongue!"

She had the grace to look taken aback momentarily by his threat, then shrugged in an infuriatingly offhand manner. "Try again, sir!" she scoffed, her green eyes bright and assessing, "For I'm certain ye can tell a better tale than that, though your lordly speech was pompous enough, I'll grant ye that. Laird indeed! I dinna believe ye, not a word! Ye look more like a . . . like a farrier, or a common woodcutter, than a laird! Lairds are much larger in girth, ye ken, wi' great barrel bellies that hang over their belts. Their voices are louder than yours. Somewhat like thunder, only more arrogant and resonant. They are often hairy brutes, too, with long whiskers, while ye . . . ! Why, ye dinna even have a beard!" she snorted smugly.

He managed to swallow the indignant oath that sprang to his lips and instead said in a dangerously

86

silky tone, "Beard or nay, my doubting Thomasina, I'm no blacksmith, nor woodcutter, nor yet any other manner of man than that which I've laid claim to being. Verily, I *am* the Gilchrist," he insisted, growing more irritated by the second, "like it or not."

"Very well. If 'tis so, then ye must prove it."

"*Prove* it? Damme ye, I am not compelled t' prove anything t' ye, ye contrary wee bitch!" he insisted, taking a purposeful stride towards her with the intent of shaking some sense — and civility — into her.

She gave a shriek of terror, and shrank back. Grasping her skirts, she would have picked them up and fled him, but in her haste to escape, her bare foot skidded on the icy flagstones. She uttered a startled yelp, but found herself caught safely in the stranger's arms and righted without injury.

"Thank ye, sir," she said grudgingly. "Ye may release me now. I am unharmed."

"And your weapon?" he challenged, his mouth twisted in a mocking smile. "Did ye lose it when ye slipped, as I lost my goblet o' wine?"

"My w-weapon?" She frowned in puzzlement, then her brow cleared and she blushed and looked away. "In truth, there was none," she admitted lamely, "but for my wee fist!" She grinned and extended that same wee fist through the folds of her mantle for his inspection, and her merry expression gave her delicate beauty a naughty, elfin cast that briefly bewitched him and made him stare at her long and hard. "Confess, sir, ye believed me armed, did ye no'? My threats gave ye pause for a wee while?"

"Not for an instant, ye dratted lunatic," he growled, disgusted. "What d' ye take me for — a callow lad? Never! I suspected from the very first ye werena armed!"

"Och, aye, happen ye did. I am, I fancy, a poor player of parts," she agreed with a sigh. "But, ye see, your sudden appearance frightened me! I could think of naught else t' buy myself some time to escape ye. Och, ye can let me go now, sir," she reminded him, for his arms were still locked about her, as they had been when he reached out to keep her from falling. "I amna afeared of ye anymore, and am in no danger of taking a fall."

"When I'm ready, I'll release ye, curse it!" he drawled softly, his gray eyes darkening as they rested on her face with something warmer than irritation in their depths.

"Indeed? And when will that be?" she cried, reading his expression for what it was and growing frightened all over again. So frightened, she struggled to tear free of his arms.

He shrugged and grinned, enjoying the feel of her petite female body pressed against his chest, his hands, affording him wickedly delightful sensations as she wriggled and squirmed to escape his embrace. "Why, when I've sampled my fill o' your soft roundness filling my arms and wearied o' the feel o' your wee bosoms pressed against ma chest, hinnie!" he countered wickedly, giving her a wink.

At once she grew very still, furious that not only had he ignored her attempts to escape, but had actually welcomed them. "Ye lecherous oaf! How dare ye make so free wi' me? Let go straightway! Unhand me this very instant, 'less I scream and call upon the laird o' the Gilchrists t' save me from ye. And be warned, sir. Ye've been overly bold in yer actions. 'Twill go badly for ye, should I scream for help!" she threatened.

"Nay, it willna go badly at all, wench, for I am whom I claim t' be, and have naught t' fear from yersel' or yer caterwaulings!" he vowed with a chuckle. "Were it my wish, I could carry ye awa' t' ma bed. I could have my way wi' ye all the night long," he winked again, "and none here would lift a finger t' aid ye, not in my keep."

Her heart sank, he sounded so cocksure of himself. "Then 'tis so? Ye are the Gilchrist? Truly?" she asked in a small, uncertain voice, her knees beginning to tremble.

"Truly!" he barked.

"Then . . . then 'twas you who found me and brought me here?"

"Aye, lass, none other."

"Then you're the one the lady Fiona calls her 'laddie'? Roarke, the Gilchrist o' Corbin?"

"Aye, aye, I am," he acknowledged impatiently, thinking, laddie indeed! His lady mother had a way of trimming him down t' size when it suited her!

"Well, now, sir! What a turnabout, for who'd ha'e thought it?" she exclaimed as if voicing her thoughts aloud. "Ye dinna look at all like a laird t' me!" She appraised him from head to toe with a frank curiosity that was disquieting, coming from so youthful a maid.

A ghost of a smile hovered about his lips. "Aye, my lass, so ye said before. But nevertheless, 'tis so. I am the Gilchrist, bearded or nay."

"Aye?" she said slowly.

"Aye!"

"Why, then, take *this*, sir, for your insolence and yer boldness!" she flared, and brought her knee up and into his groin with all the force she could muster. She would have succeeded in gelding him, had he not flinched aside at the last instant. Nevertheless, her blow didna miss its target entirely. He made an anguished moan, and released her forthwith to cradle his hurt.

"I could forgive ye your lack o' decency, were ye the uncouth woodsman or simple blacksmith I took ye for," she cried as he reeled away, clutching his aching middle. "But if 'tis laird o' Corbin ye truly are—whist, then ye should be ashamed o' yersel', pressing your 'vantage o'er a puir, sickly lass not long risen from her sickbed— one too weak and frail to fend off your wicked advances!"

"Weak and frail be damned, ye spiteful bitch!" he groaned. " 'Tis strong as a wee mare, ye are, and slippery as any eel. 'S Blood, ye've nigh unmanned me, sure!"

"Aye, mi'laird, happen I have—and will do so yet again should ye make bold wi' ma person!" she vowed with a prim little sniff.

"Ye wee shrew, I should ha'e left ye in the snow, ye cold-hearted nag," he ground out, and his wind-browned face was bleached the color of tallow when he looked up at her, his gray eyes now the color of pewter. "I should ha'e left ye t' your sorry fate, and t' Hades wi' Christian kindness, ye witch!"

"Och, aye, I'd almost forgotten 'twas yersel' who found me and brought me here," she acknowledged calmly. "Where was it ye came upon me, sir?"

"Half a league within the boundaries of Corbin's lands," he answered grudgingly, for the fierce ache in his middle had settled down to a bearable throb now. "I was out hunting that day, and was headed homeward when a blizzard blew down from the north. I whistled up my hounds, but they wouldna heed me. Instead, they kept worrying at something in the snow. That something was yersel'! When I stumbled upon ye on the moors, ye were colder than any icicle—and nigh as stiff! I feared I couldna thaw ye out, but to my great misfortune, I did!"

"Aye, sir, ye did," she agreed candidly, and added as if as an afterthought, "And I'm sure I'll thank ye for it anon. But meanwhile, tell me, was I alone there?"

"Quite alone, and wi'out mantle or furs t' keep the cold from yer bones. I carried ye on my shoulders as a shepherd carries a wee lost lamb, for many leagues! I thought t' give ye into my mother's keeping that same even', but when the blizzard didna abate, we passed the night in a tumbledown croft t' wait it out. I lit a fire t' warm ye, then at first light, I carried ye t' ma keep— fool that I was!" He grinned evilly, and added with obvious relish, "Better, mayhap, I had drowned ye in the nearest loch had I a mite o' sense!"

"Sweet Jesu! We passed a night alone together, ye say,

90

my laird?" Something half buried nagged in her memory so that she wetted her lips, and eyed him beneath her lashes before asking, "It—er—it *was* a night innocently passed, was it no', my laird?" Perhaps his bold, familiar way had its roots in the night they'd passed together and in amorous doings of which she was unaware but which he sought now to repeat!

Remembering how perilously close he'd come to taking advantage of her helpless state, Roarke bristled with guilt and gritted hastily, "Aye, my lady, it was indeed innocently spent! In truth, ye could have been a nun, so jealously did I guard yer virtue! Nor am I one t' kiss and tell. Rest assured, no mon will learn o' the crofter's hut from my lips. Or that I warmed your bonnie naked body with ma own beneath the furs and stroked ye everywhere t' warm your blood, and bring ye back from the jaws o' death." *Or that ye called upon your husband, and halted me in the nick o' time t' save your virtue!* he added silently.

"Mary, Mother of God! Naked, ye say?" she exclaimed, visibly shaken.

"Naked, my lady, as the day ye came into this world."

"But ye didna—ye didna . . . ?"

"Nay, my lady. Alas, I didna."

She almost swooned with relief, for his rueful tone convinced her he was telling the truth more effectively than his denials could have. Anxious to make amends—for, after all, lecher or nay, he *had* saved her life, and could she but admit it, she fancied now that she'd overreacted to his teasing threat not to release her—she bowed her head in embarrassment and murmured, "Then please, my laird, ye must forgive my impetuous actions, for 'tis clear ye are an honorable mon, at heart. Mayhap—mayhap I was a wee bit hasty wi' ma knee, and took yer jest too seriously t' heart? I implore ye t' forgive me, and instead accept my heartfelt thanks. My laird, I owe ye my life!"

"Nay, ye owe me naught, lassie," he dismissed her

thanks with a sour smile, "save the courtesy o' telling me what name ye bear, and t' whose clan ye claim kinship—in truth, whose daughter I have t' thank for ma wounding!"

"But did your lady mother not tell ye, sir?" she exclaimed. "I can tell ye naught, for I recall none of my life before coming here! The blow t' ma head must have robbed me of my past, ye ken? Och, sir, would that I *could* answer ye, but I canna, my laird!"

"Canna—or willna, ye obstinate wench!"

His disbelieving tone roused her dormant temper, brought color to her pale cheeks that her illness had withered. Her green eyes flashed in the moonlight. Her lips tightened. "Canna, my laird, canna! I dinna ken who I am, nor from whence I came, nor by what unhappy chance ye found me in the snow that day. In truth, 'tis as if my life began when I opened my eyes, and saw your lady mother smiling down at me."

"Come, come! Do ye play me for a fool? Would ye have me believe ye remember nothing?" he pressed incredulously.

She shook her head. "Not a blessed thing!"

"Then surely ye mock me—else lie, my lady? In truth, I've never heard of such a thing before!"

"Mayhap not, my laird, but 'tis all quite true, none-theless," she insisted, bristling now like a wee terrier. "And—despite what I've forgotten of my past—this much I know of a certainty. Whatever I might prove t' be, I'm no' a liar!"

"Ye say so? But how can ye be sure o' that," he mocked, "having forgotten all? Or indeed, how can ye be sure of anything?"

Despite her newly recovered state, she rose to his challenge like a salmon to a fly. "Why, because I know it here," she cried, touching her breast. "And 'tis a bold lout ye are t' doubt me, laird or nay! Whist, how dare ye call me liar, then stand there sae blessed arrogant and expect me t' meekly tell ye 'Aye, I am!' I' faith, sir, your beholden guest or nay, I dinna have t' listen t' your insults a moment longer! By your leave, I'm awa' t' ma bed!" she ground out, and slipped away before he could bid her halt.

Roarke, left alone on the battlements to gaze down at the sleeping white world below the walls of his keep, suddenly found its beauty dimmed, its magical luster tarnished, the air cursedly cold and damp, rather than crisp and invigorating.

Jesu! he mused. What was it about her that had made him act like a lecherous cur he scarce knew — nor wanted to know, for that matter! He'd tried to force his attentions on her, as if she were some wayside tart whose favors could be purchased for a coin, and it had taken her knee in his groin t' sway him from his purpose, so heady had been his lust!

He swallowed and flicked his head to clear it, bemused by his behavior. Until her coming to Corbin, he had never thought to seduce a maid, nor bend her to his will against her own volition. He'd usually chosen to dally with women of experience — widows like his mistress, Maggie, who enjoyed a lusty fellow in their beds and didna need much coaxing to join him there for a lusty tumble. He muttered an oath. Jesu, what ailed him? Such ardent behavior was more befitting a cowherd with the spring sap rising in his blood, rather than the actions of the dour laird of Corbin!

With no little chagrin, he admitted to himself that his attraction to her was strong indeed. And, moreover, it seemed to exist in approximately the same proportion as her ability to infuriate him! There was something about the way those slanted green eyes regarded him so coolly, the way she spoke to him as her equal wi' none o' the respect and modesty a maiden showed a man, the way she'd boldly repelled his advances without knowing if he was laird of Corbin or nay, and obviously caring not a whit should he indeed prove to be the chieftain — that both attracted him and infuriated him all at once, so that he was torn between wanting to embrace her, kiss her, and wringing her wee neck! And as for this falsehood—this mad fairy tale about forgetting her name, her past—surely she didna expect him to be fool enough t' believe her? Jaws clamped, he shook his head. Nay. Instinct suggested she was up to something, her tale a hoax. But . . . what?

Chapter Eight

"Well, mon? Did ye find the lass?"

"Aye, my laird, we did! Our horses overtook her not a league from Erskine. Runnin' like a wee crazed thing through the snow across Corbin lands she was, wi' her black, witchy tresses flyin' about her! She put up a guid fight an' all," he grinned, "scratchin' and clawin' like a wildcat, but she were no match fer us. Nay, t' be sure, she wasna!" There was enormous relish in his tone.

"Then she's dead?"

"With the foul blizzard that was a-blowin' sae hard that night?" There came a bray of laughter. "Och, can ye doubt it, sir? I fetched her a blow t' the noggin that must ha' turned her brains t' clabbered cream! The bitter cold would ha' finished the deed — if the flat o' my trusty claymore didna, which I sorely doubt!"

"Och, then ye've served me well, as always! We can rest easy now, for dead lassies carry no tales, and canna bear witness t' aught they've seen. And after? Ye didna ride straightway here, did ye now?"

"Nay, my laird, we didna. As ye instructed, we both headed south across the Tweed waters. We tarried a while at a wee village where the ale was cheap and the wenches plentiful." He winked. "And where our friend's bonnie face found favor aplenty wi' the English whores. They've a fondness for yellow hair, they have, an' were all over him, my laird—like flies t' the dung heap! Ye should ha' see it! Why, one of them even—"

"Aye, aye, I ken! But what then?"

"Well, then yester' morning, we started for home, as ye instructed."

"And no one followed either o' ye, nor remarked your part in this?"

"Whist, not a blessed soul, sir. Ye can rest assured o' that."

"Well done, my lad. Ye did right well! I'll no' forget your part in this. Now, tell me, did ye contact de Rocher at York before coming here?"

"The duke's man? Nay, sir, I didna. I thought it best t' leave that honor to yersel', sir! After all, the Norman told us that King William swore oath whoever delivered the border keeps of Northumbria to him could name his own price, did he no'? With the discord a-brewin' in his native Normandy, de Rocher says the duke must hie home t' deal with it himsel', for he hasna the army to be in both places at once! 'Tis *yersel'* who must properly be the bearer of these good tidings, my laird! 'Tis not for me t' send word that Erskine has fallen!" The man's manner was servile, obsequious, his tone crafty now.

His master smiled, and it was not a pretty sight, gloating as his expression was. "Aye, she has fallen, has she no'?" he allowed, but then his triumphant smile faded. "But we ha' taken only one o' the three border strongholds de Rocher charged us t' take fer him—and mayhap he'll no' be so generous wi' his master's favors until he has them all . . ."

The man frowned. He rested his chin on his fist and stared into space, lost deep in thought for several moments before continuing. "On second thought, we'll send no messenger south t' York with glad tidings as yet. We'll bide our time a wee while longer, laddie, until we ha'e the other fine border cocks by the throat!"

His eyes gleamed with greed, and something more.

Hatred? Aye, of a certain it was hatred, and a powerful one, too, his henchman fancied.

"All, sir? But . . . we might well wait forever, and still end up with naught! That cursed Corbin has remained inviolate for nigh on a decade. She's proven unbreachable by attacks waged from without. Forgive me for speakin' plainly, but ye know this full well, my laird! That damned Gilchrist! Och, he's no mon's fool, sir! He surrounds himself with only those he trusts as brothers suckled at the same pap trust one another. He willna let down his guard! There'll be no taking Corbin, mark my words, sir, not by ordinary means — and not sae long as Roarke Mac Gilchrist lives, and remains laird there! Come, guid sir," he wheedled, "half a loaf is better than none, is it no'? Send word t' de Rocher, and mayhap he'll gift ye wi' a fat Saxon estate afore Hogmanay!"

His master chuckled softly. "Nay, laddie, nay. Tempting though it may be, we'll bide our time a while. Patience will serve us best in this matter, I warrant! I shall ha'e all three keeps — or naught. Besides, we have old scores to settle, Black Roarke the Bastard and mysel'. I'd as lief have nothing than fail t' deliver up Corbin and Roarke's cursed head — on a platter to the Conqueror!"

His henchman chuckled. "The Gilchrist is nigh as stubborn as the Bastard Duke himself, nay, my laird?"

"Aye, that he is. Mayhap even more so! But his obstinacy may yet prove his undoing. Despite his reputation, he's just a mon. It goes against the nature of men to live always in a state of suspicion and wariness. It taxes both body and spirit t' breaking point, ye ken? Sooner or later, a chink will open up in Corbin's defenses. And when it does, why, we'll be there, ready and waiting t' pry it wide — !"

"Ah! Ye think t' persuade our friend t' aid us in this, too, do ye not, my laird?"

The other man smiled. "Why not? He has helped us

once. Why should he not again—if the price is right."

"But this is different! 'Twas not for gold he joined us this time, sir, but to revenge his blood! If we tell him we plan t' take Corbin . . . ! Why 'twill prove another matter entirely!"

"Och, I think not, my friend," the man said, a smile hovering about his lips. "Every man has his price—and his weaknesses—does he not? And either avarice or his own shortcomings can be used t' bend any man to another's will. Ye shall see, mon. Aye, ye shall see!"

"She bewitches you, does she not?"

Startled by the voice cutting into his reverie, Roarke turned back to regard his smiling *dopifer*, his steward, and shrugged. "What's this ye say? Bewitches? Och, Tavish, come now! Bewitches is far too strong a word," he denied, then cocked a dark brow in his friend's direction and admitted gruffly, "But if ye're askin' do I find her comely to look upon? Whist, mon, that's another matter! Aye, I do! What man with eyes could not, the bonnie wee shrew!"

Tavish grinned. "Indeed, my laird, indeed. And there's many a mon at Corbin whose eyes have been turned her way this last sevennight, think ye no'?"

Roarke's expression changed from easy indolence to brooding silence as he sipped the heady mead in his goblet and regarded the foundling maid over its silver-banded rim without answering his friend.

She and his mother sat side by side on two heavily carved chairs placed before the roaring fire. It was one of two hearths that blazed in the great hall of Corbin Keep, and the one favored by the ladies of Corbin on account of the clear northern light that dispelled the winter's gloom there and made sewing easier on the eyes.

His mother, Fionna, her auburn head bent close to the girl's ebony one, was teaching her to embroider, a pastime both appeared to be finding mutually reward-ing, judging by the soft bursts of laughter and the ready smiles and chatter exchanged between them.

His mother liked the lass, 'twas plain. Roarke scowled. Although he usually respected his mother's judgment of character — for Fionna had proven herself shrewder than most at reading other's hearts, no matter the good or bad reputations that preceded them — in this instance her obvious acceptance and affection for the girl annoyed him.

For his own part, although he found her lovely in-deed, since the night on the battlements he'd been unable to negate the uneasy suspicion in his innards that, like a rosy apple with a worm at its heart, the lass's beauty concealed a deceitful nature and an ulterior motive for being at Corbin. Her heated insistence that she could remember nothing of her past, including her own name, had deepened his mistrust. He'd seen more men wounded in battle than he cared to count, victims of claymore and club, mace and spear, arrow and dirk. But although many of those wounded had suffered terrible blows to the head, none that he could recall had ever claimed to have lost his memory. Was his discovery of her in the snow that evening but fortuitous coinci-dence, he wondered? Or had all of it — including the blow to her head — been part of some clever scheme, an act on her part to gain entry to Corbin, he considered? But if so, for what reason had she done so — and at whose command?

As he watched the pair, the girl stood gracefully and set her embroidery hoop aside. His gray eyes narrowed as he watched the way her skirts swung from the jut of slender hips, revealing a glimpse of the linsey-woolsey shift she wore below and the toes of her supple suede boots; the way her hair swung to and fro across her back beneath her veil. She went to the bowslit window and stood there, gazing at Loch Tully. The small lake lay in the glen below. It gleamed under a mantle of dark ice and was fringed with skeletal trees in whose bony branches perched the glossy-winged ravens who'd given Corbin their name.

Her profile was lovely, tranquil and grave, as if absorbed by the view. Her lashes were dark smudges over green irises the color of a restless sea. Her full red lips were very slightly parted. One slender, pale little hand rested against the window arch, and her petite form was half turned to Roarke's advantage, silhouetted by the bright glare of light on snow through the costly Venetian glass. Her pale throat flowed in a liquid line to meet her high, rounded bosom. Her tiny waist and the sylphlike, willowy curve of her hips were sharply defined for his admiring eye. Curse t' lass! Mistrust her or nay, he was still very much a man, and the sight of her stirred him!

Her face was uptilted, creating a lovely, fluid line that flowed down from her obstinate little chin, swept over a swanlike throat and disappeared beneath the high neck of her deep-green kirtle. Over the kirtle she wore a gunna of lighter green, laced down the sides from her hips to her ankles and girdled with a belt of golden links. All had been loaned her by his doting mother. Her glossy black hair was tamed today by a narrow circlet of flattened gold, studded with peridots. From the back of it floated a sheer white veil, drifting like a cloud of spindrift over her glossy hair. *Ah, that hair, that wild witch's mane!* he thought with silent longing. It tumbled clear past her shoulders to her waist in glossy black arabesques and fairly begged a man to weave his hands through its silkiness; to burrow his face in its scented mass and inhale its clover fragrance. To twine it about his throat as he drew off her garments and claimed her for his own . . .

Her lips, parted in a smile now as she made some amusing observation or other to his lady mother, were no less tantalizing, but as ripe and red as twin wild strawberries. Her cheeks were a paler shade of the same. Her vivid coloring, her creamy complexion, contrasted with the sooty black of her hair and the mutable green of her eyes, were in truth bewitching. Tavish had not been far wrong . . .

Roarke caught himself in midthought, and glanced guiltily across at Tavish to see if his feelings had been as transparent as he'd feared. Fortunately, although Graeme shot him a sullen scowl and quickly looked away, he had little to worry about. Tavish was mesmerized by the lassie, too, by all appearances, and far too busy watching her himself to worry about his laird's doings!

Relieved, Roarke rose and left the trestle table and the remnants of his night's fast-breaking: an emptied bowl of porridge, salty and thick the way he enjoyed it, the clean-picked bones of a juicy capon, an empty trencher that had earlier held venison stew. He strode across the rush-strewn floor to where his mother sat, humming as she sorted her colored silks. She looked, he noted, more content than he'd seen her since the year of her beloved Cam's death, but then she'd always wanted a daughter, he reminded himself. Now, in a sense, she had one to cosset and council and teach her chatelaine's arts for as long as the girl might remain at Corbin.

"Good morrow t' ye, my lady mother," Roarke greeted her fondly, bending to take Fionna's hand and kiss it.

"Good morrow, my son!" Fionna smiled up at him affectionately. She squeezed his large, rough hand in her own slender bejeweled one, pressing it to her soft cheek. Her frank blue eyes twinkled amidst a handsome face, for although full two score and eight years old, she was yet a bonnie woman by any man's measure. Her complexion was still clear and unlined. The dark auburn mane she'd prided herself upon in her youth yet had few threads of gray; what small number there were hidden now amidst the braided coronet in which she'd dressed her hair.

The girl, watching the affectionate exchange, felt a pang of longing fill her breast. She quickly looked away. Mother and son they might be, but there was great fondness between them, one they took no pains to disguise. And yet, no man in his right mind could have accused the Gilchrist of being one of those pampered, effeminate excuses for a man who dogged their mother's skirts and hung upon their every word. She sighed almost envying the quick, almost casual contact they'd exchanged without knowing why, or whether she'd ever known a mother's gentle touch or a brother's rough affection.

"Now, tell me, Roarke, what brings ye once again t' my side? Why, I wager I've seen ye rattling about my apartments and my ladies' hearth more often this last sevennight than I have in the past few years counted together! Pray tell, why is that?" Fionna asked innocently, trying very hard not to smile as she looked up at him.

Roarke bristled. His jaw clamped tight. "The lassie's . . . health . . . concerns me, madam, as does her future and the urgent need to find her kin and reassure them that she is safe and well. Surely ye'd have it no other way?"

"Och, nay, laddie!" Fionna disclaimed soothingly. "Not a'tall! I find your concern for the lassie's welfare most commendable."

It was no lie, but nevertheless, Fionna had to turn aside to hide her smile, for Roarke was so transparent in his excuses! The lassie's health, indeed! She knew her son better than most women of her class had occasion to know their sons, for Roarke had never been fostered out to some male kinsman's keep for raising and learning the arts of soldiery, as highborn lads were wont to be fostered. Aye, she knew him full well — and it was no' the wee lassie's *health* that caused his gray eyes to smolder in just such a way!

Roarke noted her amusement and bit back an annoyed oath. His brooding black brows crashed together like a pair of storm-tossed wings across his wind-browned forehead, where unruly waves crested like a midnight sea. His strong jaw tightened still more in irritation. "And . . . ?" he pressed.

"And what?" Fionna frowned. "My pardon, Roarke, but — what was it ye asked? In truth, I have forgotten!"

"I said I would know how fares the lassie this morn, my lady mother?" Roarke demanded through gritted teeth. "Is there any change?"

"The lassie? Why, she stands but two lengths from ye, my son! Why not ask her yoursel'?" Fionna suggested softly, pretending a sudden preoccupation with a knot in her threads as she added, "After all, she isna deaf, t' my knowledge, and I have a deal yet to do wi' this altar cloth for Father Augustine."

Feeling unaccountably as if he were being conspired against as his mother turned her back on him, Roarke nodded curtly and strode past Fionna towards the narrow arched bowslit and the girl gazing from it.

He opened his mouth to make his greeting and inquire after her health, but before he had a chance to voice either, the girl took it upon herself to speak to him unbidden, to his surprise. The maidens of gentle birth with whom he'd had some small acquaintance to date had been far less forward, he thought with displeasure.

"Good morrow t' ye, my laird Roarke," she greeted him softly in a lilting voice, bobbing a sketchy curtsey as she turned. Though tiny measured against his towering frame, she met him eye-to-eye in that bold, somehow assessing way he'd remarked before, a way that no modest maid should look at a man — not, that was, if she wished t' stay a maid! Her sooty lashes flickered downward for the barest instant, then swooped upward again to frame those startling green irises as her hand left the window and dropped to her side. "In answer t' your question, my laird, thank ye kindly for your concern. By the will of God, I find mysel' much recovered! The fever has left me, and with it the weakness that plagued me sae sorely. The knot upon my head has all but disappeared, too, and my headaches are now of the past. But as for the rest . . . alas . . . !" She caught at her lower lip with teeth as peerless as matched pearls and gave him a doubtful glance before confessing, "Nay, my laird. I regret there isna any change."

"Then ye still insist ye have no idea who ye might be, nor from whence ye came?" he demanded. His expression was tight-lipped, his tone laden with skepticism.

"None a'tall, sir, though I heartily wish it were otherwise — aye, even more than ye do yersel'!" She sighed. "Och, I *dream* each night o' my past, but when I waken, I find the memory fled, and no matter how hard I might try, I canna recapture it." She turned back to the window, and her eyes took on a distant, wistful expression. "This view, though. It stirred something as I looked below, my laird. I . . . I hae seen it before, methinks — or some very similar place o' which I was once fond."

"The loch? 'Tis known as Loch Tully," he supplied grudgingly, reluctant to appear to accept her claims as valid.

She shrugged her slender shoulders again. "Aye, perhaps 'twas the lake. And then again, maybe it wasna the loch at all, but the sight of the lads and lassies o' Corbin dragging home the Yule log that stirred my memory? Look, my laird! There they are again, riding down through the glen! D' ye see them, trotting their horses between the firs, wi' the sled behind them?"

Roarke went to stand next to her and looked below, seeing nothing. Instead, he was acutely aware of her nearness; of the press and heat of her arm against his, of the rounded curve of her breast swelling the cloth of her borrowed gown but inches from his hand. The scent that rose from her to fill his nostrils was sweet and warm as a child's fresh scent. He felt particularly

104

lightheaded as memories of the night they'd shared the wolfskins' warmth flooded through him. *Jesu!* He could remember the exact texture of her flesh beneath his hand and lips; the precise taste of her inner mouth, like honey on his tongue; the way the golden flecks in her green eyes had flared in the gloom . . .

Remembered sensations teemed in his head. They parched his mouth, stirring the desire he'd felt for her that night all over again and setting his senses reeling.

Giving the returning merrymakers only a cursory glance, he nodded curtly, clenched his fists at his sides, and growled, "Aye, I see them, mistress. And having done so, I must go at once t' anoint the log with wine before it may be lit. Such is our custom here at Corbin. By your leave, my ladies."

With a curt bow, a scowling Roarke left the two women alone, snapping his fingers to Castor, who dozed by the hearth, to follow him.

With a shake of his shaggy gray head and a yawn and stretch that was nigh human to see, the old hound dragged himself upright and padded obediently after his master. He gave the girl a soulful farewell glance as he left, and it was obvious to Fionna that the wolfhound would far rather have stayed close by her skirts than follow his beloved Roarke!

"He doesna like me," the girl declared with a pout and a flash of her green eyes as she returned to her stool beside the Lady Fionna.

"The hound?"

"Nay, not the hound, my lady! Himsel'—the Gilchrist!"

"Ah. And his dislike troubles ye?" Fionna asked without looking up from her embroidery.

"Och, nay! Why ever should it?" came her hot denial. She tossed her dark hair defiantly, stirring her veil. " 'Tis his mistrust I canna stomach! As for liking—why, I dinna like him either, come t' think on it, the great dark brute," she sighed, "although 'tis ungrateful of me

105

when I owe him my life! The mon's a dour, moody fellow who scarce seems t' smile at all! He scowls each time he looks at me, and growls his greetings like a grumpy old bear. As day follows night, he will then ask me most coldly if my memory has yet returned. But each time I answer him truthfully and say him nay, he stalks and strides aboot the place. Or else he , . . Oh!"

Belatedly remembering it was to the "great dark brute's" mother she was complaining, the girl broke off and reddened, looking down at her lap. Her pale cheeks were now pink with embarassment. "Whist ye, my lady, my tongue has run away wi' me yet again — an' after ye'd just explained that 'tis more seemly for a maid t' keep her opinions to hersel', too! Ye will forgive me, will ye no', my lady?" the girl implored, so patently upset her eyes were brimming.

"Aye, dearling, of course," Fionna promised, surreptitiously wiping tears of laughter from her eyes as she patted the girl's hand to comfort her.

"Great dark brute" the lass had called her handsome son — the same braw and bonnie son the prettiest lassies from Inverness t' Edwin's Burgh had always sighed after with longing! The same "great dark brute" the serving wenches connived to bed with and whose favors they fought over! Truly, the maid was fascinating, a fey little creature molded from a far different clay t' other lassies! Her vivid beauty was breathtaking, her utter candor refreshing in these times when well-bred maidens her age and younger had already been broken of conceiving a single, intelligent thought or uttering an intelligent opinion long before their first blood!

What mother could have raised such a daughter, encouraging her to develop a quick, keen mind, a will of her own, the courage to voice her opinions — but no wifely skills worth naming? And what father would have permitted his daughter to be reared so liberally? None that Fionna knew of, t' be sure! Daughters, without exception, were deemed valuable only as pawns to be used nowadays; merchandise to be bartered under the holy guise of marriage in order to bring their fathers a much-needed ally or merely as breeding stock t' whelp their husband's bairns. Perhaps the girl was, as Roarke had sourly claimed the morning he'd carried her into Corbin, a changeling? A wild and lovely half-mortal girl-child left by the fairies, her beauty destined t' drive mortal men t' madness — if her disarming candor didna do so first! And if that were the case, Fionna continued thoughtfully, an amused smile playing about her lips, Roarke was hard on the road t' succumbing to her faerie spell, or she wasna his mother!

"My lady, d' ye think I should let ma beard grow?" he'd asked her one morning, looking — she'd fancied — a little disgruntled as he'd inspected himself in her looking glass.

"Would it please ye t' wear a beard, my son?"

"Nay, it wouldna. Ye know full well I canna abide ma whiskers tickling ma nose!" he'd growled.

"Then why would ye ask my opinion? The choice is yours, and ye have made it!"

"Aye, I ken. But . . . I was wondering if ye thought I'd look more the laird wi' a fine full beard?"

"But ye *are* the laird o' Corbin, Roarke, beard or nay. A few whiskers canna change that. 'Tis a mon's actions, his honorable deeds, his wisdom and bravery that make a man what he is — not whiskers, or the lack o' them!"

"Aye, so say I!" he'd muttered with a smug grin, and stomped off to hear his villeins' monthly petitions for justice in the great hall.

"By your leave, ma'am, might I go and watch the Yule log brought in t' the hall?" the girl's wistful voice interrupted her thoughts.

"What's this? Och, child, run along with you, do! Ye didna need to ask my leave."

"My thanks, lady."

"Here now, chick, bide a wee moment! Wrap this about your shoulders before ye go — and mind, ye

107

mustna take it off! I've no wish t' see ye falling sick again, ye ken?" Fionna cautioned sternly.

The girl smiled, nodded, and gratefully took the heavy length of woolen plaid from the older woman, tossing it about her shoulders before pulling her hair free of its confines to spill over the folds of the proud red-gray-and-black tartan of Cam Gilchrist's clan.

"Och, ye scold me like a mother for my own guid — and I do love ye so for it, my lady!" she declared in a low, fervent voice. And to Fionna's surprise, she bent down and kissed her, before whirling away and running from the hall, her cheeks pink, her hair and her skirts and the plaid's fringed hems flying behind her.

Fionna reached up to touch the spot where the girl's warm lips had pressed her cheek. Och, what a strange wee lass she was, and sae tender and loving, too, despite her quick temper! Remembering the enormous bruise she'd discovered on the girl's head while tending her that first morning, Fionna clicked her teeth in dismay. Her smile became a frown. To strike such an affectionate, gentle little lassie, then leave her to die in the snow, was tantamount t' kicking a soft wee kitten that rubbed itself against one's legs. The wretch who'd done such a thing must be a terrible hard mon, aye, that he must! A loathsome, brutal animal wi' no hint o' mercy or tenderness t' be found anywhere in his dark soul. Fionna's expression hardened. He'd best pray she never discovered his identity, for if she did — why, she'd make certain the blackguard lived t' regret what he'd done t' the girl!

Jabbing her needle violently into the tapestry before her, Fionna continued her work.

Chapter Nine

Roarke was pouring wine from a flagon over the Yule log when the girl came outside into the bailey.

The brisk, icy wind lifted her hair as she left the shelter of the keep's walls, tossing it about her head and shoulders like long black ribands and giving her the look of a wild creature more fey than mortal. Holding the flapping plaid down about her shoulders like a shawl, she joined the crowd of young people who had gathered about their laird, squirming her way between them to watch the little ritual with apologetic smiles to right and left.

"Burn bright, burn long, festive log," Roarke was saying in his deep, pleasing voice, speaking in the native Gaelic tongue of the Borders. "And on these Twelve Days of Yule, we ask that ye give your pagan blessing to the twelvemonths that follow them. We ask ye t' warm our hearts even as your fire warms our hearth!"

A great cheer went up as he ended the little ceremony. With a grin Roarke tilted the flagon to his lips and quaffed the few remaining drops himself.

"And now, my lads and lassies, in t' the hall wi' ye! Graeme, bring the torch, laddie! And all o' ye bonnie wenches fetch the boughs o' mistletoe and evergreens ye've gathered! Lads, t' the log wi' ye! 'Tis a bonnie pagan time we'll be having, t' celebrate a Virgin birth and a Christian bairn most holy!"

Buoyed up by his words and the giddy excitement of the festive season, the young men and women of Corbin needed little second urging. The noisy serving wenches ran to lift great armfuls of prickly, dark-green holly, massed with bunches of bright red berries, from the horse-drawn sled they'd followed back through the glens to Corbin. Chattering like magpies, they bore them inside to deck the hall.

While some young men bent their backs to haul the massive Yule log to the great hearth — massive because, traditionally, it must be big enough to burn continually throughout the twelve days of Christmastide or ill fortune would befall the house of Corbin — other lusty youths chased after the lassies instead, the mistletoe boughs they carried so gleefully brandished aloft to good purpose. Woe betide any careless wench they happened upon standing beneath it, their whoops and determined expressions threatened, for slender maiden or plump goodwife, she'd be soundly kissed, and nae mistake! Tavish, who'd been crowned Lord o' Misrule, had thrown off his shyness with the ladies the moment he'd lifted his mask over his head, and was chasing the girls with the best of them!

A smile curving her lips, the nameless girl was left standing alone in the deserted bailey. Alone, that was, save for Laird Roarke himself and his faithful Castor, for the crowd that had surrounded her had by now dispersed like magic.

With a little nod for politeness' sake to the young chieftain, the girl turned away and started walking across the bailey, headed down the sloping ground for the wooden gates of Corbin below with a lithe, determined stride. Belatedly divining her intent and her direction, Roarke frowned.

"Hold!" he called after her.

Straightway, she halted.

"Aye, mi' laird?" she asked, turning back to face him with her head cocked inquiringly to one side.

"Where d' ye think ye're going, mistress?"

"Why, for a wee walk, sir. Now that the snows hae let up for a while, I had a mind t' take the air and stretch ma legs. This past sevennight, I've spent too long in my chamber, and I'm nae slugabed. By your leave, my laird, I willna be long . . . ?"

So saying, she dropped him another of the sketchy curtseys he found so irritating and walked on as if the matter were ended.

"Come back here, my lass! I didna grant ye leave t' go!" Roarke growled, hurrying after her. He quickly overtook her with his longer strides and planted himself in her path, his booted feet braced apart, his arms crossed over his broad chest. "Ye'll stay."

"Stay, ye say, sir?" Her delicate brows arched as if in surprise, she halted and looked up at him, wide-eyed.

"Aye. I do."

"But I wish t' take the air and walk aboot a wee bit!" she insisted. "Would ye deny me such a small pleasure wi'out cause, just t' spite me?"

"There's ample air here in the bailey for your purpose, is there no'? And distance enough that ye can stretch your legs t' your heart's content, if ye walk around and around in circles."

His suggestion seemed reasonable to his thinking. But, frowning down at her, Roarke saw a stubborn gleam kindle in her emerald eyes. Likewise, he detected a subtle obstinacy, a tiny gauntlet of challenge thrown down, in the jut of her little chin as it came up, albeit ever so slightly.

"And what if I tell ye I've nae mind to take the air here in the bailey, reekin' o' horses, hounds, and the midden, sir?"

"Then ye must pinch yer delicate wee nose, lassie, and resign yerself, for I'll not have ye wandering abroad beyond these walls! 'Tis far too dangerous.

111

Now, inside wi' ye, lass! Run and join in with the merrymaking, and enough o' your nonsense."

As far as Roarke was concerned, he had issued his command, and that was that. The matter dismissed, he turned to go, but the girl had other ideas.

" 'Tis a wee walk *outside* these grim walls my heart craves, sir — and 'tis a walk *outside* I'll have, thank ye kindly," she insisted, her green eyes narrowed. "If ye ha'e a mind t' escort me, then ye're welcome t' come along, or free t' set another t' be ma watchdog, but I *will* go — and ye canna stop me!"

"Canna?" he echoed scornfully, then added in a voice like thunder, *"Canna?* I' faith, mistress, ye dare much wi' your careless words, for *I* am laird here, and no other — beard or nay! If I should tell ye t' stand on yer wee head, why, then, ye must do it. And if I should tell ye t' cackle like a laying hen, then ye'd have no choice but t' tell me 'aye, mi'laird Roarke!' and cackle anon!" His gray eyes gleamed now, and there was an arrogant tilt to his jaw that rivaled her own as their obstinate wills clashed, the air sizzling between them.

But to Roarke's amazement, the girl was neither chastened nor cowed by his forbidding words or his angry expression. Instead, she threw back her head and laughed in scorn, the sound silvery and tinkling on the frigid air — and every bit as lancing to his male pride as shards of rare glass.

"Stand on my head, ye say, my laird?" She snorted, sounding neither silvery nor tinkling now. "Cackle like a — like a broody hen? Och, sir, happen your housecarls might harken t' your daftest bidding, but I'm no' one of them! I willna stand on ma head, nor cackle! And furthermore, I'm no' your prisoner. I shall go where I will!"

So saying, she suddenly picked up her skirts and made a mad rush for the gates, so startling Roarke that for a moment he was dumbstruck and anchored to the spot.

"By the Blessed Cross!" he growled, and sped after her, his long strides gobbling up the hoof-churned, slushy dirt of the bailey.

He caught up with her beneath the arched gateway. Gripping her roughly by the upper arm, he spun her about to face him.

"Take your paws from me, ye great bossy brute!" she hissed, her green eyes blazing into his.

"Nae, my wee dragon, I willna," he rasped, glowering down at her and quite oblivious, in his anger, to the round-eyed stare and gaping mouth of Hugh, the gate-keeper, watching them. "Ye'll come back t' the hall straightway, if I must bind ye and gag ye t' take ye there!"

"Nay, never!" she spat. "I'm no' your prisoner! I dinna have t' heed ye!" She wriggled to free herself, pounding furiously at his chest and clawing at his hand to tear his fingers from her arm and break his grip.

"Enough o' that, ye wee wildcat!" he commanded.

When she would not calm, he took her by her other arm and pushed her back against the gate's stone wall, pinning her there by his fierce grip on both her shoulders to keep her still.

Their furious faces were but inches apart now, wrath and ire locked in a fierce battle, each bent on outstaring the other as their ragged breaths congealed and commingled on the cold like plumes of smoke.

Confident he now had the upper hand, Roarke glowered down at her, his jaw hard, his eyes the color of the fog that rose o'er the loch at morningtide; hers like a cat's that glitter in the dark. But, despite his grimmest efforts, his sternest expression, she did not quail under his scathing glare, nor wilt, nor weaken. In fact, he was nigh certain she never even so much as blinked!

"Damme ye, Roarke Gilchrist! Laird or nay, 'tis a big, spiteful bully ye are! Aye, and a pompous, braying lout of a mon!" she hissed, tossing back her hair defiantly.

"And you, my *lady*," he scoffed, "are naught but a bag 'o wind! 'Tis a braw sound ye pipe, aye, t' be sure — but 'tis an empty one, for all that!"

Her answer was a resounding kick that took him full on the left knee, just above where the protective supple suede of his boots ended.

"Jesu!" he yelped. "Ye damned witch!"

"Witch, is it now, sir?" she taunted, her red lips parted in a mocking smile, her eyes sparkling, her cheeks rosy. "And what happened to the 'empty bag of wind', pray?"

Choosing that very moment when his guard was momentarily lowered due to his astonishment — and pain — she lunged forward, thrusting him back with both hands against his chest.

She almost succeeded in rocking him back on his heels. Almost. With a score of years behind him spent honing his wits and reflexes for battle — times when speed might mean living, rather than dying — he recovered far too quickly for her liking.

In a single lunge, he had her again in his powerful grip, his arms locked about her. Lifting her clear off her feet, he thrust her back against the wall, this time keeping her pinned there with the weight of his chest.

"Ye'll do as I say, lassie, and dinna forget it — ever! For as long as ye linger at Corbin, my word will be law unto ye," he rasped, "and these walls your guardians against all harm."

"Nay, they are my prison — and yersel' ma cursed gaoler!"

"Aye, that, too, if needs be!"

His hot breath fanned her cheek. His gray eyes scalded hers, hot as cinders from a fire. His broad chest crushed her breasts beneath it, and the heat of him was like pure flame against her body. Her heart began to thunder madly, her knees to shake. A damnable warmth began to gather in her belly. But then she saw his ebony head dip low to hers, and the railing words he flung at her became a distant muted buzz, like that of angry bees heard from afar.

"I hate ye!" she ground out against his marauding lips in the instant before his mouth claimed hers. "I hate ye, I do!"

"Aye, lass, aye, but nae more than I detest ye, by God—!"

Her eyes slid closed. Of its own free will, her mouth seemed to purse, to lift, to soften in surrender. Her body strained toward his, rising up on tiptoe to meet it. The buzzing sound fell away to roaring silence as the brand of his lips seared hers. He consumed her mouth with savage lips that owed more to fury than fancy; more to a desire to tame and master than any pretense at tenderness. Roughly, passionately, his tongue flailed at the margin of her lips and thrust them apart like gates flung wide. He plundered and tasted her inner mouth, wresting a response from her, demanding one, conjuring one, although she fought to deny him that victory.

She struggled, but his arms remained locked around her, inviolate bonds of steel sheathed in velvet. She screamed curses against his lips, and yet he crushed her even harder to him and silenced her cries with his bruising mouth. He meshed her slenderness to his hateful body like a second skin, using hands that were rough and urgent yet strangely exciting as he stroked and pressed her everywhere. And, when at last he was forced to yield her mouth in order to draw breath, his chest was heaving. His eyes were no longer aflame with anger as he looked down into hers, but dark as the gray mist, and wild with desire . . .

"Och, lassie, ye sorely try ma temper, do ye no'?" he growled, his breathing a husky, labored thing. "But I canna seem t' leave ye be, ye wee shrew! I must ha'e ye, or go mad wi' wanting."

"A curse on ye, Roarke Gilchrist, and on yer blasted temper, tried or nay! Aye, I curse ye t' the devil, for 'tis

115

certain sure you're no' a Christian laird!" she spat at him. "Did ye think me so low that I'd welcome your kisses and hold ye to ma breast? That I'd thank ye for savin' my life by playing the whore an' liftin' ma skirts?"

With that, she drew back her hand and cracked him full across the cheek with a blow so firm and full, it jerked his head to one side with an audible snap — and left her fingers smarting sorely! As if that were not enough, she shoved him back and barreled past him, plaid and hems flying again behind her as she sped back to the keep proper, leaving Roarke nursing his jaw and uttering obscenities under his breath.

To make matters worse, Castor — who'd followed them down to the gatehouse and sat patiently waiting for their quarrel to end — sprang to his heels. He glanced across at Roarke and barked once — threateningly — before bounding after her, deserting his master's camp for the hated enemy's.

She's a dragon, in truth! Roarke thought sourly, glowering after her retreating back and the wagging tail of his treacherous hound as he stroked his stinging cheek and jaw. *Aye, and one that breathes fire an' brimstone t' boot, the evil-tempered bitch!* he added. What, in the name o' heaven had possessed him t' try t' kiss her a second time? he wondered ruefully, shaking his head in dismay at his madness. Well, it would no' happen again, he swore, for when he next kissed a lassie, it would be his Maggie's warm lips he claimed. Aye, he'd find sweetness in her kisses, not the tart bite o' vinegar!

"Well. What are ye starin' at, mon?" he snarled, suddenly aware that he was being watched. "Ha'e ye never seen a mon steal a kiss from a lassie at Yuletide — is that what ye're gawping at, eh, good Hugh?" He flung the caustic question at the boggling gatekeeper, his expression dark as thunderheads over Ben McAlpin at Lammastide as he added scathingly, "For if not, why, I'll be verra happy t' steal another for ye, that ye may bear witness to it!"

Poor, innocent Hugh sputtered and coughed in an effort to mumble something that would appease his laird, who — in what manner Hugh couldna fathom — he seemed to have offended, albeit he'd uttered not a single word! But before Hugh could stammer an apology, Roarke had also disappeared, striding angrily for the mews.

Hugh shook his head and made the sign of the Cross. Ever since Roarke had returned the morning after the blizzard, bearing the strange lassie in his arms, it was as if all the Gilchrists o' Corbins had gone daft in the head!

Chapter Ten

On the day of Christ's Mass, the feasting began. The long trestle tables of Corbin Keep groaned under the festive bounty that would weigh them down for the next twelve days.

The heart of the feast was the traditional roasted boars' heads which the scullions carried in, borne aloft on great platters of pewter. There were apples tucked in the boars' gaping mouths, and the tusked heads rose from platters surrounded by still more apples, these baked and stuffed with suet and seasoned with costly clove and cinnamon spices from the East.

There were great slabs of juicy venison and beef, carved from the spits in the kitchens; legs of greasy yet tender pink mutton, fragrant with parsley, sage, rosemary, thyme, and other herbs garnered from Fionna's precious stores; whole swans and pheasants, grouse and partridge, all properly hung and bled then roasted to a succulent turn. There were jugged hares, blood pudding and haggis, great loaves of fresh black bread, and oatcakes drenched with clover honey. There were eels soused in vinegar, and fresh salmon tickled from the icy burns of Corbin, and salt salmon, too, preserved in casks of brine. Aye, and there was more — so much more that the girl's mouth watered and her head swam as she sat down beside Fionna and took up her eating knife. Selecting a tempting morsel of red salmon from the platter before her, she rolled her eyes in pleasure at its delicate flavor and texture on her tongue, then quickly helped herself to another piece.

"So? Is the salmon t' your liking, sweetheart?" Fionna asked amusedly, noting the girl's rapturous expression and the diligence with which she devoured the salmon.

"Aye, my lady, 'tis verra tasty!" she agreed readily, though with an embarrassed smile that Fionna might think her a glutton. "Why, I havena tasted such a bonnie fresh salmon since my father's huntsmen poached the fish from the burns' o' the clan . . . o' the clan . . . ? Oh, a pox on it, I canna remember!" Her voice trailed away, and her happy smile dwindled as she tried to recapture the memory that had teased her, then quickly fled.

"The clan Mac Donald?" Fionna pressed gently. "Or mayhap 'twas the clan Mac Kay? Or Frazier? Do any of those strike a familiar chord? And what about your father's name, dearling—can ye not recall it? Think, lassie, think verra hard!"

The girl closed her eyes and racked her mind, but alas, there was nothing, only an empty storehouse where memories should have been. Crestfallen, she shook her head. Her shoulders sagged in defeat. "Forgi'e me, lady, but whatever was there for a wee moment, 'tis now quite gone!"

"Aye, perhaps," Fionna allowed. "But happen it will return again, and no' take fright so easily the next time, aye? Take heart, my puir wee chick, for 'tis only a sevennight since ye hovered 'twixt life and death. All in guid time, your past will return t' mind, I fancy. Then we may deliver ye safe an' sound to those who love ye well." She reached out and squeezed the girl's hand. "Sup, child, sup! 'Tis but a wee mouse of a lass ye are, and I've nae mind for your lady mother t' think we ha'e starved ye here at Corbin when ye return

119

home! Bad enough the puir woman's no doubt feared ye dead these many days!"

"But . . . what if I have no fond mother who awaits my return?" The girl blurted out her deepest fear, her green eyes swimming with unshed tears. "What if it transpires I have neither kinsmen nor home t' return to?"

"Why, then, ye will stay here wi' me, child, in my home, and the clan Gilchrist will be your kin! Ye could fair worse, lassie. The Gilchrists take care o' their own, and God ha'e mercy on any who try t' harm one o' theirs! Now, enough o' your brooding, my hinnie. Sup!"

Hardly reassured—for she knew she'd sooner die than throw herself on the mercy o' the laird of Corbin, or beg his hospitality for a moment longer than was absolutely necessary—the girl returned to her meal, picking at the fine foods now with none of her former appetite. The lady Fionna was so very kind and dear to her, she thought. If only she could repay her kindness in some small fashion! It was a blessed miracle that a mother such as she could have raised such a hateful son—och, birthing such a monster didna bear thinking aboot! But then, she amended her thoughts, Fionna would hardly have had much to do with the young laird's raising. The son of a noble, as was he, would have been sent to some kinsmen's keep for fostering when he reached eight or ten years, that he might learn the arts of a man from some stern lord other than his father. Aye, she mused, for so had Fergus and Gil and young Bran been sent forth . . .

She grew very still, her heart thudding alarmingly as she caught herself in midthought. She feared she'd forget the information that had suddenly popped into her head. But this time the names remained.

Fergus. Gil. Bran?

Thanks be to God, she had them fast! But—who were these men, she considered excitedly? Brothers?

120

Cousins, at least, surely? Och, Blessed Mary be praised, *something* had come back to her, just as Fionna had promised it would! Mayhap more would follow anon, or someone would know by the names she recalled from whence she'd come?

". . . but alas, we've so few entertainments here, with Corbin so far from the nearest burgh!" she suddenly heard the older woman say, and realized belatedly that Fionna was addressing her. "Most men think only o' blood feuding wi' other clans, of siring sons and increasin' their rank, their wealth and power, while we women—! Why, we ha'e a yearning for tranquility and beauty in our lives, do we no'?" The older woman sighed wistfully. "For mysel', I've a great longing t' hear a bard's pretty voice and the melodious playing of a mandolin."

"Ye have, my lady?" the girl exclaimed. "But I'll gladly play for ye—and sing, too, if ye've a mind t' hear me? Ye've been so verra kind t' me since I came here. I would do something for you in return, my lady! I have some small talent at the making o' music—or at least I believe I must once have had such a gift. I seem t' recall a harp," she added, frowning, and then her expression cleared and she added with more confidence, "Aye, a harp fashioned of gilded wood, given the name 'Sweetsong'. . . ?"

Uncertain now, her frown returned. She'd been so convinced that she could play and sing when she made her impulsive offer, but could she truly do either—or was it but wishful fancy on her part? Would she make a fool of herself if she tried and failed? Swallowing, she closed her eyes and forced herself to concentrate. And, like a miracle, straightway she could see her hands moving surely and knowledgeably over the strings of a knee harp, and knew without a doubt what voice each string would give when plucked. Aye, she just *knew* she could play!

"Hmm. Another even', mayhap, child, when ye're a

wee bit stronger?" Fionna suggested doubtfully, for she'd seen the confusion in her face, and had blamed her expression on the poor child's exhausting efforts to recall her past. She had no wish to tax her energies further.

"Nay, lady, truly, I'm quite recovered enough t' play. Please, I would be honored t' entertain ye if a harp can be found?"

Fionna smiled at her touching eagerness to please. "Very well, lovie, if you're quite sure? Ye shall play for me upon the very harp that once belonged to my puir dear Cam, God rest his soul. I'll have my woman Flora fetch it for ye straightway."

When the harp had been brought, Fionna ordered a small stool set on the rushes below her dais for the girl to sit upon whilst she played.

Her expression intent, absorbed, the girl took her seat and arranged her topaz skirts gracefully about her. Settled, she flung back the folds of her fur-trimmed mantle to free her arms before placing the kneeharp across her lap.

Running her slim white fingers over the strings experimentally, she cocked her head to one side. First, she must listen and discover if the instrument had been recently tuned or if any loosened string rang false, for it appeared an ancient instrument indeed. Concentrating, she tried it, and found that despite its great age, the harp's voice proved true, mellow, and achingly sweet. The smile of delight that illumined her face was akin to the sun coming up over the craggy mountains, Fionna thought, and was glad she'd given the girl her way.

From the first rippling chord, the clan Gilchrist hushed. Laughter ebbed to silence. All noisy chatter ceased. To the last man and woman, they all turned to watch the foundling girl as she readied both her instrument and herself to play, for all were curious to see if — as the whisper that ran through their number promised—she had some small talent for music, or if her boasts were empty ones.

"I shall sing to ye of the last journey of the kings of our proud land," she said softly yet clearly, looking about her at the expectant faces. "I shall play for ye a ballad that tells of the isle of Iona, where our great kings—Kenneth Mac Alpin, murdered Duncan, Macbeth, and all their royal forefathers—now sleep, but awaiting the Day of Judgment, when they shall rise again t' glory."

A ripple of surprise ran through the gathering, for the ballad she'd promised to play for them was an old, familiar one. It was a difficult piece, too, a ballad that taxed even the most skilled minstrel or bard to the limits of his talents.

Her long, slender fingers flexed, then suddenly flowed over the strings of the gilded harp like purling water in a burn. Under her skilled caresses, the instrument seemed to come alive, to vibrate with passion like a lover in response to his lady's fond touch. It gave forth a silvery, rippling song that repeated and repeated on itself endlessly. The sound was liquid and sweet, akin to the rush and eddy made by waves breaking on some sandy shore—perhaps on the shores of that distant, fabled isle of Iona?

"Bear him away on the gloaming tide!" she sang, and in the sweet trembling of her sorrowful voice, it seemed they could hear the sad song of the sea, the dirge of the wind's low keening, and the mournful cry of the gulls wheeling o'erhead. In the notes she plucked so nimbly, so effortlessly, the listeners could imagine the rise and fall of the proud funeral barge's prow as it lifted and dropped, lifted and dropped, cleaving the wild waves of the Firth of Lorn to carry the dead kings of Scotland to their hallowed burial place,

> "Carry our sire
> To his kingly bed.
> There let him lay
> His noble head.
> And sleep the deep sleep
> Of the royal dead
> On the magical isle
> Of Iona.
>
> Anoint his pale brow
> With the holy oil,
> And place on his breast
> A sword sae bold,
> Bind his proud locks
> Wi' a crown o' gold
> And lay him to sleep
> Where the wind
> Blows cold
> O'er the magical isle
> Of Iona . . ."

The clan Gilchrist was as entranced as if she'd woven a spell about them all with her bewitching voice and the enchanting melody of the harp. All eyes were now riveted on the girl, and not a pair among them remained undampened by tears of sorrow.

Roarke himself was little less moved, though he'd swear fealty t' the devil himself before he'd admit as much t' anyone! He cleared his throat and reached for his goblet of mead, intending to drain it to the dregs and recover himself. But then—he put the goblet down untouched, for it suddenly seemed to him that to drain his cup in that moment would be tantamount to swilling ale in a holy kirk, so powerful was the spell she'd woven with her lament . . .

Instead, he shifted position in his carved chair, the better to watch the girl without craning his neck, thinking as he did so that he'd never seen a bonnier sight than she. Curse the vixen! He yet lusted for her, although he knew her now for a shrew!

This even', she wore her raven hair severely caught back from her finely boned face by a net of golden threads that he recognized as belonging to his mother. The style, though plain on some, when worn by her only served to emphasize the swanlike beauty of her white throat and her delicate, dainty profile. The gown she wore was Fionna's, too, he mused, yet could have been sewn for her alone, so perfectly did it suit her petite loveliness. It was a kirtle of topaz, a rich, tawny shade that brought out the striking green of her eyes and the golden flecks in their depths. It also enhanced and warmed the fine creamy pallor of her skin. Over the gown, she wore a length of wool for a cloak, dyed vivid saffron and bordered with wide bands of embroidery in gilt threads, and narrow edgings of fur. The torchlight winked off something at her shoulder, and Roarke saw that the robe was fastened on her right by a huge golden brooch — an oval one that bore a black-enameled raven with its wings spread, the red lion of Scotland rampant on its back. It was the badge of Corbin and the clan Mac Andrew, which declared his paternal grandfather's oath of fealty and allegiance to the Scottish kings and submission to their will.

Roarke's gray eyes narrowed with ire, for he knew the brooch was one Fionna cherished above all others she possessed. He'd torn it from the shoulder of Alan Mac Quinlann, the last laird of Corbin himself, the same day he'd retaken this keep from the man in his mother's name. It irked him to see it worn now by this stranger; to know that his mother, in her fondness, had impulsively seen fit to loan such a precious bauble to an upstart maid who'd come to them from nowhere, and whose very name was as yet unknown to him!

> ". . . though kings may die
>   And be laid to rest
>
> Our pride in this land
> Will weather Time's test.
> Great chieftains all,
> We ha'e buried our best
> On the magical isle
> Of Iona . . ."

Roarke looked moodily about him, noting the utter stillness that prevailed in the hall even after the girl ended her ballad—a pregnant hush that could ha'e been cut wi' a knife! Giant shadows hung like wraiths upon the smoke-blackened walls, unmoving. The torches guttered and hissed in the draft, their roar and that of the fire in the hearth as it licked at the Yule log the only sounds in the wake of her song.

Fionna, he saw, was dabbing at reddened eyes, visibly moved. That sentimental lout, his friend and steward Tavish, was wiping his eyes on his fists and wore a face of darkest melancholy. Graeme, his equerry, was dewy-eyed—in fact, there wasna a dry eye t' be seen anywhere, Roarke noted with disgust! The mood in the hall—once jolly and loud with good cheer and festive Yuletide spirit—had become a melancholy one, a circumstance that rankled and grated on Roarke's already simmering temper, for he'd yet to recover his good humor and forget the girl's impudence and defiance of the day before.

Rising from his chair, he stepped down from the dais and strode slowly across the hall to stand before her, a towering dark man in tunic and breeks of charcoal gray bordered with crimson and boots of fine black suede. He wore a length of the Gilchrist plaid, the red-black-and-gray tartan draped carelessly about his broad shoulders. Halting before the girl's stool, he reached out and took her hand in his to raise her to her feet.

"My lady, ye sing an' play like a wee angel from

126

heaven," he said gallantly and with every evidence of sincerity as he bowed deeply before her. Yet there was a wicked gleam in his eyes that struck discord in her heart as he straightened; one that filled her with forboding. "However, I would remind ye that 'tis the festive season we celebrate this even' at Corbin—the joyous birth o' the Christ Child Himsel'! We'll celebrate with laughter and merriment in my hall hereon, my lass, and I'll thank ye t' remember that! I'll ha'e no more o' your melancholy songs o' death and burial this night! Duncan! Ian! Gi'e us a lively reel t' set our toes t' tapping, laddies!" he commanded. "Andrew, t' yer pipes!"

Her face flamed with shame as he turned away. His biting criticism had quite shriveled her moment of happiness, completely doused the warm knot of pride that had kindled in her bosom on seeing the transported faces of her listeners, Fionna among them. Aye, it was a sad song she'd chosen, she admitted defiantly to herself—one quite unfitted t' the merry Twelve Days, true. And yet it had been the only one she could recall, the song she'd felt welling up in her soul as she sat down to sing! Och, that hateful, callous brute, she thought, tears stinging hotly behind her eyes, Was it no' enough that he must deny her every little freedom she craved? That he must seek t' force himself upon her wi' his hateful kisses? Must he also wrest from her each small triumph she won in this alien keep?

She bit her lip, fighting desperately to keep her tears in check. Nay, by God, she wouldna give *him* the satisfaction o' seeing her wounded, nor let him suspect that he'd stolen the pleasure singing and playing her very best for his lady mother had brought her. But . . . it was no use! Though she tried, she couldna keep a brave face! Too much had happened too soon. She was so lost, so terribly frightened, so very alone! She gave a great shudder, and with a strangled sob, cast the harp aside, letting it tumble to the rushes with a noisy twang. Her hand flew to cover her mouth and — deaf to the disappointed groans of the onlookers — she ran from the hall.

Uncomfortably, Roarke felt three score pairs of censurious eyes bore accusingly into him.

"Well, well, now, would ye look at his! All shame on ye, Roarke Mac Gilchrist" came a low voice at his elbow.

Turning, Roarke saw his mother standing there and scowled, for her eyes were more accusing than the rest put together!

"Are ye become such a petty mon, ye must take your pleasure by belittling a wee lassie before us all? In truth, it was unworthy o' ye!"

"Petty?" Roarke spluttered, his expression indignant.

"Aye, petty's what I said!" Fionna confirmed, shaking her head reprovingly. "Truly, my son, I dinna ken why it is ye've taken such a fierce disliking t' the puir wee lass! Is it no' bad enough that she has no memory o' her past? Neither name nor kin she can lay claim to? Must ye add to her burdens wi' your unfeeling words when she sought only t' give me a bit o' pleasure, ye callous lout!"

Roarke's jaw tightened. A nerve danced at his temple. His swarthy complexion grew darker still with anger. "Methinks ye make much o' little, my lady mother," he growled, trying to appear casual. "The vixen defies me at every turn — and now my own mother sees fit t' take her part against me! Jesu! The sooner the wee harridan recovers her wits and is gone from here, the happier I'll be, and nae mistake!"

His mother fixed her piercing blue eyes on him with a look that somehow managed to make him feel like a wee lad in long skirts all over again, for like then, it was as if she could see straight into his very soul and pry out the truth like sea-winkles pried forth on the point of a bodkin.

"Ah, ye can fool yersel', Roarke Gilchrist, ye great blind lout, but ye canna fool me!" she said softly. Before he could argue, she'd drifted away from him, her blue skirts whispering over the rushes.

In his irritation, Roarke turned to Tavish for solace and understanding. Friends for many years, he knew he could rely on Tavish's jovial company to return things to their proper perspective and himself t' good humor.

"Devil take the minx, eh, Tavish? She has doused our Yuletide spirit wi' her songs o' doom and gloom, an' we'll have no more of that, eh, mon? Come, laddie, you and I'll sit by the hearth and enjoy a wee dram o' the water o' life, shall we no'? I have a full cask I've been hoarding for just such a moment!"

But Tavish, rather than smiling and amicably agreeing as was his normal wont, was unusually cool. "By your leave, my laird, I am minded t' seek my bed verra soon. I find mysel' grown suddenly weary, i' faith!"

"*You* weary, good Tavish? You, my laird o' Misrule, who can dance all night and still be dancing at cock-crow?" Roarke barked, incredulous. If he was irritated before, he was livid now.

Tavish had the grace to look uncomfortable, but he only muttered "Aye!" by way of explanation, and Roarke cursed and shot him a black, brooding glare.

"So, laddie, she's bewitched you, too, has she no'?"

"Nay, sir."

"Come, Tavish, dinna lie t' me! Will ye not speak plainly — as my lady mother at least had the courage to do! — and tell me t' my face ye didna care for the way I spoke t' the lassie?" His voice had risen to a roaring bellow at the last, causing heads to turn in their direction.

"Nay, sir, I willna. Ye're a grown mon, and my laird besides," Tavish said stiffly. "It isna my place t' tell ye what ye should or shouldna do, however unfair ye may be. And so, I'll say naught."

"*Unfair!*" Roarke exploded, his eyes gray ice. "Och, Blessed Mary, I canna believe this! First, that mangy cur Castor deserts me for that wee dragon's camp. Then my lady mother takes the lassie's part over mine, and now *you* defend her, too, ye damned turncoat! What must I do t' redeem mysel'?" he ranted. "Tell me that, mon? Would ye have me hie after her like a whipped cur an' beg the lassie's pardon? Would ye no feel sae cursed 'weary' then, Tavish, and decide t' drink with me by the fire after all?" he demanded scornfully.

A flush had risen up Tavish's ruddy complexion, and now the color of his face rivaled that of his ruddy hair.

"Aye, sir," he nevertheless acknowledged firmly, to Roarke's amazement, and with even greater daring added, "I would! But somehow, I doubt ye've the spleen t' humble yersel' and do it, sir!"

He was drunk. Aye, he was! He'd long since lost count of the lonely goblets o' the fiery water o' life he'd swigged while hugging to the fire and staring morosely into its depths. He'd cursed Tavish t' the devil after his friend's desertion and wished the rest o' the clan with him, retiring to brood by the hearth alone, save for his goblet and a full cask, now half empty.

One by one, the revelers had fallen to their straw pallets or rolled themselves into their cloaks to sleep, their muffled bodies scattered all about the hall on the rushes. His mother had retired to her sleeping bower. Her cousin, the lady Elyse, had done likewise. Graeme alone had remained with him for a while, matching him goblet for goblet, and he'd felt no censure in his master-of-horse's company. But in the end, Graeme had taken himself off, too, muttering about the warm wench awaiting him in the stables. Now Roarke alone remained awake, save for Castor, his erstwhile hound, who was dozing at his feet with the other dogs.

"Ye damned betraying cur!" Roarke growled, nudging the wolfhound with the toe of his boot, though not unkindly. "D'ye forget the hunts we've shared? The years we've spent t' gether, tramping the glens and moors? The thrill o' the stag chases?"

Castor raised his head from his paws, cocked an ear, and whined softly. Roarke held out his hand, and the dog lumbered to its feet, went to him and rested its muzzle on his knee, looking up at him from soulful brown eyes.

"Is it my pardon ye ask, then, old fellow?" Roarke murmured, fondling the hound's shaggy ears and scratching him beneath the chin in the way he knew the auld dog loved. "D'ye regret your treachery now, ye soft auld brute? Is that why ye gaze at me so mournfully, hmm?"

But to his dismay, despite his petting, the hound padded away after a few moments, looked back at him once, long and hard, then trotted off across the hall. It didna take a soothsayer for Roarke to guess where the beast was headed! Springing to his feet, Roarke flung his goblet from him, not caring where it landed in his fury.

"By God and Mary, so be it, then!" he growled. "I'll ha'e an end t' this nonsense this very night, or my name isna Roarke Mac Gilchrist!"

The cause of Roarke's disquiet was, like the laird himself, yet awake, though abed in the closetlike anteroom that opened off the lady Fionna's apartments.

There was no fire in her small chamber, but in the bower beyond, one flickered, painting shadows on the ceiling and walls there, and spilling into the room adjoining. Made restless by Roarke's hurtful set-down, she lay watching the patterns made by the fire upon the walls. Her white woolen nightgown was fastened warmly at throat and wrists against the chill. A coverlet of woven wool and yet another of furs was tucked snugly around her body. Her feet should have been warm as toast from the heated stones Fionna had ordered a serving man to bring for her, along with a relaxing warmed posset to drink, but still she was cold, for it was a coldness that came from within, rather than without. The cold of loneliness and confusion.

Who am I? she asked the silence. *What name do I bear, and from whence did I come? What grave sin against God did I commit, that that spiteful, mealy-hearted brute should find me half dead in the snow, and bring me here t' torment me?*

Sometimes, as it had earlier, a fragment of memory seemed to flicker in her head like the flicker of the fire; almost touched, almost grasped, then gone like a will-o'-the-wisp or an eerily flitting bog-light. Her sleep was fraught with nightmares drenched in blood and death, sorrow and terror, yet when she tried — knowing somehow even from the depths of sleep that she was but dreaming — to recognize other names, a place — something to fit her memories to! — she couldna! She would instead awaken with a terrible jolt, a scream on her lips and her heart racing painfully, to find her cheeks wet with tears and a terrible ache in her breast that weighed as heavy as stone.

Had she lost all of her loved ones in some terrible tragedy — was that what her sleeping mind was trying so desperately to tell her and her waking mind had managed at such cost to forget? Did that explain why no one, thus far, had come in search of her?

Worse still was the other dreaded possibility — that there *was* no one who cared for her left to begin a search! Och, Blessed Mary, if only she knew her name! Even that would be better than naught, for however unloved, she must surely possess one? Aye, even the wolfhounds that hugged the hearths o' Corbin had the dignity of a name for themsel's!

As if in answer to her thoughts, she heard a snuffling on the silence and stiffened. But then it was followed by a low whining that came from close by, and she relaxed, smiling now. The firelight from beyond had caught the sheen of a soft brown eye, a plumed gray tail whisking to and fro. Recognizing her midnight visitor, she laughed softly.

"Well, well, my laddie, it seems I have a friend here, does it no', even if I can lay no claim to a name! Come, ye great daft brute, up! We'll keep each other warm t' night, shall we no'?"

Castor needed no second invitation. He sprang joyfully up onto the bed, swiped his tongue across her cheek in gratitude, circled a time or two, then curled himself up alongside her. Her arms hugged him tightly, his damp black nose resting snugly beneath her chin, the pair — warmed by the heat of each other's bodies and by the ties of mutual affection — quickly fell asleep.

Roarke stumbled down the narrow corridor, the resin torch he bore aloft guttering madly as he lurched to right and left on unsteady legs. He cursed as he slammed into a wall, bumping his brow and nose, and kicked it soundly to punish it, bruising his toes painfully in the process and punishing himself instead.

He was in a fine spate of temper when he reached the closetlike anteroom where the lassie made her bed, too furious to consider her proximity to his lady mother — and far too drunk t' care.

Coming dangerously close to setting fire to the woven hangings that curtained the room with his carelessly carried torch, he thrust them aside, sparks showering, and lumbered into the antechamber like a drunken bear.

"Wake up, ye wee she-devil!" he roared. "The laird o' Gilchrist has come t' speak wi' ye!"

To his befuddlement, the lassie answered him wi' a threatening growl . . .

Chapter Eleven

Through bloodshot eyes and with a half cask of whiskey fogging his reasoning, Roarke lounged against the threshold. Squinting into the gloom of the anteroom, he saw how the light from the fire in his mother's chamber beyond reflected off twin rows of sharp teeth set in glistening red gums: teeth that leered at him in an unholy grin from between the opened bed hangings! The shadows revealed little else but that grinning mouth . . .

"Bare yer wee fangs at me, would ye, lassie?" he growled. "Och! Is there nae end t' your temper?"

So saying, he lurched into the anteroom, his height and breadth dwarfing the chamber. Grasping one of the saint-carved bedposts for support, he swung around it and reached through the parted hangings to grab the girl by the scruff, intending to shake some sense into her daft wee head, his original intention forgotten. But before he could do so, those twin rows of teeth came at him from the gloom and sank deep into his wrist!

He yelped with pain, then cursed foully, for it was only the thick cloth of his tunic sleeves that kept those sharp, yellowed fangs from drawing blood.

"I dinna ken why ye're doing this, ye wee cannibal, but ye've done me damage enough! Cease, ye damned madwoman!" Roarke thundered, jerking his captured arm about in an effort to throw off his assailant. Nevertheless,

135

the jaws held fast, and the lass — aye, surely it must be the lass who'd bitten him, for who else could be in the bed wi' her? — worried his arm, shaking it violently to and fro.

The girl chose that very moment to rouse. Waking with a jolt and seeing a towering figure looming over her bed with brave Castor hanging ferociously to its wrist, she sprang from the bed. Clearly the intruder had no innocent purpose in mind, she thought, backing into a dark corner from which she might better defend herself! There she began screaming loudly, whereupon the hound — excited by her cries — decided to release his master's wrist and instead set up a din of barking to rival their clamor.

"Quiet, the pair o' ye!" Roarke ordered in a voice of thunder, considerably sobered by pain. Worse, he felt foolish now, having realized that it was his own faithless auld hound who'd bitten him! He pressed an unsteady finger across his lips. "Hush, will ye no'? Ye're making noise enough to wake the dead!"

"And why should I no'?" the girl challenged him hotly, seething as she realized the intruder's identity. "Any mon who'd force his way into an innocent lassie's bedchamber deserves t'be soundly punished for his sins — laird or no'!" she hissed at him. "Be gone straightway, Roarke Mac Gilchrist, 'else I'll scream again!"

"Damme ye," he growled, his expression a wounded one. "I didna come here t' harm ye, but t' beg your pardon, woman! Is this how ye repay me for ma kind intentions? For humbling mysel' t' ye? Pah, a pox on ye, ye cursed harridan! I willna ask it now!"

"My . . . pardon?" she echoed, taken aback. "Did ye say 'pardon,' my laird?" That one of his rank — let alone his arrogance — should wish to ask her forgiveness astounded her!

"Aye, I did," he admitted gruffly, though with palpable ill grace. "There are some o'erly sensitive souls at Corbin — nae but a few, mind! — who felt I didna deal fairly wi' ye this even' when I maligned your choice o' song. And so I—I . . . !"

Abruptly, he fell silent, and stared at her openmouthed as she took a step forward, moving into the ruddy light.

Jesu! he thought, *What a bonnie lass she is — all fiery spirit, pride, and temper!* Her eyes — sparking a fierce green glitter in her outrage — caught the meager light like shattered emeralds. Her nightrail made a soft white blur in the shadows. Her breasts — softly rounding out the heavy wool — were caressed by the reddish glow of the fire. Her heavy mass of ebony hair tumbled down past her shoulders like dark stormclouds, inky against the virginal whiteness of her gown. Roarke wetted his lips, for even clad in an unflattering nightsack from the neck t' heel, she was a fetching sight — a tempting vision o' womanhood t' heat any mon's blood and set his pulse t' racing! In truth, the sight of her made him quite forget what he'd come here to say, for a stirring had begun in his loins that banished all logical thought . . .

"Aye? And so ye what — ?" she persisted with a haughty toss of her head, helping him not a bit. If the great lout was minded to ask her pardon, why, she was no' about t' let him off sae blessed easily! Obstinately, she crossed her arms over her bosom and glowered at him, waiting for the promised apology with her foot tap-tapping on the rushes.

Roarke continued to stare at her, unblinking and mute. "And so I what — ?" he prompted, knowing vaguely that some answer was required of him. He'd parroted her own response like a simpleton, blinking owlishly.

"And will ye, then?" she snapped, exasperated, clenching her fists within the folds of her nightgown. Drat the man! Was he daft — or but cleverly toying wi' her for his own lecherous purpose?

"Will I what, sweeting?" Roarke queried huskily.

Ignoring his endearment, she ground out impatiently,

"Will ye say it, mon?"

"Say what, dear heart?"

" 'I beg your pardon,' ye daft great lout!" she almost shouted.

"Och, my pardon's granted ye, sweeting! And I'll grant ye a thousand more, should ye but ask me wi' your own sweet lips," he came back softly, his voice a deep, heathery burr now that she recognized as dangerous.

It seemed, somehow, as if she'd heard him speak in just such a honeyed way once before—and with hazardous results—though when that could have been she couldna recall. Apprehension fluttered in her belly like dark wings. Blessed Mary, why would he not be gone!

"I'm not asking *your* pardon, ye fool!" she railed at him, stamping her little foot and tossing her head in vexation. " 'Tis *you* who's supposed t' beg mine!"

"I am?" His gray eyes widened innocently.

"Aye!"

"But why, chick? I havena done aught yet for which t' ask your forgie'ness!" he insisted in a slurred voice, managing a roguish wink only with utmost difficulty as he added, "Though—aye! I allow my thoughts are sinful ones! Hic!"

"So!" she exclaimed, belatedly realizing his sorry condition. " 'Tis deep in your cups ye are, ye great sot! 'Tis small wonder ye dinna make sense a'tall, mon! Out wi' ye, then! Go! Be gone from here straightway! There'll be no reasonin' wi' ye this night, 'tis plain t' see!"

"Out? But I canna leave ye now, my dearling!" Roarke said with an apologetic shrug, taking a single long stride closer to her. "Ye see, ma wee sorceress, ye've bewitched me sorely! I would lay wi' ye this night an' lay your spell t' rest, once and for all! Come, ma bonnie, will ye no fly into ma arms like the wee faerie wench ye are? Will ye no' speak a word o' sweetness—grant a wee, pretty smile? — to a mon who'd love ye gently and well?"

"Lay wi' ye?" she sputtered, stunned by his boldness. "Fly into your arms? Jesu! Madonna! I'd sooner lay wi' a randy ram than beneath the likes o' ye, Roarke Gilchrist! Sooner fly from the highest crag o' Ben McAlpin to ma death than int' your foul arms! Sooner smile fer Old Nick himsel' than bare ma teeth t' grin at ye! Oot o' my chamber, ye vile lecher — or I'll loose the hound on ye!"

"Och, ye dinna mean that, dearling!" he denied softly, taking another pace towards her. His eyes were soft and misty as peat-smoke now — and doubly dangerous in their very softness, she knew intuitively. "After all, we both ken that ye desire me, too . . ." he added chidingly.

"Desire ye . . . ? Nay! Never!" she insisted, her eyes wildly searching for an avenue of escape, for she was in arm's reach of him now. "Castor! *Castor!*"

The wolfhound responded instantly to her panicked cry. He sprang at Roarke from behind with a growl, his paws slamming the man solidly between the shoulder blades. The hound's great weight knocked his unsteady master off his feet and shot him forward, into the lass. To keep herself from falling, she grabbed wildly for Roarke's arms, held fast to them, but lost her footing anyway. Somehow, her weight toppled them both sideways. He tumbled to the goosedown pallet, dragging her down after him with a wild whoop of triumph.

"Och, ma wanton wee witch!" he cried tauntingly as he leered into her furious eyes. Clicking his teeth reprovingly he added with infuriating tenderness and a wicked grin, "Ye didna have t' throw me t' the pallet t' have yer way wi' me!"

Her eyes flashed murderously as she struggled to escape the heavy male arms lolling across her, pinning her down like chains of iron. But each time she unwound an arm it was immediately replaced by its partner, octopus-fashion! "I did nae such thing," she panted, "and ye ken verra well I didna, ye oaf! Let me up, mon, before I do ye a mischief with ma knee!"

Ignoring her empty threat, Roarke leaned up on one elbow and waggled a finger at her. "Ah, sweet liar, ye wouldna harm me if ye could, for I ha'e seen the way ye devour me beneath your lashes. I've felt the heat o' rising passion fill yer blood when I stroke your silken skin. Ye burn, lassie. Admit it! Ye burn as hotly as do I!"

"And when have ye ever touched me? Tell me that?" she demanded, distracted by his outrageous claim. She frowned as vague, disturbing images, fragments of memory, again flashed to mind; a hazy reflection seen in a mirror of tin . . . a night of swirling snow . . . and running, running desperately from some . . . some terrible, faceless danger that threatened her very life! Him? she wondered? Was it him she'd feared and fled to escape, after all?

Then, too, came a vague awareness of a darkened hovel, a tumbledown croft reeking of smoke and wet furs and dampened peat . . . and a stranger's touch as warm and soft as summer rain pattering upon her bare skin. A man promising he was her beloved . . . and her own voice pleading with that stranger . . . begging him to . . . to . . . ! *Oh, Sweet Jesu, nay! Merciful Mary, nay, she didna — she couldna have — !*

A flush rose up her cheeks in the shadows. Could this rogue have taken advantage of her and seduced her while she lay helpless in his thrall, despite his promises to the contrary? Aye, it was possible — more than possible! She wouldna put such doings past a rogue like him, now that she knew him better!

"Why, when last I kissed ye!" Roarke answered glibly, cutting into her scrambled thoughts. "When else, dear heart?"

"And when might that ha'e been — and where?" she demanded, fearing the worst and dreading his answer.

"Why, where else, sweeting, but two days hence — in the gatehouse?" he supplied, smooth as moleskin.

She almost sobbed with relief, but it was relief short-lived, for it was replaced at once by consternation. She frowned. The gatehouse, he claimed? But he'd stolen only a kiss in the gatehouse, no more! His caresses were but wishful thinking on his part!

"Surely ye havena forgotten so soon, dearling," he continued, carefully watching her face, "for I willna forget the taste o' your kisses, not if I live t' be a hundred!" His smoky eyes caressed her. His handsome, swarthy face was even darker in his desire.

She stared at his lips, then blinked to dispel their disturbingly pleasing image. "The gatehouse — ? But you only kissed me then, ye didna tou — ? Och, you're mad!" she decided, giving up. "And there's nae reasonin' wi' a lunatic who's a drunkard into the bargain!" She'd best get rid of him as soon as possible instead of pursuing the truth, she decided hastily, for the look she read now in his smoky, sensual eyes was one that bothered her in some perverse way! Putting distance between them seemed her wisest course. Accordingly, she told him, "Forget why ye came here, and let me up, my laird!"

But instead the brute rolled himself *atop* her. He braced his palms on the pallet and lowered his ebony head to hers, silencing her pleas with the heated clamp of his mouth over hers and subduing her struggles with his weight. Slipping a broad hand beneath her long, silky hair, he tilted her face the better to fit her mouth to his. Then, holding her fast, he claimed her full, ripe lips with kisses that burned, scalded, and robbed her of breath, of thought, of speech.

"Ah, lassie! Ye dinna ken how many times I've thirsted for the taste o' ye on my lips these past two days!" he murmured, and resumed his ardent kisses before she could find voice or breath to utter a reply.

Truth was, despite her innermost wishes, the feel of Roarke's hard, insistent mouth moving on hers stirred her. With his kisses, a pervading weakness spread through her, filling every thirsting pore of her body like honey dripped from the comb. The rough sensuality of his kisses fired a ripple of answering sensations at the very core of her being, tightening her muscles and nerves until she grew as tense as if she'd been stretched upon a torturer's rack — but what a blissful torture was his! She

141

gasped as his mouth parted over hers. Moaned as his tongue's tip pried at the margin of her lips. Groaned as it boldly forced its way between them and beyond in an intimate kiss that left her reeling.

His tongue warred with her own briefly, before he suckled gently upon it. She shuddered, for the way his mouth teased delicately within her inner mouth was sinfully sweet. A peculiar yearning sensation tugged at silvery cords connecting her mouth to her breast and her breast to her loins. His kisses filled her with fluttery feelings she was certain she'd never felt before. Her bosom ached. The tiny crests became tight, sensitive wee buds that chafed against her scratchy woolen nightshift in a way that was torture — and sweet, so sweetly tingling, all at once. And then, as if he knew, somehow, the confusion and bittersweet pleasure his kisses wrought in her innocent body, she felt his rough warrior's hand slip down from her throat to caress her bosom. He tenderly cupped and fondled her with such gentleness, her bones felt like churned butter!

"Dear God, ye mustna!" she managed to plead hoarsely when he tore his lips from hers. She gripped the cloth of his tunic front in both hands to give emphasis to her pleas as he rained kisses over her ears, her throat, her shoulders.

"Och, but I must, my lassie! I must — and will!" Roarke threatened in a raspy groan. "Though but a month ago I hadna set eyes upon ye, since I found ye in the snow I've had not a wink o' sleep for wantin' ye! I'm under your spell, my wee witchling — and there's but one way t' escape your power!"

He breathed the ardent words huskily against her little ear. Cupping her breast, he felt the blood rush to her skin in a tide of warmth beneath his palm. Crooning endearments, he caressed her wee face, brushing back stray tendrils of midnight hair that curled wantonly about her cheeks and temples. "When I'm gone from ye, my eyes long for a glimpse o' your faerie beauty. My arms feel empty wi'out ye t' fill them. My lips hunger for the taste o' your bonnie red lips. Och, dearling, though I dinna trust ye, and though ye test me sorely at every turn, there's a demon within me—one that willna rest until I ha'e ye! Yield, sweet stranger, whoever ye might be! Changeling or mortal, faerie or woman, noblewoman or wench, yield all, an' fight your laird nae more!"

He gathered her up into his arms, and kissed her again. Weaving his fingers through her hair to arch her head back, he brought her mouth fully to his. His wild lips were like raging storms that wreaked their havoc with savage, hungry beauty, brutally drawing the passionate, sensual woman within her fully to the surface and leaving the bairn forever behind.

With an anguished cry, her arms came up. Sobbing his name, she cradled his dark head, tugging it down to hers so that their mouths could meet in a fiery kiss. Little cries of wonder uttered in her throat as, still kissing her, he slipped the skirts of her nightrail up about her thighs. Sliding his hand beneath them, he lightly stroked her silken legs from ankle to thigh.

His low groan broke against her mouth as he caressed her, like a wave breaking against the shores of Paradise. His arms encircled her. His fingers splayed across the twin mounds of her bottom, touching and kneading, cupping and stroking her where no one had ever touched her before.

She wrapped her arms about his throat, sobbing as he clasped her buttocks in both of his hands and drew her hips hard against him. Sweet Jesu, what madness was in her heart—her soul—her treacherous body—that she should feel so wild and wanton? Was this the shame that her forgotten past would reveal—a wanton wench who hungered for the touch of men? Oh, she knew she should gainsay him, knew she should tell him nay, should call him vilest lecher and force him—somehow!—t' halt what he was doing! But nay, she couldna . . . nay, she wouldna, for she could feel the proud rise and thrust of his manhood nudging her belly; the heat of his flanks as he moved his hips against her, and an answering pulse had begun in her loins. It throbbed like the beat of a pagan heart, a chant that kept time to the male rhythm of his body in perfect harmony, partnering it measure for measure. Its beat rose, its tempo mounted, until its song of desire filled her veins like a litany. *I want him! Och, how I want him!* it throbbed.

Her eyelids slid closed against the murky light, shuttered out the wavering shadow-beasts drawn by the fire on the cold stone walls. Now she saw only Roarke's darkling face, poised but inches from hers. His smoke-gray eyes were half closed. The thick black lashes curled like sooty moths above the jut of his high, wind-browned cheeks. The irises glittered beneath them like dark-silver coins, glimpsed amidst the coals of a fire. His mouth — so masterful, so firm! — was slightly parted, his breathing ragged as he crushed her to him.

"Och, ma bonnie, ye feel sae blessed sweet!" he groaned, nuzzling her hair.

"My laird!" she whispered. "Oh, my laird, I canna bear it! Surely I ha'e gone mad! Ye must stop! Nay, nay, ye must go on! Och, I dinna ken *what* ye must do, but for the love o' God, help me!"

"Down wi' ye then, my bonnie," he commanded in his masterful voice. "Lay ye down, dear heart, and I will gi'e ye the ease ye yearn for."

Loath to release him, she nodded and sighed. Obediently, she lay back as he'd commanded, her will now his in every way. Her fingertips trailed down over his chest, drifted like wings over his oaken belly, until — her eyes still fixed upon him — she was forced to relinquish him as he moved away. To watch, strangely bereft, while he rose and left her side to strip off his tartan mantle, his tunic and breeks, his boots.

Her bosom rose and fell rapidly with excitement as, unclothed, he turned. Towering over her, he stood looking down at her beneath the flickering firelight. His fists were knotted, planted on hips where old scars gleamed silvery-white, crisscrossing the darkness of his flesh. Had she ever seen a man unclothed before, she fought to recall, wetting her lips? Nay, she thought not, for surely she would have remembered such masculine beauty!

Darkly handsome as any centaur, beard-shadow lent Roarke's face a rugged, manly cast, one contrasted by sleepy, hooded eyes that any woman would envy. His fine head was capped by an unruly thatch of ebony curls that spilled about his broad brown brow and clung about his shoulders like commas drawn on finest vellum by a monk's firm hand. The teasing, ruddy light played over broad, wiry shoulders and a well-muscled torso — paler than the weather-bronzed flesh of his face. Sometimes the capricious light hid the firm ridges that stood out across his abdomen and hard belly, then boldly revealed the broadness of his chest and the thick T of hair that furred it, though mercifully cloaking the rest of him in darkness . . .

Before she could catch her breath — stunned by his almost tangible aura of maleness and power — he came to her. Standing beside her couch, he loomed over her like some great dark god of yore; one of the dark and bloody gods of the Vikings who'd sired his granddam. She felt the down-filled pallet give to his weight, and then he stretched his full length beside her. Gently, he turned her to face him.

"Ah, my bonnie, 'tis fair ye are indeed! The fairest flower the Borders ha'e ever seen . . ."

With whispered endearments in his lilting Gaelic burr, he caressed her hair, tilted her chin. And, when he dipped his head to kiss her again, full upon the lips, she eagerly parted her mouth beneath his, surrendering to his tender ravishment. As he kissed her, he unfastened the laces that gathered her nightshirt at the throat and loosed it. His mouth was hungry against the pulse at its base as he worked the garment from her.

She gave a muffled little cry of protest when she lay

bared beside him. Hands fluttering like pale butterflies, she would have shielded both breasts and womanhood with her hands if he had let her.

"Nay, my lassie, nay. Dinna cover yersel' from me — ever! 'Tis a beauty ye are, my wee wren, and soon your Roarke shall drink that beauty t' its fullest measure! Aye, my bonnie, I shall savor ye wi' my eyes. I shall taste your nectar on these lips, and love ye with the touch o' these battle-scarred hands. I command ye, dinna hide yersel' in shame, my sweet, but yield . . . yield all . . ."

He kissed her brow, and the tip of her little nose. He kissed her cheeks, her chin, his lips like the brush of a wizard's wand against her skin, weaving a glamour about them both. Sliding down, he kissed each bared, snowy breast where it nestled in his hand like a wee dove, teasing the flushed, stiffened peaks of each with his tongue and thinking they were a bonnier pair than any he'd seen, all cream and roses in the flickering light. His tongue traced down over her rib cage, then darted into the tiny well of her navel, lapping it with ticklish caresses before moving lower to swirl over her belly like whirl-pools of fire.

When his hot breath fanned the fluff of curls that crowned her womanhood, she stiffened and pleaded with him to cease, trying to drag his mouth from her body. But Roarke shook his head and firmly removed her hands. With tenderness, he parted her thighs and traced his tongue around and around the satin flesh of their inner columns. Then, with a low, lusty growl, he dipped his dark head and supped on the honeyed heart of her.

A stunned cry was torn from her lips, a cry of wonder that pealed on the darkness like a joyous bell as a golden wave moved through her. Pleasure rippled through every part of her, turning her loins to molten fire. Sunbursts exploded against her eyelids as she whimpered and clutched for him, finding him looming above her now, his hard male body poised between her thighs, his shoulders a bastion that blotted out the light.

146

"Dearling! Dearling! Ah! Such wonder!" she moaned raggedly, and her body arched and grew still beneath his.

His gray eyes dark with desire, he kissed her closed eyelids, then drew back, hungry now to claim her for his own. To his joy, she surrendered all to him in her rapture, opening like a shaded flower that finds at last the golden light of the sun. She embraced his flanks with her slender, milk-white thighs and embraced his chest with her eager arms, knowing he alone could extinguish the blaze that consumed her.

Sweat forming in beads across his brow, Roarke fitted himself against her. Winding her long black hair about his hands to bind her to him, he thrust forward. Aye, he would take her now — at last! — at last! he thought. And in the taking, he would burn her enchantment from his soul forever!

But to his confusion, something thwarted his entry.

The sweat rolled from his brow as, for a fleeting moment, he pondered if the wench might yet be virgin? But nay, it wasna so, *couldna* be so, for had she not called him "husband" that night in the crofter's hut, when she lay rambling with fever? True, he'd be guilty of adultery come dawning, but couldna be called t' account for ravishing an innocent maid!

Reassured, he thrust again. And, with this second practiced thrust of his flanks, she cried out — but the barricade was sundered. He lay sheathed within her sweet loveliness t' the hilt, breathing heavily as he waited for his heart to cease its deafening gallop. Now there could be nae turning back, nor regretting, nor gainsaying! Married or nay, nameless or known, liar or guiltless, for this night, if no other, the foundling lass was his, and he her lover!

Tamping the pressure of his own desire, he forced himself to ride her slowly, deeply, mindful of his lady's pleasure. He filled her to the depths with himself at every thrust, then flexed his muscled flanks to slowly withdraw, only to plunge into her honeyed sheath again and again

147

and drown anew in her searing heat and sweetness.

"Ah, dinna leave me, my love! 'Tis good, sae very, very good!" she moaned when he would have withdrawn to tease her again. Wetting parched lips, she clung to him ardently and implored, "Kiss me again — aye, kiss me, Alan, my own, my love!"

He kissed her, although her use of another name at such an intimate moment — the same cursed name she'd murmured the night he'd found her in the snow — rankled sorely, needling his male pride. It stirred the beast of jealousy within him. A fierce need to take her and leave some brand of his possession upon her suddenly consumed him! Gathering her up into his arms, joined now at mouth, at breast, at belly and loins, he loved her wildly, fiercely, vowing she wouldna forget this night sae readily as she'd forgotten his kisses — or his name!

Their panting breaths, the sensual slap-and-slither sounds of their lusty mating, rose loud on the murky shadows. The whispered endearments he uttered, her gasping or breathy responses, were the only other sounds in the little anteroom for many long moments.

But all too soon, Roarke could no longer curb his body's clamor for release. His heart thundered. Sweat glistened in the meager firelight as it poured from him. The heavy ache at his groin was exquisite in its agony, demanding ease. Fiercely, he gripped her waist, lifting her higher and still higher to possess her utterly. He rode her swiftly now, scaling the craggy tors of passion to stride its shining peak and conquer its glittering promise for his own.

"Alan! Alan!"

"Nay, my lass! 'Tisna your cursed Alan, but Roarke MacGilchrist who takes ye!" he growled, stern of voice as his hands tightened jealously about her hips. "Remember this night, ma wee dragon, if ye forget all else! And remember, too, that 'tis Roarke — the laird o' Corbin — who gi'es ye pleasure . . . and no other mon!"

"Aye!" she moaned. "Aye!"

"Ye will say it, my lass!" he demanded roughly. "Ye will speak my name! Who is it who pleasures ye?"

"Roarke!" she sobbed, her voiced strangled with mounting passion. "Dear God in heaven, 'tis — 'tis Roarke and nae other!"

"And who is it who gi'es ye your ease?"

" 'Tis Roarke! Only *Roarke!*"

With her impassioned acknowledgment of his mastery, the moment came for him. Roarke shuddered and gave a great, roaring cry of triumph as the storm within him broke. An enveloping blaze of pleasure drained him, left him empty — yet somehow filled as never before.

Panting, he rolled to her side and lay on his back, gazing up at the play of shadows on the rafters while his chest heaved and he fought to recover his breath. *Christ's Blessed Mother, 'tis magic, in truth!* he told himself, his senses still reeling. *This lovely witch must surely possess the gift o' sorcery!* he pondered, his thoughts careening like leaves tossed in a gale, for never had he tumbled a wench and felt this way before, tho' he'd tumbled a goodly number in his day . . .

Warlock! she thought bleakly, tears of shame filling her eyes now as she stared morosely at the rafters. Cold reality had returned in the aftermath of their delirious passion, and the full import of what he'd done t' her slammed home like icy water dashed in her face. *Aye, surely he's a warlock — one of the devil's own! An incubus! A demon-mon who's bewitched me wi' his touch and claimed me, body and soul, for his own dark purpose!*

"Well, my laird, 'tis done!" she announced bitterly on the shadows but moments later. "And although I loathe ye t' the very depths o' my being — I will throw mysel' from McAlpin's highest crag before I play the whore for ye again! — ye must wed me now, sir, and wi'out delay!"

"*Wed* ye?" he exploded, shocked by her words and instantly sobered by them, too. He sat up, stunned. "Did ye say *wed?*" he growled in an incredulous tone.

"Aye, sir, I did," she ground out, likewise sitting up. She held a woolen covering-up to shield her nudity. "Ye ha'e taken your brute's pleasure o' me this night against my will. Ye ha'e shamed me, ha'e ye no'? Well, sir, now ye must right the wrong ye ha'e done me and pay fer your pleasures wi' a ring o' gold and a priestly vow!"

"Och, lass, dinna ask it, for I canna," he groaned, grinding out the words through clenched jaws. His face wore a scowl as black as the bottom of a well.

"Canna — or willna?" she cried, her voice rising in anguish, and he was minded of the time he'd asked her exactly the same question.

"Both, wench, both," he repeated crossly. "Come, now, 'tis late. Sleep ye anon, and we'll talk more on this matter at 'morrow's first light."

"Nay, Laird Roarke, we'll talk more on it now — this verra night," she argued hotly, "for 'tis this *night* ye ha'e taken my maidenhead, and it canna be returned t' me at daybreak like a — like a lost riband!"

"Maidenhead?" Roarke scoffed, shaking his head. "Och, wench, do ye take me for a fresh-cheeked youth, t' fall for your protests of innocence? A bairn of a laddie who canna tell a fearful virgin from a well-used wife?"

Her fist launched out of the shadows and landed with a ringing smack across his ear. " 'Well-used wife', d'ye say? Why, and be damned for yer insolence, sir!" she railed. "Does a 'well-used wife' bleed when her husband takes his pleasure — I ask ye that?"

"Christ's Wounds, dinna damn yersel' further by lying t' me, lassie, for I heard ye well enough when ye tossed wi' the fever! Ye called on some mon named Alan — aye, and 'twas 'husband' ye called him, and 'heart o' my heart!' " Roarke rasped, uncomfortably remembering now his first attempt to enter her, and the fleeting notion he'd had that she was untouched; a circumstance he'd been all too happy to disregard in the heat of the moment. Having been denied her once, he'd been half mad t' possess her! Could she be telling the truth? Nay! It wasna possible!

150

"Husband I have, mayhap. Of that, sir, ye would ken the answer better than I, having eavesdropped upon my fevered ramblings," she accused bitterly, "for as I have sworn t' ye, I canna recall aught of my past in my waking hours. But, sir, wife or nay, I tell ye truly, I was yet a maid until ye ravished me this night! A virgin, pure and innocent o' sin, whose deflowering ye undertook without thought or care for the consequences! Deny me if ye will, my laird, but the light o' dawn will prove my claims — and the depths o' my shame!"

"Aye, my puir lamb! As will dawn's first light also right all wrongs — or my name isna Fionna Mac Gilchrist!" came Roarke's mother's tight, angry voice from the door-way to the chamber beyond.

Chapter Twelve

"Damme ye, woman! I willna be cooerced by ye, my lady mother or nay!" Roarke bellowed.

Pacing back and forth, he swung on her with a fierce black scowl, looking as if he'd dearly like to wring the neck of the serene, comely woman who'd birthed him and now met his glare not only unmoved, but with an amused little smile playing about her lips that infuriated him.

"Och, dinna raise your loud voice t' me, Roarke Gilchrist, for 'twill avail ye naught," Fionna scolded calmly, her hands clasped before her. "I amna afeared o' ye, as well ye know. And besides, lad, ye canna gainsay the truth! The proof is here, for all who care t' see!" she added pointedly, indicating with a graceful sweep of her beringed hand the bloodstained white linens she'd taken from the girl's chamber. "The lassie was chaste—until ye forced yer sotted way into her bed, the puir lambkin! Now ye must make amends for your rutting ways and wed the girl—or will your royal sire's blood prove the stronger, after all? Will ye take your man's pleasure then desert her, as your father once bedded and deserted me?" she challenged.

Roarke shot her a darkling look. So! She sought to make him feel guilty did she, by reminding him of his bastardy and her own desertion? Well, by God, she wouldna succeed!

"Ye dinna play me fair, my lady, t' remind me of the unhappy circumstances of my own begetting!" he rasped.

"Nay, I dinna!" Fionna admitted with marked relish. "But nor did ye play the lassie fair! From the first, ye lusted after her, then took her innocence whilst knowing full well that the poor bairn is at your mercy here at Corbin, a homeless waif dependent on your good will for her shelter and the very victuals that pass her lips!"

"Puir bairn!" Roarke scoffed, shaking his head. "I' faith, my lady, 'tis a good jest ye make! Your puir wee bairn is like unto a wee dragon—one well able t' see t' hersel'! Aye, my lady, despite what she may ha'e claimed while ye whispered together so cosily in your chamber," he scoffed, "the maid wasna forced, I tell ye true! She came into my arms like a wee wayside wanton, eager and willing t' have me tumble her and—!"

"For the love of God, Roarke, hold your tongue!" Fionna cried, aghast to all appearances, though inwardly she shook with laughter rather than outrage, for she'd never seen Roarke so plagued by guilt, so confused, that he must explain his actions to anyone before this. "Must ye dishonor the lass further wi' your vile and false accusations? She was chaste, a virgin maid until last night, as the stains of her maiden's blood upon these very sheets has proven! An innocent maid, Roarke, and one unable t' resist the wiles of a rogue well schooled in the bedding o' wenches—and unprincipled enough t' use his experience against her!"

So saying, Fionna advanced on her towering son, shaking her finger at him reprovingly and with a stern expression. Roarke clenched his jaw and planted his fists upon his waist, his strong legs planted aggressively apart like twin oak saplings braced for a coming storm.

"Dinna waggle your finger in my face, madam!" he growled threateningly, his gray eyes snapping, "for I'm nae longer a wee laddie that ye can scold and see thrashed

153

for his pranks, but the laird o' Corbin, and master of this keep! I willna pay through the nose for my one night o' pleasure by placing a band o' gold about a foundling's finger. And nor will I take as mother t' my bairns a wench whose name and pedigree I dinna ken. Enough! Have an end t' your railings, madam, fer there'll be only one cock in this barnyard. Aye, and that one, mysel'! I willna be ruled by a brace o'clucking *hens*, d' ye hear me, madam?" he thundered.

This time, Fionna was forced to retreat, backing away as he advanced upon her.

"Well, my lady? Do ye?" he repeated in a voice that shuddered the rafters, towering over her like the wrath of God.

"Aye, I hear ye full well, my son," Fionna spat back through tightened lips, though her blue eyes blazed. "I hear ye—but I canna believe 'tis the laddie I raised t' honor and justice who speaks! I thought ye an honorable mon, Roarke Mac Gilchrist. A finer mon than the royal bull who sired ye! But ye are nae better than he at heart, where it counts! Like the high king, Duncan, ye would ravish an innocent maid, plant your brat in her belly, then leave her t' her woman's sorry fate! Ye shame me, Roarke Mac Gilchrist! Ye shame the name o' the guid, decent man who raised ye, loved ye like a son, and whose name ye took for yersel'! If my puir Cam could see ye now, God rest his soul, he'd be turnin' cartwheels in his grave!"

She swirled about and, with her hand clasped to her mouth as if to stanch a sob, she fled the solar where they had convened to discuss the night's events, her skirts flurrying in her haste to be gone from him.

"Cursed women!" Roarke growled, made uncomfortable by her mention of Camden Gilchrist, the man he'd loved and respected like a father. He slammed one knotted fist into the open palm of his other hand. "A pox on them all—aye, an' t' devil take the lot o' them! Tavish! *Tavish!*" he bellowed, striding across the flagstone floor and taking the stairs down in haste, three treads at a time, to reach the hall below.

Well aware of the curious eyes of the clan Gilchrist upon him as he crossed it, he roared, "Damme ye, Tavish, attend me straightway! Graeme! Ready my horse! Jesu, I would quit this perfumed bower of mewling she-cats for the fresh air o' the glens! Damn your eyes, Tavish, where are ye, mon?"

Fionna was surprisingly composed when she reentered her bower moments later. The girl lay comfortably tucked in the noblewoman's own bed amidst fur coverings, as pampered as any beloved invalid.

Her green eyes at once snapped up to meet the blue ones of the older woman as she swept into the chamber, a peculiar mixture of dread and anticipation in their emerald depths.

"Well, my lady?" she asked softly. "Did ye — did ye show him?"

"Aye. I did."

"And . . . and is he reconciled? Will he . . . will he — ?"

"Wed ye?" To the girl's amazement, Fionna's haughty composure crumpled. She giggled like a serving wench, flinging herself down to perch on the bed beside the girl with an expression of glee. "Aye, lambkin, aye! I dinna doubt it now!" she confided, "tho' my great brute o' a son willna be led t' the altar like a bull led by a ring through its nose! Nay, chick, he must bluster and roar a wee bit first, and protest t' the rafters that he willna be yer mon. For, ye see, my Roarke canna abide being thought one who comes running at a woman's beck and call! At heart, however, 'tis a different tale. My Roarke's a man of honor, one who despised his sire till the day o' his death for using and deserting me, and even more for his refusal to acknowledge the child I bore him as his own royal get. Och, lass, dinna fear, ye'll see! My Roarke willna allow history t' repeat itsel'. He willna cast ye aside, nor send ye from Corbin, never fear. Before too long, ye'll be his bride—and my dearest daughter!"

"But perhaps ye—we!—shouldna compel him t' wed me, my lady?" the girl suggested worriedly, frowning. "Ye ha'e been good t' me, and I would do anything for ye, but—but I yet have my pride, although the Mac Gilchrist has taken my maidenhead." Her little chin came up obstinately. "Madam, I've had second thoughts since ye left me here to go speak with him. Despite what I swore in shame and anger last night, I willna wed a mon who cares nothing for me! I' faith, there would be no happiness nor joy t' my life, were that the case!"

Fionna smiled and squeezed her hand to comfort her. "Och, my lassie, d' ye think I dinna ken my own son? Roarke's done more than his share o' wenching in his day but has never met his equal in obstinacy or spirit—till now. The simpering beauties of Malcolm Greathead's court swoon like wilted daisies at his feet, offering him their all. But thus far, he's found none among them t' stand up t' his bluster—none t' cause him the loss of a single wink o' sleep for more than a day or two! While ye—! Why, ye have done *both,* bless ye, my clever dearling!"

"I have?" the girl echoed wide-eyed with surprise.

"Aye, lovie, for I ha'e seen Roarke many a night since ye came here, pacing the battlements sleepless, when all else at Corbin lie deep in slumber. And I ha'e seen the jealous way he looks upon ye, too, when ye dinna ken he's watching! 'Tis the look of a hungry wolf, one plotting and scheming how best t' devour an unsuspecting lamb, and slaughter the other wolves who rival him! I dinna ken if Roarke even knows it himsel', but he wants ye, lass—aye, he wants ye wi' a powerful hunger! Last night, wi' the water o' life to weaken his will, he succumbed to his heart's desire!"

"But he said—he swore!—that I called upon a husband when I lay sick of fever! If that be so, then how can I wed him?" the girl pointed out.

"Aye, so ye said. But I've thought on that, and am convinced it must have been your *betrothed* ye called upon, lassie. After all, do maids not call the mon t' whom they've plighted their troth 'husband', long before they take their wedding vows? Rest assured, my lovely," Fionna added, brushing back a dark strand of hair from the girl's rosy cheek, "with such beauty as you possess, ye wouldna have kept your maidenhead this long, were you in truth any man's wife! And, if 'twas but betrothed ye were, then that betrothal must needs be broken now, must it not? My wretched son," Fionna smiled, eyes twinkling, "has robbed ye of your dowry of innocence. And consequently, your father — when we ha'e discovered the puir mon's name! — will be outraged. He'll demand that the Gilchrist make ye his bride wi' all haste and honors, will he no'? Och, you'll see, my chick! All will be well!"

The lady Fionna smiled at the promise of a successful conclusion to her plans, blissfully ignoring the girl's doubtful expression.

She'd decided soon after the girl came to Corbin that she was all she could ever ask for in a daughter-in-law. Gentle of nature, yet proud and spirited; intelligent and lovely, yet capable of great compassion, with none of the false, simpering airs so many of the chieftains' daughters possessed these days. Moreover, on a more selfish note, Fionna had quickly grown fond of the girl and enjoyed her companionship and teaching her the chatelaine's arts of which she was sadly ignorant. Add to that Roarke's obvious obsession with the lassie, and the lassie's marked and powerful reactions to him, her denials notwithstanding, and, why . . . ! It seemed obvious to the noblewoman that the pair were meant for each other! Besides, Fionna had rationalized, she was of an age herself when she should have had a half-dozen grandchildren to dandle upon her knee and indulge, as granddams were fond of doing. Roarke had shown little inclination as yet towards providing her with any of his own free will, for all that

Corbin badly needed an heir. Could she be blamed for giving him a wee nudge in the right direction?

"But I amna sae sure I want him for husband, willing or nay!" the girl blurted out, struggling to cast aside the furs and sit up. She blushed furiously as she added, "He isna — he isna the mon of my dreams, ye ken, madam? I — I find him quite hateful, in truth — even ugly t' look upon! He's — he's overbearing, too, an arrogant lout who . . . who — ! Oh, forgive me, my dear, kind lady, for I know full well he's your only son but — but I confess I *detest* the mon, and would nae sooner choose him for husband than ask for the moon, if he didna rob me of my innocence!"

"There, there, my bonnie, dry your wee eyes," Fionna soothed, gathering the weeping girl against her bosom and stroking her hair. "I know how it is! Aye, and I know how ye feel. But even were matters otherwise, few lassies are fortunate enough t' love the mon their father chooses for them, is it not so? In time, however, most come to love their husbands. Mayhap time will also change your heart, think ye no'?"

"Never, my lady! Forgive me, but nay! I fear that day could never be!" the girl insisted with a delicate shudder that stirred the cloud of midnight hair tumbling down about her breasts.

"Och, chick, dinna say never, lest ye tempt the spiteful Fates t' make a liar of ye!" Fionna warned. But she was smiling as she said it.

Still angered by the unsettling confrontation with his mother, Roarke kicked his huge black horse into a thundering gallop. Its hooves churned up drifts of snow as they raced across the rolling moors, followed by Tavish and Graeme upon their own sturdy chestnut mounts — massive horses more suited to the fields of battle than riding abroad.

In the distance, the mountains rose in purple splendor, their crags bearded with gray mist, their peaks capped with snow. Below, in the shallow dimple of the glen that lay beneath their path, were several crofts belonging to the shepherds of the Clan Mac Gilchrist. The cottages snuggled under deep mantles of white, with only their turf roofs left visible. Peat-smoke rose from small chimneys to purl away on the crisp wind. Flocks of sheep with snow-encrusted fleeces huddled against the frost-laden hedges, scores of them in every direction, with the small black-and-white sheepdogs native to these parts keeping a watchful eye on the flocks in the shepherds' absence.

His eye coming to rest on one croft in particular, Roarke's furious, tight-lipped scowl abated. He grinned, although it was a thin-lipped grin. The vigorous ride in the crisp wind had made his breathing heavy and brought a ruddy flush to his cheeks beneath his beard-shadow. Cold and sudden lusty anticipation lent a sparkle to his eyes, too.

Well, now! What lucky stroke of fortune had sent him riding in this direction, he considered, his smile broadening?

Below lay the croft of his bonnie Maggie, a widow these past three years and his mistress for the last twelve-month. In Maggie's plump and tender arms, he'd surely find solace and forgetfulness — a means t' drive away the lingering image of slender white arms and a faerie face that bewitched him even now . . .

"Ride on, my laddies!" he ordered stony-faced Tavish and a grinning Graeme with a roguish grin of his own. "I've a mind t' inquire after the — er — the health o' Mistress Maggie, puir widowed soul that she is. Ride on! I'll catch up wi' ye anon."

Graeme nodded. "As ye will, my laird! We'll ride clear t' the borders o' Corbin's lands, and see t' it that the beggarly McNairs arena trespassing upon them. And if we should find — by some sorry chance! — that they are — why, then there's a dirk fairly itchin' at my side that will see them set t' flight, and nae mistake!"

The equerry's brown eyes burned with anticipation. The clan feud between the McNairs and the Gilchrists was an old and bloody one in the Borders; a feud in which both sides had eagerly taken part for over a decade now, with no hint of a truce on the wind.

The bitter feud had been started shortly after Roarke became laird of Corbin. Angus McNair, chieftain of Clan McNair and laird of Erskine — yet another keep whose demesne lands straddled the marches between Scotland and England — had trespassed on Gilchrist lands. Ruthlessly, he and his clansmen had ambushed a hunting party of the clan Gilchrist who were pursuing a fleeing stag through one of their own glens.

Before the Gilchrists could recover their wits and repel their attackers, the McNairs had sprung from tree and bush and slain eleven of Roarke's closest, most faithful companions and followers, hacking them down with no chance given them to defend themselves. The McNair's two oldest sons, Fergus and Gil, had sent the rest running for their very lives. Then, with macabre humor, Laird Angus had ordered the ears lopped from each of the dead man's heads, and had sent the bloodied bodies home to Corbin lashed to their own horses. The last corpse had carried a hastily penned missive, destined for Roarke's eyes. The scrap of parchment, pinned to the bloodied and soiled plaid of one man, had read:

"Greetings Gilchrist! We would inform ye that the hunt was a poor one this day, our quarry cowardly sport that afforded small challenge. This time, we ha'e culled your herd o' its puniest bucks and clipped their ears for our trophies. Be warned that next time, 'twill be the stag o' Corbin himsel' whose antlers we nail t' Erskine's door!'

The lamenting of the dead men's womenfolk had been heard for miles across the moorlands that day, Graeme's mother and sisters among them. Roarke had rallied the remainder of his clan and retaliated, seeing a goodly number of McNairs dispatched to an uneasy rest in the weeks, months, then years following the senseless massacre. But there were times—when the wind was right—that Graeme, whose brothers and father had been among the hunters that fateful day, fancied he still heard the ghostly echoes of the women's shrieks and wails of sorrow. Times when he thought bitterly than nothing short of complete annihilation of the clan McNair would fully end his grief.

"'Tis a bitter cold day, is it no', Tavish? I, for one, wouldna take it amiss t' heat my blood wi' a bit of sword play!" Graeme continued with grim-faced relish, blowing on his knuckles to warm them.

"Nor I," Tavish gritted with a sour look for his lord, and Roarke knew his friend would welcome a fight to drain off the anger that still simmered in his breast from the even' before, an anger born of jealousy over that cursed foundling wench.

"Aye, no doubt ye would. But have a care, laddies," Roarke cautioned the pair. "Dinna go looking for trouble, lest it take ye unawares. I've nae wish t' lose my right-hand men—nor my two guid friends."

The pair muttered sober agreement. Following Roarke's curt nod of dismissal, they rode off.

He watched them until they'd vanished from sight over the crest of the next hill, and then dismounted from his horse. Its leather harness creaked in the cold, damp air; its frigid bit jingled as he led the animal to the door of Maggie's humble croft. Looping its reins about a broken cart wheel that lay half-buried in snow before it, he beat upon the plank door with his gauntleted fists.

"Why, an' there ye are at last, my handsome laird!" Maggie greeted him, flinging wide the door with a broad smile of welcome. Hands on her plump hips, she eyed him flirtatiously while he peeled off his gloves, her wide red mouth pouting while those ample hips swung slowly to and fro. "Why, an' I thought ye'd forgotten your Mags, sir, 'tis been so verra long since last ye came t' me. Och, my puir heart was sore, it was, and fair t' breakin' wi' longing for ye!"

Roarke stepped inside the smoky hut and roughly kicked the sagging door shut behind him. Grasping the brown shawl that cloaked her shoulders, he yanked the edges aside and roughly caught her to him, his mouth hot over hers. With a groan, he plunged his hand down the front of her bodice to fondle a full ripe breast, and boldly tweaked the swollen nipple that crowned it.

"Ah, Maggie, ye lyin' wee bitch," he said fondly in a husky, purring tone that Maggie had grown to recognize over the past months. "Yer wee heart isna broken, lassie! Nay, ma sweeting — it lies full and fair and beatin' strongly in ma hand!"

The wench giggled, her bosom quivering, her plump arms going up about his throat to tousle his damp black curls. "Och, sir, ye're daft, ye are! 'Tisna my heart ye have there, but ma bosom!"

"Aye, Maggie, aye. I ken full well!" he agreed amiably, and without further ado, he tumbled her down to the straw that was her bed.

Chapter Thirteen

Tavish and Graeme rode on, scanning the white-mantled hills and glens all about them with no sign of the enemy clan's green-and-yellow tartan, much to Graeme's disappointment.

"These cursed winters!" he growled. "A mon could die o' boredom wi'out a McNair t' sharpen his . . . wits upon!"

"Aye," Tavish agreed dourly. But then his eyes narrowed as he looked ahead to where the forests that lined the banks of the Tweed began. All trees save the sturdy firs were leafless skeletons now, bony and forlorn-looking, but the ground about their trunks was littered with brown, snow-laden bushes. Something had darted between them and caught Tavish's eye.

"Ho! What's that—over there? D' ye see it, mon? Something dark and moving?" He reined in his horse, and squinted against the blinding snow the better to see, suspecting an ambush.

"Whist! 'Tis naught but an auld hag," Graeme responded with open disgust, perhaps disappointed it was not a stray McNair Tavish had spotted as he returned the long dirk he'd drawn to the cuff of his boot. "Auld Morag, or my eyes deceive me!"

"Aye, ye're right. But what is it the witchwoman's searching for?" Tavish wondered aloud, frowning. The old crone had grown closer. Now he could see that she was ferreting about between the sagging bushes and prodding at deep banks of still more snow with her stick of peeled ash.

"Dry kindling? A snare she set last even' that mayhap holds a hare for her supper? Och, lad, I dinna ken what the old dame's aboot, but mayhap we may while away a dreary moment in the asking. Come!" Graeme responded with a bored sigh.

The two men cantered their horses over the white drifts. Snow sprayed from beneath the destriers' feathered hooves, and the breath of both men and horses rose in steamy clouds on the frigid air about them.

As they drew closer, it soon became apparent that Graeme's first impression had been correct. It was the auld witchwoman, Morag, all bundled about in her bits of tattered rag, who tramped the snowy moors and foraged amongst the hushed woods. A moth-eaten blue shawl was tied about her head, with hanks of thin, yellow-white hair escaping it at the brow. Her nose was hooked, her toothless mouth sunken in at the lips like a withered chestnut. Her ancient face was a morass of lines and warts and wrinkles, all wind-wracked to a leathery brown.

"Why, and good day t' ye, old mother!" Graeme greeted her cheekily, sweeping his woodsman's feathered cap from his head as if in welcome to a grand dame. "What are ye aboot? Ha'e ye lost aught o' value? A string o' pearls, mayhap? Some precious jewel ye value, for surely 'tis treasure ye seek sae diligently in the snow?" And he winked at Tavish, enjoying his childish sport as he teased the old woman.

"Some might say so, aye," Morag responded with a hostile, shrewdly-searching look for the two of them, cast from watery blue eyes. "Aye, some might — tho' others wouldna!"

"Has that old bastard, the McNair, hidden a stolen fortune hereabouts, then?" Graeme bantered, for they'd ridden far since they'd left Roarke at Maggie's croft, riding perilously close to the borders of the clan McNairs' vast holdings.

"Nay, good sirs—but he ha'e lost a treasure! One he ne'er recognized whilst he drew breath! Aye, and nor will that auld devil ever recognize it now, not where he be gone!" the old woman responded mysteriously. She cackled with bitter laughter, waggling her wand of ash up and down in a clawlike hand as she spoke.

Tavish, a great lover of riddles and mysteries in any form, perked up on hearing this, his dour mood dissipating. "A treasure ne'er recognized by Angus McNair," he pondered thoughtfully. "Now, what could that treasure be? Tell me, Grandmother, did the McNair receive this treasure of the king, or did he relieve some enemy clan o'—"

"Och, be done wi' yer cursed riddling, mon!" Graeme growled, his former merry expression now faded. "Did ye not hear what the old hag said? She said 'twas a treasure the McNair never recognized whilst *he yet drew breath*. What did ye mean by that, Grandmother?"

"Why, the McNair's dead, is he no', laddies? Aye, ye ken very well he is, so dinna make sport wi' auld Morag! And this being so, how can the auld fox recognize aught?" Morag demanded with a bitter twist to her mouth. So saying, she turned quickly from them, hobbling off between the snow-laden bushes that fringed either side of the path as if she'd suddenly taken fright and was fleeing for her life.

The two men exchanged puzzled glances. The Mac-Nair dead? The chieftain of their enemy's clan, dead? Why, these were tidings indeed!

"Wait, Grandmother! We would speak more wi' ye!"

"Ye would, would ye now?" Morag snapped, whirling to face them with her stick held defensively before her and an expression of foreboding in her eyes. "What aboot, pray?"

"We would hear how and when Laird Angus met his

end?" Tavish asked, kneeing his horse after her. Halting alongside the crone whose assorted rags flapped in the wind, the massive beast was unsettled. It tossed its head and curveted, pawing its feathered hooves at the hard ground. The battle-horse towered over the old woman who barely reached the top of its chest, she was so shrunken by age, yet she glowered at the beast as if daring it to trample or bite her.

"How? Why, how else but by the dirk, my fine masters, for them that live by murder shall die by it, shall they no'?" She eyed them craftily, with, Tavish fancied, somewhat less fear than before.

"Ah! A dirk, was it? Whose dirk, pray tell, auld one, for I would thank the whoreson rogue who held it in his fist, and kiss the bonnie blade that did the deed!" Graeme said with macabre humor.

Morag snorted in derision, shaking her head to and fro. "Ye ask me that? You, of all men, Graeme o' the Gilchrist?" the old hag hissed. She spat into the white of the snow. "If not Gilchrist dirks and claymores, then whose weapons did the bloody deed, I ask ye?" she accused, noting how the steward's jaw dropped and his eyes widened, though the other one seemed not a whit surprised. "The McNair and his litter were slain in their own den, taken unawares by the clan Gilchrist whilst they supped! Now the walls o' Erskine weep wi' their blood! Their ghosts cry fer vengeance on their murderers!" She raised her fist and brandished it at the pallid sky with a vehemence that dried the spittle in Tavish's mouth.

"McNair *and* his sons?" the steward echoed, his eyes widening with horror. He wetted his lips and cast a startled glance at Graeme. "Sweet Jesu! Their slaughter was not the doing of our clan! Snowbound we've been, auld one — aye, snowfast and blizzard-besieged for this sevennight past! This morn is the first that any of the clan Gilchrist have left the walls o' Corbin since the Twelve Days!"

"Pah! Snowfasted or nay, the McNairs are no more!" Morag insisted bitterly. "And all signs point t' yoursel's as their bloody butchers! Go see, my laddies. Go see what ye've wrought! There be none left standing t' bar your entry t' Erskine now. Nor a soul left alive t' tell what befell the laird and his clan, if not the wrath of the Gilchrists — whose memories are as long and unforgiving as their blades."

She wrung her gnarled, liver-spotted hands before continuing, "Och! Och! 'Twas a terrible dark day for the Borders when Erskine fell! Tell the Gilchrist that auld Morag prophesies he's gone too far this time! Tell himsel' she foretells a dark blot of shame cast upon his name for all time, with these cowardly doin's! His blind ambition will be the rue o' Scotland, his begetting forever cursed in the hills and glens of our people, mark my words! Wi' the border chieftains and their keeps laid low by the clan Gilchrist, who now will keep the Norman wolves from o'erunning our southermost marches, even as they conquered King Harold this year past? *Who?*" she shrieked, angrily shaking her fist at the pair, and the ash-wand with it.

"Damme ye, auld hag, 'twas none of our doing, I tell ye! Enough o' your dark prophecies!" Graeme growled, making the horned sign to ward off her evil eye before gathering his reins in his fists. His blue eyes crackled. His lips thinned. A nerve danced at his left temple. "And as for long and unforgiving memories — ! Pah! A pox on ye, for surely ye forget who started the feud betwixt our kinsmen? 'Twas the McNair who slaughtered the flower o' the Gilchrists this ten years past! 'Twas your bonnie butcher-laird who fell upon them whilst they hunted and sent their mutilated bodies home t' Corbin, lashed to their own mounts! Mark well what ye say, auld woman, for my own brave father, my own three brothers, were among the slain that day! One took a McNair coward's dirk in his back, and the others were skewered 'pon McNair claymores — !"

"Enough, Graeme, enough!" Tavish murmured, disturbed by the hatred in his companion's tone. "Ye waste yer breath on this old one. 'Tis clear where her sympathies lie. Words willna change her heart, not now."

"Aye, I suppose ye're right. As ye wish, then. I'll say no more," Graeme agreed tightly. "We'll ride on!"

"T' Erskine?"

"Aye, laddie, t' Erskine! Where else?" the equerry acknowledged grimly. "I would see for mysel' the bloody butchery that's been laid at our door!"

"Then look well about ye when ye enter those sad walls, Graeme Gilchrist," Morag railed after them. "Aye, look well! But tho' ye look all ye may, ye'll nae find the laird's fair daughter among the dead. Auld Morag ha' been there, and she ha' seen for hersel'! My maid's gone, she is — ! Aye, my wild, wee Catriona's gone as if she never drew breath! Vanished in' t' thin air like a changeling brat! Poof! Just so!" Morag screeched, snapping her bony fingers and whirling about. "Seven days I ha'e spent, searching for her! Och, my puir, puir bairn!"

Tavish and Graeme exchanged puzzled glances once again. They turned their horses' heads back to the old woman.

"Hold, Grandmother! Who is this Lady Catriona ye seek?" Tavish demanded.

"Why, who but the McNair's daughter, as I told ye!" Morag muttered. "And a fairer lass ye never did see — a treasure, i' faith, for some fine mon t' wed!" Her bleary blue eyes gleamed accusingly as she cocked them at the clansmen.

"McNair's *daughter?* Whist, now I know of a certainty ye lie t' us, Morag," Graeme accused sternly. " 'Tis known the length o' the Borders that Laird Angus sired only sons!"

"Fergus, Gil, and young Bran. Aye," the crone admitted, nodding sagely. "But his lovely lady birthed a daughter, too, that she did! I know full well, for 'twas I who attended her at her laying-in. The wee lass was the thirdborn of the McNair's litter. Then came young Bran, and the puir lady Moira died giving him birth, God rest her soul."

"The McNair had no daughters, I say! 'Tis still lies ye feed us, hag!" Graeme protested. "We would have heard o' the lassie — seen her — long before this, did ye speak truly!"

"No lie, but truth!" Morag insisted. "As God bears witness, I lie not! With his woman gone, the McNair hadna time nor heart t' spare for a wee lassie that so resembled his dead woman. Let her run wild, he did, t' be raised by whatever slattern would tend t' her needs, puir lambkin, never sae much as letting her leave his gloomy keep while he carried on his blood feuds far and wide. But then when she were sixteen years an' grown t' womanhood, his eyes were opened. When he realized what a wild young beauty he'd sired, the auld fool tried t' tame her, ye see? Had a mind t' marry the lassie off t' his 'vantage, he had, and break the betrothal her mother had arranged on her deathbed. But — 'twere far too late fer Angus t' bring her t' heel! My wee Catriona had grown as stubborn as her sire by then, and wouldna heed him! Said she'd marry the mon her poor mother had chosen, and nae other!" Morag grinned toothily, remembering.

"Sweet Jesu!" Tavish cursed, then added hopefully, "She is fair, ye say, this maid? A beauty wi' golden hair, and eyes o' blue?" He held his breath while awaiting Morag's answer, dreading what she would tell him.

Morag cackled, throwing back her head. "Why, bless ye, nay, Master Tavish Gilchrist! The lass isna a beauty such as the simpering bards sing of, but a beauty in her own right and fashion. Black hair, she has — black as the deepest, wildest waters o' Loch Ness! Black as the corbie's glitterin' wings! Yet her skin is fair — aye, as flawless and fair as the virgin snows all about ye, with lips as red and ripe as a summer rose!"

"And her eyes?" Tavish pressed anxiously. "Mother of God, what color are they, old Grandmother?"

"What else but *green* would suit, my laddie, for a faerie beauty such as my wild Catriona? Green as the leaves of springtime, and slanted as any cat's!"

"Jesu! Green?" Tavish exclaimed, unable to help himself.

"Aye," Morag confirmed, and her rheumy blue eyes narrowed craftily. "Why, laddie?" she whined slyly. "Ha'e ye see such a green-eyed lass at Corbin, then?"

"Nay, old woman," Tavish blustered, "I havena!" But his discomfort with the lie showed plain on his guileless face and Morag was not deceived.

"Alas! Alack! By now, my pretty's been used by her father's murderers—or else was ravished, then murdered hersel'! Which was it, pray, laddie? Tell me, I beg ye?" she implored, clawing at his stirrup strap as she gazed up at him beseechingly. There were tears swimming in her eyes.

"I dinna ken what ye're talking aboot! She isna at Corbin, I tell ye!" The steward of Corbin added with unusual harshness, "Be gone wi' ye, ye troublesome auld witch!"

With his command, the hag flew off down the rutted track in a flurry of grimy rags, bewailing the girl's loss loudly and mournfully on the wind.

"Christ's Sacred Blood!" Graeme cursed. 'Tis the foundling wench she spoke of, or I'm no' Graeme Gilchrist!"

"Aye, my friend, none other!" Tavish agreed with a similarly grim expression. "The clan McNair lies dead t' the last mon, she claims, while their laird's daughter, the Lady Catriona, still lives. And—or so 'twould appear for all intents and purposes!—she is our prisoner at Corbin. An enemy hostage who but awaits our laird's pleasure!"

"Hmm. Does this have the stink of a clever plan t' discredit us, think ye, Tavish—or is it all but an unhappy coincidence? Full well we know that 'twasna our clan did this foul deed! But there's no' a mon the length and breadth o' the Borders who'll believe us innocent, not wi'

170

the stolen lassie at Corbin!"

"I think mayhap ye have the rights o' it, Graeme! 'Twas of a certainty all cleverly plotted that the dice would fall this way — planned by the same clever bastards who slew McNair and his men t' discredit us! It could well be they left the lassie in the snow for Roarke himself t' find and carry home, and thereby make our guilt appear complete. Madonna Mary! D' ye think she was one of them? A party t' their villainy, or but their innocent pawn?" The hope that Graeme would deny such an idea was evident in his tone.

"Chance or plot, it doesna matter now, does it? The end will all be the same," Graeme observed heavily. "The clan Gilchrist will bear the blame for both! The McNairs' blood will be on our innocent heads!"

"Aye, laddie, aye," Tavish agreed soberly. "But we can do naught about it here. What say we ride on t' Erskine and see this carnage for ourselves, the better t' advise our laird?"

"Lead on" came his companion's reluctant reply.

Morag was crooning to herself when she returned to her cave in the lee of a hill. She hefted a sorry bundle of damp kindling, stuffed beneath her arm. Tears coursed down her crab-apple cheeks, icy tears shed for the bonnie maid she'd loved, and whom she was now convinced was not dead in the snow somewhere, as she'd feared, but a hostage t' the laird o' Corbin.

"He'll ha'e taken yer maidenhead, ma bonnie, aye, long-since," she moaned, shaking her head. "An' when the Gilchrist has wearied o' ye, he'll slay ye sure, my dearling! He'll take your innocent life in vengeance for the bloody murders yer father did his clan, curse his soul! Och! Och! These are dark, dark times we live in, just as the long-haired star foretold two summers hence!"

Still muttering under her breath, Morag thrust aside the ragged hanging that concealed the entrance to her cave and ducked inside the musty darkness. She fumbled about, setting the kindling down and rubbing her bony hands together to warm them. Then, of a sudden, she stiffened, her head snapping up.

"Badger? Who's there?" she hissed on the gloom. "Show yersel'!"

A low, mirthless chuckle shivered on the darkness, raising the hackles on Morag's neck and down her knobby spine.

"Och, that willna be necessary, Grandmother. I ha'e but a question t' ask ye," the disembodied voice came to her. "There's nae need t' see my face. None a'tall."

"Question?" Morag echoed faintly, her old heart leaping about beneath her shriveled paps like a salmon in the spawning season.

"Aye, hag, a question," rasped the voice. "I would know of what ye spoke wi' the Gilchrist's men?"

"Spoke? Och, I spoke wi' no one, good sir," Morag protested in a whine. "I'm an auld woman. I but—"

"You're a liar, that's what ye are, hag! I saw ye wi' my own eyes, up yonder where the forests grow thin. There were two o' them, both mounted on fine chestnut horses. Ye spoke wi' them at length."

"What—? Och, aye, sir, 'tis right ye are, now that I ponder on it!" Morag blustered. "These days, my auld memory isna so sharp as it once was, I do confess. Aye, sir, there were two o' them, right enough. And we talked a wee bit, just as ye said."

"Ye told them of the McNairs' slaughter?"

"Aye, sir, I did," Morag admitted in a whisper.

"And why did ye see fit t' tell them of it, when ye ken full well 'twas the clan Gilchrists' doing?" the faceless voice demanded silkily.

Morag shrugged, at a loss to explain. Dare she tell this—this—voice that the astonishment in the clansmen's faces when she'd spoken of the McNairs' massacre had given her second thought? Should she tell him that to her eyes and ears, they'd seemed as innocent as they'd claimed t' be? "I . . . well, sir, I . . ."

"You what?" snapped a voice like a clap of thunder.

"I—I thought mayhap I could trick them, ye see, kind sir! I'd hoped t' make them tell me—!" she babbled, deciding 'twas wiser to tell the truth.

"Tell what?"

"Why, sir, t' trick them into telling me—if—if their laird yet kept my puir bairn hostage, sir," the old woman mumbled. "Or if she were—were dead!"

"What bairn is this? That Badger dolt ye raised?"

"Nay, my lady Cat, sir, who else? My puir, bonnie wee Cat!"

"Not—the lady Catriona?"

"Aye, sir, the poor lost lambkin!"

"Lost? But the lassie's no' lost, she's dead! She has been dead this past sevennight, God rest her soul."

"Aye, I thought 'twas so myself, at first, good sir," Morag cackled. "But praise be, I was wrong! The lass isna dead, bless her!" she finished in a confiding whisper. "She lives!"

"God's Blood! Your wits are addled, hag! The McNair's daughter was slain by the Gilchrists the night of the blizzard. Killed the selfsame night that the rest o' her clan met their deaths, after they'd taken their pleasure wi' her in the snow!"

"Nay, sir, nay, 'tis wrong ye are!" Morag crowed with a chuckle of triumph. "I thought so mysel' when I didna find the puir lamb's body among the others, and after searchin' the moors high and wide for her these past days. But I was wrong, praise be! The laird o' Corbin holds her in his donjon!"

"Black Roarke?" the voice rasped.

"Aye, sir, none other!" she agreed eagerly. "Och, that Tavish Gilchrist—! He tried t' say me nay. Aye, lied, he did! Wanted me t' believe he saw no green-eyed beauty in his lord's keep. But I'm nae fool, for all I might be auld! Aye, I could tell by his eyes 'twas a lie he told me! Laird Roarke stole my puir wee bairn away from Erskine that dreadful night — and she isna dead, not yet, tho' happen she wishes she were by now, poor lambkin! She is the Gilchrist's prisoner."

She saw the darker bulk of the speaker leap up from a corner and lunge towards her from the shadows.

"You're certain of this?" he demanded urgently.

"Aye, sir, she's not dead — my auld life on it"

"By all that's holy — !" the man cursed. "Brand!"

"Here, sir. But — but I swear t' ye, my laird, the maid couldna have survived both my blow and t' blizzard!" came a second protesting voice at Morag's back.

For all her frailty, the old woman spun like a top in the direction of the sound. *"Yer* blow?" she screeched, but the two ignored her.

"Couldna? Och, but 'twould seem she did survive, laddie! And 'twould seem ye bungled the job I set fer ye, after all, ye stupid oaf!" the voice sneered. "Pah! A pox on ye, simpleton! I should never ha'e trusted ye! I should ha'e done the bloody deed mysel', and made sure o' it!"

"Please, sir, ye must forgive me! We thought . . . !"

"Aye, I know what ye both thought, but ye were wrong, laddie, and mistakes are dangerous and costly! Ah, well. What's done is done, I suppose, and canna be changed. But ye ken what ye must do t' make amends, lad? The old witch here, she knows too much . . ,"

"Aye, sir, I know. And I swear I willna fail ye, not this time."

"Very well. See to it! And after . . . aye, after, we must make plans t' silence the other one . . ."

Morag felt the man move past her in the gloom of the cave. She felt the heat rising from his body, the rush of air his passage stirred, and heaved a sigh of relief. Thanks be, he was leaving — and not a moment too soon! Her knobbly old knees threatened to buckle beneath her with relief, so frightened had she been . . .

But then, she caught a fleeting glimpse of the man's profile etched against the pallid daylight beyond. She gasped in recognition as he raised the ragged hanging to go from the cave.

"You!"

Her cry of accusation became a gurgle of pain as a garrot came out of the blackness. The leather thong bit hard across her scrawny throat. It smashed her windpipe, then drove the breath from her ancient lungs in a whistling rush, silencing her forever as the hands holding it tightened . . .

Pitilessly.

Chapter Fourteen

"Holy Mother of God!" Roarke ground out, gripping the arms of his chair until his knuckles were bled white against wind-browned flesh. His expression was drawn, his gray eyes dark with unease beneath brooding brows as he added softly, "If any but the two o' ye had told me, I wouldna ha' believed it!"

A grim-faced Tavish gave a slight nod. "Nay, sir, nor I, unless I'd seen for myself. But alas, all was as we told ye on the ride home. Erskine's great hall was littered with rotting corpses. Although 'tis winter and cursed cold, I'll carry the sight an' stench wi' me to ma grave!" He hurriedly crossed himself. "We found the McNair abed in the west donjon tower. His throat had been slit from ear to ear, and his chamber's disarray told the whole sorry tale. The auld devil had fought hard and long for his life, Roarke, Jesu, he had! Stools had been overturned and broken. Rushlights had been dashed t' the ground. The hangings t' his bed were shredded. And . . ." Here he paused and exchanged doubtful glances with Graeme.

"Aye? Go on! What else?"

"Well, we found this clasped in his fist, sir."

Reaching out, Roarke took the carved wooden comb Tavish handed to him and held it up to the firelight. He turned it about this way and that.

It was a beautifully crafted piece wrought of finely

polished rowan wood, a bauble that had obviously belonged to a noblewoman, for it was too daintily made for a man's usage, too costly for a peasant wench. The handle bore a design of rowan buds and tiny thistles, each one carved in heavy relief, then delicately painted. Between the teeth, several strands of long black hair had been snared. Roarke smiled thinly. A comb of rowan wood—what irony? From ancient times, the rowan tree was believed to possess magical powers. As a consequence, anything fashioned from its wood had the ability to ward off evil. Alas, it had done little to protect Angus McNair from its owner's evilness . . .

"Ye pried this from Angus's fist, ye say?" Seeing Tavish nod in confirmation, Roarke added thoughtfully, "Then 'tis probable he tore it from his murderer's hair as he fought for his life?"

"Ye believe it could ha'e been a wench who killed him, sir?" the steward exclaimed, then swiftly realizing the turn his chieftain's thoughts had taken, his eyes widened and he insisted, "Nay, sir, never, not in ten thousand years! Och, my laird, I know what ye're thinking, and why, but 'tis wrong ye are! A dirk isna a woman's weapon . . . and nor is slitting a mon's throat a wench's way o' doing murder! 'Tis poison a woman uses, sir, or a pillow slipped over a sleeping mon's face to stifle his breath. Both methods are easier, less bloody and distasteful, and they dinna rely upon brute strength, which a wench lacks! What ye're thinking . . . ! Why, Roarke, 'tis madness! Have done wi'ye, sir! The mon was the lassie's father, for the love o' God!" The sandy-haired steward's face was red with indignation.

"Aye, my friend, she was. And who would the McNair trust more than his own daughter, the lady Catriona, I ask ye?" Roarke demanded. "And who would have had more reason t' want him dead? If 'twas as Morag told ye, Laird Angus was threatening t' find the lass an advantageous match of his own choosing and renege on the betrothal her lady mother had made for her. Perhaps she had no wish t' wed, and decided to take matters into her own hands? Or mayhap her betrothed realized he stood to lose her considerable *torchia,* dowry, if she married another, and so was her accomplice in these murders?"

Tavish opened his mouth to protest, then abruptly closed it again. What could he say to refute Roarke's claims? The hairs snagged in the comb were every whit as dark as the foundling lassie's ebony locks, their very color a damning clue to the murderer's identity. And Roarke was right on the other count, too. Of a certainty, Angus McNair would have trusted his only daughter! And of certainty, her dowry would have been a goodly sum. The McNair had been a wealthy man . . .

Tavish clamped his jaw and closed his eyes. He tried to conjure up an image of that faerie lassie with her delicate, pale hands clenched around the handle of a bloody dirk, her green eyes ablaze with murderous hatred. But his mind refused to accommodate him; refused to accept the possibility of any such thing. He could see those graceful little hands only as they'd looked flowing over the harpstrings on the Eve of Christ's Mass, or gently fondling Castor's shaggy gray head, not dealing in death!

"For the time being, I charge ye both t' say nothing of this matter — or of my suspicions — outside these four walls," Roarke instructed sternly, rising from his seat to go and stand by the hearth in his chamber. He planted one palm against the chimney breast, then dropped his head to rest upon his upper arm as if suddenly overwhelmed by weariness. For a few pregnant moments, silence reigned in the firelit chamber, broken only by Roarke himself when he at last continued. "Tell me instead of the lad ye found?"

"Very well, sir," Tavish agreed. "It happened just as we told ye earlier as we rode home t' Corbin. All was deathly quiet when we entered Erskine, not a living thing stirring anywhere! The cows left in the byre had starved t' death, ye see, as had the geese and hens in their coops. And the hunting hounds had been slaughtered along wi' their masters! Graeme and I—well, we didna . . . we didna tarry any longer than was necessary t' confirm the truth o' auld Morag's claims. Once we'd found the McNair, we—er—we rushed out o' the hall and back into the fresh air. We were standing there in the bailey, trying to recover our stomachs, for ye ken, sir, the—er—the clan McNair had been dead o'er a sevennight—when . . ."

Even as he described the ghastly scene for a second telling, Tavish appeared a mite greenish about the gills. His Adam's apple bobbed up and down as if he were but a swallow away from losing his gorge once again.

". . . and we were standing there, looking for some inkling as to who might ha'e killed them all, when we heard a sound, sir. Like a child weeping, it was! Well, as ye can imagine, we were overjoyed t' hear that cry, for 'twas proof o' life yet remaining within those silent gray walls! We tracked the sound t' the well, sir, but when we tried t' pull up the bucket t' discover its source, it wouldna come. Instead, a lad clambered up the rope, a-weeping and a-babbling and a-carrying on he was, too. From what we can piece together, my laird, the boy feared we were the same men who'd slain his clansmen, now returned to take his life. He'd climbed into the well t' hide from us. Wet and frozen he was, and half starved, besides. But at the sight o' our Gilchrist plaid, why . . . ! He were that frightened, he tried to climb back down into the well and risk his neck rather than face us!" Tavish shook his head ruefully. " 'Twould seem, sir, that the sole survivor of the massacre is a wee bit simple, ye ken." He tapped his temple.

"Tetched?"

"Aye, sir. Why, he must be a score—maybe more!—years old, and yet he speaks and acts like a bairn o' six or seven years."

"He has the look of a simpleton, too, sir," Graeme confirmed, "what wi' his mouth hanging half open all the while, and a sort of—a sort of emptiness t' his eyes."

"Hmm. But 'tis cursed strange him being there, is it

179

not?" Roarke observed thoughtfully. "The same butchering curs who'd slay bairns, defenseless women, and hunting hounds wouldna hae been so careless as t' overlook a half-wit lad who might yet identify them! And, since it seems they were intent upon seeing our clan shoulder the blame for the murders, they would have taken pains t' silence anyone that could. Curious, don't ye think, my riddling friend?"

Tavish blushed. So aghast had he been at Roarke's suggestion that the lass had murdered her father, he'd given thought to naught else! "Come t' think on it, aye, sir, I do," he admitted slowly. " 'Tis a mite odd!"

"Mayhap more than a mite?" Roarke mused. "But nevertheless, fetch the lad here to me, Tavish. I would put him a question or two, simpleton or nay."

"Very well, sir. But I doubt ye'll get much sense from him! We both tried, and didna learn a blessed thing more."

From the first, it was obvious to Roarke that Graeme and Tavish had assessed the fellow accurately. The youth with the stringy mouse-brown hair whom two burly housecarls wrestled into Roarke's chamber was obviously backward, clearly terrified, and made no attempt to appear otherwise. He fought the men who restrained him like a trapped animal, threshing his arms wildly about and uttering squeals and moans.

"Nay! Nay! Please, let me gooo!" the youth whimpered as the two men jostled him to stand before Roarke. "I didn't do anything bad, sir, honest I didn't. Ow! Ouch! You're h-hurting me!"

"Release him," Roarke commanded softly, gesturing to his servants.

Obediently, the two unhanded him, and the short, slight fellow scuttled into a dark corner like an ungainly crab. He cowered there in the shadows, blubbering and sniffling, his arms wrapped around his head, his eyes darting in all directions.

"Don't hurt me, master, please don't! Hal's a good lad, he is, truly he is! He didna hurt the laird, I p-p-romise he didna! I never hurt no one!"

Roarke strode across the chamber and squatted on his haunches beside the fellow. He reached out to touch his shoulder in a reassuring way, but Hal flinched from his hand so violently and with such tremors of fright, Roarke thought better of it and resorted to soothing words instead.

"No one means t' harm ye, laddie, least of all mysel'. Ye've naught t' fear from anyone here at Corbin, my word on it, if ye speak the truth. I but wish t' ask ye a few questions, lad, that's all. D' ye understand me, Hal? No one will harm ye."

His tone was soothing, as if he spoke to a wild animal. Little by little, Hal ceased his shivering and drew his arms from about his head, risking an uncertain glance from beneath his stringy locks.

"Nothing t' fear?" he murmured, then carried on so eagerly, droplets of spittle flew from his lips in every direction. "Aye, master I understand! After all, Hal's not stupid! Nay, he isna! He's but a wee bit . . . slow. Aye, that's it! *Slow.* Mother said so, she did, so it must be true. Mother was learned, she was, and she said many, many times, 'Hal,' she said, ye arena simpleton. 'Tis but a wee bit slow in yer thinkin' ye are, my son!' So ye see, I'm no' a simpleton!"

He sounded almost defiant at the last and was scowling fiercely at Roarke, as if daring the laird t' challenge his claim.

"Nay, laddie. I didna think for a moment ye were stupid," Roarke soothed, looking serious. Hal appeared to be about twenty years old or thereabouts, he judged. Although his body was that of a lean, undernourished young man, his upper arms were wiry, powerfully muscled, an incongruous feature when coupled with the naive expression he wore; that of a young child. But then, that could be accounted for quite reasonably. A serf lacking in intelligence would most certainly have been employed in tasks that called for brawn, instead of wits.

He glanced directly at the lad, and saw that the blue-gray eyes that stared so uncuriously back into his were not the shrewd eyes of a thinking man, but the puzzled, hurt eyes of a half-wit. "Tell me, Master, Hal, are ye hungry?" he coaxed.

"Aye, sir, verra hungry, that's what I am! Ma belly's nigh empty. Ye hear it, master?" He stood, clumsily divested himself of the ragged cloak slung about his shoulders, then yanked his tunic of serviceable, filthy homespun free of its belt of frayed rope. He bared a decidedly bony rib cage and a fish-pale, grubby belly, which he thumped with his fist, declaring with a gleeful smile, "Ye hear it? Sounds empty, it do, like a wee drum. Pom! Pom! Pom! Ye hear it, master?"

"Aye, laddie, I hear it. But we've victuals aplenty here at Corbin — more than enough to fill ye t' burstin', if ye'll but tell me this. What happened at Erskine, laddie?" he coaxed. "What did ye see the night the McNair was killed alòng wi' the others?"

A sullen look wiped the slack-mouthed stare from the youth's face. "Nothing," he muttered, pouting. "Hal saw nothing! He was fast asleep. And," he added and brightened, beaming now, "ye canna see or hear anything when you're asleep, can ye, master!"

"That's true — *if* Hal was truly asleep," Roarke agreed mildly, yet his eyes had narrowed now and were riveted on the lad's face, watching the play of expressions he saw cross it as he spoke. "Now, if I was Hal, say, I wouldna ha'e slept sound in ma bed and missed all the excitement that night — och, never! I would ha'e woken when first I heard the horses and the jingling of their harness. I would ha'e jumped right up with the voices of their riders and crept from ma bed to discover who came t' the keep at such a late hour! There must have been many horses that night, and many riders, too. How many would ye say, my friend? This many?" He held up both his hands, fingers splayed. "Ten? A score, mayhap? More?"

Hal side-eyed Roarke craftily, as if he suspected the laird's trickery. Something sly and feral kindled in his eyes for a fleeting instant, but was as swiftly replaced by wide-eyed innocence again. "Och, nay, master! Hal was fast asleep all night in the byre, he was. Warm in the straw it be, see? Hal saw nothing. Not horses. Not riders. Hal woke up in the morning when the cock crowed, just like always. He went t' the kitchen for his morning bread, but they were—they were all . . . stiff and bloody. I was afeared—like when those men came. They . . . they made me get out of the well!"

His eyes moistened as he nodded accusingly towards Tavish and Graeme. Meeting their gaze, he squirmed and hurriedly looked away, not seeming to know quite what to do with his hands. At length, he opted to busy them in donning his ragged cloak once again, fumbling as he tried to swing it around his shoulders and tie the fraying ends in a knot beneath his chin. At last, with difficulty, he succeeded. "Hal wants t' go home now," he whined. "He doesna like it here. You ask him things he doesn't know about, and he's verra hungry."

Shuffling away from Roarke with a lackluster gait, Hal made as if to leave the chamber. But straightway, the two housecarls stepped forward to prevent his exit. Roarke waved them back.

"Nay, lads, let him pass! Follow him, and see to it that he finds the kitchens before too long. I want him fed, and fed well. Mayhap after he's a trencher o' victuals beneath his ribs, he'll find he remembers a wee bit more. Och, and Ogden—?"

The towering housecarl turned and bowed to his lord. "Aye, sir?"

"See to it that our young friend doesna leave Corbin just yet, should he seem so inclined. I may wish t' question him again."

"Aye, my laird."

When Roarke was alone with his two companions once again, he bade them find their suppers, promising to join them shortly in the hall below.

After they'd gone, he went to the narrow, arched window that faced westward — in the direction of Erskine — and stared from it, pondering all that the pair had told him.

Who, he wondered heavily, had slain the clan McNair and its chieftain? And why had they done so in such a fashion, the blame for the deed would logically fall on the Gilchrists, rather than taking the credit for their bloody acts themselves? 'Twas common knowledge that the Frazier chieftain, Laird Hamish, had harbored little love in his heart for the McNair. He might well ha'e done the deed, Roarke considered, but — bold, boastful Hamish would have made no secret of it! Nay. Hamish would have relished the success of a well-laid plan t' infiltrate Erskine that had succeeded in obliterating the Border McNairs from the face o' the earth. He would have crowed his triumph from the top o' Ben Mac Alpin, rather than let another take credit for it. Something else was afoot here. Something, he fancied, that had nothing to do with either the clans or their feuds. Something that made no rhyme or reason in his head as yet — but would, 'ere long, he promised himself. Tavish was not the only one at Corbin who enjoyed the unknotting of a riddle or mystery! Meanwhile, however, there was the girl to consider . . .

"Lady Cat," Tavish had told him the old witchwoman had called her, and Roarke smiled cruelly, thinking how appropriate the name was as he murmured it in his lilting Gaelic: "Catriona o' Erskine. Catriona McNair, my wee Lady Cat, what ever are ye up to, eh, my tricksy lass?"

Aye, that sly wee baggage was the key t' all o' this. He was even more convinced of it, now that there was something more to his suspicions than a nagging unease in his vitals! Catriona of Erskine and no other could give him the answers he sought — and by God, she would tell him

184

all this very night, he vowed, her convenient lapse of memory be damned!

Taking up the wooden comb, he strode from his chamber.

Chapter Fifteen

"Thank ye, Flora. The water's perfect," the girl praised. She lowered herself into the huge wooden tub that had been set before the crackling fire in Fionna's chamber — now her own for the duration of her stay at Corbin.

That morning, after Roarke had left his keep in a fine dark mood, the lady had graciously insisted that she have the use of her chamber. And, despite her protests that such upheaval was unnecessary, Fionna had instructed her servants to move their mistress's belongings to other quarters. And so, here she was.

In the corners of the chamber, pale-yellow candles of expensive perfumed beeswax, not smelly sheep's tallow, glowed against the rose damask hangings that concealed bare stone walls. The candles scented the air with a pleasing herbal fragrance as they burned. The chamber was filled with mellow, overlapping pools of amber, candlelight puddles that gleamed on her bare arms as she raised them above her head and made diamonds ropes of the water that streamed from them or caught in spangled droplets in her midnight hair.

Flora, a dour, practical woman from the Highlands, thought nothing of the charming picture the lass made at her toilette. Rather, she sniffed piously and crossed herself when she thought her young mistress wasn't looking.

No doubt Flora was convinced she was a witch, the girl thought, hiding a smile, for she'd seen the superstitious gesture and knew full well what had caused it: her requests for hot water and a tub in which to bathe!

"Ye dinna approve o' cleanliness, I fancy, do ye, Flora?" she observed without looking up.

"Nay, mistress, I dinna," Flora boldly admitted in a snippish tone. She crossed her beefy arms over a shelf of a bosom better suited to a cow than a woman, confident that the weight of the powerful Catholic Church was behind her convictions as she continued. "I dinna hold wi' a body bathing more than twice in a single twelve-month. And neither do others with a deal more learnin' than I, mi'lady — men o' the cloth and the church! They do say," she added in a hoarse whisper, "that prideful acts such as bathing oneself sae regular and sae thorough as ye do attract the notice o' Satan himsel'! Och! It — it isna natural for a guid Christian lass t' be wallowin' in a tub o' water! 'Tis more akin t' them godless norsemen, wi' their strange habits!"

"Aye, Flora, perhaps 'tis not natural," the girl agreed, but there was a wicked little sparkle in her green eyes as she added, "But then again, since I havena any memory o' my past, who's t' say if I'm guid — or even a Christian, come t' that? Happen I might well be a very wicked woman — even a pagan! One much taken wi' midsummer dancing aboot the standing stones in unholy blood rites? Or mayhap a witchwoman who rides a-cock her broomstick t' the devil's sabbats every full o' the moon, with auld Castor here as my loyal familiar! Are ye no' my companion in wickedness, then, Castor, laddie?"

She threw back her head and laughed merrily, for Castor raised his head and whined softly in answer to her question, for all the world as if he'd truly understood every word! It was immediately obvious, by the serving woman's expression, that Flora was now more than half convinced she was truly a witch. After all, who but a witch would talk wi' a dumb animal, and more damning

187

yet, receive what sounded like an answer!

Again, Flora surreptitiously crossed herself. She wetted her lips nervously and eyed the girl askance. Och, by the Virgin Mary, she were too bonnie by far t' be o' this world, the serving woman considered jealously, her with her eyes so green and her skin so white and her hair as black as the darkest night! Flora looked towards the door, suddenly anxious to be gone from the foundling wench's presence. After all, who knew from whence she'd come, and who she really was—or what dark powers she might possess t' cast spells upon them what crossed her?

"If ye've nae need o' me for a wee while, mi'lady, I'll be away t' help t' mistress wi' her hair?"

At once, the girl felt ashamed of herself, guilty for having taken the serving woman away from her proper duties for so long. Flora attended the lady Fionna, assisting her with her toilette, her gowns, and her hair, as well as a hundred other tasks she performed for the chatelaine of Corbin with calm if bovine efficiency. It was spiteful t' tease her so, when the puir woman had two of them t' see to, instead of just the one.

"Thank ye kindly, Flora," she said sweetly. "And please, forgive me my wee bit o' teasing, will ye no? I'm as Christian as yersel', Flora, I promise ye truly, and certainly nae more wicked!"

Flora looked disconcerted to hear her pardon requested—and her own somewhat gray character held to light as an example—but she was obviously still unconvinced the girl was not a witch. Her doubtful eyes betrayed her, although she insisted primly, "Och, mi'lady, I knew very well ye were but funnin' wi' me, I did! Ye mustna apologize! But now, mistress, by your leave, I must awa'?"

The girl sighed. "Be off wi' ye then, Flora. Oh, and ye dinna need t' come back and help me t' dress after ye've seen t' your mistress. I can dress mysel' well enough, thank ye."

"As ye wish, m'lady" Flora mumbled. She was secretly

188

overjoyed to hear her services would not be needed further that evening but took pains not to let it show. One less chore to perform would leave her a few free moments in which to dally wi' her handsome sweetheart, Ogden! Eeh, she could imagine it now, just the two o' them cuddled cozily together in some dark, private corner of Corbin! Right bonnie Ogden was, aye, and proper taken with her, too, besides. He called her his "Sweet Flora, ma buxom wee flower!" every time their paths crossed about the keep, and gave her a wee pinch on her rump, too, more oft than not, the saucy rascal! He had quite the broadest shoulders she'd ever seen, and the strongest arms, and the bonniest pair o' legs beneath his kilt! Mayhap she'd find out this even' if the rest o' him was as braw and bonnie, she thought, smothering an excited giggle as she scurried from the chamber.

With a suddenly beaming Flora gone, the girl lay back in the water until it rose up about her neck. She lazily stirred it around her from time to time with an idly drifting hand or a playful toe and inhaled its perfumed scent with obvious pleasure.

Jesu! Such a simple luxury, this Norse custom of soaking one's body in clean warm water to wash away the sweat and grime and refresh oneself, but how delicious it was! And yet, anything that was the least bit pleasurable was frowned upon by the pious old men o' the kirk, who — nae doubt! — practiced every vice and sin known t' man — and mayhap some as yet t' be discovered! — behind their sanctified walls! Hypocrites they were, aye, and that overblown Flora little better than they!

She smiled, for she'd seen the sly gleam that flared in Flora's eyes as she made her hasty exit. And, since she'd noticed on more than one occasion the way a certain master o' the keep guard — what was he named? Oswald? Osbert? Nay, Ogden! — ogled the woman and her ponderous bosom, she fancied she knew what was in the wind. Her smile deepened. If she wasna mistaken, it was t' seek out her admirer Flora had hastened, not t' dress her mistress's hair! And mayhap, in her anticipation of Ogden's powerful arms, she'd forget her suspicions, the girl thought hopefully.

Humming, she lathered her face, neck, and shoulders, her hands gliding over the creamy froth that coated her body. Unbidden, she was reminded of the feel of *his* hands as they'd grazed her body. Her movements slowed, and a knot tightened in the pit of her belly, creating a tension that she was afraid she recognized all too well, for 'twas the stirring of desire. She was suddenly reminded, too, of what had caused the slight soreness between her thighs that had lingered all day, and the gentle touchings and arousing kisses that had led her to succumb and yield him her maidenhead.

"Damme ye t' hell, Roarke Mac Gilchrist!" she muttered on the shadows. "I dinna want t' be your bride — but nor will I play the whore for ye a second time, either!"

That cursed dark brute had awakened something within her; roused a sensual part of her nature she knew she'd denied before. Cupping water in her hands, she rinsed herself off, gasping at the pleasurable feeling of warm water trickling down her nude body. The water felt akin to the way his fingertips had felt skimming over her flesh! Her nipples grew tight. Her blood began to throb with a quickened pulse. "No, no, I dinna want t' feel this way!" she moaned, and closed her eyes as a sweetfire longing sang through her, nigh causing her to swoon as she leaned back against the sides of the tub.

Harlot! Jezebel! she railed at herself silently. *Ha'e ye no pride? How can ye desire a mon who seeks only t' use ye for his pleasure, simply because he saved your life?*

Because his touch excites me so, I canna think straight when he's near me! came a swift, unwanted answer. *Because I could spend an eternity drowning in the silver sea of his eyes and never want to surface! Because the music that filled my soul last night when he touched me, claimed my body, is the sweetest song I ha'e ever heard . . . and because I long t' hear its ballad over and over again!*

Och! It didna make sense! She could make a list of the things she disliked about Roarke Mac Gilchrist, starting with the obvious: his looks. Did he not have thick, curling black hair, while she favored men whose locks were fine and straight and gold as the summer wheat standing in crooks in the fields? And did the chieftain not have brooding gray eyes that changed color with his moods, growing pale and cold with anger, or soft and misty as a silver fog with desire, while it was steady, calm eyes of cornflower blue that made her heart sing? And was his body not tall and wiry as a forester's, the well-muscled body of a man who was no stranger to battle and sword-play, the horse, or the hunt, while she found men less overtly male, less rough and rugged, far more pleasing to her eye?

In temperament, he didna appeal t' her either. She didna care for his dour Border moods nor his brooding silences, nor the sudden hot flare of his anger when pressed. And what could the chieftain Gilchrist know of the gentle arts of courtship? The magic that sweet songs and the playing of the lute, harp, or mandolin could weave to make a woman's heart grow tender and her eyes soft and misty with love and desire? Aye, indeed, what pretty words could that Border ruffian possibly utter that would set a maid's heart t' fluttering and cause her to yield him her all in joyful surrender? None — none at all! So why, *why,* had she surrendered?

'I would lie wi' ye!" he'd declared roughly last night. Not that he found her lovely, och, nay! Not that he yearned t' worship at the temple o' her body, och, dear me, no! That would be too refined, too delicate, for the likes o' him! He'd simply said that he wished t' lay with her. *Lay* wi' her — a crude declaration that a barbaric chieftain might utter to a comely bower-slave, or some easy wayside wanton who'd caught his lustful fancy before he mounted her like a rutting stag! Well, she didna ken who she was, but of a certainty she wouldna play the wanton for him!

"Enough, my laird," she declared in a firm voice. "I willna marry ye, no matter what pressures your lady mother brings t' bear upon ye, not unless ye've already planted a bairn in my belly! Nay, and I willna warm your cursed bed! Ye have robbed me of my precious maidenhead. T' my thinking, what ye took from me is more than ample for saving my life. We are quits hereon, my laird, and I willna change my mind!"

Stepping from the wooden tub, she knelt beside it. She took up a pitcher filled with warm water, shivering as the cold air fanned her damp body. Bending low, she dipped her head and poured the water through her hair before lathering it with soap. The knot on her head had almost gone, she noticed, exploring her scalp with her fingertips. Only a tender spot remained where a lump the size of a goose egg had once been.

She soaped her hair, then rinsed it free of lather with jugfuls of water scooped from the tub. The lather gone, she squeezed her long tresses out then shook her head like a wet hound, teeth chattering now in the chilly air as she fumbled about. Where was the drying cloth, she wondered? With her eyes squeezed tightly shut, she couldna find it. She opened them, and at once felt a smarting sensation. Och, drat it! Some of the soap must have found its way into her eyes!

"Yer drying cloth, my lady Catriona!" came a deep, mocking voice.

Her eyes still smarting, she blinked rapidly, cursing herself for letting *him* — for the voice belonged t' the laird o' Corbin — catch her at such disadvantage. Nude, and with her eyes so sore and streaming from the soap, she couldn't meet him eye-to-eye, drat the mon!

Snatching the length of linen from his hand, she wound it about her, at once casting about for a less revealing garment.

"What do ye here, my laird?" she demanded in a tight, controlled voice as she finally found a voluminous fur-trimmed chamber robe and slipped into it. "I wasna

192

aware we were already husband and wife, and yet ye seem t' consider yersel' free t' visit my bedchamber at will!"

"As laird o' Corbin, I go where I please in this donjon, mistress, invited or nay. I'll thank ye t' remember that," he said coldly.

"Your pardon, sir," she gritted, cheeks flaming.

"And as for becoming my wife—!" he continued. "I dinna ken what your schemes are as yet, wench, but I'll tell ye this much. I wouldna take a McNair bride were she the last wench on the face o' this earth! In truth, I'd sooner clap an adder t' ma breast!" He paused, then added hatefully with his gray eyes heavy-lidded and dark with lust as his gaze ravished her, "Though I wouldna deny mysel' the pleasure o' *bedding* my enemy's daughter!"

"What—?" she whispered hoarsely. Her voice rose louder and shriller as she repeated, "What are you saying? Your enemy! What enemy? And what name was it you called me? McNair?"

"Enough, lass, enough!" he growled, his expression disgusted and impatient. "Have done wi' your wee deceit, for you are discovered. I know it all! Who ye are. What cursed name ye bear. Where ye come from! Everything!" he rasped triumphantly.

He was pleased to see the blood drain from her cheeks in the candlelight with his words, leaving her face as waxen as the tapers themselves.

"Ye do? Then, sweet Jesu, tell me what you know, sir, for I have no such knowledge!" she cried vehemently, her hands clasped before her.

His sudden appearance and startling announcement had thrown her thoughts in utter turmoil. Her heart began to beat faster—more from fear, to be honest, than anticipation. What had he discovered about her identity and her past since he'd ridden hard and fast from Corbin's gates this morn, furious at his mother's insistence that he wed her? What if—she wetted her lips and swallowed nervously — what if his discoveries revealed a shameful past she wanted no part of? A life she loathed? A family she didna care t' claim as kin? Or — worse! — some horrid truth about herself she couldna bear t' live with?

Of a sudden, she hated him, loathed him — the Gilchrist! — with a raging, bitter passion; hated him almost as much for his cleverness in ferreting out her identity as she did for any other reason. Nay. She didna want t' know what he'd learned! She didna want t' hear!

And yet — the alternative was even less palatable. As long as she remained nameless, homeless, devoid of kith and kin, Lady Fionna would insist she tarry at Corbin, remain near *him* every day, that great, dark brute! Remain within arm's reach o' Roarke MacGilchrist, dependent on his good will for every morsel she ate, each thread of clothing upon her back, the victim of his lust. In truth, his lowly leman, his kept whore, his woman, wi'out the honors due a bride.

She looked up at him from beneath her lashes, which were spiked with tears as yet from the suds, and regarded him apprehensively. His eyes, those gray, gray eyes like the streamers of mist rising o'er a loch on a damp autumn morn, were watching her intently. They were cold, ruthless eyes now, the fathomless leaden hue of pewter, empty of all emotions but suspicion and mistrust. Nay, she thought with a shudder, those were not the fiery, hungry eyes of the man whose glance had made the bones melt within her as he fitted himself to her virgin flesh in the dark of night! His mouth was narrowed now, too, an angry slash well suited to cruel words and heartless mockery. 'Twas not the masterful, heated mouth that made her lips hunger for his kisses, nor his lips the gentle lips that had made her body tremble with desire, but the mouth and lips of a stranger!

"For the love o' God, be done wi' ye, mon! Speak!" she beseeched him, suddenly impatient when he said nothing, suddenly unable to bear a moment longer without knowing the truth, however unwelcome it might prove. "I'm no' a spider that ye can pluck the legs from, one by one, t' see how long it may dither and dance! Tell me who I am! Put me out o' my misery, or t' Hades wi ye," she flared, "and the devil take yer tongue!"

"Verra well. Yer name is Catriona, wench," he ground out, adding in a mocking tone, *"Lady* Catriona, that is, mind ye. Ye were the only daughter of Angus McNair, curse him. Laird o' Erskine Keep — and my sworn enemy this ten years or more!"

His eyes narrowed. His upper lip curled with contempt as he glowered down at her. Standing there, with her black hair damp as strands of kelp falling about the pale flower of her face, the velvet robe clinging to her damp curves, she was still beautiful, still had the power to arouse him as no other woman had done, curse her. Poor Mags, his bonnie mistress, had wept as he bade her farewell that morn. She'd pleaded with him t' stay, not caring that she'd lost the power to stir his passions. Nevertheless, he'd turned a deaf ear t' poor, loyal Maggie's sobs and left her anyway, wanting — wanting what — ? Wanting whom? Whose lips? Whose arms? Whose softness?

He shook his head, furious at himself, for he knew whose lips, whose arms, and hated himself for it. He lusted after the daughter of Angus McNair, the same cursed McNair who'd slain the flower of his clan some ten years past, leaving him but a handful of green young fighting men and old warriors too feeble t' bear arms, and with their weeping mothers and widows t' provide for. But even now, even knowing who she was, even knowing whose hated blood ran in her veins, he wanted her with a reckless craving he'd never felt for Maggie . . . or anyone else!

Knowing he must say something, do something, or lose his temper, he growled, "So silent, my lady Catriona! How so? Has the cat claimed yer tongue? Have I dumbfounded ye wi' my discovery? Or do ye yet cling t'

195

yer lies, and swear your own cursed name is no' familiar t' ye?"

"But it isna, damn ye!" she insisted hotly. "T' say it was would be a lie!"

"I'll tell ye more, then, and happen 'twill come back t' ye," he scoffed. "Your laird father's name was Angus. He was the McNair, chieftan of his clan. He was—"

"*Was,* ye say?" she echoed, dry-mouthed. Her brow creased. "Then—then he is long dead?"

"Not so very long, wench, nay. He was slain the night o' the blizzard—as were all his kinsmen with him! By some great good fortune—or so 'twould appear—you alone of your clan survived. Fortunate, was it not?"

"Jesu!" she cried, her hands flying to her throat, then to cover her quivering mouth and the scream aborning there. "Tell me, how—how was he slain?" she whispered, dreading his answer. "In battle? A clan skirmish?"

"Nay, my lady. What happened at Erskine canna decently be called a 'battle' by honorable men. Not when corpses lay with their dirks still sheathed. Not when the dead carried not a single arm among them!"

"Who was it who killed him—them—then? Can ye not tell me that?"

"Nay, I canna, for I know not. In truth, I wager you might supply the answer t' my questions, lady!" Roarke tossed at her, making no attempt to be kind or spare her feelings. Rather, he wanted to see her expression as he flung the hard, cold facts at her; to read the guilt or innocence in her face and in the emerald depths of her eyes.

"Your brothers were hacked down like wheat before a scythe, mistress," he gritted, noting how, at the mention of her brothers, she'd grown suddenly so pale; her eyes were hectic, dark-green jewels ablaze in the chalky pallor of her face. "Fergus, the eldest, was brained wi' a claymore. And Gil—"

"Aye, sir, aye, but what of Bran . . . the youngest?" she whispered, tottering on her feet as a wave of dizziness

196

swept over her. Close to fainting, she managed to murmur, "He had but thirteen winters, nae more! He was just a bairn! Not him, too? I beg ye, say it isna so?"

So, he thought heavily, his gut lurching, she remembered her kin well enough now, the wee bitchling! Aye, she remembered her litter of brothers full well! He'd been right all along, he thought bitterly, and anger filled him anew. Her claims that she'd lost her memory, forgotten all, had been naught but a ruse! She'd tried to play them all for fools, for her own dark purpose.

"Aye, young Bran, too! Dead at Fergus's feet, my men found him, his arms wrapped around his brother's legs. And Gil — aye, I see ye ken who Gil was, too, do ye no'? — was likewise slaughtered, skewered like a fish in a barrel."

She crossed herself, and appeared close to swooning as she whispered, "And my father?"

"The McNair was found sprawled across his own bed. His throat had been cut from ear t' ear — do ye remember that now, my lady Cat? Do ye recall the blood that was everywhere? The auld man spitted to the walls like a suckling pig? A young reeve wi' his throat likewise cut? Do ye remember them!"

"Please . . . enough . . . no more!"

"And what of the women, Catriona? What of the wee bairns, the little children, even the cursed, dumb hounds! For the love o' God, wench — what of them — ?" he thundered.

"As God is my witness, sir, I can tell ye naught, I swear it — !"

He swung around and slammed his fist down on the surface of a small wooden table. "Enough o' your lies! Tell me what ye know! Why ye wormed your way into my keep? Who put ye up to this? Tell me!"

"Stop it! Stop it!" she moaned, covering her ears with her hands. "Please, my laird, dinna do this t' me, I beg ye, for I canna bear it! I have done nothing, conspired with no one, I swear it!"

Great glassy tears pooled in her eyes, slipped down her

cheeks, and splashed onto the furred edges of the velvet robe she'd hastily donned.

"If ye canna remember aught, why then do ye weep?" he rasped.

"Because ye . . . ye have told me what I've longed t' hear — who I am," she sobbed, "and to what clan I belong. But then, in the selfsame breath, ye cruelly disclosed that — that those I surely held dear have all been slaughtered to a man! That both family, clan, and kinship are lost t' me forever! That I — that I ha'e no one! Sweet Jesu, have ye no pity nor compassion in ye, sir? D' ye think me stone, that I have no heart wi' which t' greave for what might have been? Och, 'tis a hard, cruel brute ye are — and 'twas a hard, cruel day that ye found me in the snow! Better I'd died wi' them than survived for ye t' torment! Aye, better I was dead — 'else gone from here!"

She made to rush blindly past him, to flee Corbin as she once must have fled Erskine. Yet Roarke was not done with her yet. Not nearly! He had one more test t' put to her. He reached out and grasped her wrist as she flung herself past him, pulling her up short and yanking her about to face him.

Her eyes blazed into his, startling in their brilliance. "Unhand me!" She spat the words at him.

"Nay, not so fast, my lass! I have something of yours I would return before ye run. Here! Take it!"

So saying, he thrust the comb Tavish had found towards her, holding it up to the candle's light before she could compose her wits or mask her reaction. She took it from him while he carefully watched her face.

To his surprise, her green eyes considered the trinket curiously yet dispassionately, although her bosom still heaved with anger. Then, after a few moments, she looked him full in the eye as she dropped the comb into his hand.

"Keep your cursed bauble, my laird Roarke, for I regret you are wrong. The comb doesna belong t' me. I've never seen it before in my life — and nor do I covet it

198

at any price! Ye must find another t' earn this pretty favor on her back, if that was your intent!"

"How can ye be so certain 'tis not yours, when ye claim t' remember naught?" he challenged, his eyes withering her. "Look! These strands here. Were they not wrest from your hair?"

She took the comb from him, and drew one of the hairs that were caught in the teeth from it, testing it between her fingers. It was very long — equally as long as her own, true. But whereas her hair was slightly curling, silky and fine, this hair was thick and coarse and straight as an arrow.

A slim, bitter smile of recognition curved her lips. "God knows, I didna expect flattery from any mon, least of all from yersel', my laird Roarke," she said huskily. "But still, I have my wee morsel o' pride! Can ye no' tell the difference between a woman's hair, and that clipped from a common palfrey's tail?"

For once, Roarke appeared taken aback, though she was still too shaken, too numbed, to savor her tiny victory.

" 'Tis horse hair, ye claim?"

"Aye, mi'laird. 'Twould appear so to me. But — since ye havena believed aught else I've told ye, why, then I doubt ye'll believe that, either!"

She turned away, desperate to hide the telltale quiver of her lips, the sobs that begged to be set free and lift the weighty stone lodged in her heart. Dead, he'd said, all of them! Her kinsmen . . . her father . . . her brothers. Their clansmen, all dead! God forgive her, but she could summon up no loving memories of them; could feel no true sense of loss. To her, the dead men he'd described meant nothing, were but meaningless names. And yet, they belonged to her family, to those she must once have loved. Even should she someday remember them fully, she would never have them by her to love again. That was why she felt such terrible emptiness, this crushing sense of grief and loss! If she was Catriona, daughter of the

McNair of Erskine, as he'd claimed, she was now alone in the world. She had no one she might call family, her own, nor even a memory to which she might cling for sanity. Only an empty, frightening future loomed ahead of her, as blank as the parchment of her past!

With a moan, her knees buckled. She sank to the ground. She bowed her head and knelt there, as if in prayer. Then her shoulders began to heave, first with silent sobs, then with muffled, noisier ones.

Roarke's shoulders sagged. He coughed and shook his head slowly from side to side, his discomfiture marked. Then, reaching out, he took her hand and raised her with peculiar gentleness to her feet.

"Enough, my lady. Ye've convinced me! I was prepared t' believe ye guilty o' murder when I entered this chamber, but now . . ." He paused, for, despite himself, the anguish in the emerald eyes she lifted to his moved him. Either she was a consummate player of parts — or had been telling the truth all along, as his warrior's gut instincts had suggested. No player, however skilled in her craft, could summon such a look as she wore!

"But now what?" she whispered.

"Though I doubted ye sorely, Catriona, I fancy I believe ye now." He crooked his thumb beneath her chin and turned her damp face to his. "Ye truly have no recollection of your family nor your past, do ye, lassie?"

"None," she swallowed as a wave of relief swamped her. "Naught but the names of those three puir laddies, and the knowledge that one had but thirteen winters t' his span. But . . . but before ye told me, I didna ken who the names belonged to, or if they were my brothers, my cousins, or what-have-ye! These and that melancholy ballad of the Isle of Iona and the dead kings of our land are all I can recall. Mayhap the ballad came t' mind because the song struck a chord of sorrow in my breast, though I didna ken why till now. But I swear t' ye, upon my oath, my laird, these things are *all* that I recall! Jesu, what will become of me now?"

She shuddered. Her voice cracked. With eyes downcast, she hugged herself about the arms and fought the tears that welled in them.

"Och, lassie, dinna fight it!" Roarke urged. "Weep and have done wi' it."

"Tears willna help me!"

"Nay, but they'll ease the heartache."

In truth, he wished she'd managed to staunch her weeping. Her tears weakened his resolve to stay aloof from her. They melted his determination to resist her loveliness, her vulnerability, henceforth, as he must. Knowing who she was, whose blood ran in her veins, the question of marriage, or indeed any relationship between them, was unthinkable. But — despite himself, and nonwithstanding the vows he'd made — he held out his arms.

To his surprise, she came into them. The fresh, herbal scent of her damp hair was all around him. The warmth and softness of her body pressed against his as she burrowed her face against his chest like a frightened wee mouse. With a muffled sob, she clung to him. Her fingers tightening about his arms, pressing hard into his back, were like a velvet net enfolding him — one he had no wish to escape. Her defenselessness, her very need of him, his own treacherous desire for her, were dragging him down, pulling him into the dangerous undertow of some bittersweet current that might drown him, even as he welcomed its liquid embrace.

"Roarke!" she wept. "Oh, Roarke, Roarke, what am I t' do?"

He held her close, and felt warmth flood through her, replacing the chill of moments before. She stirred in his embrace, meeting it, accepting it, and he knew that she'd welcome his offer of comfort in whatever form it might take.

Aye, he thought heavily as he felt his gut tighten in response to her nearness, even that.

Chapter Sixteen

"Flora? *Flora!* Och, where is that lazy slut?" grumbled a voice.

"Holy Mother o' God, 'tis Cook hersel'!" Flora hissed, disentangling Ogden's beefy hands from her bodice and shoving her rucked-up skirts down t' cover her knees. "Leave go o' me, ye randy great lummox, 'else t' puffed up auld toad'll catch us, she will!"

Flora and her burly swain had finally come together in one of the storerooms built below Corbin, their love nest concealed by a mountain of sacks containing flour, barley, oats, and the like. Against the wall were piled barrels of salted fish and meats, and kegs of strong drink. It was not a very romantic place for the lovers' tryst that Flora had fondly imagined, for the sacks of dried stores gave off a musty earth-and-damp odor about the pair, and the dirt floor had proven cursed hard on her ample buttocks. But still, Flora was loath to end what had promised to be a very energetic conclusion to their first coupling!

She muttered a curse as she scrambled to her feet, consigning Cook to a variety of excruciatingly unpleasant and very permanent demises as she blew Ogden a tender kiss and stepped out from behind their hidey-hole. Her frantic movements to thrust Ogden off her had disturbed several brown mice as they supped on the barley that had spilled from a hole in one of the sacks.

They scampered away as Flora scurried around a tower of barrels, almost slamming into Cook's considerable girth as she made her sudden appearance.

"Och!" Flora gasped.

"Och, yersel'!" snapped Cook, red-faced from supervising the spit-boy at his duties beside the roaring kitchen fires. "What are ye aboot down here that's takin' sae blessed long, Mistress Flora?" She looked about her suspiciously, her small, dark eyes bright with eagerness to find something amiss, but Ogden was well hidden by the stores, and gave no sound to betray his presence.

"What I'm aboot is none o' your concern, Mistress Joan," Flora snapped back, her own cheeks ruddy now with indignation. "And I'll thank ye t' remember I'm t' lady's bower servant, and dinna have t' answer to the likes o' ye in the kitchens for aught!"

"Och, now, d' ye hear this!" Joan exclaimed, her plump white hands planted on her enormous hips. " 'Tis high and mighty ye've grown, have ye no', *Lady* Flora!" she jeered. "We're a mite stuffed wi' pride t'day, and must ha' forgot we was birthed in a dirty highland croft an' raised among heathen savages by a father who slept wi' his cattle!"

"At least I ken who ma father was!" Flora flared, setting her jaw pugnaciously. "Och, and speaking o' dirt . . .! These store chambers are a disgrace — scarce better than a privy! Why, there's a plague o' mice down back, scampering in and out o' *your* precious stores! Happen I'll drop a word or two in ma lady's ear about this, and see how she feels about mice droppings wi' her barley bree!"

Joan, however, was not to be sidetracked. "Ye must do as ye feel fit, Flora dear," she said with a malicious smile. "But meanwhile, mayhap ye should know that your dear Lady Fionna has been searchin' the keep high and low for ye since Terce. Aye, and proper vexed she is that she canna find ye, too! 'Tis fortunate for ye that I saw ye come doon here, and oot o' the kindness o' my heart, thought t' follow ye, and tell ye she was callin' fer ye." Joan sniffed.

"Kindness o' your heart', my arse," Flora countered rudely, "for ye have no cursed heart, ye windy auld sow! I wager there's naught but a lump o' lard where yer heart should be! Well? Oot with it! What did my lady want of me?"

"Ye're t' fetch a platter o' victuals up t' the foundling lassie's chamber, and quick aboot it, she said. Ye ken how she cossets the lass?"

"Aye, I ken," Flora acknowledged sourly. "Though why, I canna fathom!" She pursed her lips, and folded her arms across the shelf of her prodigious bosom — the bosom Ogden had been fondling so enthusiastically when they were interrupted — and added tartly and without a shred of graciousness, "Weel, Mistress Joan, I suppose I should thank ye for telling me?"

"Ye should — but I doubt ye will!" Joan shot back. "And I canna stand here till doomsday waitin' for ye t' find your manners, ye Highland baggage! I've a kitchen t' tend to, and more t' do than bears thinkin' aboot — unlike some I could mention!"

She started back the way she'd come, weaving her ponderous path between the sacks and barrels with surprising grace for one so large. But by the opening that led out to the stairway, she halted and grinned. "And by the by, Master Ogden," she cooed in a loud voice, "do ha'e a care tumbling this wench, will ye no'? After all, she's been well used, ye ken — and likely t' be poxy, too!"

With that parting blow, Joan made a hasty exit, leaving Flora red-faced with rage at her insults.

Ogden emerged from his hiding place, looking shame-faced and ready to bolt. On seeing his expression, and hastily judging from it that her fond plans were about to melt like snow in the sunshine, Flora cast aside her anger at the cook and ran to him. Coyly, she slipped her arms around his broad waist and pressed her head to his chest.

"Och, now, lovie, ye didna believe her spiteful talk, did ye now?" she cooed in Ogden's ear. "Why, I'm nae more poxed than the lady o' Corbin hersel'! And as for 'well-used'—whist, drat the woman! God knows, I've kept mysel' chaste as a blessed nun, I have, since the sad day my puir mon, Georgie, were taken by the flux and breathed his last, God rest his puir auld soul!"

"Nay, lass. I shouldna linger. I should be awa' t' ma post before the Gilchrist has need o' me and wonders where I am," Ogden suggested doubtfully.

"Why, bless ye, lovie, he's been brooding in his chamber since Master Tavish and Master Graeme returned from riding this morn'!" Flora reassured him. "And believe me, laddie, I know himsel'. When these dour, brooding lowland humors take hold o' him, he doesna show his face till even', at earliest. We've a while yet t' pleasure oursels'. And besides," she cooed, stroking his muscular thigh and batting her lashes at him, "I wouldna ha'e ye leave me so . . . discomforted, my lovie?"

Ogden hesitated, loath to depart without the lusty tumble Flora's actions and coquettish smiles dangled like a carrot before a donkey's nose. She was as plain as Lenten bread, and na'e mistake, but her teats—! Why, he'd never seen their mammoth ilk afore today, though he'd dreamed o' them a time or two! "But the victuals the lady was askin' after—?" he reminded her.

"Och, 'tis o' no import! I'll ha'e that half-wit McNair lad they brought from Erskine run t' the kitchens and tell that auld cow Joan t' make the platter. And after I've fetched it up t' that foundling bitch—ooh, we'll ha'e us a fine auld romp, will we no'?"

The enormous bulge in Ogden's breeks was answer enough. Ogden gulped, nodded, and returned to his hiding place, while, both giggling and flushed, Flora sped away t' find the half-wit lad.

She collared him stuffing his face in a corner of the great hall. Yanking him up from where he squatted by one ear—which she soundly gripped in her calloused fingers—she boxed the other ear with the flat of her palm.

"Owww!" Hal yelped.

"None o' your lip, laddie," she ground out sternly, "but listen, or 'twill go hard on ye here. Ye're a McNair, are ye no'? Well, we o' the clan Gilchrist have nae fondness for your bloody butcher clan! I'm mistress Flora o' Corbin, and I've a task for ye. If ye wish t' find yer bed tonight wi'out a whipping, ye'll be aboot my bidding straightway."

Catriona stood in the center of a circular tower. The windeyes and doors had all been flung wide, and yet there was not a sigh of wind to stir the air. High walls towered above her, so like those of a deep dungeon that standing there, looking up, it felt as if she were standing at the bottom of a well.

Far above, she could see a narrow opening framing a wintry night sky. Gray moonlight streamed through it to illuminate her cell, picking out sparkling chips in some of the rough-hewn blocks that formed its walls. Curiously, the tower was completely without ornament or furnishings, save for a looking glass that hung on the wall directly before her. It was fashioned from a large oval of polished tin and framed in ornately carved, then gilded, wood. The surface shone like a clear pool beneath the moon's frosty light.

Catriona stepped closer and peered intently into the looking glass. She saw her own image reflected in the polished depths momentarily. And, though there was no breeze in the tower, she saw that her reflection's hair swirled about in wild, dark pennants, as if whipped by a blizzard, though her own was still. Her mouth was moving in silent entreaty. Her green eyes were wide and terrified.

Puzzled, she reached out to touch her false reflection. But as her fingers brushed the icy metal, the image disappeared. It was replaced by another, far more ancient reflection, of a withered crone; an old, old woman with

206

grizzled white hair and skin as creased and leathery as a crab apple. The crone was clothed in motley-colored rags, and about her throat rode a necklace of purple welts, livid against her spotted old flesh.

"Who are ye?" she heard herself ask the reflection. Her words, though whispered, were thrown back to her with a rustling, "Are ye? — ye? — ye?"

"I was once called Morag," the image responded with infinite weariness.

Suddenly, every door and casement in the tower flew shut with a thunderous boom that made Catriona's heart leap in fear! Sweet Jesu, what sorcery was this, she wondered, trembling, for the movements of the crone's puckered lips were out of kilter with the words they uttered! A shiver crawled down the girl's spine as the reflection continued:

"Auld Morag, the Healer, some named me. Others were less kind, curse their black hearts! They called me 'witch' or 'hag.' But by either name, I was once midwife to Moira of Erskine, your own lady mother. Auld Morag, who brought ye safe into this world o' wickedness and sorrow, rue the day!"

"My . . . mother? And where is my lady mother now?" the girl asked breathlessly, fearing the answer she would receive. Her heart was in her mouth with eagerness. A mother! She had a mother! She was not alone!

"Alas, your bonnie mother is dead long since, lambkin" came the image's sorrowful reply. Her voice was like the soughing of the wind through somber pines.

Heartsick with disappointment, Catriona crossed herself before continuing, "And my — my laird father?"

"Ye ask after him, the auld devil, when your sire's heart was barren of love for ye?" the image hissed.

"Aye, Auld Grandmother, for whether he loved me or nay, he was yet my father, his blood my own," the girl responded. Despite the sweet sadness to her tone, there was a firmness to it, also.

"Aye, lassie, aye, 'twas so. 'Twas so indeed! But ye were no' t' blame, dinna think that! A better daughter never lived than ye were

207

t' him — nor a poorer, meaner father than he proved t' yersel'! Tell Auld Morag, hinnie, Would ye see what befell the McNair?"

"Aye," Catriona murmured as firmly as she was able, for her knees trembled so, she feared they would buckle. "Show me, auld one!"

"Come closer, then, daughter. Gaze deep into the mirror's depths!"

The blood began to pulse in Catriona's ears. Although it was nigh deafening, she stepped closer to the looking glass, wanting to see for herself the man who'd sired her, and whom she had no memory of.

Slowly, slowly, the mirror image of the old hag vanished. It dissolved, as one's reflection in a still pond vanishes when disturbed by a pebble dropped into its depths — fragment by fragment, wavering ripple by ripple. For a moment, there was nothing in the mirror but a smoky haze, then the haze was shredded as if banished by a gale.

Swimming deep within the mirror's shining depths, Catriona saw a familiar chamber reflected. It was the twin of the Spartan cell in which she now stood, though this was comfortably appointed. Beautiful, rich tapestries worked in vivid silks graced the walls. Tall yellow candles in silver candlesticks spilled golden light everywhere. The chairs, padded footstools, and coffers were of carved wood, as was the enormous bed. The posts that rose from each of its four corners were the Apostles, Matthew, Mark, Luke, and John, their tonsured heads bowed in prayer, their hands raised in benediction. Upon the feather pallet sprawled a stocky man of middle years. His ruddy beard and locks were long and unkempt. His cheeks were florid from the bitter border weather, and overindulgence in strong drink and rich victuals.

"Och, ma laird Angus, ye ha'e whiskers enough for any auld goat!" Catriona heard a sultry female voice murmur in a petulant tone. "I willna warm yer bed 'less ye trim them!"

Straining her eyes to see deeper into the mirror, the girl could dimly make out a woman, standing in the shadows beyond the bed. Her features were cloaked in darkness, but she was clinging coyly to one of the bedposts, twining a finger through her long, straight tresses, midnight-black tresses that were caught back at one temply by a comb of rowan wood, patterned prettily with buds and thistles . . .

Something worried in Catriona's memory. Something jangled an alarum bell within her mind, but she could not fix her attention upon it, for the man was moving now — and she couldna bring herself t' take her eyes from him! This, then, she thought eagerly, straining to see his features more clearly, This man was her father!

Rising now, Angus sat upon the edge of the bed. With a lusty rumble of laughter, he reached for the wench, who hung back in the shadows. Planting his hands on her ample hips, he dragged her to him. He squeezed her plump buttocks and leered up into her hidden face.

"Och, lovie, gi'e me a wee kiss, will ye no', an' t' Hades wi' ma cursed whiskers," he coaxed. He made to plunge his hand down her bodice to squeeze a plump breast and to tug her down beside him on the feather pallet, but she gave a husky giggle and squirmed free of his clutches. Drawing something metallic from her belt that glinted in the candlelight, she took up position behind the bed, just beyond his reach.

"Patience, ma lusty laird, patience! I'll trim yer shaggy locks an' barb wi' ma own wee dirk first!" the wench trilled. *"And then, when ye're as bonnie an' soft-cheeked as a bairn, why, I'll gi'e ye kisses t' spare, lovie — an' more besides!"*

The laird chuckled indulgently. He leaned back upon his elbows, tilting his shaggy head back to offer the lass his throat and jaw.

"As ye will, then, lassie, as ye will!" he acquiesced. His ample belly shook with mirth. *"If I can ha'e ye no other way, then go to it! But . . . take care ye dinna nick me, nor draw blood,"* he bantered, waggling a scolding finger at her. *"I 'faith, I dinna trust a dirk in a lassie's hands. More at home wi' a distaff, they are!"*

209

"Och, ye great daft beastie, dinna fear! Ye can trust me, my laird!" the woman promised. Her voice had a breathless, excited edge to it now. *"I gi'e ye ma word, sir, ye willna feel a blessed thing. And after . . . ! Why, we'll have a fine auld time, we will!"*

Catriona saw the wench's russet sleeve slowly rise; saw a pale, soft fist brandishing a dirk at its cuff in the candle's light: saw then the throat of the man she'd called Father bared and vulnerable, his windpipe angled as if in — in *sacrifice* to that blade!

The clamor of warning that had jangled in Catriona's head finally birthed a scream:

"Naaay — ! Jesu, naaay — !"

In the selfsame moment that she cried out, the wench's dirk came down in a silver-streaming arc! Catriona sprang towards the looking glass, but the tower room, the pair, the magical images within it, had vanished as if they'd never been!

Sobbing, she tore the looking glass from the wall and gripped it in both hands, shaking her head helplessly from side to side as she held it before her and whispered, "Father! Blessed Mary in heaven, she has murdered ye, Father!"

As she stared at the looking glass, she saw that blood was streaming down the surface of the shiny oval in her hands, like rain pouring down a wall. It rose up the confines of the carved frame as wine rises up the sides of a shallow basin. The dark, ruby cascades lapped the polished surface then brimmed over the gilded edges, splashing her hands, her gown, with red —

Terror-struck, she flung the looking glass from her. She rubbed her palms together, scrubbed at them with her fingers, tried desperately to eradicate the stains of her father's life blood from them . . .

"Catriona? What saw ye, maid?" demanded another stern, eerie voice that was somehow familiar.

She looked about her, but there was no one there. The voice came from thin air!

"Whatever the lassie saw, 'twas far too much!" cut in a second, harsher voice.

"Nay! I saw nothing! I swear it!" she pleaded, looking wildly around her again for the speakers. But still, she saw no one.

"She lies! She must be silenced!"

Silenced. Silenced. Silenced. The word pounded like a drum in her mind, each beat a knell of doom.

Catriona began running for her life, running around and around the circular stone floor, searching and clawing frantically for a way out, an escape from her faceless enemies. But the doors had slammed shut and vanished when Auld Morag first spoke; the wind-eyes had likewise disappeared. The stone walls were blank now. There was no way out — no opening left by which to flee!

"Help me!" she screamed, running around and around like the hapless cur that turns the knife-grinder's wheel. "Blessed Mary — somebody — *help meeee!*"

"Lady Catriona! Lassie, wake up! 'Tis naught but a dream ye're after having!"

Roarke's stern voice, his urgent shaking, finally brought her back from the edges of madness to waking and reality.

"Please, ye must hide me!" she whimpered, her green eyes huge by firelight as she plucked fearfully at his sleeves. "Ye must help me, sir, I beg ye! Jesu! They mean . . . they mean t' kill me! And I have no sanctuary, no place to hide! 'Silence her!' they said. 'Silence her . . . silence her!' " She babbled on, trembling so violently her teeth chattered.

"Hush, now, hush. There's no one here but the two o' us, lassie," Roarke murmured. "Come, dearling, open your eyes and see for yersel'. Ye're safe at Corbin in my mother's chamber. There's mysel' and two score men-at-arms t' keep ye from harm." A rueful smile played about his lips as he added, "And if we're no' enough, why, there's your loyal Castor asleep by the hearth, ready t' protect ye."

"Safe, ye say?" she echoed in a small, uncertain voice. She looked apprehensively about her as if expecting ogres to spring at her from the shadows, then her eyes snapped back to his. She wetted her lips uncertainly. "Ye're sure?"

"Aye, lass, aye." He stroked her dark hair away from her face and met her terrified, searching look with a steady one of his own. "I promise ye, wee Catriona," he vowed earnestly, his gray eyes calm with assurance as they locked with her own. "McNair or no, I willna let aught harm ye wi'in these walls. I swear it, on my honor as the Gilchrist!"

With a sob, she threw her arms around his neck and clung to him, her tear-stained face pressed to his chest, her dislike and mistrust of him forgotten for the while. God only knew, she needed to trust someone! "Nay, my laird, I amna safe anywhere! They'll come here! They'll seek me out, I know it! They'll find me and they'll slay me, lest I tell who they are!" she cried brokenly, her words muffled by the cloth of his garments.

"They shallna, for I willna let them," he soothed simply, his voice firm. Stroking her back as he might a small, frightened child, he held her tighter so that she'd feel his strength and be comforted.

Jesu! he thought, *Her slender body trembles so, 'tis like a willow battered by a gale!* When she'd first come into his arms earlier, though, it had not been so.

Her hair had still been wet as strands of dark kelp against his cheek, her damp body clad in only her chamber robe when he'd carried her to the bed. There, he'd stretched himself out and gathered her into his arms, meaning but to comfort and hold her until her weeping ceased and either sleep or composure claimed her. Poor wee lassie, he'd thought, his heart softening in the aftermath of her tears, he hadna been kind in his actions, telling her of her clansmen's deaths in the blunt, deliberately callous way he had. But he'd had his reasons for being cruel, and what he'd done couldna be undone, he'd

212

rationalized. At least now, he was almost convinced of her innocence.

Accordingly, he'd held her, stroking her hair, clucking meaningless words, until she'd had no more tears to shed. Soon after her sobbing ceased, he'd known by the deep, even rise and fall of her bosom that she slumbered, and that her slumber was deep and dreamless. Her body had been still and warm, her limbs loose and heavy, curled against his own.

Fascinated, he'd watched her in the firelight and enjoyed the play of its flickering caresses over her delicately boned face. He'd also seen how the light gleamed upon the ivory length of her thigh where her robe had fallen back. And, to his chagrin, he'd known again the quick, hot upsurge of desire for her that he'd felt so many times since the night of the blizzard. Blessed Mary, what ailed him? His desire for her was dangerously powerful, always but a heartbeat away, always perilously close to the surface of his every waking thought — and ofttimes his sleeping ones, too!

Unwilling to take advantage of her helplessness again — for, aye, in his heart of hearts, he admitted guiltily that he had on more than one occasion before — he'd attempted to slip his arm from beneath her and leave the chamber before he did something he might later regret. He'd meant to go below the hall and sup, certain if he did so, he could put her from his mind.

So much for good intentions! Of a sudden, she'd begun whimpering and murmuring in her sleep. She'd thrashed about and cried out in a voice made hoarse with terror. So distraught had she seemed, he'd been forced to waken her, reluctant to leave her to battle her nightmares alone . . .

"Come, my lady, dress yersel'," he urged. "We'll go below and sup. Good victuals, a goblet o' mulled wine, and ye'll forget the dreams that plagued your sleep."

He set her from him, holding her at arm's length. But at once, he regretted doing so, for as she leaned back, the fronts of her robe fell away. The change of position exposed her perfect, rose-tipped bosom and the darker wee valley between them, framed by the garment's edging of silky fur. He swallowed and reached out to restore her to modesty, yet she caught his hand instead and drew it within the folds to cover her breast. The contact of her hand upon his own, her warm flesh cupped in his, made his mouth grow dry. And, lifting his eyes to gaze deep into her slanted, thick-lashed green eyes, he felt the full magic of her allure strike him like a blow to the belly.

"Nay, lass, ye shouldna . . ." he began uncertainly, withdrawing his hand. He remembered all too clearly how she'd succumbed to his caresses once before, only to gainsay her willingness come dawn's sobering light, and claim ravishment and seduction.

"Aye," she murmured, her emerald eyes shining. "I say Aye, Roarke Mac Gilchrist! I bid ye take me, my laird! Hold me! Love me wi' yer bonnie lips. Hold me to yer fine, braw body, as ye did last night! Och, sir, please — I beg ye!" she implored, tears filling her eyes. "Only your strong arms can exorcise my demon this night! Only ye can make me forget the terror that fills me. I — I — *need* ye t' hold me!"

Her eager fingers worked his tunic up, burrowing beneath it to bare his hairy chest. She sighed as her arms slid around him and she felt the broadness of his torso, the strong play of muscle rippling beneath lean, hard flesh, as she caressed him. There was such life there, such power, such vigor! Her fingertips grazed over his shoulders, brushing his throat like wands of thistledown. To Roarke, it seemed an eternity had passed before she finally framed his ebony head within her palms! Then, lacing her fingers through the crisp curls at his temples, she drew his mouth down upon hers. With a whispered, "Please, oh, please, my laird Gilchrist . . . ?" she closed her eyes and gave him her lips.

Her kiss, so freely, so eagerly given, shook him to the core, so wondrous sweet it was.

"Love me, Roarke o' Corbin!" she murmured huskily. "Love me the night long, I beg ye, and dinna say me nay! For, like a small ship, I am adrift, and ye must be my anchor . . ."

Roarke was a man lost! Her loveliness dazzled him. Her husky entreaties stirred him. Her touch enflamed him. Her scent dizzied him. Moreover, he had never felt such an overwhelming urge to protect, defend, and cherish any woman as he felt for the wee wren curled beside him now! With a groan, he caught her to him. Winding his fist through her hair, he arched her backward to fit his mouth more fully over hers.

His breathing was shallow as he gently devoured her lips, seasoned with salty tears. His tongue surged between them as he covered a breast with his hand. He ravished the inner softness of her mouth with a tender ardor that stirred her blood, until it pulsed like molten pitch through her veins.

Sweetly, her breasts rose against the ball of his thumb, the tiny, rosy buds that crowned them blossoming at his touch. Dipping his dark head, he took first one velvety nubbin then the other deep into his mouth, drawing gently upon them in turn until her soft moans became breathless gasps. Whispering ragged endearments, Roarke dragged the robe down from her ivory shoulders, his hands rough and unsteady with desire as he caressed her slender back. He traced the knobs of her spine lower and still lower, until he held the firm mounds of her buttocks in his hands. With a growl deep in his throat, he brought her hard against his flanks that she could feel his rising passion. Crying out, she moved against him, arching her soft curves to his hard hips in a way that drove him to distraction.

"Free me," he commanded hoarsely. "For the love o' God, free me, lass!"

Swallowing, she gave a murmur of assent. He drew back, then her hand burrowed beneath his tunic once again, this time grazing over his oaken belly. With a

215

muttered oath, he tore the hampering garment off, tugging it over his head and flinging it aside. Her palms trailed fire over his belly and down to his flanks as she sought and found the laces to his breeks. With trembling fingers, she loosed the knots. The hardened shaft of his manhood sprang forth to fill her hand. And somehow, she knew instinctively what it was he craved of her, and that touching him as he'd touched her would give him pleasure. The breath catching in her throat, she caressed the velvet length of him, her nails lightly scratching, the groove of her palm enfolding him in heat and sensation.

Roarke began to tremble uncontrollably, so great was his desire. Sweat sprang out upon his brow, for all that the season was winter. The feel of her hands upon him almost undid his control, for 'twas as if he'd been stroked by lightning . . .

"Jesu! Ye rouse me so, I canna delay, ma bonnie!" he growled against her ear. His hot breath made goosebumps rise and break in waves down her arms. "I would take ye now, lassie, wi' none o' the pretty fondlings a woman craves, 'else shall spill mysel' like a callow lad!"

"Then take me, my laird," she whispered with little less fervor. "Dinna hold back! Let it be now!"

With a groan, he lay back and lifted her from the rumpled folds of her robe to bestride his flanks, possessing her utterly even as she fitted herself over him.

Poised above him, her firelit form was sleek and taut, arched backward in her ecstasy as he came into her softness. Her throat was a fluid curve, her hair a soft, dark cloud spilling down her back. Her breasts were thrust up and forward, the nipples taut as they crested her bosom's creamy swell. Her teeth had caught her lower lip and were clamped deep in its tender flesh as she fought her deepest instincts; a woman's desire that commanded she let passion rule, and the 'morrow be damned! In truth, she was glorious, a vision to behold and keep forever in his mind!

"Och, but 'tis bonnie ye are, my sweet, my love," he

whispered, caressing her high, proud breasts and running his hands down over the silken sweep of her belly and hips. "A mon could go mad wi' wanting ye, ye lovely witch!"

"Are ye mad, then, Roarke o' Corbin?" she asked throatily, her eyes dancing as they rested on his handsome face.

"Aye, by God, I fear I am! Mad wi' desire — !"

Looking up, he saw the passion fill her face, enflamed by his caresses, the naked desire blazing in her emerald eyes. A desire that, in her nigh innocent state, she knew not how to ease.

He gripped her hips, and with knowing hands he taught her how to move upon him; showed her what her body had always known, in its deepest, most primitive heart.

Flinging her head back so that her hair swept in a glorious waterfall to her buttocks, she undulated her hips, taking him deeper, deeper, until they were one, a creature without beginning or end; dancing the mating dance with a sensual, feline grace that was cat and woman, woman and cat, commingled.

As she moved above him, perspiration beaded her pale brow. The runnels poured down her throat to trickle between and over her breasts, as if dew glistened in sparkling trails down the pale, pale petals of an ivory rose. Her musk filled his nostrils. It was wild as the sea, sweet-scented as clovered meadows wrapped in the spell of summer. She flung her head forward, poised above him, a low pleasure-purring escaping her lips as she crouched there with her raven hair spilling about them both in a midnight cascade, caressing, swirling, pooling over Roarke's chest.

With a lust-filled growl, he caught her teasing tresses in his fist and hauled her down across his chest, hungrily devouring her lips as he rolled her beneath him, still joined to her flesh.

She did not lie submissive beneath him, meekly giving

217

him his man's way as Mags had been wont to do. Jesu, nay! Tonight, with grief and terror firing her passions, adding a desperate, fevered quality to her needs, the McNair's daughter fought him, met his thrusts, matched his driving maleness measure for measure, then finally surrendered her all with a fierce, sweet yielding that was all fire, all woman, all hungry passion! She curved beneath him like a nocked bow to take him, make him one with her in body and heart.

Where now her love of cornflower eyes and hair of wheaten gold? she thought dreamily, drowning in the pleasure of him, and of it all. Where now her yearning for gentle ballads and the soft strummings of a lute? Fool, aye, 'twas a fool she'd been, to ever think him uncomely! It was his eyes of smoke and his raven-black hair she craved now! Not gentle words nor sweet music, but the earthy tremor and the ardent, manly timbre of *his* voice when he'd murmured that he couldna wait t' take her, but must claim her as his own! That urgency, that ardor, the look in his eyes as he voiced his desire, were the sweetest of love songs, the most wonderful wooing of all! After all, what more could a woman ask than to be wanted so fiercely, desired so impatiently, by her man?

Love! a small part of her whispered. *A nobly bred young woman would ask for love at least, Catriona o' Erskine, if she took a mon without benefit o' wedlock!* But what good was love, if it didna protect one, reason argued? What price love, when it couldna keep your enemies from taking your life? Whereas strength . . . ! Aye, strength was what really counted in these harsh times; strength and power, a man's protection, the sweet pleasures of passion. And this dark, handsome brute could render them all . . .

The flames danced and writhed on the hearth in time to the music of the crackling logs. Upon the pallet, the lovers danced and writhed to music of their own making, the sweetsong of their passion soaring them to rapturous heights, building and swelling until, at last, the final note was sung, the ballad played out, the last chord thrummed. A dreamy languor and contentment filled them both in the drowsy hush that followed.

Quietly, they lay twined together, both lost in their own thoughts, both sated, both a little stunned by the power of the emotions that had been unleashed by their joining as their heartbeats slowed.

The gloaming had faded whilst they sported, Catriona noticed, glancing dreamily at the narrow windeye. Where had the moments flown? The gray afternoon sky had grown dark. The first star was out. The distant sounds of the clan Gilchrist at their supper carried but faintly to her here. And where was Flora at this very moment, she wondered idly, for the wooden tub still sat before the hearth, the water long since grown cold. The serving wenches hadna come t' empty it, as Flora'd promised before she left — unless they'd knocked and left unheard?

She snuggled closer to Roarke for warmth, for with passion spent, the air in the chamber was markedly cool. Again, her mind was drawn back to the hateful Flora. She wondered if the serving woman was even now at her supper, or if she'd sought out her strapping guardsmen, Ogden, as the gleam in her eyes had suggested she intended to do when she scurried off? Was Flora gobbling down her victuals — or enjoying a clandestine tryst with her Ogden that was very similar to the one her mistress had just enjoyed with Laird Roarke?

A guilty smile curved Catriona's lips, but it did not remain long, alas. Thinking of Flora had put her uncomfortably in mind of the strange dream she'd had of her father, sporting with an unknown wench, and of — and of what had come after.

She swallowed, a knot forming painfully in her throat. Nay, what she'd seen wasna true — it couldna be! Her dream had been woven of her fears, its fibers strung on the warp and weft of Roarke's shocking revelations earlier. If she went to this Castle Erskine, she would find nothing there as it'd appeared in her dreams! Or . . .

would she? Suddenly, she was gripped with the desire to *know*, to see for herself if the strange dreams she'd had were really dreams, or if they were memories, instead? What if she had witnessed her father's murder the night of the blizzard, and fled the keep to escape his slayers?

"My laird. Do ye sleep?" she asked hesitantly, pushing herself up on one elbow to peer into his face.

"When a wench fidgets like a hound plagued wi' fleas, how can a mon sleep?" Roarke grumbled, opening one eye. "And furthermore, my wee lassie, I was baptized 'Roarke', not 'my laird' nor 'sir.' If we're t' share a bed and its pleasures, can we no' share our given names?" he teased with mock sternness.

"Aye, my—! Aye, Roarke," she amended hurriedly.

"Hmph. 'Tis well, then," he approved with a sleepy grunt. "Now, what is it that's sae blessed urgent, ye would wake me from ma hard-won rest?"

"Castle Erskine," she explained in a breathless rush. "Before we—we . . . I dreamed that I was there and—and that—!" She fell silent again, her head bowed, her eyes averted from his. Surely he would think her foolish if she told him!

"And what?" he asked, gently tilting her face to his.

Encouraged by his serious expression, she told him, "In the mirror, I saw m-my father slain, his throat slit by the wench who wore the comb ye showed me!" she whispered, swallowing. "Like so!" She pantomimed holding a dirk in her right fist, her arm raising, coming down in a deadly arc across an unsuspecting throat.

Her actions vividly described the scene for him, and he was filled with pity. So that explained her tormented sleep, her terror on waking! "Come, now. 'Twas but a dream, lassie, no more, I promise ye. A horrid dream, made up o' the things I told ye."

"Aye, mayhap it was. But still, I would go there, by your leave? I want—I *must!*—go t' Erskine, and see for mysel', ye ken?" she implored him, praying he wouldna refuse her point blank.

He considered for a few moments, before nodding in understanding. In her place, would he not do likewise? Would he not want to learn the truth. And besides, he was curious to visit Erskine himself, and witness the slaughter he and his clan had been accused of.

"Very well. So be it! And the sooner 'tis done, the better, I fancy, for your peace o' mind. We shall ride for Erskine on the morrow, if the weather proves clement," he decided. "And who knows? Mayhap being there, in familiar surroundings, will cause your memory t' return?"

"Aye, my laird. 'Twas my own hope exactly!" she cried, smiling in gratitude now, for she'd been certain he would deny her request, and was so relieved he hadna. "Och, thank ye, my laird!"

"Roarke, lassie, Roarke!" he scolded.

"Aye, *Roarke*. My thanks t' ye . . . Roarke."

Grinning so that his eyes twinkled in a way she'd never seen before, he sat up, running his hands through his disheveled black hair to tidy it. The fur coverlet he'd dragged over them as they slept had slipped down, baring his loins. She blushed and quickly glanced away, grateful for a timid knock at the bower door.

"Aye?" Roarke growled, pulling the fur back over his flanks with a careless tug.

"By your leave, my laird, your lady mother bade me fetch up a trencher of victuals for the lady's supper" came Flora's startled voice. Clearly, she had not known Roarke was within the chamber. Her tone betrayed as much.

Roarke glanced across at Catriona. He saw that she'd sprung from the bed like a leaping hart, and had already retrieved her chamber robe and slipped into it, taking up a demure pose upon a low stool close by the fire. Furthermore, her eyes implored him to also dress and pretend that they hadna shared an afternoon of lusty bedsport. Ignoring her silent pleas, he grinned wickedly, lay back, and folded his arms beneath his head, as relaxed and at home as if the bower were his own.

"Enter!" he barked, ignoring the furious look Catriona

shot him from across the chamber.

Flora bustled in, her eyes growing round and disapproving as she took in the cozy little scene, then frankly aghast as she saw that apart from the fur coverlet, the Gilchrist was unclothed. In her suddenly unsteady hands, she carried a wooden board bearing a trencher filled with broken cold meats, some bread and cheese, a bowl of what smelled like barley bree, and a goblet of something steamy. *Hot milk,* Catriona realized, wrinkling her nose in distaste. She was fond of cold fresh milk, chilled in a sparkling burn, but not when it was heated.

"Och! My laird Roarke!" Flora exclaimed, obviously flustered. "I didna ken ye were — ye were here, sir. I sorely doubt this wee platter will suffice for two. Shall I awa' t' fetch ye more, my laird?"

"Nay, Flora, there's nae need t' bother yersel'. I'll be down t' sup directly. Off wi' ye now, there's a good lass. I would don my breeks, ye ken?" He winked roguishly, and Flora's wind-reddened cheeks turned scarlet.

"Aye, sir," she acknowledged primly, her mouth puckered in disapproval. She bobbed him a sketchy curtsey, then made another in Catriona's direction. "By your leave, my lady — ?"

Catriona nodded, unable to meet the woman's censurious eyes. Flora left in obvious haste — no doubt headed straight for the kitchens to spread this new morsel of gossip among the housecarls, she thought ruefully. By Compline, all at Corbin would know she'd shared a bed wi' the laird himself — if they didna already!

"Did ye ha'e to ruin my guid name before that — that pious auld hen?" she asked him with a reproachful sigh, shaking her head.

"Flora? Och, lassie, dinna worry about that auld biddie, nor spare a concern for what she thinks of ye! The woman's a hypocrite! Why, I warrant she's been tumbled more times and by more lads than there are stars in the sky, for all the pious looks she gives ye! Why my lady mother's kept her for so long, I dinna ken. But, enough of

222

Flora! Come, up wi' ye, lass, an' dress yersel'. I willna have ye brooding up here all alone. Ye'll come down t' the hall and sup wi' me this even', lass. Ye'll sit at my side as if we were sweethearts, an' I'll feed ye only the choicest morsels, served up on the point o' my own eating knife? What say ye?" he cajoled.

"Och, very well," she agreed after only a moment's hesitation. His offer was strangely appealing. His smile seemed genuine and warm. Perhaps she could even come to like him a wee bit, if he was often so gentle and understanding? "Will ye take a bite or two t' hold ye while I dress, sir?" She picked up the platter and carried it to him, prettily offering him his choice of the victuals upon it.

"Nay, lass, leave it here. Flora or another of the servants can see to it later."

Soon after, with Roarke serving as her lady-in-waiting—a task he performed with surprising expertise, much to her dismay—she was dressed in a kirtle of turquoise and a surcoat of pale blue. A mesh girdle of knotted dark blue threads rode low at her waist, defining the slender shapeliness of her figure. A narrow filet of silver threads encircled her head, like a shaft of moonlight glinting amidst the waves of her midnight hair.

Admiration in his smoky eyes, Roarke took her hand in his and drew it to his lips, murmuring, "Turquoise becomes ye well, my Lady Cat. With such a beauteous creature dangling on my arm, I'll be the envy o' every red-blooded Gilchrist o' Corbin!" He kissed her fingertips, before whistling over his shoulder and commanding, "T' heel, Castor!"

The old hound glanced up from his warm spot by the hearth, but he made no attempt to obey Roarke's command. Rather, his soft brown eyes met his master's for only an instant before he gulped and quickly looked away, a picture of guilty reluctance as he rested his nose on his shaggy gray paws.

"Och, my laird, the old fellow's cozy enough here,"

Catriona observed with a beguiling smile. "Let him stay by my fire, if ye have no need of him, will ye no'?"

Her coaxing tone won him over completely. Truly, the lass could charm the birds from the trees, when she'd a mind to! And he liked her fondness for hounds, a rare trait in a woman. 'Faith, he could almost forget why he'd ever christened her his 'wee dragon'!

"So. D' ye hear that, Castor, laddie? This fair lassie has pleaded in your favor, ye wretch! And, since her smallest wish shall be my command this even', I must obey! Dream on, auld friend. And come along wi' ye, Lady Cat! My growling belly will sanction no further delays."

So saying, he placed her hand upon his and led her below to the hall.

Chapter Seventeen

With the red-black-and-gray plaid of the clan Gilchrist flapping furiously about her, Catriona wound her reins around her fists and set her palfrey's head at a steep, rock-strewn incline powdered with snow, urging it on when it balked with a quick drumming of her heels against the mare's flanks.

Rider and horse took the icy slope at a swift gallop more daring than prudent, with Roarke racing after them on his own great battle-horse.

His stern expression betrayed his concern for Catriona's safety, but he need not have worried, he realized with a rueful smile. She rode as if she'd been birthed on a horse, and handled her mount with a careless ease and grace granted few women, mounted a-cock horse like a man with her skirts rucked up beneath the fringed tartan *arisaid* she'd flung about her shoulders at his mother's urging.

The cold air, the swift ride over snowy moors and then on through the hushed, deep-green pine forests that lined the winding Tweed Valley had all combined to fill Catriona with an exhilarating sensation of freedom after endless days spent within Corbin's walls. Her eyes shone. Her cheeks were whipped cherry-red by the chill wind. Her lips were curved in an irrepressible smile, as if the grim errand they were about promised to be a pleasurable outing, rather than a task to shy away from.

For Roarke's part, he secretly dreaded the moment not long hence when he must tell her that Erskine lay beyond the next stretch of forest, and watch her smile dwindle, her eyes dim, her cheeks grow pale. Their ride alone together had revealed yet another facet of her mercurial nature, for her intelligent conversation and her keen and ready wit had made the leagues pass swiftly for him, although he'd never been overfond of the twittering companionship of women before — save in his bed! A dullard the lass might well be when it came to a chatelaine's duties, but he'd been damned if she was dull in any other way! Nor, for that matter, did she twitter.

"Beautiful morning! Wondrous morning! Och, Roarke, will ye just smell the air? 'Tis as cold and tangy as wine from Francia! And the pines? Did anything ever smell sae blessed crisp and fresh t' ye before?" Turning in the saddle, she reined in her mount at the crest of the hill. With her head cocked to one side and her hair blowing out behind her before the scudding clouds and the blue-washed sky like a black pennant, she waited for him to draw level with her, watching how his stallion's feathered hooves beat back the drifts of snow and sent it flying like the prow of a warship creating a trough through the waves.

"Nay, lassie, never!" he declared, buoyed up by her high spirits for all that he wondered at her ability to forget the reason for their journey. "Fickle Lady Weather has smiled on ye this morn, 'tis clear!"

"Aye, she has, bless her. But . . . tell me, Roarke, is it many more leagues distant t' my father's keep?" she asked suddenly, the question tumbling from her.

He knew by her anxious expression then that she'd not really been able to forget their true purpose after all; only to deny it for a moment or two.

"Half a league. No more. Ye havena changed your mind? There's time. We can yet turn back, if ye wish?" he offered.

She shook her head, holding her hair down about her shoulders. "Nay. I canna be a coward. Canna take the easy way out. I must go! I have t' see the place where my laird father and my clansmen were slain — and not only to set my own mind at peace. If I'm who ye say, 'tis my duty t' see my clansmen buried and shriven, is it no', as the clan's only survivor, and the McNair of Erskine's daughter?" Her chin came up, and he glimpsed again the pride and iron stubbornness of will that underlay her faerie beauty; gifts her father had bequeathed her along with his thegn's noble blood.

She had said it all, and Roarke could think of nothing he need add. He simply nodded gravely and led on, his two young wolfhounds racing ahead of their horses with tails held high and whisking to and fro. The hounds' pleasure to be abroad was little less than the lassie's, if their joyous baying was aught to go by, he observed, a twinge of sadness filling him. He sighed, his gray eyes darkening. No more would his favored companion of the chase go with him through the glens and o'er the braes t' hunt the mighty stag or rout the evil boar.

"Poor auld Castor," Catriona said softly as her horse drew alongside his. It was as if she'd read his thoughts. She also sighed heavily. "I'd grown fond of the puir beastie. 'Tis truly sorry I am that he's gone. I'll miss him, for he was my first friend at Corbin." Her mouth turned down in sorrow now as she remembered the evening before . . .

She'd returned to her chamber after supper to find the tray of victuals Flora had brought her earlier spilled, half-eaten remnants scattered over the rushes.

"Ye thieving rascal!" she'd accused the dog. "Were ye so blessed hungry, then?" So saying, she'd knelt to fondle the dog's shaggy head, only to find the faithful old wolfhound cold and unmoving to her touch.

"Och, Castor, what is it? Are ye sickly?" she'd cried.

With her words, she'd heard something topple behind her and crash to the floor with a thud. She'd whirled about to see a scrawny, lank-haired lad standing, poised for flight, in a corner of the gloomy chamber, obviously terrified — or guilty. The goblet that had contained her hot milk posset was rolling about at his feet.

"What do ye here?" she'd demanded, and when the lad made a break for the doorway without answering, she sprang after him, took him by the elbow, and spun him around to face her. "I asked, what do ye here, lad?" she'd repeated, shaking him in her annoyance.

"Mistress Flora sent me, she did. 'Hal,' she said, 'ye must fetch the platters from the McNair wench's chamber,' she told me, 'an' bring them down t' the kitchens. So, Hal came.'"

Catriona had noted his vacant expression, his lackluster manner, and had realized belatedly that he must be the lad Roarke had told her of as they sat at supper, the half-wit youth found hiding in the well at Erskine.

"Ye didna harm the hound, did ye?" she'd demanded sharply, for in her heart, she knew that Castor was dead.

"Nay, lady, I never! Sleeping it was, same as now. Please lady, Mistress Flora will box ma ears if I dinna hasten!"

"Take the platters and be gone wi' ye, then," she ordered, and released him. The youth had snatched up the trencher, board, basin, and goblet, and fled . . .

"Aye, lass, I'll miss him, too," Roarke's voice cut into her reflections. "But, well, Castor was an auld dog — ten winters at least, if memory serves. He had a good life — far better than many who walk on two legs, I warrant! He never went hungry or thirsty, nor wanted for a warm hearth t' dream by. Nor did he ever lack for a comely wee bitch t' breed his whelps upon!" he teased with a wink, trying to cheer her. "Och, lassie, it canna be helped. Dinna mourn him, for nothing lives forever, though Castor had pups enough t' ensure himsel' a kind of immortality!"

"Aye, I suppose he did," she agreed, bravely summoning a smile, for Roarke was trying so very hard to be kind and cheer her, when he was the one that needed her consolation. "Could I — would ye let me take one of his pups for mysel'?"

"I dinna ken why I shouldna, do ye? Ursa, auld Castor's favorite bitch, should whelp in a sevennight or so. I'll gi'e ye your pick o' the litter when she does, if it please ye."

"Aye, it would, verra much." The prospect of owning one of Castor's whelps delighted her, for she'd have someone t' call her own when that day came — albeit that someone walked on four legs, and had a tail t' wag!

She smiled as if he'd promised her a shower of pearls, or a rainbow at the very least, and Roarke wondered — not for the first time — what kind of life she'd led at Erskine as the McNair's only daughter — a daughter the neighboring clans had not dreamed existed until after the father himself was dead!

Had Laird Angus doted upon her so jealously, he'd kept her hidden away t' protect her from their enemies such as himself, he wondered? Or had he instead considered her value of so little worth, he'd all but forgotten her very existence until others had opened his eyes to her beauty, and thence to her value as some man's bride? Graeme and Tavish's conversation with the old hermit woman, Morag, had implied the latter. That would explain why a maid of her breeding would smile at the promise of a hound pup as if she'd been promised a casket of costly jewels! Doubtless she'd not been gifted with much in her life, nay, not with that pinchpenny Angus for her father! While he lived, Angus had been known for his ability to take a groat and squeeze it until it squealed for mercy!

"Thank ye . . . Roarke," she murmured, bringing him back to the promise he'd made her. She quickly looked away, unsettled by the frank curiosity in his gaze as he stared at her. She wondered what he saw with those smoky gray eyes beneath their fringing of long lashes that any woman would envy. Did he see her as a woman in her own right, or merely as the daughter of his hated enemy?

Suddenly, she wanted desperately for him to see her simply as a woman, with none of the spiteful feuding and emnity t' come between them; yearned desperately for him to want her for herself, not because he found her bonnie, nor because she was the McNair's daughter, nor because he wanted t' prove his mastery over his foes.

But he only blinked and grunted, appearing embarrassed by her thanks. "Erskine lies ahead, my lady Cat. Ye'll see her towers between the trees in a short spell."

Catriona stood in the tower of her nightmare, staring into the polished metal looking glass that had figured so prominently in it. Only this time, she was wide awake and only wishing she was dreaming.

Palls of black smoke had hung in the damp air above the donjon as they'd ridden up a rocky incline to Erskine some while before, their color ominous against the pallor of the wintry sky. The gloomy keep that perched on a high bluff overlooking the rushing Tweed had seemed little less ominous.

'Tis a cold, forbidding place, without warmth or laughter, or smiles, she'd thought with a shudder. She could not imagine herself ever living here, let alone growing from bairn t' girl t' woman within these oppressive walls. The place was an impregnable fortress, a prison. Surely no one could ever have called it home? And surely she could never have been truly happy here, she with her love of beauty and color, music and song, light and open space?

Catriona had wondered why they'd ridden from Corbin with no escort to attend them when they left shortly after Nones that morning. But as they entered the gatehouse, her question had been answered. There had been no clansmen left for that duty, for either late last night or in the gray hours of early morning, Roarke had dispatched all of his men who could be spared from their duties about his keep to Erskine, and had commanded them to attend to the distasteful task of disposing of her

230

clansmen's bodies. The smoking black ruins of a fire-gutted barn just within the donjon's walls told in what manner they had done so.

Roarke had ordered it done before her arrival to spare her further pain, she knew it without a doubt, and she bowed her head and felt tears fill her eyes. How empty the great hall had been! How eerily silent! How marked had been the knowledge that she was truly all alone in the world, standing in that vast emptiness where her every footfall carried on an echoing silence. And yet, standing within those once-familiar walls, a healing had begun. A knot had been loosened somewhere in the tangle of her thoughts, allowing memory to return.

She knew now that she'd never loved her father, nor felt any great fondness for her trio of brothers — how could she have loved them, i' faith, when she scarce knew them, for they'd had precious little time t' spare for her, and no inclination to let her love them! Nor had they ever shown her any affection whatsoever. And yet, she grieved for them all, after a fashion, mourned the life they *might* have had; the love and strong bonds of kinship that could have flowered between daughter and father, sister and brothers, now lost to her forever . . .

At the sound of footfalls, she blinked away her tears and straightened her spine. She gazed into the looking glass again, knowing even before she raised her eyes to it that she would see a reflection of Roarke standing behind her, tall and handsome with his fine ebony head set proudly atop his broad shoulders. He wore the favored saffron shirt of the men of the north beneath a knee-length tunic of black wool this morn. A *breacan* of the clan Gilchrist's tartan was pinned at his left shoulder with the enameled raven badge of Corbin. A gray bonnet with a similar badge and a long, elegant partridge feather was angled jauntily atop his black hair. His fists were planted on his hips above legs clad in black breeks. His feet were shod in supple knee boots of black suede, braced apart now as he tactfully waited for her to notice him, reluctant

231

to disturb her thoughts. His *sgian dubh,* his dirk, was thrust down the cuff of his right boot in true Border fashion. Och, he cut a bonnie figure, he did, with the wintry gray sunlight limning him all about like some god of old.

"I wish t' thank ye, my laird," she murmured, talking to his reflection without turning around to face him directly.

"Ye do? But for what, my lady?" he asked softly, his gray eyes meeting hers in the mirror.

"For much more than I can ever repay ye, I fear, sir! For sparing me what would have proved too terrible a sight to bear this morn. For sending your men here ahead of us in the cold and dark of night, t' see my kinsmen given a decent burial." A sob caught in her throat that robbed her of speech momentarily before she continued brokenly. "The McNairs were your enemies, sir, as was — am — I! There are precious few men in the Borders who would have done as you have done. And so, I gi'e ye my heartfelt thanks, for 'tis a man of honor and Christian goodness ye are, Laird Roarke. And, I confess, I ha'e misjudged ye sorely in the past!"

Still facing away from him, she swept him a deep curtsey, her head humbly lowered, her woolen skirts spread. Still standing, staring at her reflection, he gently bade her rise, embarrassed by her humility towards him. He much preferred her fierce and proud, with her head held high and her eyes spitting fire at him, than meek and humble and so very, very still and quiet.

"I did no more than any honorable mon would do. Speak nae more of it, pray, my lady, for there's no need for thanks. By your leave, I took the liberty of having my *dopifer* summon one of the Cistercian brothers from Melrose Abbey to speak holy words over your kinsmen's ashes. And my piper waits t' pipe them . . . home . . . when ye are done here. I trust my arrangements meet with your approval?"

She nodded, swallowing the strangling knot in her

throat. His unexpected kindness pained her more deeply than his cruelty could ever have done! She knew full well how to deal with the unkindness, the thoughtlessness of men, for her father had been a learned scholar in those arts. But to accept help graciously, to sincerely express her gratitude, were pretty talents she had yet to learn. But she would, she vowed, she would, and in the learning, discover what it meant to lead a normal life. "Aye, sir, they do, most heartily. I'll be but a — a moment more here."

Tactfully, he made to leave her to her thoughts. But as he turned away, she suddenly called after him, "Laird Roarke! Another word, by your leave?"

He halted and faced her. Their eyes met once again in the polished mirror of tin, and she could see the pity and compassion in his — emotions she had thought him quite empty of, until the past few hours. And, to her surprise, she didna resent him feeling that way, for she knew his feelings were genuine. Jesu, how wrong she'd been about him — about so many things! He had plucked her from the snow, bore her at cost through the drifts, and labored sleepless t' chafe the warmth and life back to her body. He had been there when she wakened from her terrifying nightmare, and had set aside his hatred of her clan to hold and comfort her, and keep her terrors at bay. He had sworn to defend her from her enemies, and had been gentle in his passion when she'd begged him to give her solace. And then — then he'd shown her the ultimate kindness; he'd spared her the pain that looking upon her kinsmen's bodies would have dealt her, and seen that they were properly disposed of himself before the sight of them could fill her mind forever. He was a rare man, was Roarke Mac Gilchrist.

"Aye?" he answered her.

"When we met on the walk above Corbin that night, my laird, I was convinced I'd seen ye before the blizzard. Do ye recall?"

"I do."

"I was right," she told him softly, venturing a wan smile. "I had seen ye before then. Just once."

He smiled. "In the market square at Kelso perhaps? Or at Malcolm's court in Edwin's burgh?"

She shook her head. "Neither, sir. 'Twas none of those places. 'Twas here, in this very mirror, that I saw ye, some two years past!"

"Here? How could that be so?" He'd never set foot within Erskine's walls until this very day, and her claim puzzled him.

"The night was the Eve of St. Agnes, sir. And, if ye recall the custom, as silly young maids are wont to do I'd chanted spells t' summon up a vision of my future husband that eve. As midnight changed night to day that January, I saw ye in the mirror's depths, my laird, I swear it! There was only a smoky swirling at first, but when it cleared, I saw ye most plainly!"

He smiled in sudden understanding. "Ah! So ye've remembered your past, have ye, lass?"

"Aye, sir, I've remembered much of it," she confessed. "It — it was as if my thoughts were tied in a knot. Coming here, surrounding myself with the familiar trappings of my former life, untangled them. Only one piece of the cord yet remains missing, alas."

"The night your clansmen were slain?" he guessed. "The identity of their murderers?"

"Aye." Her slender shoulders sagged with exhaustion brought about by her emotions. " 'Tis as if the march of my life came to a halt the morn it happened! I remember that I was angered with my father that day. We had quarreled two days before, ye see, and it had not been mended between us. Nor did it seem probable that it would ever be mended! He . . . he had told me he wouldna honor the betrothal my lady mother had arranged for me upon her deathbed, ye see. Instead, my lord father planned to find me a more advantageous match — advantageous t' him, that was, with no thought for my wishes!"

234

"And ye defied him?" Roarke added, smiling at her reflection. He saw her blush and look demurely away, yet there was an obstinacy to her tone that he knew well when she looked up again and answered him. Aye, she would ha'e defied the auld fox — and t' the bitter end!

"I did," she confirmed. "The man my mother had chosen as my betrothed was one I'd grown t' favor over the years. He was gentle and kind, and although many years older than I, we had a love of music and beauty in common that boded well for a happy future for the two of us. I didna fancy being wedded to another not of my choosing, and I told my laird father I would marry Alan or no man. He was furious, and banished me to this same tower," she gestured about her. "He bade me remain here for as long as it took t' learn a daughter's obedience. He swore he wouldna permit me t' leave until I'd pledged t' do his bidding without question." Her chin came up. Her green eyes sparked. "Jesu! I would ha' stayed within these walls until I rotted, rather than obey him!"

"Perhaps in this instance, your defiance saved your life," Roarke pointed out. He realized as he did so that he was glad she'd defied her father; glad beyond measure that she'd not met the fate of her clansmen. "If ye'd been below that night, ye wouldna be here now, I fear."

She shrugged. "I dinna ken, sir. Perhaps. Perhaps not. I wonder, shall I ever recall what happened, or will it always elude me?"

"Time will tell in this, as it does in all things, Lady Catriona. And, speaking of time, Brother Ambrose is awaiting us. But . . . before we go below, I have a question I would put to ye."

"If it is in my power to answer ye, I will. What is it ye would know?" She expected him to ask if her recovered memory had given her any inkling as to the identity of her clan's murderers, but his question surprised her.

"When ye saw me in the looking glass that Agnes's Eve — what thoughts filled your head?" he asked, curious to hear her answer, although he felt daft for asking it.

235

To his surprise, she gaped at him round-eyed for a moment, then giggled. "Och, ask me another question, for I canna answer ye that one, sir!"

"Canna? Or willna?"

"Both!" she declared impishly, twirling around to face him.

"I see. Then from your reluctance, I must presume your opinions were not . . . favorable?" he gritted, cursing himself for a fool.

"Far from it, alas, sir!" she admitted, gentle laughter in her voice. "As I recall, I — er — I called ye a 'great, dark ugly brute' and swore the mirror played me false and that blessed St. Agnes lied!" She paused. "And —"

"Go on," he growled. "Pray, dinna seek t' spare me now!"

"I — er — I tugged off my boot and flung it at the mirror with all my might! Look! The dent yet remains in the tin, if ye'd care t' see it?"

"Nay, I dinna care to, lassie. I was . . . curious, 'tis all." His tone was gruff now, and a little lame. His eyes refused to meet hers.

"Och, bless ye, ye're angered wi' me now, are ye no', Roarke, laddie?"

"Angry? For what reason should I be angered? A mon who asks a lass such a leading question should be ready for an answer not to his liking!"

"Aye, sir, he should," she agreed solemnly, but with a twinkle in her green eyes now. Jesu! He looked as cross and sulky as any old bear, she thought, and 'twas clear his pride had been wounded by her flippancy. Poor, proud Roarke! He'd been so kind to her, she couldna let him suffer!

"However, my laird," she added, "I should be fair and remind ye that, at the time, I was yet a silly young maid. I had but sixteen winters t' ma span, and was heartsick with love for my betrothed. I wanted t' wed him straightway, because I feared he'd tire of waiting for me to . . . to become a woman —" she blushed, "and marry another instead. Och, have no fear! Ye're a right bonnie mon, Roarke Mac Gilchrist, in truth ye are! Had my eyes not been blinded wi' love for my betrothed . . . well, I would ha' blessed St. Agnes for the fine promise of a husband she sent me that eve, truly I would! Bonnie ye are, both in face and in deed, Roarke, and I'll scratch out the eyes o' any lassie who gainsays me!"

"Aye, nae doubt. But . . . who was this paragon o' monhood ye were t' wed?" Roarke demanded dourly, not a whit mollified by either her cajoling or her flattery. "D' ye recall his name — or dare I hope 'tis yet t' be remembered?"

"Aye, I know it. He is Alan Mac Quinlann vic Andrew, the Mac Quinlann of his clan. His manor lies north of here, and is called —"

"Rowanlee," Roarke breathed, and she saw how, in a heartbeat's span, his eyes had changed, grown cold as black ice.

"Aye — ?" she whispered, fearful as she looked up at him, for he was angrier than she'd ever seen him. "Ye know of him?"

"Know of him?" he ground out, his fists knotted now. "Jesu, woman, would that I didna!"

"Ah. Then there is bad blood between ye?" she asked in a hushed voice.

"Bad enough! Ye see, 'twas Alan of Rowanlee who inherited Corbin from my grandfather, Kevin McAndrew, upon his death. And 'twas that popinjay fop, my lady mother's distant cousin, from whom I won back her holdings in battle!

"Corbin was my mother's birthright, lass. And yet my noble grandsire turned her out when he learned her belly had been sown with King Duncan's bastard seed. The auld devil sent her from Corbin wi'out a siller penny t' her name, and nae roof over her head. And on his deathbed, he named Mac Quinlann as his heir! Corbin should have been my lady mother's, and mine after her. Had my royal father but acknowledged me as his get, it would have been so!

"Your Alan thought a plump prize had been handed him on a platter when he inherited Corbin — a fine Border stronghold in which t' set himself up as laird. But true laird he never was! In three short years, he'd leeched my grandfather's holdings of their wealth like a parasite gorging on its host. With each passing harvest, the hides yielded smaller crops, but nonetheless, your bonnie Alan blithely feasted King Malcolm in royal fashion, and quartered him and his enormous retinue most comfortably from the bounty of Corbin's storehouses. He increased the lord's shares each villein must pay him t' cover his extravagances, until my puir people couldna eke out enough t' feed themselves or their bairns, for they'd been bled dry!"

"Och! Surely your hatred o' him colors your opinion, sir?" Catriona exclaimed. She felt uncomfortable hearing Roarke malign the man she'd once vowed she loved, and had hoped someday to marry. Besides, Alan had always been most gentle and courteous to her on his rare visits to Erskine; kind and patient and . . . affectionate. Her loyal heart couldna bear that she stay silent and hear ill spoken of one who'd done her no wrong — not without a word in his defense!

"His soft looks and bardish manner ha'e gulled ye, Cat, for he was no' a mon well loved by any but yersel', least of all the people of Corbin! All about him, the serfs and crofters starved, for he ordered all grain taken t' the mill, and there was none left for the next spring's planting. Corbin's flocks grew smaller and smaller, their yields of wool and mutton less, their lambs fewer in number, while Quinlann grew fat and sleek, and enjoyed a soft, carefree life with music and dancing and revelry. He shirked his responsibilities, lass. He betrayed the people that 'twas his sworn duty t' care for, and let Corbin's walls and lands fall into disrepair. For what he'd done t' those puir folk, I couldna forgive him! He didna deserve what he'd been freely given, and so I did what I had to do. I

238

rallied a band of fighting men t' my cause, and we took Corbin from him by force! Aye, and after we'd won the battle, I tied your pretty Alan backward upon a spavined donkey, and sent him back t' Rowanlee with a well-placed boot against his rump. I made him appear the backward jackass he was, while his men looked on and hung their heads in shame!"

The ghost of a smile hovered about Roarke's lips as he remembered that day. Then he gritted, "Corbin wasna Mac Quinlann's, curse his soul! And never will be, sae long as I draw breath! Black Roarke, Bastard of King Duncan, I might well be — but Corbin is mine! And so, my lady, are you."

As they rode back to Corbin, he told her of the years that came after; of how he'd petitioned King Malcolm III, Duncan's grandson, for lawful title to Corbin, and of how, after several years, he'd finally won the right to hold the donjon in his own name, and to bequeath it to his heirs.

"I dinna ken if it was guilt at his grandsire, King Duncan's, refusal t' own me as his blood, or if Malcolm is that rarity among men, a man of justice. Whatever the reason, Corbin belongs to me now. I willna let Mac Quinnlan — or the cursed Normans — wrest her from me, as God is my witness!"

"Your grandfather was a hard, unforgiving man," Catriona observed, her expression a rueful one. "I' faith, he sounds much like my own father!"

He nodded, and Catriona lapsed into a thoughtful silence. Hearing his tale had gone a long way to explain what events had shaped him into the man he was today. It could not have been easy for him to grow t' manhood with the stigma of bastardy, denied his royal father's name and love, or even his acknowledgment that he was his sire. And poor Fionna! Almost the same age as Fionna had been then, Catriona could readily imagine Roarke's mother as a beautiful young woman, frightened and heavy with child, but having no one to turn to for help, nor anyone to take her in. Little wonder the lady of Corbin had treated her so kindly! Fionna must have understood how she'd felt far better than anyone else could have done! She had trod the path of loneliness herself.

They rode on, still in silence, for over a league, a companionable silence broken only by the blowing of their horses as Roarke led the way along the banks of the Tweed. They did not return directly to Corbin, she observed, but were following the river to its outpouring in the North Sea.

The river that twisted and turned across the borders, separating Northumbria and the land of the Scots from Saxon Britain to the south, roared like a great gray dragon between its banks in these months of winter. It lashed its tail furiously, throwing showers of icy spume above its course, winding itself in serpentine coils of fury in some places to form seething whirpools.

And yet, the Tweed was a tamer, gentler beast as they neared the coast, flowing in a cold, swift rush between small hamlets and farms and empty fields that gave way at last to fishing villages, with stone huts clinging like limpets to a single steep and narrow street. There were small boats beyond, clustered about a stone quay. They were bobbing about as they fought their moorings on a wind-whipped sea the color of Roarke's eyes. Fishermen were mending their nets, while the fishwives gutted herring for salting in great barrels, or skewered them on racks for smoking.

They turned off the path that led down into the fishing village. Instead, they followed a winding, stony track up a cliff face overhanging the crashing waves. There were jagged rocks below; above, a snowswept headland rose high and proud as a giant's brow. There the wind was wild and icy as pellets of hail dashed against their cheeks. Hungry gulls swooped and screamed above them, cutting arcs of silver from the grim iron pallor of the sky.

At the top of the path, Roarke reined in his horse. He dismounted and lifted Catriona down after him. As if by mutual agreement, they walked side by side to the very edge of St. Abb's headland and stood there, their feet braced apart against the furious wind that threatened to steal their breath away and whirl them into the air like weightless leaves.

She watched him as he stood beside her. Like a proud sea hawk, he faced into the wind. His cheeks were ruddy with cold. His long, curling black hair was tossed about his head as furiously as her own. Their tartan mantles and her skirts flapped about, tangling together, flying apart. It was exhilarating and frightening all at once to stand there, facing the weather's fury, risking that a careless gust would hurl one to the rocky jaws below. And yet, instinctively she knew why he'd chosen to bring her to this place, after the unpleasant task she'd had to face that morning. Tears pricked behind her eyelids once again as she remembered.

Dry-eyed, her *arisaid* drawn up to cover her head, she'd stood straight and proud — the last survivor of her Border clan — while Brother Ambrose uttered words of farewell over the smoking ashes, for ashes were all that remained now of her kith and kin. Tears had flown freely and without shame afterward, when Roarke's young piper had appeared on the battlements of Erskine far above them. Sweetly, mournfully, Andrew had piped the fallen home with the song she'd sung at Corbin on the eve of Christ's Mass. The wailing lament of the bagpipes had filled the glen as it told of the kings of Scotland, borne to their last resting place on the sacred isle of Iona aboard a funeral barge. The skirl of the pipes rising on the frosty air to the standard of the McNair — lowered now to half-mast and drooping forlornly in mourning — had all seemed a fitting farewell for a warrior chieftain and his clansmen who'd go a-feuding no more along the Border glens.

"Goodbye, Father," she'd whispered. "Ye're with Mother now, and happen ye'll find peace at last . . ."

"In a day or two, I'll have their ashes brought t' ye at Corbin," Roarke murmured. "If it please ye, I thought ye could bring them here, and scatter them on the sea."

"Aye. It pleases me well," she agreed softly. "My father was descended from Thorwig the Red, a viking, ye ken? 'Tis well known that the Norsemen burn their chieftains' bodies t' honor them, then set their longships adrift upon the sea t' carry them t' Valhalla. I think . . . I think he would ha'e wanted it this way."

He nodded in understanding.

"I come here when my thoughts trouble me," Roarke murmured some while later, the soft burr of his musical Gaelic as he bent low to her ear a sharp counterpoint to the wail of the wind. His eyes were fixed on the distant, murky horizon out to sea. "Even at the height of summer, the wind blows wild here at St. Abb's — though somewhat warmer than now! Somehow, t' stand here in this fashion untangles my raveled thoughts. I come away eased, and thinking far more clearly than before. D' ye ken what I mean?"

"Aye, I ken, my laird, for I feel it, too."

"Ye do?"

"Aye. The wind cleanses one's soul, I fancy. It blows away the useless chaff that clouds one's thinking, leaving only that of import behind."

They stood side by side, without touching. Yet, in some inexplicable way, both felt as if they were bound together by invisible cords, by the warp and weft of Fate that had thrown them together on a night of murder and blizzard.

Roarke was the first to move again. He reached out and slipped his arm about her waist, drawing her gently against him. Then he unpinned his flowing *breacan,* and wrapped its warmth about them both.

"When ye're ready, Catriona, we'll go home."

"T' Corbin, ye mean?" she murmured, looking up into

his eyes.

"Home," he repeated softly, "for I meant what I said at Erskine, lassie. Ye belong t' me. I willna let ye leave me for another!"

He held her close, and bent his head to kiss her icy lips, replacing their wintry chill with the warmth of springtime.

Chapter Eighteen

Spring came early to the Borders in the year of Our Lord 1068. High in the mountains, her warm sunshine melted the snowcaps and swelled the waters of the Tweed so that she rushed and tumbled in icy torrents on her winding course throughout the vale, threatening at times to flood her banks. Sparkling burns burbled over beds of smooth pebbles in the glens below, the chuckle of spring's song merry in their throats.

Spring spread a tartan mantle of greens throughout the glens and dales and over banks and braes. The bright green of new grass vied with the tender, paler green of the new leaves that uncurled on the boughs of the oaks, the ash, and the graceful birches. Deep in the forests of fir and stately pine that grew the length and breadth of the Borders, and beneath the white-blossomed hawthorn hedgerows, the first wildflowers peeked shyly. There the delicate, pale-yellow primrose, Catriona's favorite, showed its demure face amidst the harebells, wild hyacinth, snowdrops, violets, and pastel-blue liverwort. The rowans, too, with their long, trailing brambles, burst into blood-red buds.

The rams battled violently when the warm promise of spring perfumed the air. They locked curly horns in fierce rivalry to become lords of the flocks and win their chosen ewes. And, having won them, they mated. The crofters threw off their winter lethargy and tended their flocks with renewed vigor, using sling and club to protect the slow, lamb-heavy ewes from the predatory wolves who'd grown winter-lean and bold on account of their hunger. On the wild moorlands, patches of springy turf and heather, still brown from winter frost, now showed between the melting snows. Upon them, the shaggy wild cattle with their huge, curved horns grazed and dropped their calves. Within an hour of their births, they were tottering after their mothers on stilt legs, whisking their tails and mooing to nurse.

Birds wool-gathered and built their nests, chirruping as they flew from thorn-thicket to branch with twigs and wattle. The stags rutted. Their mating bellows and the challenging crash of their antlers against tree trunks as they practiced the tactics that would win them their pick of the does could be heard on the early-morning air, ringing out through the glens over which they were kings. In the river at its foaming spate, the fishermen of clan Gilchrist spread their nets and trapped the red salmon as they leaped upstream against the rushing current to spawn in quiet inland waters. And at Corbin, fresh salmon and trout, rolled in oatmeal and fried, and fresh watercress from the spring, tempted palates grown weary of winter's endless salted meats.

Catriona, too, felt the season in her blood. Spring fever rose through her as strongly as the sap rose through the young trees and filled her with restless energy! She was eager to be out and about in the fresh air now that winter's fierce hold upon Corbin was broken and the short gray days and long dark nights of the past. It was not easy to regain the freedom she remembered enjoying in her father's keep, however!

Growing up at Erskine, no one in the keep from her lord father down to his lowliest stableboy had ever given second thought to the wisdom of her wild rides alone wherever her fancy led or whither the winds blew her. It was not so here. Having people care for you, she realized, had its disadvantages, too.

The lady Fionna, who still cherished the fond hope that she and Roarke would wed someday, especially now that they were on more amicable terms, kept a mother's protective eye on her; Roarke an affectionate if watchful guardian's one. Tavish and especially Graeme exhibited an annoying brotherly concern in regards to her comings and goings, while even Flora, the serving woman, drat her, offered unwanted cautions and seemed intent on keeping her in sight at all times.

Hal, the half-wit, dogged her path, too. Roarke teased her mercilessly when they were closeted alone together that the daft lad fancied himself in love with her. This, he insisted gravely, explained why Hal followed her everywhere as faithfully as the mischievous bitch pup, Lyra, that she'd chosen from Ursa and Castor's last litter in mid-January.

But, try as Catriona might, since the night she'd found Castor dead in his sleep by the fire, she hadna been able to summon up any fondness for Hal. And worse yet, it made her feel guilty that she couldna! After all, the laddie couldn't help being born daft, now could he, any more than he could help his vacant gaze and the way his mouth hung slack, letting his tongue protrude?

Despite his appearance, she'd endeavored to behave kindly towards Hal even when he tried her patience. It was her Christian duty to be charitable to those less fortunate than herself, however disagreeable they were. Moreover, although she didna remember him at all, she felt obligated to treat him kindly, for Roarke had told her that, like her, Hal had survived the massacre at Erskine, and been found by Graeme and Tavish hiding in the well there. Because of this twist of fate, and because she was now, to all intents and purposes, the McNair of Erskine, she felt compelled to be patient with Hal — and not box his ears as she oftimes itched to do!

She grimaced. The lad wouldna be so cursed irritating if he didna jump out at her from dark corners when she believed herself quite alone, an annoying habit that left her weak-kneed and with a wildly pounding heart, more oft than not. Or if he'd leave off standing so close behind her, he was nigh breathing down her neck! She'd tried countless times to explain to him that she had no objection to him attending her, if he would but keep his distance, but with little measurable effect. He'd simply nod, that vacant look in his eyes, and tug on his forelock as he mumbled in a dull monotone, "Aye, lady, aye. Hal understands, he do. He isna a simpleton, Hal isna! Just a wee bit slow. Mother said so."

After a few weeks of "Mother said so," Catriona considered with a sigh, she'd come to hate Hal's dratted mother—whoever she might ha'e been—and wi' a vengeance! So now, she just pretended Hal wasn't there, and after a while, it almost seemed he wasn't.

So although she was not truly a prisoner, despite Roarke's stern warning that she belonged to him, Catriona chafed under the yoke of cautions and restraints and endless warnings that she not leave the walls of Corbin unaccompanied.

"Whist ye, I'm no' a bairn in small cloths t' be coddled and cossetted! Would ye prefer I don a ball and chain, mi'laird?" she demanded impudently of Roarke one morning when the April sunshine was drenching the greening moors beyond her windeye, and her heart and spirit were bursting to be free of Corbin's confinement.

Roarke had already noted her restlessness, seen the bright, defiant sparkle to her eyes, and, fearing the worst, he proceeded to deliver a lengthy lecture on the dangers of leaving Corbin's wooden palisades unescorted. There were bands of robbers roaming the Tweed Valley, he warned her, and possibly Norman spies abroad, too, sent north by William of Normandy and England to secretly gauge the Scots' numbers and their means of defense. Moreover, her clan's murderers yet remained at large, unknown and unpunished for their bloody deeds. If, as she feared, she had seen who they were, surprised them at their butchery, they might yet seek to kill her.

"Well, why dinna ye lock me awa' in your wee dungeon, then," she flared, "just t' be certain I canna escape ye, and be done wi' this nonsense?"

Roarke shot her a dour look, his former preoccupied expression gone for the moment. "A sharp tongue doesna become ye, lassie," he said sternly. "Ye know full well why ye must be cautious and no' ride abroad by yersel', do ye no'? 'Tis for your own safety and well-being I caution ye, not t' keep ye ma prisoner!"

"Aye," she muttered with a mutinous expression. "I ken right enough. But . . . I dinna have t' like it, do I?"

"Nay, ye saucy minx, ye dinna — but ye *do* have to obey me!" he growled in a voice so unlike the gentle, indulgent Roarke he'd been of late, she decided it would be prudent not to try his temper by arguing with him further, in case she lost the small liberties she'd won along with his trust that day at Erskine.

Setting her jaw, she turned away from him, biting back a torrent of arguments that would have served little purpose as she made to leave the bower. Roarke, she knew now, was a man who made up his mind but once, and kept to it. And, though she itched to belabor her point, she was not sae stupid as to bang her head against a stone wall for naught! Besides, there were other means, she'd discovered, little by little, by which t' get one's way, especially with a man like Roarke who, for all his manly pride and potential for ruthlessness, had a tender heart he kept well hidden where lassies were concerned . . .

Sure enough, Roarke saw how her green eyes — true windows to her soul! — betrayed her disappointment and became dangerously bright and dewy with unshed tears. Saw, too, how the corners of her lovely mouth turned down now, instead of dimpling up in a merry smile. His impatience ebbed. His irritation softened. "Och, Catriona—!" he called after her in a gentler voice. "Where are ye off to?"

"I promised t' help your lady mother this morn, and am already tardy, sir. She must list all she needs t' replace her stores before the spring fair in Kelso next sevennight. I am to count what she has on hand for her."

"Ah. I see. And I suppose ye couldna asked her t' spare ye t' go hunting wi' me instead?"

A thrill leaped through her. Hunting! He'd said hunting!" She was hard put to smother a grin of wicked triumph as she shook her head in utmost regret and summoned a serious mien with her hands modestly clasped before her, her dark head bowed. "Alas, sir, I regret I couldna. I ha'e given my word, ye see, and canna break it."

"But ye havena left Corbin since ye came here, save to visit your father's keep on that dark day we laid him t' rest!" Roarke argued, vaguely wondering how the tide had been turned, and why he was now arguing *for* her to accompany him, rather than bidding her stay safe within Corbin's walls!

"Well, sir, I do so love t' hunt . . . but nay, your lady mother has done too much for me already! I couldna disappoint her, Roarke, truly I couldna."

Minx! Roarke thought, belatedly realizing the wee game she played. Well, if one could play, then so could two!

"Very well then, my lady," he said levelly. "I would ha' welcomed your company, but if ye're committed t' helping my mother, then 'twould be churlish o' me t' tempt ye away. Anon, sweet Cat! I'll see ye 'ere I return in the gloaming!"

He made to drop a kiss on her brow as he passed her, headed for the doorway. And Catriona—realizing he had called her naughty bluff — gave way to a wail of disappointment as she saw her plans in ruins.

"Oh, Roarke — ! Say ye willna leave wi'out me!" she cried, clutching at his sleeve to detain him.

"But ye begged me to!"

"Aye, but I didna mean it, truly I didna! Oh, Roarke, please take me hunting wi' ye, 'else I'll die o' boredom here!"

"And what o' your promise to my lady mother?" His brows rose questioningly. A smile tugged at the corners of his mouth.

"I confess I lied, sir! I made no such promise — 'twas all falsehood," she admitted, reddening, "to persuade ye t' give me a wee bit o' freedom!" Her sooty lashes fluttered like coquettish fans as she placed her hand over his muscular forearm and leaned against him, imploring prettily, "Please, my laird?"

"Whist, come along wi' ye then, ye conniving minx — and be quick aboot it. Dally, and I'll leave ye here — after I beat yer wee bottom for your trickery!" he threatened, hiding a grin as he strode away.

Pausing only to snatch up her *arisaid* and her hunting dirk, Catriona sped after him, not at all certain he wouldn't keep his threat and leave without her . . .

'Twas a brisk morn, and the wind was bracing tho' the sun was bright as she bathed the moors and riverbanks. The scarlet pennants of Corbin Keep furled brightly in her welcome light so that the raven emblazoned upon them with wings raised and spread seemed to fly.

Boarhounds and wolfhounds alike milled around the horses' hooves in the outer ward of Corbin, nipping at each other's rumps, yipping and yapping and ignoring the kennel-master's whip and stern commands. They were baying excitedly, the sound deafening, when Andrew rose in his stirrups and brought the curling hunting horn to his lips.

Hallooo! Haloooo! sounded the horn's nasal notes.

At last they were off! Catriona thought excitedly, gathering the reins of her mare, Kelpie, securely in her fist. The hounds streamed past her through Corbin's gates, eager to be away, and within moments the cavalcade of brightly dressed huntsmen and women rode out after them, followed by the kennel lads and the serfs who would carry home the game.

Fionna's cousin Elyse was among their number, looking happier and more at ease than she had since the day she'd arrived at Corbin with her sad tidings. She was a fine horsewoman with an excellent seat, despite her timid manner. Her two small grandsons, Masters Michael and Christopher, rode beside her on shaggy, barrel-bellied moorland ponies, shooed and chivvied along by their loyal nurse, Betty, who—not to be left behind her charges!—rode astride the lumbering cart-horse that had brought her safely across Britain and north to Scotland, much to everyone's amusement.

The lady Fionna accompanied them, too, looking queenly and beautiful in a leaf-green gown, mounted upon a game little palfrey the color of clotted cream. Tavish and Graeme, Roarke's reeve, the solemn Master Ian, Roarke's men-at-arms and a number of others were there, too, cheeks flushed and eyes bright with anticipation of a stirring day of sport; the first such sport of the new year.

They'd followed the hounds for over a league when the lead dogs routed a boar and began baying and salivating with excitement. Sure enough, an old, one-eyed male exploded from a thicket of thorn brambles and took flight, head down. It was squealing in fury, black and bristly with long, fierce tusks and trotters that were pumping so rapidly as it fled, they became a dark blur.

Andrew sounded the gone-away. Before the notes of his winding call had died on the air, the excited hounds had broken free of the kennel-lads' restraint and stretched out in pursuit, bounding over hedge and style, struggling through muddy ditches, springing across small burns and through leafy copses, after the boar. The huntsmen followed, urging their mounts to keep up with the disappearing hounds. Tavish and Graeme rode well to the fore of the hunt, while Fionna and Elyse, their ladies and menservants, brought up in the rear at a slower pace. Roarke, Catriona noticed, had fallen back, letting the others sweep past him, and had ridden to his mother's side. She followed suit, pacing her horse at a walk to keep abreast of theirs.

"Is all well wi' ye, my lady mother?" Roarke inquired.

"Not altogether, my son!" Fionna confessed with an embarrassed smile. " 'Twould seem my auld joints are badly in need o' oiling after a winter spent rusting in my sewing bowers! In faith, my puir netherquarters are sae blessed numb, I canna feel them!"

"Would ye return t' Corbin, then?" Roarke asked. "But say the word, and I'll escort ye home?"

"Nonsense, ye daft lad! I'm no' sae old yet I'd give up such an outing as this! Elyse and I will follow the hunt — but at our own more leisurely pace! Ye and Catriona ride on. We'll catch up wi' ye anon."

"I'll gladly stay back wi' ye, my lady?" Catriona offered, concerned for the dear lady.

"I wouldna hear of it!" Fionna insisted firmly, waving them on with her riding crop. "Be gone, the pair o' ye!"

"We must make haste, or miss the kill!" Roarke called to her.

"Then ride on ahead o' me, sir, if ye will," she called back across the expanse of moorland that separated their horses. "I dinna care t' watch a poor beast die, not on such a bonnie spring morn o' birdsong and new life growing everywhere. Besides, I ha'e no stomach for bloodshed." She wrinkled her nose. " 'Tis the thrill o' riding fast and far that endears the hunt t' me, ye ken?"

He nodded and reined in his horse, eyeing her speculatively, and with a look that made goosebumps rise on her arms. "Would ye rather we found some quiet woodland spot instead, and enjoyed the wonders of spring?"

She blushed, looked down, and gave a small nod, saying in a low, soft voice, "I can think of nothing that would please me more, my laird."

"Then come, sit before me upon my horse, and I will bear ye away t' a secret place that is dear to my heart, and known to few."

The nearness of his body to hers, his teasing caresses and kisses as she leaned back against his chest, had stirred her passions to brimming by the time he declared that they had found his secret place.

A small glade opened up in the woods before their horses, circled by lofty trees whose branches all but met way above them like a lofty hall. Around the boles of the trees were tussocks of lush spring grass and clumps of wildflowers, snowdrops, violets, harebells and primroses everywhere the eye chanced to look.

Without further ado, Roarke dismounted and spread his tartan *breacan* upon the grass. Lifting her down from his saddle, he bore her to his mantle and, still cradling her in his arms, set her upon it as gently as if she were made o' eggshells, murmuring, "Your bridal bed, sweet heart!"

"Ye dinna play fair, my laird," she accused him without rancor, looking up reprovingly from beneath her lashes, tho' a tiny smile dimpled the corners of her mouth. "How can a lassie deny ye, when ye press your suit sae winningly?"

The laughter came up from deep in his throat, husky and laden with a sensual, manly timbre that made her heart skip a beat, for 'twas a roguish, wicked sound — and one she'd grown to cherish. His strong brown fingers pushed back the tousled hair that framed her face, baring her temples and the sweet curve of her jaw that he might brand them with his lips. He did so linger-ingly, framing her face between his palms.

"Och, ma wee wren, where ye're concerned, I wouldna play fair were the devil himsel' my rival for your heart!" he murmured, his breath warm against her skin. "If I can sway ye t' ma cause wi' kisses, then kisses ye'll have," he promised, soft and low, brushing his lips against the fluid line of her silken throat. "And if 'tis caresses that'll win your love, then I'll caress ye till the moon turns blue and ye swoon wi' longing! And if 'tis pretty wooing your fickle heart desires, I'll be your rough and ready lord nae more, but a lovesick swain who'll weave flowers through your bonnie curls, and call ye 'love.'"

So saying, he reached beyond her to pluck the pale-yellow primroses that peeped shyly from the grass — her favorite of all the springtime flowers. One by one, blossom by blossom, he tucked them amongst her ebony tresses. There, they shone out amidst the inky mass like creamy stars, pricked against a dark night sky.

"Eostre, ma wee pagan goddess o' spring," he declared, leaning back to admire his handiwork when he was done.

Shyly, she smiled her pleasure at his silly, tender words, and then he took her in his arms again and kissed her most thoroughly. His warm palm slipped down over her shoulder, moving to cup her breast through the cloth of her kirtle, even as his mouth covered hers once again in the sweetest of lingering kisses.

"In truth, yer boldness leaves me breathless, my laird!" she gasped shakily when he drew back, though her arms continued to hold him as tightly as when they'd kissed. "Aye, and confused, too, ye bonnie devil ye!"

He smiled, and his gray eyes sparkled with a teasing glint. "Only breathless, ma lovie? Naught but confused? Alas, I'd hoped for more. . . !"

"Och, ye canny rogue! Ye ken full well it isna only breathlessness ye make me feel, nor but confusion!" She sighed heavily, reaching up to caress his rough, swarthy cheek. She traced the tiny sun furrows that winged away from the corners of his beautiful, brooding gray eyes, and smoothed an errant ebony lock from his wind-browned forehead. "Ye make me want ye, damme ye, Mac Gilchrist," she whispered.

"Aye, but no' so sorely as I want ye, I wager, ma love," Roarke said with feeling. Taking her hand, he kissed her palm and drew it down to cover the hard shaft that rode beneath the lacings of his breeks.

As she touched his loins, felt the hardness of his manhood, a shudder of passion moved through her. Dizziness swept over her, and with it an unexpected yearning to abandon all attempts at modesty and restraint for once and return the passion and pleasure of Roarke's loving twofold. Why oh *why* did she yet lie to hersel'? Why could she not admit it wasna Alan she wanted anymore, but Roarke? Why could she not relinquish her foolish control, and be as wild and free as Roarke with her kisses and caresses, show him just how wonderful he made her feel?

"Aye, my love, I ken ye want me," she whispered, sitting up and turning to face him. Kneeling before him, she leaned over and pressed her mouth to his in a fleeting kiss. Her green eyes locked with his gray ones in a sultry look that spoke volumes as she promised, "And ye shall have me . . . soon."

Never had he seen her look at him as seductively as she did now! Her slanted green eyes were bright beneath half-lowered sooty lashes. And, as he watched, he saw the tip of her pink tongue dart out to moisten her lips as delicately as a wee kit washing itself. Both glance and gesture were provocative enough t' make a mon lose hold of reason!

"What mischief are ye aboot now, lassie?" he asked, clenching his fists to master his desire, and wondering what had come over her? His heart, already thundering with the promise of passion, skipped a beat, then two, like a frisking colt. His manhood bucked, for she was no longer sitting there, meekly watching him, but had risen to her feet. Standing now in a patch of sunlight, she began removing her garments, one by one. She undressed so slowly, so gracefully, that he realized, suddenly, what she was about. Why, the naughty wee minx sought to give him the pleasure of watching her disrobe! Accordingly, he smothered his lustier impulses, and, with a grin, lounged back upon his elbows to enjoy her seductive gift.

Already her suede boots lay in the grass, tumbled carelessly aside. Slowly, she drew up her skirts and unfastened her garter ribbons, drawing them free only to let them drift slowly to the dew-damp grass in weightless curls. Daintily raising one foot and planting it atop a grassy tussock, she rolled down her white hose to bare her shapely calves and small pink feet. Looking up, she saw Roarke swallow, saw how his eyes darkened to the color of silver rain as he watched her. The smoldering intensity of his heavy-lidded gaze thrilled her! Jesu! Her wee attempt at seduction was working even better than she'd hoped! She felt her pulse quicken, her skin grow rosy with warmth.

Turning her back to him so that her hair lifted and swirled about her in an inky mantle, she unfastened her girdle of braided silk and let it fall at her feet, before raising her surcoat over her head and tossing it to the winds. Reaching down once again, she gathered up the hems of her kirtle and slipped it slowly up, then off, her body, over her head, casting him a sultry glance over her shoulder as it, too, fell to the grass in a puddle of color.

Roarke's chest was rising and falling rapidly now. His fists were yet clenched. He wetted his lips, and Catriona was hard put to forego voicing the chuckle of delight that welled in her throat. Who'd have believed it! She *enjoyed* the heady sensation of power over him that her newfound seductiveness gave her—though she thought of it as power only in the gentlest, most loving sense of the word. Why, in this moment, if she bade him cluck like a hen as he'd once boasted he could command her, she fancied he'd cluck aplenty, bless the rogue!

Now she wore only her filmy veil, held in place by a narrow circlet of silver, chased with a pattern of thistles, and her thin undergown. This last garment was woven of such delicate, fine thread it was nigh transparent. As she turned slowly to face him, her arms held wide in invitation, she knew full well that her breasts were visible as darker mounds glimpsed through the cloth.

"Come t' me, Roarke o' Corbin!" she commanded huskily.

"Sweet Jesu!" Roarke groaned, drunk on the sight of her standing there, offering herself to him so sweetly. "Ye are Eostre, in truth!"

Where the filmy white cloth clung to her slender curves, her body was dappled with green-and-gold coins of sunlight and shade, spilled through the leafy boughs of the oaks above them. It gave her an insubstantial quality, made her seem not quite real; a faerie maid, a sylph of the woodlands, with the primroses starring her long black hair, and that dreamy 'come t' me, sweetheart' look for him in her green, green eyes.

"Aye, young laird, I am Eostre!" she teased him as he suddenly started forward. She laughed merrily as she slipped away between the trees, for Roarke had clambered to his feet and strode purposefully towards her. He looked lean and dark and deliciously dangerous as he crossed the greensward — ready for something more t' his liking than games! "I'm a pagan goddess, beyond the reach o' mortal man — and ye canna catch me!" she flung over her shoulder as she evaded him.

Her arms embraced the trunk of first one tree, caressed it fleetingly, then slipped gracefully about another as, barefoot, she twisted and turned between the sapling oaks and the silver-trunked birches to escape

257

him.

The sight of her ivory arms entwining the rough bark of the trees was peculiarly erotic to Roarke. The breath catching in his throat, his heart hammering, lust a powerful aching in his groin, he began the pursuit in earnest. Feinting a break first to left, then right, he gave a roar and sprang towards her. He lunged for the hem of her kirtle, managing only to grasp a handful of leaves from an intrusive bush, and a pinch of air, rather than the folds of her filmy linen as she shrieked and fled.

"A moment more, and, mortal or nay, I'll hold ye fast, my goddess!" he threatened wickedly, casting about for her.

"Think ye so, my laird?" came her voice, husky with merriment, from somewhere behind him now. "Then surely ye arena mortal, after all, but a god! After all, no mortal man could catch the spring, and hold her hostage for his pleasure!"

He spun about on his heel, spying her perched on a steep, mossy bank above him now. One of her arms rested along the bough of a tree that grew up to it from his level, while with the other, she blew him a kiss. With a roar, he leaped up the bank in pursuit, losing his footing in the slippery damp moss momentarily before recovering his balance and plunging on.

But to his dismay, he discovered she'd vanished when he breasted the slope. Not a sight nor sound of her could he see anywhere!

Breathing heavily, he waited, his ears cocked for a telltale rustle. But he could hear only the distant winding of the hunting horn, the fluting of a cuckoo's woodwind call, the song of water purling over a pebbled streambed somewhere close by.

Slowly, he turned full circle. And then, just when he'd given her up for lost, he glimpsed a flash of white through some bushes below. Quietly, he sprinted down to them and thrust them aside. Och! The wee minx!

Somehow, she was below him once again, balancing precariously on tiptoe as she sprang from steppingstone to steppingstone to cross the chuckling burn he had heard but been unable to see between the trees! She looked every whit the nyad there, where the willows dipped their spindly tresses low to wet them in the chilly flow.

Along the banks, irises bloomed in purple splendor. Cushions of deep-green cress mounded in the shallows. It was a bonnie place for a trysting bower, he thought with a wicked smile, for 'twas enclosed by leafy trees and briars and hidden from curious eyes . . .

Moving quietly, he slithered back down the slope. Circling around ahead of her, he leaped the burn in two long strides, just above the point she'd forded it.

He was waiting for her when, humming, she gained the opposite bank. He'd crouched down behind a cairn of heaped stones that had been left there long before by some pagan worshipper to appease the spirit of the burn. The wide-eyed look of astonishment, then delight, that crossed her lovely face as he sprang up and caught her in his arms was worth a king's ransom!

"I have ye, ma sweet!" he whispered triumphantly. And without further ado, he bore her down to the water's edge.

There were mossy green banks beneath them as her arms came up to encircle his neck, and her sweet mouth lifted for his kiss.

"Kiss me, ye cheating varlet!" she demanded, and the cheating varlet complied.

Her under-kirtle was damp in places, transparent now where water had splashed the cloth over her bosom. Her breasts were deep-rose shadows beneath it, the nipples tiny hillocks that begged his lips to taste them! With a groan, Roarke thrust up her skirts and parted her thighs, covering her lips with his own as he lost himself in her sweetness.

That morn, in their woodland bower by a pagan

spring, he claimed her with the wild, sweet fervor of the hunt and capture thrumming in his veins—and with the fierce passion of love, at last acknowledged, bursting full in his heart.

His loving had a piercing beauty that spring morn, transcending all the other pleasure-filled couplings they'd shared, Catriona thought dreamily, cradled secure in his arms. The scent of spring was everywhere, filling her nostrils; 'twas in the sharp green smell of the cress, in the fragile petals of the irises and wild hyacinths blooming all about them at water's edge, in the creamy-yellow of the primroses decking her midnight hair. The sky was a mantle of blue, a ragged-edged robe they glimpsed way, way above them between the lofty green boughs of the trees as they loved, and the sun was a badge of gold fit for a Border laird and his Border bride.

"Ye willna leave me, lassie," Roarke whispered as he made love to her, his words half threat, half entreaty. "Ye willna go t' him, I command ye, for if ye do, I'll never take ye back!"

"To who would I flee?" she asked, her brow knitting in puzzlement.

"T' Mac Quinlann," he growled, his fingers rough and biting now where they gripped her.

"I willna, never fear, ma sweet laird!" came her low promise in reply. "I couldna, I wouldna, for I—love thee!"

"Ye're certain?"

"Och, aye, I am, i' faith! More certain than of anything before. 'Tis you I love, my Roarke, heart o' my heart! I'll never leave ye . . . never . . . never . . . nev—Oh!"

Her fingers tightened on his upper arms as her words became little birdlike cries of delight. He kissed her hungrily as the storm broke between them, their bodies arching fiercely together, their mouths joined.

Their panting cries mingled with the chuckle of the

busy burn as rapture claimed them. And, in rapture's shimmering wake, a sweet, exhausted lethargy o'erpowered them.

"I wager ye've missed the thrill o' the boar-kill, my laird," she reminded him impishly much later as he turned her about to pluck the wilted primroses from her hair once she'd dressed.

They had woken to discover—judging by the sun's set in the sky—that the hour was close to Terce. So well and lustily had they loved, they'd slept far longer than they'd intended!

"I dinna give a damn, madam," he growled, grinning as he lifted her hair and dropped a kiss on the nape of her neck. "The sport in these woods was far more t' ma liking—and the game more tender t' ma teeth!"

"Varlet!" she accused, whirling around to face him.

" 'Varlet' is it, mistress?" he countered, retrieving his feathered bonnet from the grass and dusting it off by slapping it against his thigh. "Ye'd have called me worse had I said I'd rather ha'e followed a reeking boar!"

"Aye, I would," she confessed, grinning. "Give me one last kiss, then, mi'laird, and we'll be awa' t' Corbin."

Chuckling, Roarke drew her into his arms and kissed her in a leisurely, thorough fashion. So intent were they on that kiss, they did not notice they were no longer alone until Tavish's horse whinnied a greeting to their own. Guiltily, they sprang apart, to see the steward leading his mount across the sward to the spring. His fair complexion was red with embarrassment.

"Forgive this intrusion, my laird, my lady Catriona," he asked them each in turn. "But Dearg was in need o' watering." He nodded to his mount, its head bent low to the water. "I didna ken ye were here."

"Och, no matter, laddie. We were about t' return t' the hunt, anyway," Roarke dismissed the matter. He winked. "Were we no', my lady Cat?"

"Aye, sir," she agreed, smiling fondly back at him. "Were the huntsmen rewarded wi' a boar for their trouble, Master Steward?" she asked Tavish.

"Aye, my lady, long ago! In truth, all the huntsmen ha'e already returned t' Corbin with the kill! One was an evil, bristly auld brute, wi' tusks this long!" He spread his hands to demonstrate. "He gored two or three o' the hounds afore they had him"

Catriona shuddered. "Then 'tis glad I am I didna see it!"

Tavish nodded soberly. He yet seemed uncomfortable with them, felt like an outsider, perhaps, and so instead of looking directly at the pair—whom he must have guessed had been sporting—he stared into the water instead, suddenly quoting:

"In my face are
All men reversed—
Nay, not in fortune
But in form!
Look deep within me
And be shown
How evil left becometh right,
And stalwart right,
The devil's own!"

"Oh! A riddle!" Catriona exclaimed, delighted.

"Aye," Tavish agreed, seeming relieved to have something to discuss with the pair and lessen his discomfort while his horse drank. He played with his mount's reins, blushing under her gaze. "I—I am fond of riddles and such. Can ye guess who 'I' might be, my lady?"

"I shall try! How did it rhyme again? 'In my face are all men reversed'? Was it so?"

"It was."

"Hmm. Then we must ponder what it is reverses, must we not, Roarke?"

"The Wheel of Fortune," Roarke suggested. "It spins

262

men one way, then the other, bringing good luck then bad, in turn."

Tavish grinned. "A worthy try, my laird, but a wrong one!"

"Aye, for it says ye must look deep within my shining face," Catriona reminded Roarke. "And a wheel has no face! Is it mayhap an amulet, Master Tavish? One with pagan runes scratched upon its 'shining face' t' ensure good fortune and repel evil?"

"I regret, my lady, ye are also wrong!" Tavish said gently.

She frowned, and for a moment both she and Roarke were silent, thinking hard.

"Well, my laird and lady? Do ye give up?" the grinning steward inquired at length, his confidence growing by leaps and bounds. "Do ye admit I've bested ye?"

"Nay, not so soon!" Roarke growled. "And furthermore, I willna guess on an empty belly, mon! This even' at supper, I will gi'e ye your answer."

"And if ye canna guess . . . ?"

"Never fear, 'twill come t' me, laddie!"

"Ye wouldna care t' place a small wager on that, would ye, ma laird?"

"Aye, I would!" Roarke declared rashly, goaded by his steward friend's smiling confidence. "A gold piece says I'll win!"

"Certain as that, are ye, sir?" The steward's brows rose. "Och, verra well, 'tis agreed!" Tavish said. "And here's my hand on it!"

The two men clasped hands to seal the wager, and then, whistling jauntily, Tavish led his horse from the water, swung astride it, and rode off with a doffing of his cap.

"That cocky young whelp!" Roarke muttered. "But this time I shall prove him wrong! He may best me at chess a time or two, but he willna confound me wi' his cursed riddling, that porridge head!"

Smiling in amusement, Catriona watched as Roarke

untethered their horses. He led them to her side and held her stirrup, offering his arm to help her to mount. Settled comfortably in the saddle, she watched him do likewise, then urged her horse to follow his as he led the way between the trees.

The day had been idyllic, a day t' cherish in her memory, which contained few such glorious days.

"Roarke?" she called after him, ducking to avoid a low-hanging branch that crossed their path.

"Aye?"

"For a gold coin, I'll tell ye the answer myself," she offered.

"Now who's the wee cheater, eh, Lady Cat!" he accused, his eyes scorning any possibility that she might know the solution when he did not. But despite that, he didna refuse her offer, she noted!

Chapter Nineteen

"Well, my laird Roarke? D' ye have an answer t'. ma riddle for me?" Tavish challenged after supper that even'. "Or will ye add your gold coin t' those wee lovelies in ma sporran?" The steward tapped the coin purse of fur that hung at his belt and winked.

Roarke set down his goblet, playing for time as he made a great show of wiping his lips on his fist and pushing back his chair. He stood and came slowly around the trestle to stand before his companion, tapping him in the chest with his index finger.

"On the contrary, Master Steward, 'tis *your* gold coin that will keep *mine* company this time," he countered, grinning.

"Then ye've solved my riddle?"

"Aye. I have. After all, it wasna difficult," Roarke said pompously with an airy wave of his hand. "Any but a fool could solve it!"

From somewhere at his back, he caught the sound of a feminine giggle, hastily smothered and disguised as a fit of coughing. *Jesu, that wench!* he thought with a flicker of irritation, *Could she no' contain hersel' for a wee while?*

"Very well, then, my laird. Let's have your answer! Who am 'I'?"

"Weel, it came to me that ye'd been gazing into

265

the water when ye set us this puzzle, laddie, and I began t' wonder if 'twas not the pool that had brought this simple riddle t' your mind. Who are ye, ye ask, Master Riddler? Why, 'tis a *looking glass* ye are, to' be sure! When one looks into the mirror's 'shining face', he sees an image of himsel', does he no'—but all parts are reversed! So does the left hand—which all know is the hand used by the wicked who do the devil's work—changed to 'stalwart right', and right t' left in its turn!"

Tavish's expression was as easily read as a mirror now—and his "shining face" reflected his disappointment, Catriona thought guiltily as the puir laddie delved into his sporran and drew forth the promised wager. He tossed the coin to Roarke, who caught it in midair, bit its edge to test its gold content, and straightway tucked it into his own bag of coinage.

"Ye win, Roarke, fair as may be!" the steward conceded. "But now, just t' prove yer arena a poor sport, what say ye t' another riddle and another wager? We'll double the purse this time?"

"Enough, good Tavish, enough! My lady can scarce keep her eyes open, and I have pressing business t' tend to on the morrow. Some other time, mayhap?"

"Very well, sir. A guid night t' ye, and t' yersel', Lady Catriona. May sweet dreams attend ye both."

He made them a bow as Roarke took Catriona's arm and raised her to her feet.

"What's ails ye, laddie? I'm no' in the least tired!" she hissed as they left the hall, offering "Goodnights" and "Sleep-ye-wells" to one and all as they did so.

"Aye, I ken," Roarke acknowledged, taking her elbow as they mounted the stairs and all but chivvying her up them in his haste. "But there was something I wished t' ask ye."

"What?" she demanded, her curiosity piqued, her green eyes searching. "What is it that couldna wait?

"Ye'll find out soon enough, ma curious wee Cat. T' your bower wi' ye!"

Once within her bower, he made no attempt to kiss her, as she'd half expected he might. Rather, he led her across the chamber to the looking glass she'd brought from Erskine, along with her harp and some of her garments. It hung now upon the wall in its gilded wooden frame, much as it had once hung there.

"Look!" he commanded, standing behind her with his hands planted on her shoulders.

"Aye, sir, I am."

"Guid lass. Now, raise your right hand."

She did so, and simultaneously her reflection raised its left.

"Ye see? In my face are all men reversed!" Roarke declared with obvious satisfaction. "Tavish's riddle was right!"

"Aye, and what of it? 'Tis no mystery t' *me*, as well ye ken," she reminded him with a sharp look. "Unlike yersel', I've known the looking glass reverses all things since I was no more than a bairn. It used t' fascinate me t' gaze into it and wonder if another world existed within! My own belonged to my lady mother. One of a pair, it was," she added.

"Aye. And did its partner hang in the tower chamber your father slept in?"

"I suppose it did, tho' I never gave it much thought before," she allowed, wondering what all this was leading to.

Roarke grunted. "Now, lass, I want ye t' think back a wee bit—and think verra, verra hard. D'ye recall the day I told ye who ye were?"

"Most clearly. Jesu! How could I forget!"

"Aye, how could ye! And the dreams that came after—d' ye recall them at all?"

"I do indeed, sir—and far more vividly than I care to!" She shuddered delicately, and crossed herself.

"Ye told me that night ye saw a woman slit her father's throat, and ye mimed for me how it was done." Seeing her nod agreement, he continued. "Show me again, exactly as ye did that night."

"Very well," she agreed, and, eyeing the dirk at his belt asked, "May I, sir?"

He drew the dagger forth and handed it to her by the blade. "I'll play the part o' your father, and ye shall be the wench."

"Then ye must lounge across the bed — aye, like so, but lean up a wee bit on yer elbows — that's the way!" she approved. "Now, angle your jaw up, like so, as if ye were offering your whiskers t' be shorn. Perfect! Now, the wench was here, in the shadows, just as I am now. I couldna see her face, ye understand, only her hands — so pale and soft! — as she raised the dagger and brought it down across my father's throat. Like — so!"

Her hand swooped down, the blade slicing air scant hairbreadths from Roarke's windpipe, but then she gave a small cry and flung the dirk across the chamber, as far from her as she could. She rubbed her palms together as if they were in truth stained by blood, and implored him, "Oh, Sweet Jesu, enough! Dinna ask me t' show ye again, for I canna! 'Tis . . . tis far too painful!"

He went to her and, standing behind her, encircled her trembling body with his arms. Drawing her close, he promised, "Nay, dearling, I will ask ye but one thing more. Are ye *certain* the wench held the dirk in her right hand as ye saw her?"

"Aye," she said after a few seconds' thought. "Why?"

"I may be wrong," Roarke said slowly, "But I'm nigh certain ye didna witness your father's murder directly, but reflected in a looking glass. Why else would ye dream of the mirror so vividly? And, furthermore, if what ye dreamt of really happened, then

268

ye saw the wench's *reflection*, not her true self — and therefore she slew your father wi' her left hand, no' her right! D' ye see now, my love? Precious few favor the devil's hand, and far less women do so than men. 'Tis a clue t' her identity, I tell ye!" he declared, the excitement in his gray eyes marked. "And with it, we draw closer t' finding her out!"

"Aye, but your reasoning is all founded on 'ifs' and my shadowy dreams, my laird! How can we tell if any of it were so?"

"We canna" he agreed heavily. "But what else have we? A comb of rowan wood, clutched in a dead man's hand. A few strands of night-black hair snagged in its teeth, which ye claim were taken from a horse's tail. Precious little t' find the murderers with, before they strike again!"

"Ye believe they will?"

"Aye, lass, I do." He smothered a yawn, and stretched. "For now, enough of this ugly matter. 'Twas a long day, and we should away t' bed. Besides, as I told that pup, young Tavish, I've pressing business t' tend to on the morrow."

"Ye do? Och, I thought ye but made excuses, my laird!"

"Excuses? For what purpose? T' steal ye away t' ma bed, ye insatiable wee minx? Och, lassie, my pardon, but ye ha'e drained me sorely this day," he apologized with a grin. "On the morrow, mayhap?"

His clothing removed, he tumbled to the bed and stretched out his limbs with a groan of sheer, manly pleasure, his eyes fluttering closed.

"What business?" she inquired curiously, tending to her own disrobing.

"On the day following Candlemas, I sent riders far and wide along the Borders to Corbin's sister keeps. Under flag of truce, these messengers carried greetings from mysel' to both allies and to enemy clans in their keeps. They requested that the lairds join me here at Corbin in the month of April."

"Ye did? But for what reason?"

"To discuss pressing matters that concern us all."

"Ah. The Normans?"

"Aye, my wee wren, the Normans. Now, will ye come t' bed and keep me warm?"

"I will, sir, if ye'll answer but one question more."

"Ask it," he urged her with an enormous yawn.

"Where's my gold piece, ye cheating rogue!"

Chapter Twenty

True to Roarke's promise, the first of the great Border lairds came riding up the steep hill to Corbin the following morning. Hamish, the Frazier of Glenmuir, was the first to arrive, Fionna noted from her bower casement, resplendent upon a white horse with a *breacan* of his clan tartan flung proudly over his shoulders. He showed not an inkling of fear as he rode beneath the gatehouse, although as agreed upon, he'd brought with him only two of his men. Arrogantly, he entered Corbin's gates like a conqueror, rather than a once-time enemy, flying a white banner of truce.

He was cordially — if fleetingly — greeted in the inner ward by the gracious lady Fionna herself, who had, along with the lady Elyse and their womenfolk, seen the brace of boars killed the previous day butchered and roasted for a fine feast, along with numerous other dishes to tempt the appetite and palate. No one would have cause to mock the hospitality of the Gilchrists, a furiously blushing Fionna had vowed as she fled the admiring eyes of Hamish Frazier to supervise her cooks and scullions in the kitchens.

Edwin of Dunnroth, Tam of Aberbrae, and Diarmid of Ban, all lairds of keeps that straddled the redstone cliffs along the easternmost marches, came next, followed within the hour by the Carmichael of Dearg Cruach, and the Elliot of Buidhe Clachan. By nightfall, over a dozen Border chieftains had congregated within Corbin's walls. And—though some might well have slept uneasily or not at all that first night, for fear of being murdered in their beds whilst they slept—not one of them had seen fit to leave come cockcrow of the following morning, much to Roarke's satisfaction.

Fionna beamed with pride as she looked down from the gallery of Corbin's chapel at the sea of bowed heads in the nave below. Here stood the strongest, most powerful men of the Borders; great men who were princes in their own demesnes and who had, for the greater part, never exchanged a civil word with each other till now, let alone come together to worship! And yet, as Father Augustine ended the Mass with the Blessing, and added a heartfelt plea that God would see fit to unite them all in brotherly love against their common enemy, to a man they answered with a rousing "Amen!" Roarke had, it seemed, accomplished the impossible task; that of bringing bitter enemies together beneath one roof, and of persuading them to set aside their differences and halt feuds of decades' duration in order to discuss the growing threat of a Norman invasion of their lands.

Fionna was lingering by the kirk steps in what appeared to be earnest conversation with her cousin, the lady Elyse, when Laird Hamish exited the chapel in the company of his men. As he drew level with her, she turned as if to take her leave and return to the hall, but drew up short on seeing the impressive chieftain standing before her with his sturdy legs braced apart, and his fists planted on his hips, effectively blocking her retreat.

"Good morrow, 'Ona," he boomed, grinning broadly. "A bonnie day, is it no'?"

"Why, Laird Hamish!" Fionna returned warmly, as if she'd just that second spied him there. "Good day t' ye! And aye, it is a bonnie spring morn — the bonniest we've had thus far!"

Hamish grunted agreement. "Aye, mistress, and one made all the bonnier for the sight o' ye standing there. Ye havena changed a morsel, 'Ona, not in all these years, by God!"

"And no more have ye changed, Ham — er . . . my laird Frazier." She dimpled and lowered her lashes, before adding teasingly, "Och, ye're a wee bit stouter aboot the middle, mayhap, but . . . ! Who isna these days?"

Hamish chuckled, and signaled impatiently to his men to leave him alone. To Elyse's astonishment, then amusement, he did likewise to her, before taking Fionna's elbow and leading her in a promenade across the bailey, away from the others.

"I meant it, 'Ona," he continued when they were out of earshot of the others. "Ye havena changed a wit! Ye're still the comely lass I knew and loved." He eyed her intently. "We would ha'e been guid together, ye and I."

"Aye, we would," she agreed. "But for King Duncan and his lechery!"

Hamish nodded soberly. He squeezed her elbow. "Aye, and but for my father and your own. Did ye ken I refused t' permit my father to withdraw my offer for your hand, 'Ona — even after we heard what had come aboot? I came here, t' Corbin and demanded t' see ye, but your cursed father refused me audience. I would ha'e wed ye, lassie, virgin or nay, wi' or wi'out the king's bastard in yer belly, I loved ye so well!"

"Aye, dear Ham, I dinna doubt ye would, nor that ye loved me. But . . . I couldna ha'e wed ye! Ye were your father's heir, after all. The future laird o' Glenmuir and the clan Frazier. Ye deserved better

273

than a soiled bride and another man's bairn. Ye searched for me, I heard tell, high and low, for many months."

"Aye, I did. Ye knew, but didna come t' me?" he exclaimed, his hand tightening angrily about her elbow as they walked.

"I knew, aye — and loved ye all the more for it! But — things had t' be the way they were, Ham. That night — well, suffice it to say King Duncan's actions changed everything. I knew that. I came to accept it, too, by and by, even if you could not. Come. Be honest wi' me! Your life hasna been so very bad, has it now?"

"In some ways, nay," he admitted reluctantly. "Mary was a good lass, in her fashion. Three sons she gave me, aye, and a half dozen daughters, too. All wedded, save for my second laddie, all mothers and fathers themselves, now. I have a full score o' grandbairns, 'Ona — an' no' near enough knees t' dandle them upon!" he declared proudly.

Fionna smiled. "Och, I envy ye, then, Ham, for I have not a blessed one as yet. But tell me, how has it been for ye since Mary — left ye?"

"Lonely, lass. Terrible lonely. I've thought often o' ye down the years — even before my Mary died, God forgive me! — and still more so since her passing, and your husband's death. Many's the time I've hated my father for the feud he started 'twixt himsel' and your father's clan. So, when your Roarke's messenger came t' Glenmuir at Candlemas, 'twas all I could do t' bide my time and wait upon this day!"

"Ye were so anxious for a truce, my laird?" Fionna inquired mischievously.

"Nay, ye wee redheaded minx — I was anxious t' see ye!"

"Och, ye flatterer! Ye can still make me blush wi' your bold words!"

"I'd do more than make ye blush, sweeting, gi'en a

274

nod and a wink, and half a chance."

"I dinna doubt it, sir — ye were ever a rogue!" Fionna accused with a trill of sparkling laughter, like that of a young girl.

"Will ye come t' Glenmuir, then, 'Ona?" he asked earnestly. "Will ye bide wi' us a while there in the summer? Ye'll have all the bairns ye could ever ask for t' cuddle and cosset!"

"I dinna ken if I should . . ." she began, startled that after all this time, Hamish Frazier should still harbor such obvious affection for her — and no reluctance whatsoever about showing it! Her heart had begun thrumming madly with his invitation, spurred on by the bright glimmer in his eyes. Her knees felt weak! She was no longer young, 'twas true, and yet she *felt* perilously light-headed and giddy this morn, walking beside him with her arm in his, like a lass with a third of her years. Two score and eight, she was, and her youth had fled. She'd been lonely since Cam's death, besides, for she had loved her husband well, and had ached to know a man's love in her life again. Still, she had waited, promising herself she wouldna remarry, would accept no other man's court, until Roarke was wed and a father himself. There had been offers of marriage aplenty, but she'd refused them all till now, yet what was the point in denying herself a chance at happiness? Time was flying by, and would wait for no one. What was she waiting for? What was she saving hersel' for? For old age to wither her last claims to beauty? For Death's cold arms, when she could have the warm, lusty arms of a lover such as Ham Frazier promised to prove? Impulsively, she nodded. Smiling, she told him simply, "Aye, my laird, I'll come — should ye send for me," and drifted away, leaving him staring after her with a broad and foolishly happy grin spreading 'cross his face.

* * *

275

As the McNair's daughter, Roarke had suggested the morning of the chieftains' arrival that Catriona take part in the talks to represent her Border clansmen. She'd agreed to do so without hesitation — though not without a good deal of anxiety!

Much had changed in the over twenty years since Kevin McAndrew had died and disinherited his daughter, Fionna, in direct opposition to the laws of heredity set forth by King Duncan's great-grand sire. Women could now inherit their fathers' or husbands' manors and lands, failing male heirs, and frequently did so. Accordingly, in the eyes of the law, Erskine now belonged to Catriona. She was the Lady of Erskine. It would be well, Roarke advised seriously, that Catriona learn all she could about the running of a great demesne — and what better place to start than with its defenses? Although somewhat nervous as to her ability to live up to her new position and its responsibilities, Catriona had agreed, and joined the rough lords about the trestle that morning.

All clad in their various clan *breacans* and bonnets sporting their clan badges, made jaunty with cock feathers, the Border chieftains brought a splash of bright color to the gloom of the hall, where a pale spring sun fingered its way but dimly. Catriona, proudly wearing her own green tartan *arisaid*, pinned with the silver wild-rose badge of the clan McNair at the shoulder, did her part to add to the display of Border clan pride. In Roarke's opinion, she was living proof of the fabled beauty of Scottish womanhood, with her heavy hair piled elegantly upon her head in a regal coronet of braids, over which she wore a sheer white veil held in place with a filet of gold, studded with green glass stones. For her part, Catriona was grateful now that Roarke had ordered her *arisaids*, much of her clothing, and some of her personal belongings — including her harp, Sweetsong, and that cursed looking glass!—loaded into coffers and brought to Corbin the day her memory had returned. No longer was she forced to rely so heavily on borrowing what she needed from Fionna, though her own garments were ugly, shabby things compared to the lady's finery, she thought wistfully. Her father had cared little whether she donned sackcloth and ashes, or velvets and gems . . .

Seeing all the chieftains lining the trestles in his great hall, Roarke stood and began the talks with a greeting to one and all.

"Ye have shown great wisdom and love for your land and your people by coming here t' day, my lairds," he told them, looking about the company, and silently marveling to see Fraziers seated next to Murrays, Douglases sharing a trencher with Gordons. "What we are met here t' discuss will change the future of our beloved Scotland. Whether that change shall be for good or ill rests in our hearts and hands, and upon the will o' God.

"I have here a proclamation for us all, sent from our king," he announced, holding up a rolled parchment which bore a scarlet ribbon and the red-lion seal of the Greathead himself. "Curiously, 'twas brought by messenger t' Corbin this very morn, just as we left the chapel. In it, Malcolm urges us all t' join forces. To prepare vigorously for a Norman invasion of our lands that will, he prays, be strongly rebuffed by the strength of a united Scotland. D' ye see, my lairds? The king's will and our own are in perfect accord. His wishes on this matter arrived as we were about to gather here! Surely 'tis more than coincidence that it should do so? I say 'tis an omen of good fortune! A sign that the course we take is right and just and wise, and that Scotland willna suffer the same fate as the conquered English!"

His words, their optimism, their patriotic fervor, stirred many hearts. Several of the chieftains felt compelled to stand and speak out, swearing allegiance to all men present for as long as Scotland needed them. Other Border chieftains were more pessimistic. They brought news from the south, rumors and facts that, stirred together, formed a heady broth that was hardly reassuring and Corbin's great hall rang with their horror stories in turn.

They told of vast Saxon manors—lands and keeps which had formerly belonged to dead King Harold's closest followers—being burned to the ground; of their Saxon lords being hunted down and taken in chains to France, or ruthlessly slaughtered when they resisted capture. Of their womenfolk suffering rape at the invaders' hands, or of being forced into marriage with the Conqueror's earls. They spoke of grain byres being emptied across the width and breadth of England, of herds of livestock being slaughtered indiscriminately to feed William's vast armies; of stables being emptied to provide fresh mounts for the warriors; of coffers of gold and silver, coinage and jewels being taken to swell the royal coffers of the new and greedy king. And everywhere the Normans went, they left a trail of blood and terror behind them.

"In truth," the Frazier of Glenmuir growled, his black eyes glowing with ire as he thumped his fist on the trestle before him, "William and his fyrds are like bloody locusts! They descend upon the Saxon manors and fields," he gestured with a sweep of his hand. "And when they rise again in their vast numbers, glutted, the land lies empty and scarred in their wake. Naught remains for those poor fellows who must struggle t' survive on their lordships' leavings! Hear me, fellow Scots! We mustna stand idle, and let these Norman curs do likewise with our lands! We mustna—nay, and we shallna, eh, laddies?"

"Nay!" his fellow chieftains roared in unison,

278

springing to their feet and clashing their arms together with a mighty clamor of metal against metal to signify agreement.

"Then, come, laddies! Let all those in favor drink a pledge, here and now! A pledge to remember this day at Corbin when our clan hatreds were cast aside and we took oath t' unite against the Normans, instead!"

"T' Bonnie Scotland, and our king—and t' Hades with the Bastard Duke and his Norman rabble!" cried Diarmid of Ban.

"Aye!" they roared as one. "Aye! T' keep Scotland for the Scots, we shall be one!"

They raised their pewter cups to the rafters, and drank deep of the potent "water of life," the *uisqe beatha,* that brimmed over them.

'Twas after the Terce bells had rung and daylight was beginning to give way to the amethyst gloaming before the threat of a Norman invasion had been fully discussed and a plan of action formulated to repel it; strict measures taken to drill their garrisons to peak performance, and a series of beacon fires and tolling bells agreed on for warning of any forthcoming Norman attack to be passed from one Border keep to the next. At last, when there was nothing more to be said on this matter, on Catriona's behalf Roarke brought up the matter that was secondmost in everyone's mind: the cowardly massacre of the clan McNair of Erskine and its chieftain's family.

Looking about the circle of faces, Roarke asked if any man present knew who had done this deed.

"Whist ye! Would that I could claim such glory for mysel', Roarke Gilchrist, but alas, I canna!" Hamish, the Frazier, growled with marked regret, casting a speculative eye at Catriona.

At once, she sprang to her feet, incensed. Two spots of angry color rode high in her ivory cheeks. Her green eyes crackled. Abruptly, she shoved back her chair and strode around the trestle to stand before Hamish's seat with the regal bearing of an enraged queen.

"Do ye forget sae soon, my laird," she asked quietly as her eyes blazed into his, "that we are met here under pledge of truce? And yet, damme ye, ye dare t' sit here in my verra presence and make sport o' the murders o' ma clansmen! By God, sir, ye lack discretion and honor both! 'S Blood, would that I were a mon! I'd cut out your cursed tongue an' feed it t' the corbies!"

"By the Cross, lady!" Hamish growled, grinning and not a whit abashed by her angry outcry, seeming more amused than anything. "Had your brothers possessed your fire and spirit — yea, or one tenth of your spleen! — the McNair would ha' taken me by the throat and slain me long since! Come, bonnie mistress, what say ye t' a wedding, and an end t' the feud betwixt our warring clans for all time? Would ye take my braw secondborn, Donald the Tall, as yer mon?"

In answer, Catriona drew back her hand and slapped the Frazier hard across the mouth. Her actions drew a shocked gasp from the onlookers that dwindled to a pregnant hush, yet she did not seem in the least cowed by it, nor by Hamish's livid expression.

"Damme me, sir! Ye willna speak o' marriage and the deaths o' those dear t' me in the same breath wi'out answering for it!" she gritted. "And as for your son . . . ! Och, I'd sooner mate wi' a viper, than wed and bed a Frazier!"

"Aye, *lady*, mayhap ye would," Hamish snarled, springing to his feet with his fists clenched. All pretense at good humor had vanished now. His lip was bleeding where his teeth had dug in from her blow. His expression was ugly. "But the keen knife o' your tongue has a one-sided edge t' it, does it no'?" he

280

jeered. "Ye dare speak sae loftily o' honor and respect for the dead, when 'tis rumored that ye bed willingly wi' the Gilchrist — the mon who slew your kinsmen!"

Roarke saw the hectic color that filled her cheeks, while all flesh around it paled to the color of chalk, and sprang to his feet.

"Enough!" he intervened, coming to stand between the pair and raising his hands to keep them from each other's throats. "We are met here t' join in peaceful discussion, and peaceful 'twill remain! Under threat of death, I willna permit any mon — or woman — t' pervert our true purpose: the freedom of Scotland. Hear me and hear me well, Frazier of Glenmuir, Catriona o' Erskine! Within these walls, we are not enemies, but allies. Within these walls, no feuds exist! D'ye hear me?" he thundered, his eyes glacial. "Lady Catriona, ye'll return t' your seat straightway," he commanded. "And ye, Laird Frazier . . . ?"

"Aye?" Hamish snarled.

"I charge ye t' ask the Lady of Erskine's pardon, 'else leave our company at once — willingly, or otherwise." Though this was softly spoken, not a man present doubted that Roarke could make good on his implied threat.

A crackle of expectancy ran through the gathering, for it seemed certain Hamish would refuse, and both men would unsheathe their swords, with bloodshed the outcome.

"A silver penny says Frazier draws metal," whispered Diarmid of Ban behind his hand to Edwin of Dunnroth.

Edwin eyed Hamish speculatively. Already, the Frazier's fist had closed over the hilt of his claymore. His jaws were clenched. Moreover, Edwin knew the Frazier for a proud, unbending man who'd hated the McNair and his clan with a passion.

"Nay! I'd be a fool t' wager against ye, mon," Edwin hissed back, his expression disgusted, "when the outcome's nigh certain! Whist! The Frazier will never back down, not now—!"

But to everyone's amazement, Roarke's stern reminder had tamped Hamish's anger. After a few tense moments, the Frazier relaxed and his shoulders slumped.

"Och, as ye will, then, Gilchrist," he agreed soberly, the fire doused from him. "As ye said, we've more pressing matters t' see to here than squabble among ourselves." He turned to face Catriona's seat and doffed his feathered bonnet, making her a stiff-legged bow. "I beg pardon of thee, my lady, for my rash words. In truth, 'twould seem old enmities canna be readily forgot on my part."

To Roarke's relief, Catriona responded far more graciously than he'd feared. Nor, to his surprise, did she demand Hamish take back his slurs upon her honor or even mention that he had, indeed, insulted her.

"Nor is it easy for me to forget my own, sir," she said coolly but with a regal inclining of her head. "However, in these hard times, we must all endeavor to cast old differences aside, for the good of all Scots. I accept your apology without rancor, and will speak nae more of it—or of anything else."

She didna, Roarke noted, hiding a smile, beg pardon for striking the Frazier, and in all honesty, he could not fault her! Hamish had deserved the blow for his sneering words.

"Well said, and there's an end t' it," Roarke declared with approval, returning to his place at the head of the table. "And t' my mind, such amicable settlement of our differences augers well for our future alliance, and should serve as an example to all men—" his lips twitched with a smile—"and ladies present. Now, to return to the matter we were discussing. The massacre of the McNairs. As the Frazier implied, many of ye have heard rumors, nae doubt, that 'twas my clan did this evil deed?"

A spattering of sober "ayes" circled the trestle.

"However," Roarke continued, drawing his claymore and holding it up by the point of the blade, " 'Tis a lie! There are those among ye who know me well. Friends as well as men who have been my enemy and faced me in battle more than once. Men who ken 'tis not my way to stab my enemies in the back whilst they sit at table, nor t' murder their women and innocent bairns. Nay, my lairds, when the Gilchrist has old scores t' settle, he faces his enemy. Meets him eye t' eye and hand t' hand! Therefore, I take oath before ye now, upon my *claidheamh mor*, that no Gilchrist mon took part in this butchery. That before God, we are innocent of wrongdoing!" So saying, he pressed his lips to the cold steel of his sword to seal the oath. " 'Tis done! Now will ye, as honorable men all, swear likewise upon your hilts?"

One by one, the Border lords drew their swords, upended them, and took oath upon the holy cross formed by the crosspiece and blade of their weapons that they were innocent of the deed.

When each man had sworn, Diarmid of Ban suggested that perhaps the deaths had had nothing to do with clan blood-feuds, but could have been the work of a wandering band of cutthroats.

"After all, my friends, wouldna a rival clan ha' claimed credit for the deed, were they responsible?" he pointed out.

Remembering the Frazier's earlier comment, many of the Border chieftains nodded agreement and seconded Diarmid's suggestion.

"Mayhap 'twas so, but think again on this. If 'twasna one o' us, nor a band of robbers, mayhap 'twas the Normans?" suggested Edwin of Dunnroth.

"Mayhap William's fyrds arena across the channel and busily occupied wi' defending their own Normandy, as our spies report? Perchance the information we've received is false—clever lies planted to start rumors. Rumors sent north for Scottish ears t' hear, as part o' a plot t' keep us off guard? Mayhap the Normans are *already* aboot their mischief in Scotland, and Erskine but the beginning!"

The men gave Edwin's suggestion careful thought, for he was a shrewd laddie was Edwin, and all present knew it.

"Och, surely not!" Catriona argued, surprising the lairds by her willingness to voice her opinion. They regarded her with interest of another sort as she continued. "For what possible reason would the Normans slaughter my clan, then vanish back o' er the Borders wi'out laying claim either t' Erskine or her lands? Or indeed, t' any of her riches? After all, lands and wealth are the very prizes the Normans covet, so t' strike and run makes no sense!"

"Aye, lads, the lady Catriona is right, it doesna make sense," Roarke agreed. "What think you now, Diarmid? Garreth?"

"Mayhap 'twas Norsemen, then?" Hamish suggested, speaking for the first time since his apology to Catriona when Diarmid and Garreth only shrugged in answer. "This bloody business reeks o' their barbaric ways!"

"Aye, it does," Edwin allowed, frowning. "But I fancy the Norsemen are too busy trying to wrest York back from under William's controls t' bother wi' us! And when did ye ever hear o' Norsemen slaughtering women, when they could carry them off t' the Danelaw for their pleasure? Nay, lads, we must think again!"

"I canna forget the hall at Erskine that day," Tavish said heavily, and to nobody in particular. "And I promise ye, I have seen my share o' battlefields!

284

There were bodies everywhere—some still with their eating knives in hand, their meats skewered upon them. Upon the rushes, there lay a young reeve with his throat cut from ear t' ear. And, scattered all aboot him, a wee bairn's playthings. Wooden balls, my lairds, of red and yellow and blue. A bairn's fairrings, in the midst of a slaughterhouse!" He shook his head morosely. "In faith, 'twas an incongruity I shall never forget, that innocence, that evil, side by side."

"I had hoped ye could cast light on this matter, my lairds," Catriona observed, "but alas, we have drawn no closer t' finding an answer t' our riddle," she finished, blinking back the tears Tavish's descriptions had stirred.

"Nay, my lady. But in time, as with all riddles, we shall have our answer," Roarke vowed. "Somewhere, there is someone who knows. And, sooner or later, a careless word exchanged in a tavern, or a pillow secret whispered t' a wench in the dark o' night, or a friendship grown bitter and sundered, will gi'e us the answer we seek. For now, I charge each one o' ye t' keep your eyes open and your ears pricked for any tidbit of information that will throw light on this matter. If any man should hear aught, he is honorbound t' pass on what he learned to each one of us. Is it agreed, my lairds?"

They cried "Aye!" to a man, and turned to the discussion of other matters.

And so, the mystery of the clan McNair's murders yet remained unsolved.

Chapter Twenty-one

"Ye seemed vexed, Cat?" Roarke observed that night when they'd retired to her chamber to sleep. His comment was somewhat foolish, considering she'd made little effort to conceal her anger since they and the Border lairds had turned from discussion to feasting in the great hall! The moment they had been left alone, her composure and genteel, charming manner had vanished. She'd become, in effect, an ill-tempered shrew—a woman he scarce knew, and wasna sure he cared to!

At supper that even', she'd declined even the choicest tidbits he'd offered her upon the point of his knife, scowled at each compliment he paid her, spilled the water from the fingerbowls into his lap, and intentionally kicked him in the shins more than once when he'd led her onto the rush-strewn floor to dance. That she had flirted with Tavish all night long, and smiled winningly at that cursed Edwin of Dunroth, had further brought home to him her unspoken message: I am sorely vexed wi' ye, Roarke Mac Gilchrist!

Now, with Master Longstaff making his lusty desires known as she undressed before her looking glass, and causing him considerable discomfort, Roarke was anxious to discover the reason for her ire, resolve it, and get on with more pleasurable diversions! Catriona having been tight-lipped and patently bent on hugging the cause of her anger to herself, he'd had no choice but to remark on her mood, and pray she'd be forthcoming.

"Vexed?" she snapped in answer to his comment, two red roses suddenly blossoming in her cheeks. She tossed her head irritably as she tore the veil from her head and hurled it from her, a shower of hairpins following as she unplucked her braided coronet with furiously trembling fingers. "Vexed?" she repeated scathingly. "Och, whatever was it gave ye *that* idea, mi' laird?"

"Was it aught I said?" he carried on, patiently ignoring her sarcasm, though his own irritation was building apace now.

"Hmph. Rather 'twas what ye *didna* say, but should have!"

"On what matter?" he demanded, feeling unjustly accused of a crime he didna commit.

"Ye but stood there," she seethed, spitting the words through clamped lips. "Ye but stood there, and let that windy auld bastard malign me! Ye let him call me harlot before all, and though ye vowed ye loved me, ye didna speak a word in ma defense, God rot ye, Roarke Mac Gilchrist! Not a single, blessed *word!*"

His jaw clenched. His gray eyes turned to pewter. His fists knotted. "So that's what's riled ye, is it!" he snapped. "D' ye count your blessed guid name worth a mon's life, then?" he demanded, rising to his feet and advancing upon where she sat. "Was it worth another slaughter such as that at Erskine, t' see yer reputation scoured t' lily-whiteness?"

She sprung from the stool, whirled on him with her green eyes blazing. "Aye—t' me it was!"

"Mayhap—but not t' me!" he growled. "Had I demanded Frazier beg your forgiveness for his insult, he would have refused. Marry, he would have laughed in my face and scoffed at our hypocrisy. Then I would have had no choice but t' challenge him, and the truce and unity for which I have planned since Candlemas would instead have become a bloody melée!" He turned her about to face him, his hand firm upon her shoulder as he did so, and looked down into her furious face with a stern expression. "I *have* bedded ye, Cat—aye, and done so more than once. And, so long as keeps have serfs, the bower walls have mouths and ears t' spread gossip on the four winds! Our lusty trysts havena been secrets since the first, lassie! Would ye have a man die by my hand, when he has spoken only the truth, however uncouth and intentionally cruel his chosen words? When he but said what every man in that hall knew t' be true? That we are lovers!"

"Nay—that I'm the Gilchrist's whore!" she cried bitterly. "That's what he implied. That—and that I'm sae lacking in honor and decency, I would sleep wi' ma kinsmen's butchers! 'S Wounds, could ye not have said something—spoke some lie, mayhap—t' salve my pride . . . to save my feelings?"

"I couldna," he denied bluntly, a muscle dancing in his jaw. " 'Twas a delicate moment. You're no fool— can ye not see that, woman? A word too much or too few . . . !" He shrugged and shook his head. "Experience has taught me that 'tis far better t' say too little, do too little, than say or do too much. If I wounded ye by saying naught, then I ask your pardon. And if ye thought me disloyal and uncaring for not defending ye, then I beg your understanding for my silence. Hamish Frazier is, at heart, a guid man, lass—one of the Border's best, though he has been both the McAndrews' enemy and the Gilchrist's in turn. He's Border-blunt, and oftimes speaks without giving thought to what he means t' say. But nevertheless, he'll make Corbin a fine ally, Catriona. I'd as lief have him fighting at my side than ag'in me!"

"Then go sleep wi' yer 'Border-blunt' sweetheart this night, since ye defend him so prettily and well!" she flung at him. "Let it not be said that ye slept this night wi' yer wee McNair harlot, curse ye!"

So suddenly, she cried aloud in shock, he lunged forward and grasped her by the upper arms. His face a swarthy mask of fury, he shook her till her teeth rattled. "I'll sleep here, wi' ye," he ground out, "and enough o' this nonsense! T' your bed, woman, and await my pleasure!"

"I'll not!" she cried. "I am done wi' ye! Sleep here ye may, ye bastard, but ye'll sleep here alone!" she spat, tearing free of his arms and running for the door. "I canna bear t' make my bed beside ye this night, ye . . . ye traitor!"

In three swift strides, he caught up with her at the door. He wound his fist in a handful of her chamber robe, jerking it down to bare her shoulders as she was brought up short by its folds.

"Ye think t' run through Corbin halls half dressed, and with a keepful o' lusty rogues who'd welcome ye in their beds? Damme ye, woman, ye'll go no-where — not like that! Not if I have t' chain ye to me this night!" he swore.

"Nay?" she jeered, her eyes brilliant as she glared up into his face, just inches from her own. "But what would ye care for whom I played the whore, sir? You, who canna defend me for fear o' a wee bit o' bloodshed!"

Her naiveté, her unthinking, careless words, incensed him as nothing she had said or done to date had succeeded in doing. Christ's Blood, she surely knew not of what she spoke . . . had surely never seen a mon dead of the sickening, gaping wounds made by a sword, else she couldna — wouldna! — speak sae rashly! A red rage filled him, swimming before his eyes. A red rage, and a powerful lust t' tame and tamper her fury, to teach her once and for all time that he was her laird, and wouldna be summarily disobeyed.

"If 'tis whore ye'd be, then 'tis for me ye'll spread your thighs, my lass, none other!" he vowed grimly. "And 'tis for my coin and favor ye'll lift yer skirts."

She sucked in a horrified gasp as he shoved her roughly back against the cold stone wall, breathing heavily as he thrust up the hems of her chamber robe, baring her to the waist. She cried out as his cruel knee forced her knees, then thighs, apart, but then her cries were stanched by his mouth as he forced it down upon hers, hungrily forcing her lips to open. His kisses were brutal, hurting. The hand that found the softness of her breasts beneath the parted fronts of her robe and caressed them was not tender and gentle with her sensitive flesh, but greedy and marauding. He didna go so far as to hurt her, thank God, but he came close enough t' make her cry out in upset and dismay, silently yearning for the tenderness and gentleness with which he'd always made love to her before.

"Please, Roarke, dinna!" she whispered. "Not . . . not like this!"

In answer, he grunted and reached to unfasten the lacings of his breeks, baring his ready staff and bringing it hard against the joining of her thighs, which trembled violently as she stood there, pinned against the wall by his chest. With long, lean fingers, he sought out the fluff of curls that hid her mound. With deft moves, he had found her secret flower, had parted its velvet petals and released the nectar that lay within. Quite against her will, she gasped, for though rough and ready his touch was this night, he was yet so damnably exciting!

"Ofttimes ye've complained that ye're the Gilchrist's whore, mi'lady," he rasped, his eyes burning like banked coals as he gazed pitilessly down into her tear-streaked face, continuing to enflame her with his intimate touchings. " 'Tis a word ye bandy carelessly about, tho' with little understanding o' its true meaning. I have dealt gently with ye, Catriona, since ye came here. I havena ravished ye, nor debauched ye for my perverse pleasure, nor cast ye aside to be serviced by my garrison, though this be the sorry fate of most other lassies who fall into enemy hands. Now, ye shall have a taste o' the dark side o' passion, where a man's will is all, and a woman but a vessel for his lust for the price o' a coin!"

So saying, he reached behind her and gripped her buttocks in both his powerful hands, raising her up so that her feet left the floor and she was braced against him for support. In an instant, he'd thrust forward and was buried deep within her; so deep she cried out and gripped his upper arms with fingers like talons. Raising her legs, he wrapped them about his waist and began moving against her, covering her mouth once again with his own as he kissed her savagely. He thrust hard and deep between her thighs, until he knew the rough wall of stone behind her must surely have burned her lower back. Stepping backward, he kicked his breeks aside and staggered with her to the heap of furs strewn before the hearth and the warmth of the fire crackling there, lowering her onto her back.

"How now, my bonnie harlot?" he panted. "Have ye had enough o' your laird's punishment?" Her eyes were shut. Her lower lip was caught between her teeth. He couldna judge if she was transported by ecstasy, or rigid wi' hurt.

To his surprise, her green eyes flew open, and a wicked smile lit up her face. "Nay, my laird, not nearly enough!" she vowed naughtily, wriggling in a blatantly wanton fashion beneath him that nigh caused Master Longstaff to give his all straightway.

Astonished, he threw back his dark head and

roared with laughter, all anger forgotten as the minx surprised him yet again. So, she'd enjoyed his lusty punishment, had she? Thrilled t' the new lesson he'd taught her? Well, by God, he'd show her another! He withdrew, grinning as he saw the disappointment fill her face.

"Turn, ye exasperating, wee she-devil!" he commanded huskily, fondling her breast while his eyes held hers captive. "If ye've a mind for some lusty loving this night, then I'm of a mind t' teach it to ye! Over, my lass, onto your belly wi' ye."

She rolled over, and at once he was upon her, his hands sliding beneath her to cup both swollen breasts and fondle her aching nipples. A moment more, and she felt the graze of his hands upon her buttocks briefly as he positioned himself between her legs, and then a mindless blaze of desire surged through her as he slipped into her sheath from behind.

"Oh!" she sobbed, and ground her face into the silky pile of furs beneath them. Gritting her teeth, she arched backward, taking him deeper than ever before.

With such passion and novelty, the end was not long in coming. Like a blast from a furnace, lusty passion swept them up in a breathy roar that scorched them to the core, then spat them out with a roaring breath that left them spent and steaming.

In the aftermath of their frenzied coupling, Roarke lay back and stared at the shadows made by the fire overhead, each breath wheezing from his lungs as if from a cracked bellows — and hers little less marked! She giggled on the ruddy shadows, and Roarke swatted her rump with a playful palm.

"By all that's holy, woman!" he managed to utter finally. "If ye ever decide t' take on that ancient profession, ye'll grow rich as Midas!"

She rolled over to lean across him, and playfully tickled his handsome face with a strand of her inky hair. "Thank ye kindly! I'll keep that in mind, good sir," she promised cheekily.

Several moments of silence passed before either of them spoke again. It was Catriona who broke the silence, raising her head from Roarke's chest where she'd been listening to the thunder of his heart gradually returning to its slower pace. "Roarke?"

"Aye?" he mumbled.

"I was wrong."

"Wrong?"

"Ye were right."

"Right?" He was too drowsy for sensible speaking.

"Aye. Aboot the Frazier."

"I ken."

" 'Twasna worth a mon's life to deny what everyone knew anyway."

"Hmm."

"I'm sorry, Roarke."

"Hmm."

"Can ye forgive me?"

"Can ye forgive me?"

"For what?"

"I hurt ye . . . ye know, at first—did I no'? 'Twas unforgivable!"

"Och, ye daftie, ye didna harm me at all! Truth was, after I realized ye didna have it in ye t' really hurt me, no matter how angry ye were, I . . . I found it most pleasurable!" In the shadows, her cheeks grew crimson.

"Hmm."

"Roarke?"

"Aye?"

"Ye didna answer."

"Answer what?"

"Can ye forgive me? For being a porridge-head? For not understanding why ye couldna speak for me?"

" 'Tis already forgiven, ye wee goose. Sleep, will ye no'?"

"Roarke?"

"Aye?"

"I love ye, my dearling."

"As I love you."

"Truly?"

"Sleep, Catriona. Sleep!"

In the days that followed that night and the subsequent departure of the Border lairds to their own keeps, life at Corbin changed. Though Roarke had always devoted time each month to drilling his men in swordplay so that his keep would be well defended in event of attack, now he worked them in deadly earnest. He did not give much weight to Edwin's suggestion that the McNairs had been killed by Normans, but he preferred to take no chances. When—and if!—the Normans came, he'd be ready for them!

Each day, the men practiced their warrior's skills in the outer ward. The spring air grew blue with their yells and curses, grunts and ululating war cries. The spring sunshine sparkled on helm and breastplate, sword and dirk. The ground became a morass of churned mud beneath their boots.

At first, Catriona liked to climb the stairs to Corbin's battlements and lean from her favorite embrasure there to watch Roarke drilling his men, for he cut a bonnie figure in his battle helm and armor. Also, she never ceased to marvel at the strength it took to wield such weighty arms as they must use, let alone swing them aloft to strike a blow, for she'd helped Roarke off with his weapons and armor enough times by then to know full well the considerable weight of his two-edged sword, his claymore, alone.

Day after day, the men of Corbin trained on foot. They trained on horseback. They practiced with spear and dirk, with claymore and longbow, with the spiked mace and the dreaded crossbow. They wrestled. They marched. They practiced riding at speed.

By the time spring gave way to the first warm days of summer, no able man would have been spared rigorous training, Roarke vowed, from the youngest groom who had but ten winters to his span, to the oldest graybeard who numbered seventy. Even the simple crofters who tended the flocks were taught to defend themselves and protect the precious strips of earth that grew the barley and oats they farmed, and without which there would be scant food come autumn.

Graeme volunteered to ride out over the moors to set up targets upon which the serfs and crofters could hone their marksmanship with the deadly sling, the simple but effective weapon the shepherds used to slay marauding wolves, along with their hefty wooden clubs. He took his task most seriously, and was oft gone from the keep.

Sometimes, Roarke would have one half of his garrison play the part of hated Normans storming Corbin's walls, while the other half played the "noble defenders." Catriona—long since grown bored with watching them—grew to dread the sound of Roarke's bellowing cry of, "To arms, laddies! To arms!" each morn after they'd broken the night's fast, for she knew now that that bellow meant yet another day would pass without seeing him, except from a distance. Yet another day would go by without having him near. And, if that were no' bad enough, it also meant that more often than not, at night he'd be too exhausted to take her in his arms and make love t' her—and truth was, she'd grown to welcome his caresses and lusty love-play with an eagerness that sometimes frightened her! Blessed Mary, how quickly she'd changed from innocent to wanton with such an accomplished tutor as he!

Still, she could see the effects of his rigorous drilling, and knew that what he was doing was right and good. In but a few weeks, the men of his garrison who'd puffed and wheezed and fallen exhausted to the ground after but a few moments of these strenuous mock battles now managed to stay upright without sign of tiring for the duration of the supposed attack. Their stamina was much increased by practice. If the Normans came, Corbin would be ready for them — and with a "welcome" they wouldna expect!

Chapter Twenty-two

It was on a day in spring, when Roarke was still much preoccupied with his preparations for battle and she was feeling somewhat neglected by his perpetual absences, that Catriona awoke feeling out of sorts and sickened to her stomach for the first time. I' faith, she was barely able to fling aside her coverlet and spring from bed to chamber pot before she was overwhelmed by nausea!

Afterward, her belly feeling as hollowed out as an All Hallows' turnip, she shakily made her way back to her bed and crawled beneath the coverlet. Like a frightened child, she lay there all morning, staring bleakly at the smoke-blackened ceiling, refusing all offers of food and pretending illness when Fionna came to gently inquire after her. She was too preoccupied with wondering and fretting if what she'd feared had finally come to pass to think of aught else! Did she but have a bilious stomach? Was it the spring sickness of the belly that ailed her? Or . . . was she with child, as she feared? Her monthly courses were a whole sevennight past due, she discovered, counting on her fingers with a mounting sense of panic. Aye, surely she was breeding!

Her heart pounding, she slipped trembling hands beneath the cover and felt her stomach for some sign of a bairn quickening within it. But she found her belly still as flat and firm as it had ever been, and hope flared, briefly. Mayhap she was wrong? Mayhap she had miscounted the days? But alas, that hope was soon extinguished. She had counted properly and she — whose courses had never been tardy by so much as a day since her woman's bleeding began — was seven days past her time! And her flat belly proved naught, for if she was with child, 'twas yet early days. She'd seen enough of the serving wenches at Erskine swell up with her brothers' bastards t' know her belly wouldna begin to show for a month or two yet. Meanwhile, sweet Jesu, what should she do? If she told Roarke of her suspicions, would he make her his bride and give their child his father's name? Or would he turn her out, send her from Corbin to the cold comfort of a convent, as his grandfather had once cast out his lady mother, there to suffer the shame and hardship of giving birth to a poor wee lamb the world would cruelly christen "bastard"? With this awful thought, she cradled her stomach and wept until exhaustion overwhelmed her, for she couldna clear her mind of the look in Roarke's eyes on the day he'd sworn he'd never wed a McNair were she the last woman on earth. Nor could his avowals of love quite blot out the hatred she'd seen in his eyes then . . .

All that day, she kept to her bed. She did not leave it until the wee hours of the following morning, when the desperation of her plight and the loneliness of her spirit, combined with her terrible fears for the future, drove her to seek the consolation of Corbin's chapel.

Dressing, she made her way down the torchlit stairs to the great hall, cautiously picked her way between the sleeping servants and men-at-arms all huddled in blankets or furs about the fire there, and went out into the bailey.

No one was up or about yet, she saw, yawning and shivering, for the early morning air was chill. Already the last stars were melting from the sky. The moon's pale glimmer was dwindling, the sky growing faintly pink in the east. She inhaled deeply, fighting the dizziness and nausea that had assailed her as she left her bed, revived by the scent of dew on good, dark earth, so sharp, clean, and wholesome in her nostrils, it quelled her nausea. Picking up her skirts, she scurried the short distance to the wee kirk.

The tiny chapel of Corbin appeared to have been built far earlier than the rest of the demesne. Constructed in the shape of a cross with blocks of sculpted gray stone, it nestled alongside the great hall and reminded Catriona of a small gray sparrow tucked beneath the wing of a great dark raven. It boasted a tiny pointed turret, surmounted by an ancient cross.

Drawing her *arisaid* over her head, she turned the huge twisted-iron ring set in the arched door and shoved it open. It swung inward with a groan.

Inside was gloomy, the air heavily scented with incense, burned wax, and the mustiness of great age and dampness. The only stained-glass window faced east and took the shape of a many-petaled flower, somewhat like a daisy. Each of the petals contained a colored-glass rendering of one of the disciples. What little light there was at this early hour filtered through that window and took on the colors of old wine, aged mead, the blue of a deep loch, the rich green of damp moss. The tiny altar below it was covered with the altar cloth the lady Fionna had labored upon so long and diligently over the months of winter, snowy linen from Flanders embroidered with metallic threads of gold and silver about the borders, all beautifully worked. The crucifix and

299

communion platters, the crucibles placed upon the altar, the holy relic—a scrap of St. Cuthbert's robe, sealed within its reliquary—were all of chased silver, their luster the only brightness winking in the gloom.

Thinking at first that she was alone in the chapel, she made her way down the aisle towards the altar and one of the rows of rough, high-backed wooden pews that filled the nave, there intending to pray and beseech God to help her in her dilemma. But the low yet heated murmur of voices coming from the tiny west transept to her left alerted her. The solitude and privacy she sought wasna to be found here! Father Augustine, Corbin's priest, was no doubt hearing an early confession. She had no wish to intrude on so personal a moment—nor have some shame-faced penitent intrude on hers!

Casting about her, she spied a short stone staircase, leading above the west transept to a narrow gallery that overlooked the nave. Perfect! It was a place where the sick could be carried to worship without mingling with the hale and hearty worshipers in the chapel, or where the lady of the manor might pray, if reluctant to show herself in public—or where a sorely troubled young lass might sit in solitude and search her heart.

Lifting her skirts, Catriona mounted the stairs and went out onto the little gallery through a narrow archway. There, she knelt at the carved rail that fronted it. From here, she was afforded a view of the lower floor of the chapel, for the little gallery overlooked the apse and the nave, and the dark recess of the west transept beyond it on the other side. To all intents and purposes, she could be alone here with her thoughts and her God, she thought, gratefully kneeling, her ebony head bowed on her clasped hands.

Closing her eyes, she tried very hard to pray, but

soon realized, to her annoyance, that the hum of voices she'd heard from the west transept below were not fainter here, as she'd hoped, but rendered — by some trick of architecture or sound — more distinct, and doubly distractive. Snatches of conversation carried to where she knelt. She tried to deafen herself, to block out the voices in devout prayer, but she had never been very devout, if truth were known, and had always been readily distracted, and so in the end, she gave up all attempts at prayer and eavesdropped instead.

". . . warn ye, laddie . . . leave off wi' following! . . . I gi'e ye fair warning . . . 'twill go badly . . ."

"Ow! Ow! Please master, I didna mean t' vex ye . . ."

". . . nevertheless, ye have, runt, an' . . ."

"I swear . . . ! I'll be good . . ."

"Desist . . . will he believe? A misbegotten oaf such as yersel', or . . ."

Such strange fragments of conversation! Catriona was at once overwhelmed by curiosity to identify the speakers, and to hear the rest of what they spoke and decipher what it was they discussed so heatedly!

She peered between the carved wooden spindles of the railing, but could make out only the back of one of the speakers, a short man whose features — like the entire person of the other speaker — was cast in the deep shadow of the transept. Frustrated, she stood and leaned over the railing, craning her neck while hoping they wouldna see *her*, instead, but she could see nothing more standing than she could kneeling.

"Damme ye! I willna stand for it . . . Once was enough! . . . next time . . ."

"I beg ye . . . nay master! Dinna . . . Ow!"

She hurriedly ducked back down moments later, kneeling again, for a heated quarrel had now been enjoined, judging by the raised voices. It seemed prudent not to reveal herself for the moment! Undoubtedly, her presence would embarrass the speakers — perhaps even turn their anger on her, if they believed she was spying upon them from the concealment of the gallery!

But then, as she listened, she heard someone rasp an oath, another squeal out in pain yet again, followed by the rapid, clipped footfalls of an angry man as whoever had cursed left the western transept and strode through the nave. Moments later came the thunder of the door as he flung it open and passed through it, letting it slam shut loudly in his wake.

Now, only the shorter man whose back she'd seen remained. And, in the ringing silence following the other man's explosive exit, this one rubbed his ear as if to soothe a hurt, yet chuckled as he did so, the sound echoing over and over in the chapel's hollow belly. Jesu! It was laughter t' set the hackles on Catriona's nape rising in prickly waves, and make her pulse suddenly quicken in apprehension!

Dry-mouthed, she peered down into the transept, wondering if the second man would hurry after the first to continue their quarrel outside — or, mayhap, end it in blows? In either event, she had no wish t' be a witness! Perhaps 'twould be better if she went away, and returned to the chapel at some later hour?

She rose from her knees, using the railing for support, yet even as she did so, the man who'd chuckled left the shadows of the transept and stepped out into the rainbow-colored morning light, now falling through the stained-glass window to pattern the nave with mottled, watery hues. She gasped, for he was no stranger to her. One of the voices she'd heard belong to the half-wit, Hal!

He stood there, his shoulders thrown back, his fists planted on his hips. A small, smug smile played about his usually slack mouth. His blue eyes were no longer vacant, but alive and lit with—intelligence!

She hesitated for an instant, uncertain now whether to make her exit or remain where she was and hope he would not see her. But as if alerted by some sixth sense that she stood there, looking down on him, Hal happened at that inopportune moment to glance up. Their eyes met, a startled, then accusing blue-gray to widening green.

"Good morrow, my lady," Hal greeted her with a sketchy bow, tugging on his lank forelock. His tone was almost that of a normal country youth, she fancied, crisp and alert as any lad's. But then—in a single, quicksilver moment—he was again the slack-mouthed, vacant-eyed lout he'd always appeared, with shoulders slumped, with arms dangling, his manner servile. Blinking, Catriona wondered if she'd misread his expression and his arrogant, cocksure stance—or the intelligence in his tone?

"Good morrow, Hal," she said curtly, nodding. "What do ye here at this early hour?"

"Hal can come here if he wants. Father Augustine said so," he told her sullenly. "The lady can come. And so can Hal. This be God's house. All are welcome within. Mother said so."

"Your mother spoke truly," Catriona acknowledged, although tight-lipped with irritation. "The House of God is open to all. But . . . who was it ye were talking with, Hal?"

"Talkin?" he repeated slowly, scratching his head as if he had to think through what she'd said.

"Aye, talking?" she gritted, wondering if he was, perhaps, playing some game with her, and not near as dull-witted as he appeared.

"Hal talked with no one," he muttered, cocking an eyebrow up at her as if to gauge her response to this patently false answer.

"Dinna lie t' me, laddie!" Her grip tightened on

the railing. "I heard ye."

"Heard Hal, my lady?" His expression was impassive.

"I did. Ye were quarreling."

" 'Twas Father ye heard, mistress! Hal was talkin' wi' the good priest. Kind t' Hal, Father is, not like the others here. Father Augustine doesna box Hal's ears like that bitch, Flora, nor call him a 'stupid runt', like others are wont t' do."

"Hal! All shame on ye! D' ye not ken 'tis wicked t' speak falsely o' others when they arena here t' defend themselves! Whist, laddie, enough o' your fibs! I canna believe Mistress Flora would be so unkind t' ye!"

"I dinna care! 'Tis true! I hate her! She boxes poor Hal's ears, she do. Makes puir Hal do all the work ye set for her. 'Fetch up the witch-woman's victuals, Hal!' she sez. 'Hasten and draw water, 'else she'll "witch ye, sure!' she sez. But 'tis her that's wicked, mistress! Her and that Master Ogden, I seen 'em in the stables, och, aye, Hal has! They make the two-headed beast together, bumping up and down in the straw, all naked and moaning. 'Aaah, ye great brute! Aah! Faster, my laddie, faster, harder!'" Hal mimicked in a high, feminine voice. "That's what Flora says, just like so, mistress. 'Tis no lie, for Mother said 'tis sinful to speak falsely, and Hal isna sinful . . ."

"Enough!" Catriona snapped, angry color and embarrassment staining her cheeks. Although she hadn't believed Hal at first, his words sounded far too like Flora and so unlike anything dull-witted Hal could fabricate, she couldna discredit him entirely. After all, Flora and Ogden *were* lovers, she was certain of it, so perhaps if he was telling the truth on that score, he was also honest about her spiteful treatment of him? Still, she was not about t' be diverted from asking him questions about what she'd over-heard by either his comments or his graphic descriptions of Flora's lusty trysts with her swain!

"Dinna try to turn my questions aside wi' yer complaints and tattles of Flora's doings, my laddie!" she continued sharply. " 'Twasna Father Augustine ye quarreled with here but moments ago, I know—and nor was it Flora. I ask ye again. Who was it ye met with?"

In answer, his expression became stonily blank. His lower lip jutted mutinously, giving his narrow face a pugnacious cast.

"Hal!" she warned again, her voice stern. "I'm the McNair o' Erskine now, and your lady. Ye must answer me! I command it!"

Without another word, Hal spun on his heels and ran from the chapel. And, by the time she'd run down the gallery stairs and out of the west door after him, he had gone. There was no sign of him in the bailey, either, where the sky had lightened to a rosy pink since she entered the chapel. Squinting, she saw that the sun had risen over the mist-shrouded peaks of Ben McAlpin, saw the cocks stretching their necks to crow, heard the hounds yawning, and the smithy firing up his forge. The yeasty aroma of fresh morning bread baking in the ovens carried on the breeze. Like Hal, night had fled.

Shaking her head, Catriona made a mental vow to question Hal further about the peculiar conversation she'd overheard when next he put in an appearance. But her intention was soon forgotten when she returned to the great hall to find the lady Fionna, her cousin, the lady Elyse, and their ladies-in-waiting already up and abroad, and breaking the night's fast at the long trestle tables with bowls of porridge sweetened with honey, broken meats and cheeses, and hunks of dark bread.

"Good morrow, dearling!" Fionna greeted her fondly, and the lady Elyse also cast her a shy smile of welcome. She moved over to make room for the girl to sit beside them on the bench. " 'Tis a bonnie spring day, is it no'?"

"Bonnie indeed, my lady, and the sun already up and shining, too," Catriona agreed, smiling wanly in return. "Ye keep early hours, madam, to be up and about at cockcrow!"

"Aye, chick, but no more than do you! Tell me — are ye quite recovered from your sickness?"

"So 'twould seem, my lady," she hedged. "But nevertheless, I couldna sleep. In truth, I tossed and turned the whole night long!" She sighed. "And so, at first light, I sought out the solitude o' the chapel."

Looking at her weary but lovely face, with faint lilac shadows like pale bruises beneath her green eyes, Fionna had no reason to doubt that she had indeed spent a sleepless night, or that she had been sickly.

The three women looked up at the sound of footfalls. They saw Roarke striding towards them across the hall, accompanied by Tavish. The two men bade the ladies a good morning, doffing their caps.

Roarke took his carved chieftain's chair, helping himself to cold mutton while asking a serving man to bring bowls of porridge for himself and the steward. Taking up the eating knife that hung from a chain at his belt, he speared a piece of mutton and observed, "Ye look a wee bit peaked this morn, ma lovely." His brows raised in inquiry. "Did ye no' sleep well wi'out me beside ye, sweet?" he teased, for he had passed the night in the garrison with his men — a valiant gesture designed to boost morale and foster a spirit of comradeship.

"Nay, my laird, I didna," she admitted, lowering her lashes and staring at her trencher of victuals as she felt heat and color rise up to fill her cheeks.

Och, she couldna bring herself t' look him full in the face! If she did, she knew that she'd be lost, for every line of his handsome features had grown sae blessed dear to her in the past months, she couldna bear even t' think of leaving him, of never seeing him again! And yet, she thought, moistening her lips, could she be certain he'd let her stay if she told him she suspected she was carrying his child? Could she bear to have him wed her for the child's sake, when in his heart he felt nothing for its mother, other than a sense of duty and obligation? Nay, she decided. She'd say naught, for the time being. She must think things through more carefully, make the decision of whether to tell him or nay wisely — not allow herself to be swayed by his handsome face or his nearness, or even her own burgeoning feelings for him. Her decision must be one that would stand the test of time, the one best for herself — and the well-being and future of the puir wee bairn she was nigh certain she carried.

Chapter Twenty-three

The first day of May dawned bright and sunny with fleecy white clouds drifting upon a field of azure sky, much to the delight of everyone at Corbin.

In the past s'ennight since Catriona had overheard that peculiar quarrel between Hal and the unknown man in the chapel, Corbin had begun to receive a thorough spring cleaning at the lady Fionna's command. Every serf from the youngest spit-boy to the oldest graybeard had been set some task or other by the chatelaine or her ladies. One and all, they fell to cleaning and scouring with a will, for woe betide those who were caught slacking! Those sluggards might well find themselves forbidden to take part in the May Day revels as their punishment, and none at Corbin wanted to be left out of the fun!

Accordingly, the great hall had been swept clean, thoroughly dusted, and scrubbed of winter smoke and grime, as had both family and guest bowers. The garderobe had been shoveled out, the midden's bounty carted off t' fertilize the newly planted crops, and the stables thoroughly mucked out and spread with fresh, fragrant straw. The kitchens and store-rooms had, under Mistress Joan's eagle eye, likewise undergone transformation, then all doors had been flung wide open to allow the stale air of winter to depart, and permit the fresh flower-and-grass-scented air and sunshine of springtime to enter.

On the last day of April, Fionna's ladies had gone a-Maying along the hedgerows of the Tweed Vale, returning to deck Corbin's walls with boughs of the seasonal mayflower — sweet-smelling white hawthorn blossoms — and see her flagstoned floors scattered with fresh rushes and herbs to replace the old ones. That day had also seen the Queen of the May crowned.

Some days earlier, one of the crofters' daughters — a shy, bonnie lass named Kirsty — had been chosen Queen by the common folk of Corbin, and there was great excitement in the air that lovely May Day morn as Ogden and some of his lads erected the Maypole in the center of Corbin's inner ward, and hung from its top the rainbow-colored ribands of the Morris dance.

When Queen Kirsty arrived in her flower-trimmed cart, all decked out in her prettiest kirtle with a garland of snowy mayflower crowning her golden hair, she would lead her chosen maids-in-waiting in an intricate dance about the pole, each maid carrying the free end of a riband in her hand as they pranced to the music of flute and tabor, and the pan-pipes of the shepherds. And, when the dance was ended, the pole would be left prettily braided after the ancient pagan customs of spring, and a lively feast would follow!

There was also a May Day fair in progress in a wee glen just outside the closest hamlet of Kelso, and the lady Fionna had given her gracious permission that all who'd worked well and hard the previous week might leave the keep to attend the fair after the Maypole dancing.

Each year, stalls laden with fairrings — ribands and

flower posies, velvet purses, glass-jeweled combs and other such frippery — were heaped with treasure trove to delight the wenches' eyes and tempt their pennies from their pockets. Other stalls groaned under mountains of bread wheels and cheeses, eggs, fresh fish, and savory smoked herrings, or "smokies," brought from St. Abb's, pickled eel from the marshes, and other produce arrayed for the good-wives' shrewd inspection, while the laddies could go there simply to fill their bellies on meat pies and blood sausage, bannocks, and scones and buttery shortbread, or to test their agility by climbing from one side to the other of a swinging Jacob's rope ladder, strung between two poles at a sheer angle and craftily designed to topple an unsteady lad to the mire!

There'd be contests to see who could catch a lard-smeared, squealing piglet, and another to discover who could climb to the very top of a well-greased pole without sliding down it. There'd be caber-toss-ing, tugs-o'-war and mountain racing, too, so that the young men might practice their skills and test their endurance before the great gathering of all the clans, presided over by King Malcolm at Glen Braemar each year in the summer months. And, after darkness fell, ale and mead would flow like water, and there'd be sword dancing about the fires on the heathery heaths: the proud sword-dance the men o' Scotland now danced on such festive occa-sions to commemorate their sovereign's victory dance some fourteen years before. Back then, it was said by those who were old enough to remember, the Great Head had crossed his sword with that of his fallen enemy's on the turf following a fierce battle and danced a spritely jig over the blades with both arms held aloft, one finger of each pointed skyward. The king had looked, the storytellers claimed, like a stag with its antlers proudly raised after it has successfully challenged a rival buck for a favored doe!

Whist, ye had t' be daft to purposely catch the lady's stern eye for some wrongdoing, and miss such funning as they'd have, the serving lads and wenches of Corbin told each other. Accordingly, they'd seen the keep scrubbed and dusted and swept until she fairly sparkled, and not one among them had been singled out for punishment—when the day at last came. Spirits at Corbin were therefore high on that first day of the month of May, save for one who couldna find it in her heart to smile, not even at the prospect of Morris dancing and a fair, for she and Roarke had quarreled bitterly the day before . . .

For a full week, Catriona had miserably hugged her lonely secret to her breast, sharing it with no one, hoping against hope she'd been wrong, and that her flow was but tardy. Alas, she'd been forced to admit by now that this was an unlikely prospect, for a full fourteennight had passed since her expected day had dawned. And so, for the past two days she'd been steeling herself to make her condition known to Roarke, before it became obvious.

Alas, 'twas not easy t' find him alone, much less broach such a delicate subject, for he was ever absent from her side, busy with his men and his preparations for battle! And then, as they sat at the morning meal on the last day of April, to her relief he leaned down and whispered in her ear that he would come to her bed that night. He promised to leave off drilling his men for the day following, that they might enjoy the May Day dancing and the fair together. Would she find such an outing pleasing, he'd asked, his gray eyes twinkling with certainty of what her answer would be.

"Aye, my laird," she'd accepted flatly, and had heaved a sigh.

311

Her lack of enthusiasm had caused him to wonder about the reason for her lackluster response. With raised eyebrows, he'd cast a sharp look her way, but her expression had revealed nothing. *She is but weary,* he'd decided, and with a shrug he dismissed the matter. Faint lilac shadows rimmed her eyes, standing out against the pallor of her complexion. Surely naught but weariness explained her lack of vivaciousness, that pinched look about her? Accordingly, he'd dropped a careless kiss on her cheek, promising, "Anon, then, sweet mistress. Await me in your bower this night, and we will renew our acquaintance most . . . memorably!" Without further ado, he'd left her for his men once again.

Before Roarke appeared on the threshold that night, a nervous Catriona had labored to make the bower a place that was both inviting and cozy. As the lady Fionna had taught her, she'd cast herbs and dried flowers onto the fire, so that when they burned the smoke would perfume the bower pleasingly. She'd doused all but a half dozen candles so that the light was mellow, the shadows warm and intimate, and had arranged soft pillows upon the bed to cushion her laird's head. A flagon of wine and a platter of tasty tidbits had been readied to delight his palate.

For her part, she'd gone to great pains to make herself beautiful—both to please Roarke and to bolster her own flagging confidence! After bathing herself in water scented with honeysuckle, she'd brushed out her long black tresses until they crackled and shone like polished jet, then donned a kirtle she knew Roarke favored—one of primrose yellow that he'd vowed made her look like the Queen of Elfland! She'd pinched her cheeks until they stung to bring the roses back to them before, certain all was in order, she'd finally ordered water heated and brought in kettles to her bower, seen the wooden tub filled for

312

her laird's bath, and perfumed the water herself with drops of mint oil.

She timed her preparations so well that the moment Roarke entered the chamber, he found her perched on a stool beside the hearth. Her skirts were draped prettily about her. Her harp, Sweetsong, was cradled in her lap. She was strumming and singing his favorite ballad, the rousing "Beowulf" when he flung the door wide, and the rush of surprise, then pleasure, then tenderness, that filled his face in turn as he looked about him gave her cause to hope he would deal kindly with her news.

"At last ye're come t' bed, my laird!" she cried, forcing a shy smile of welcome and wishing her lighthearted tone hadn't sounded so brittle and false. "Och, let me help ye off wi' yer helm, and see ye into the tub before the water cools!" She gestured to the wooden tub Flora's girls had filled with steaming water just moments earlier. "There! A good hot soak will rid ye o' all weariness, and set ye speedily t' rights."

Too exhausted to protest, Roarke gave her a lopsided grin and staggered forward to drop a teasing kiss upon the very tip of her nose. "Och, lassie 'tis guid t' me ye are indeed! Sweet songs t' lure me to your bower. Warmed water t' wash the reek o' sweat from my body — aye, and the bonniest lass o' the Borders to feast my eyes upon! Mayhap I'll please my lady mother and wed ye after all, eh, love?" he'd teased, chucking her beneath the chin.

With her painfully sensitive and uncertain mood, he could not have chosen his words more poorly that night! Not only did his flippant teasing vex her, it served to double her anxiety, for he'd implied that the only possible reason he would marry her would be t' please his lady mother! And, since he'd vowed he'd never wed a McNair, she could not help believ-

313

ing his careless words were more than half true and took them at face value.

Blinking back tears of hurt, she bit her lip and bustled about to help him off with his heavy helm, his surcoat, shirt, and breeks, finally straddling each of his legs in turn to haul off his boots. She hid her face with her hair as she did so, hoping he would not see that she fought tears. That great, unfeeling brute! Jesu! How sorely his careless words had stung! So sorely, she didna ken if she could bring herself to tell him about the babe now. And yet, somehow, she must, she thought desperately!

Unclothed now, Roarke strode across to the tub, brushing her cheek fondly with his knuckle as he passed her. As always, the sight of him weakened her purpose, destroyed her resolve to remain quietly practical and emotionless until she'd done what she intended to do. Dry-mouthed, she watched him move about the bower with the light from candle and fire oiling his well-muscled body. She was all but transfixed by the way the sinews and cords rippled beneath the firm, manly flesh of his back and shoulders, mesmerized by the brawny width of his hairy chest, the lean span of his waist, the virile spareness of flanks patterned with old, silvery scars, as he stepped into the tub. He lowered himself gingerly into the steaming water, wincing at its heat, casting her a rueful little-boy grin when he glanced her way and caught her staring at him.

"Will ye join me, then, ma wee Cat? There's room and t' spare, if we cuddle close!" He winked at her.

Just to look at him like this, just to hear the sensual timber of his voice, stirred a wild passion in her blood! Her feelings shamed her, for they knew not inhibition, nor modesty, nor restraint. They were all hunger and pleasure-seeking. All reckless abandon and wanton yearnings. All manner of things she shouldna be thinking of at such a time!

"Nay, sir," she muttered. "I willna."

With rather more vigor than gentleness, Catriona at once snatched up soap and cloth when Roarke was settled. She knelt beside the tub and scrubbed his back and neck as if she were a sailor under threat of the cat-o-nine-tails, holystoning the deck of some leaking, barnacled barge. She studiously ignored Roarke's muffled grunts and groans as she buffeted his throbbing bruised body to and fro.

"For the love o' God, have a heart, lassie, lest ye bruise me anew!" he grumbled. "Even Graeme's stout staff didna thump me aboot today as ye do this even'! Enough, sweet Cat, enough! I'm no' a pot ye have t' scour, woman!"

But Catriona was merciless. "Lean back, sir, and let me scrub your chest," she snapped, tight-lipped, ignoring his pleas.

"Och, very well! I'll do as ye command, ma cruel wee dragon," Roarke resigned himself. Then he added with a drowsy chuckle, "But first, a kiss t' balm ma bruises, by your leave!"

He puckered his lips expectantly, leaned back and closed his eyes, only to open them again in disappointment moments later when the kiss he'd demanded was not forthcoming.

Ignoring both his wounded expression and his heavy sigh, Catriona kept her gaze riveted on his broad chest, pretending a sudden fascination with the way the whorls of dark hair upon it tossed in the water like sea anemones as she soaped him vigorously.

"Catriona? What ails ye, sweet?" he asked after some moments of quietly contemplating her expressive face. She had a sulky, brooding look to her, he fancied, though he could not fathom a reason for it. Several moments passed, but she did not answer him. "Damme ye, lass, when I speak, 'tis only right and proper ye should look at me!" he said sharply when she still made no response.

"I'm busy, my laird," she ground out, keeping her head lowered.

"So cursed busy, ye willna heed your laird's commands?" Roarke growled, a warning in his tone.

Reddening, she jerked her head up and glowered at him, making her eyes overly wide and staring — boggling, in fact! "There. Are ye content now, my laird? I'm looking at ye!"

"Aye, so I see — and wi' a sour and owlish expression t' curdle fresh cream!" he teased, not unkindly. In a gentler tone he asked, "Come, lassie, ye can tell me. What's gnawing at ye?"

"Naught t' bother yersel' aboot, I'm sure," she spat.

"Ye're no' wi bairn, are ye?" he demanded, eyeing her astutely.

Her head jerked up as if sharply jerked by a leash, her frightened eyes meeting his, then hurriedly looking away. Jesu and Mary, what magic was this? Was he a sorcerer, that he could read her mind so perfectly?

Stunned by his question, she hesitated, torn agonizingly between flinging a defiant, "Aye, sir I am indeed! And what will ye do about it?" at him, and in fiercely denying his accusation. Denial won out, however, for fear was her champion in this tourney. Catriona could not read the expression in his eyes, could not determine if an affirmative would please or infuriate him, and so cowardice and uncertainty compelled her to answer, "Nay, praise God, I amna!" in a vehement tone.

"Is there something else awry, then? Some hurt I've done ye that ye'd have me beg yer pardon for?"

"Naught!" she insisted, angry with herself now at missing such a God-sent opportunity to empty her heart, but unable to swerve from the course she'd taken.

"Then why d' ye not smile for me, my bonnie?" he asked, nonplussed. "Where's the fond, merry wee lass who lay wi' me in a woodland bower, and vowed she was Eostre? Where flown my Queen o' Elfland, who ensorceled me wi' her teasing smiles and bewitched me wi' her laughter?"

"Gone, Laird Gilchrist! Gone forever!" she flung at him crossly, though she was more angry with herself than with him. "Blessed Jesu, must a woman smile simply because *ye* ask it of her? Does what she wants count for naught? By your leave, I would be finished wi' yer bathing and seek my bed, sir."

"Weary, are ye, lovie?" he asked in a low, taunting drawl.

His sensual expression was so potent, so virile, she felt her blood leap in response.

"Why else would I seek my bed, ye lummox?" she tossed back at him.

"Och, ma wee wren, I can think o' another reason—can ye no'?" he purred.

She blushed. "Aye, I can. But surely my laird is too blessed weary from his swordplay t' think o' bedsport, or his lowly Catriona?"

Her caustic tone made him flinch, for she was not a lass give to sarcasm. That she did so now, he took for a sign that she was indeed sorely wounded—or angered—though the reason she should be so yet eluded him. Trying to draw out whatever hurt or lack of attention had soured her by gentle teasing and affectionate banter, he insisted in a husky timber, "Whist, I'm never too weary for swordplay o' that lusty sort wi' ye, ma elfin queen! 'S Wounds ye've stirred ma blood t' boiling! 'Tis like a cauldron, all a-simmer—and I've no woman but yersel' in mind t' cool ma broth!"

Her hands had fallen away from his body as they conversed. Now, they dangled slackly in the water. But as her green eyes met his smoldering gray ones, he moved his flanks. She felt his hardened shaft nudge against her hand — leaving her in no doubt that he was fully aroused, and ready t' make good his word! She cried out, and withdrew her hands from the water as if they'd been dipped in boiling pitch.

"Whist! What is it, lass?" he demanded, trying to sound innocent although shaking with laughter. "Was ma bonnie sword not what ye were after? Och, but if it wasna, then why were ye dabbling in this wee pond, ma lady? Were ye thinking t' tickle up a wee trout!" So saying, he flung back his head and roared with laughter, the laughter cut short and transformed into a choked gurgle as she slapped the wet washcloth across his face and left it there, dripping.

"*Trout!*" she exploded, furiously drying her hands on a clean cloth. "Och, but ye've a foul mouth t' ye, Roarke Mac Gilchrist! Ye're vile and uncouth, and think o' naught but your own pleasure, as do most men!"

She turned to leave the fireside and the tub in a fine spate of temper, but his hand snaked out and snared the hem of her kirtle, holding her fast. Though she tugged and yanked and jerked, he would not release her, curse him!

"Foul or nay, ye want me sorely, do ye no', Catriona Moira?"

"Never!" she insisted hotly.

"Aye, lassie, aye, ye do, though ye willna admit it! Why else would ye douse the candles and perfume the air, and pretty yersel'? Why else would ye try sae hard t' run from me — 'less ye were also running from yersel'?"

"Ye're conceited, sir, as well as lecherous!" she

318

insisted a little shakily, tugging at her skirt to free it from his grip. "Unhand me, I say, and be done wi' yer pranks! I'd sooner lay wi'—"

"Aye, I ken, Mistress McNair! Ye'd sooner 'mate wi' a viper than lay wi' a Gilchrist'!" He parroted her own words at her, those spoken in anger to Hamish Frazier when the Border laird had come to Corbin.

"Yea, verily!"

"Then ye lie, ye wee vixen! Ye canna deny ye want me, for I can read ye through an' through. When I look in your eyes, ye feel a quivering deep inside ye—even to here," he told her, drawing her closer by her skirts so that his other palm could rest lightly upon her lower belly.

She swallowed, for his feather-light touch was like the kiss of hot coals through the cloth of her kirtle. Sweet Jesu, she could almost feel her flesh sizzle at the contact!

"And when I touch ye, yer wee bosom blooms . . ." he continued, his hand gliding up over the curves of her body. It skimmed her hips, roved fondly over her bottom before encircling her waist and rising to lovingly cup her breast.

And damn him, bloom her bosom did, tautening with almost painful pleasure in answer to his bold caress, so that, involuntarily, she gasped.

"Aye, that's why ye're out o' sorts wi' me, my lass! There's no shame in admitting it! For once, accept that your needs are a woman's needs now—and that ye want me t' love ye," he accused with a grin of such utter relish, her palm itched to sting his hateful, handsome face and wipe the smug smile from it. "That ye want me as a woman wants a mon—with a raw, fierce hunger that's all pounding blood, all sweat and musk and passion's heat. Ye want me abed wi' ye, as Mother Nature intended. Ye want me inside ye, lovin' ye. Ye're weary of the celibate nights we've

319

passed of late, within arm's reach, but never touching, or playing, or coming together. Admit it — are ye no'?"

Aye! she longed to scream. *Aye, but that's but a part of it, can't ye see? Aye, I want ye that way, damme ye, Roarke Mac Gilchrist — but I want ye for husband, too, not only as ma lover. I want ye as a father t' the puir wee bairn ye've planted in ma belly! Oh, God, unlock my tongue, I beg ye! Oh, pride, be gone and let me find the words t' tell him! Release me from this tongue-tie, that I may hear his answer and be done wi' this agony of doubt!*

The words trembled on the tip of her tongue, but waiting to be said aloud. And yet, she feared so deeply that Roarke's answer would be the one she dreaded, the one that would see her sent from Corbin to a convent's cloistered walls, she couldna utter them! Roarke lusted after her — och, aye, there was nae doubt o' that! He was a man, after all, and what man didna think of wenching? But had he not sworn he'd never wed a McNair, would not marry the daughter of his enemy were she the last woman on earth? And was he not a man rarely given to changing his mind? She bit her lip. Hot, salty tears pricked behind her eyelids. What else had she expected? After all, what mon had ever loved her — truly loved her — for hersel'? Not her own father, t' be sure, and certainly not her brothers, she considered, filled with bitterness and heartache. Nay, not a fond word had they ever uttered to her, so why should she have expected more from the Gilchrist, who — when it came right down t' it — had but chanced upon her in the snow, and carried her home like a lost pup? Mayhap . . . mayhap there was some sinful flaw within her? A fault that made her unworthy of being loved by any man?

" 'Tisna true," she denied, trembling, damning the words even as they forced their way from her mouth.

320

"I dinna want ye! I've never wanted—"

"Shut yer wee trap, Catriona dearling, and kiss me instead!" he commanded, his tone rough and impatient with desire. "Kneel down beside me, lass, and press your bonnie lips t' mine."

"I willna."

"Aye, aye, ye shall," he coaxed. He hauled on her skirts until she had no choice but to kneel beside the wooden tub.

Water slopped over the edges as he drew her against its sides. Gazing deep into her eyes, he murmured, "This night, we'll make redress for all the nights we've spent apart. Tonight, I'll pleasure ye as never before, ye'll see. Och, ma wee bonnie wren, I ken I've neglected ye of late. In truth, I dinna blame ye for being riled, and I beg your sweet pardon. But dinna deny ye want me, lassie. Never deny me that, 'lest I come t' believe ye . . ."

As if in a dream, he framed her face with his large hands. His dark head dipped as he pressed his lips to her own, nuzzling their softness.

In that moment, Catriona was lost. The moment when she might have uttered her secret had passed into memory. There was no going back. The words she'd intended—ached!—to say had been locked inside her forever when he kissed her. Her secret was now walled up in a dungeon of pride and fear that would remain inviolate till time and Fate conspired to bring it tumbling down.

Sooner or later, Roarke would know of her condition without need for words on her part. Time would see to that! And, sooner, or later, he would either take her as his bride or revile her as his enemy's daughter, and send her hence. Fate would decide which! She would let both run their course, and deal with it when the time came. But meanwhile—och, so sweet, so wondrous sweet were his lips, she could forget her misery when he kissed her! And how she loved to lose herself in the warmth of his strong embrace! His arms were her bastion against all fear, her protection against all harm—albeit their safe, tender haven was but a lovely illusion that would vanish when tried or tested by adversity . . .

With a muffled sob, she let him take her in his arms, let him hold her lovingly. His hard mouth parted hers as he slipped his tongue between her lips. He tasted the velvet honey of her inner mouth with mounting ardor.

She felt a shudder move through his upper body, pressed so fiercely to hers. That he desired her so powerfully made her pulse leap in response. Still kissing her, he unlaced the ties to her kirtle and slipped it down, baring her shoulders and breasts. His loins tightened, for she was bare beneath that single garment, dressed in naught but her silken skin and the glossy mantle of her glorious black hair. With a tortured groan, he gathered her up and drew her over the sides of the tub to nestle, naked, in his lap, her head cradled against his damp chest, the curves of her bottom pressed to the aching heart of him.

"Sweet, ma love! Ye're sae blessed sweet!" he murmured, burrowing one hand beneath her hair to turn her head to his. He kissed her but briefly, then raised her above him that he might suckle her breasts, might draw each rosy crest into the heat of his mouth and savor its sweetness on his tongue.

The gentle tugging of his mouth, its drawing heat upon her bosom, made her breathless with excitement. She twined her fingers in his inky curls and gripped him tighter as her passion mounted. "Roarke?" she whispered, watching as his eyes closed in pleasure, as his mouth moved upon her creamy bosom, enflaming her. "D'ye . . . d'ye love me?"

"Aye, my sweet, I'll love ye well," he vowed, his head pillowed upon her breasts.

"Nay, my laird, ye mistake me. I didna ask *would* ye love me, but *do* ye love me?" she beseeched him again with some urgency, cupping his face in her hands to force him to look at her. Her green eyes were apprehensive, searching, as they plumbed the smoky depths of his.

For a moment, he made no answer. He simply returned her questioning gaze with a like one of his own before replying, "Catriona, I am what I am. Ye ken full well I'm no' a bardish lover who would haunt his bower and write ye sonnets of love. Nor am I some moonsick swain t' strum ye ballads upon a lute and praise the glory o' your eyes, your lips, your hair. Nor am I one t' play pretty games with words, as Tavish does, and make a tricksy riddle of my thoughts. I am but a plain man—a rough and ready Scot who loves this life and lives it just as it is— plainly, wi'out need o' frills or falsehoods or changing. So do I accept others for what they are, and so do I accept thee, wi' all yer tempers and flights o' fancy, and for all that ye're a 'cursed' McNair, and for all that ye're a plaguesome wee dragon more oft than no'." A ghost of a smile hovered about his lips as he added, "Aye! My answer's aye, Catriona. In as much as a plain man like mysel' is capable o' love, then love ye I do. Is that answer enough for ye, hinnie? Am *I* enough for ye?"

"I don't understand ye," she murmured, confused.

"Nay, lass, I dinna suppose ye do, for ye're a dreamer. But . . . how do I tell it? I sense ye ask more of me than I can give ye. That ye willna be happy nor satisfied if forced t' settle for less."

"But I seek only happiness from life! I crave no wealth! I ask no position!"

"Nay, lass, it isna that." He frowned. "When I

323

make love t' ye, ye ken, I sense there's a part of yersel' ye willna yield. A secret part ye're saving that ye willna share wi' me. Ah, Catriona, ye carry in your heart a portrait of the mon ye yearn t' wed and call yer own, do ye no'? An image of the perfect man who you'll call 'love' and 'heart o' my heart' and give your all. But . . . that man isna me."

"Nay? Who is he then?" she cried, pushing him from her in anger.

"I dinna ken, lass. Perhaps he doesna exist, except in a lonely wee lassie's fondest dreams."

"It isna so, my laird!" she protested hotly. "I love ye!"

"Do ye, lassie? Just as I am? Wi' my love o' battle and swordplay, and the thrill o' the hunt? Even wi' my fondness for bawdy talk, and despite my disdain for the gentler arts and the pretty, posturing peacocks who practice them?" His gray eyes glazed, his jaw was granite-hard as he glared down at her, looking much as if he'd love to shake some sense into her although he added in a gentler tone, "Even wi' my lusty way of loving ye and my bold, rough words o' passion? Can ye accept me, lassie, utterly, no matter what flaw or fault or freckle I own, as I accept ye? Wi'out wanting, deep in your heart, t' change me to your image, as once ye sought to banish me from your mirror and replace my image wi' another's face?"

"Ah ha!" she exclaimed. "Now I see it! Ye willna freely confess what is in your heart because ye seek t' punish me! And why, mi'laird? Because jealousy devours ye, that is why!" she tossed back at him, giving a triumphant little toss of her head. "Since I admitted at Erskine that another had once held my heart, ye canna forget it, can ye? Ye would have me squirm and beg and implore ye for your favor—a smile, a kind word, a gentle touch—like a worm pricked by a fisherman's hook! And so, ye'd rather confuse me with your raveled talk than speak plainly!"

"What other?" he demanded as if he'd heard not another word she'd said, setting her from him and rising from the tub. Water streamed from his magnificent body as he stepped from it.

His question took her aback for a moment, but she recovered with only the barest hesitation and cried, "Alan! Alan of Rowanleee! 'Twas him ye spoke of, was it no'?"

"The Mac Quinlann?" he said slowly, as if the name had not occurred to him until she uttered it. "Ha! By all that's holy, lass, that sniveling excuse for a mon isna so worthy he commands *my* thoughts — though I wouldna doubt he commands others!" He snorted his disgust as he wound a linen drying cloth about his flanks. "And nay, I dinna fear ye comparing me t' him, for ye see, the Mac Quinlann ye dreamt of doesna exist — save in your pretty fancies!"

"Aye, ye've said as much many times, Laird Roarke," she ground out, dashing tears of hurt and anger from her eyes with her knuckles. "However, both you and my father were mistaken! The Mac Quinlann was ever gentle, ever kind in his dealings with me. Just because he's different t' the pair o' ye doesna make him any less worthy!"

She saw how her words in Alan's defense caused him to tighten his grip on a chairback so that his knuckles were bled white. He did not turn to face her when next he spoke, but remained uncannily still. " 'Tis easy t' be 'kind' and 'gentle' when a plump dowry is dangled in front of a mon's nose like a carrot before a donkey. And 'tis no great task t' play the fond suitor when the lady in question is emminently bed-worthy."

Hectic color bloomed in her cheeks. "Damme ye, sir!" she hissed. " 'Tis a cruel bastard ye become when jealous!"

"Jealous?" he echoed, and gave a chilling laugh. "Hardly, my love. Ye see, had not your father met his untimely end, ye would be *my* bride now—had I agreed t' take ye to wife as your father wanted."

She blanched, incredulity stamped on her lovely, angry face. *"What!* What? Damme ye for a liar, Gilchrist! My father hated ye—hated your clan, hated everything ye stand for! He would never— *never!*—have wed me t' ye! He would ha'e sent me to a priory first!"

"On the contrary, Angus McNair was a canny man. Not likable, nor entirely noble, certainly, but shrewd, very shrewd, when it came t' warfare. He obviously realized that wi' England firmly beneath William's heel, the Normans would set their caps at Wales and Scotland. He also must have realized that the Borders were the key to Scotland's remaining free. Accordingly, he had his reeve draw up the necessary documents, offering me the hand of his only daughter, Catriona Moira. With our marriage, he hoped to achieve a dual purpose. One, an end to the feud between our clans for all time. And two, the gaining of the Gilchrists as his allies against the Normans. Alas, he was murdered before the missive could be sent and his plan acted upon."

"I dinna believe ye!" she hurled at him, feeling betrayed beyond all reason by a man who'd been dead over five months.

He shrugged. "Believe or no, it changes nothing. I found the parchment in your father's chamber at Erskine the day we went there, along with another from the king himself, granting his approval of the marriage. The first was signed with your father's mark, sealed with his wild-rose seal and witnessed by one Master Gordon Alistair McNair."

Gordie, she acknowledged with a sinking heart.

Roarke's knowledge of Gordie's name confirmed the truth of his claims! With a bitter heart, she realized that her father's threats had not been empty ones that fatal Yule. Nay, he would have carelessly betrothed her to another — given her as wife to his most hated foe! — had not death confounded his intent!

"I see," she said shakily. "And what would your answer have been had my father lived long enough to see this parchment sent?"

"At that time?"

She nodded.

"I would have thrown it back in his face," Roarke admitted, his jaw hard. It was no lie. He would have done just that, rather than risk alienating his clan by marrying the daughter of the man who'd had their loved ones slain, their bodies mutilated. Aye, and he would still have reacted thus today — had he not met Catriona, and fallen under her spell . . .

"Then mayhap 'tis for the best that my father is dead now, sir," she said tightly dragging on her chamber robe as if it were her shroud, for she knew now that he would never make her his bride, "for his intentions for my future died with him. As for marrying ye — God's Blood, for once we are in accord, sir!" she babbled on, her tongue running away with her in her eagerness to wound and cut and slash him as his declaration had wounded her, and in so doing, assuage her own hurt and pain, "for I would never willingly be your bride. I' faith, I'd suffer the rack before I wed ye!"

"As would I, my lady!" he snarled. "A thousand times o'er!"

"Would that I had fled Erskine and gone t' my beloved before that fateful day!" she cried. "Oh, would that I had gone t' Rowanlee, married the Mac Quinlann and never set eyes on ye!"

"Amen t' that," Roarke said acidly. "I'll leave ye

now, and find my bed in the hall amongst my fellows. Although 'twill be chill there, despite the fire, 'twill be far warmer than here wi' ye! And there, at least," he added cuttingly, "I dinna have t' fear to awaken wi' a McNair dirk at my throat."

"Go, then, damme ye! Go!"

"I am gone," he ground out.

She'd been alone when she awoke the following morning. The pallet beside her had been chill and empty, and the downy goose feathers, however comfortable, had felt as unyielding as a bed of nails without Roarke's deep depression beside hers. Her heart ached, but her McNair pride had strengthened her as she went about the mundane tasks of making her toilette.

The lady Fionna had survived when Laird Kevin disowned her, she told herself. Then so would she survive without *him*, curse him, with no need of his care and protection, much less his love. Aye, somehow she would! The McNairs didna give up, and, after all, she would at least have a roof over her head, with Erskine now her own. Fionna had not even possessed that luxury. If Roarke didna love her, then the devil take him! She would leave Corbin and go to Erskine. If she but asked, Auld Morag, the witch-woman who lived in a cave in the woods, would help her when her time came, she knew it.

We didna need him, my bairn, she said silently, pressing her palms to her belly and closing her eyes. *We have each other!*

Her stomach rebelled once again at sight and smell of the night's fast-breaking spread upon the trestles, and she turned green at the sight of kippers and pickled eel floating in their drippings or vinegar sousing. Accepting only a morsel of dry bread and a spoonful or two of porridge, she gave the lady Fionna the mumbled excuse that her head was plaguing her and escaped the hall for her bower once again, only too well aware of the sharp, searching look Fionna gave her, and of Graeme's curious gaze as he gnawed at a leg of capon.

"But ye'll miss the May Dance, lambkin, and I did so want fer ye t' see it!" Fionna said, disappointed.

"And so I shall, my lady," Catriona promised, "when my head has ceased this wearisome throbbing. I'll watch the revels from above, I promise, where my long face will bother no one."

"Would ye have me bathe yer temples, chick? Or mix ye a sleeping draft?"

She shook her head. "But enjoy your morning victuals, my lady, and I'll join ye anon, I promise."

After the girl had left the table, Fionna and Elyse exchanged meaningful glances.

" 'Tis not the first time the lassie has come t' table looking peaked and bilious of a morning!" Elyse whispered so that Graeme, the master-of-horse, who sat close by at the trestle, breaking his fast, could not overhear her words.

"Nay," agreed Fionna slowly, her lips pursed in thought. "It isna."

Flora, the serving wench, was setting her bower to rights when Catriona returned to it. She was in a thunderous temper, Catriona saw, if her glowering expression and the lethal way she was plumping pillows was aught to go by.

"Good morrow, my lady," Flora gritted. " 'Tis a fine day for the Maying, is it no'?"

"Aye, so it appears," Catriona agreed absently, flopping listlessly onto the bed.

"Why, mistress, are ye ailing?"

"Nay, I am not."

"Well, ye look it, ye do. Proper peaked ye look, if I do say so mysel'," Flora insisted with a sniff, casting Catriona a sly, spiteful look. "And the Gilchrist himsel' didna look much better, stormin' out o' Corbin the way he did at daybreak, galloping off on that great black beast he favors as if the hounds o' hell were snappin' at his heels! Whist! 'Tis an ill omen, all this discord coming on Mayday, or my name isna Flora—!"

"Oh, hush, do, Flora! I'm in nae mood for your dire predictions. And furthermore, what the Gilchrist does is none of your concern—nor mine, come to that! He can ride t' the devil, for all I care!" Catriona declared crossly, stretching out with one arm shielding her eyes from the spring sunshine streaming through the wind-eye. Her excuse of a plaguesome headache had been a lie, but was fast becoming fact. Her temples throbbed, and Flora's grumbling grated on her shredded nerves.

"Very well, mistress," Flora said primly, her task of setting the chamber to rights completed. "And I'm sure you're right. It's none o' my concern if Laird Roarke's off t' his leman's bed, after all. Highborn or peasant, men are all the same when ye get right doon t' it, are they no'? 'Tis what dangles 'twixt their legs that rules them all! Whist, even my bonnie Ogden proved nae more faithful than most. Surprised him in the stables last even', did I no', tumbling that Saxon slut, Betty, what came here wi' the lady Elyse from England. Naked, they were, and he was calling that strumpet his 'wee flower o' the Borders' as he once called me, that dung heap!" Tears swam in Flora's eyes as she whirled away toward the door.

"Wait!" Catriona cried, springing from the bed. "Where did ye say Roarke had gone?"

330

"Why, t' his leman's bed, I have no doubt!" Flora revealed, turning back to the girl and endeavoring to muster a look of great indignation. "Och, ye poor lady! We've both been sorely wronged by men, we have!"

"What leman? What name does she bear?"

"Why, bless ye, surely ye ken who she is? Himsel's been visitin' her cot nigh two years come Lammas Day, after all! 'Tis the Widow Maggie he goes t'— that plump slut what lives oot wi' the crofters?" Seeing her mistress's distraught, stricken expression, the knot in Flora's own jealous heart loosened a little. "Och, ma puir mistress, did ye not ken the Gilchrist had another leman besides yersel'?" she purred.

In her hurt, Catriona failed to respond to Flora's subtle insult. Instead, she demanded, "And has he continued to visit the Widow Maggie since I came here?"

"Why, bless ye, my lady, naught but a time or two, no more, in truth!" Flora insisted with too much vehemence for honesty.

"I see," Catriona breathed, shaking all over as she staggered to her feet. The breath seemed knocked from her, as if she'd received a blow to her belly. "That's enough for now, Flora. The chamber is t' rights. Leave me now," she whispered.

"But I—"

"Be gone!"

"As ye will, mistress," Flora mumbled, her head downcast to hide her glee at seeing the McNair bitch so shaken as she did as bidden, and scurried from the chamber.

Like one in a dream, Catriona flung a mantle around her shoulders for warmth and left the bower in Flora's wake, taking the spiral stairs that led to the battlements of Corbin. Her chamber had become a prison. Sweet Jesu, she craved air! Distance! Space!

331

Up she climbed, breathless with agony, the sobs coming hard and fast as she gained the topmost tread. A cool breeze buffeted her as she stepped out onto the ramparts, snapping the scarlet pennants of Corbin high above and riffling her hair. Slowly, she made her way across the battlements to her favorite embrasure, one from which she had watched Roarke drilling his men-at-arms many times and that would give her an unimpeded view of the Maypole dancing—while also allowing her the solitude she sought to shed what little tears still remained.

Grains of something gray and rough were scattered at the base of the wall beneath the embrasure. Though her slipper scuffed over them with a harsh, scratchy sound as she stood there, looking down for a moment at the revelers below, she did not remark them in her upset.

Kirsty, with her bonnie golden hair, was below, radiant as Queen of the May crowned in her garland of mayflower, with a kirtle of sky-blue girdled with daisy chains. Her maids were little less bonnie, a pretty bevy of fresh-cheeked lassies with flowers in their hair, who giggled and blushed under the watching lads' admiring eyes.

Beware, lassies, for they'll make ye love them, give yersel's t' them, then wound ye t' the quick! she thought silently, locked in her misery.

A cheer went up from the crowd of spectators below as the lady Fionna took her seat. The loud, sudden sound startled a flock of swallows into soaring flight from their mud-nests beneath the eaves of Corbin. Soon after the pom-pom-di-pom of the tabors began. The flute and pan-pipes joined their woodwind voices to the small drums' skipping beat. Each maid took up the end of her colored riband, watching Kirsty expectantly for the signal to begin the dance. Queen Kirsty gave a smiling nod, and with one accord, the lassies began tripping lightly about the pole in time to the music. In the wake of their steps, the colored ribands twined about the maypole in the beginnings of a complex braid.

The sounds of revelry snapped her back from her jealous imaginings of Roarke with a buxom shepherdess. Blinking rapidly, she turned to seat herself in the alcove made by the embrasure's thick walls, there to watch the dancing as she'd promised Fionna.

With a sigh, she leaned back against the wall that framed the stone shelf, but was poised there only a second — no more! — when she felt the loosened stone suddenly move beneath her, wrenched free of its mortar. The motion thrust her off balance. She pitched forward. Her arms flew out. Her frantic hands grappled wildly for some hold. Yet there was only the morning air that slipped between her fingers like water, and was as swiftly gone . . .

Chapter Twenty-four

Catriona's piercing scream cut through the lively music in the inner ward way below. Flutes fell silent. Tabors hushed. All motion ceased. As one, all heads turned to look upward. Eyes widened, mouths gaped, faces paled as they saw a massive block of stone loosed from its mortar come crashing down to the ground amongst them. Its thunderous landing made the ground shudder and sent folk leaping backward, out of its crushing path.

"Look! The McNair lass! She's fallen!" someone cried as the dust settled.

Roarke's blood ran cold with the cry. He jerked his head back, squinting against the bright sunlight to see. *Sweet Mother of Christ, nay!* Catriona had fallen from the embrasure far above him! She was even now dangling from it by her trapped skirts — fragile cloth and the hidden projection that had snagged them all that stood between her and certain death! She was frantically windmilling her arms and scrabbling for purchase.

"Be still!" he roared. "Dinna move! For the love o' God, *dinna move!"*

Like a man possessed, Roarke threw himself across the ward at a ground-eating lope, taking the outer stairway up to the battlements with great, powerful strides that swiftly bore him up.

Heart pounding, he exploded onto the battlements and ran to the embrasure. At once, he realized that her skirts were not trapped by some projection, as he'd thought, but *held,* wound in the fragile, bony fists of the half-wit lad.

Hal's face was pouring with sweat and purplish with strain. His feet and thin legs were braced against the wall, calves bulging beneath ragged hose in his valiant efforts to keep her from falling—a superhuman effort that Roarke knew at any second must surely be lost!

In but a heartbeat he'd joined Hal by the embrasure and added his mighty strength to the lad's. Roarke took up the strain, grasping her ankles. Together, muscles bulging, veins standing out upon their necks and temples, the man and the lad dragged her back over the ledge to safety.

"Roarke, oh, God, Roarke!" she sobbed when she stood beside them. She tottered into his arms, trembling so violently in reaction to her brush with death, her teeth chattered. Her face was the color of chalk.

Shaken himself now, his chest heaving, he realized how very close he'd come to losing her. Swearing under his breath, he held her fiercely to him, hugged her so tightly she wondered dimly if her bones would snap—and yet didna give a damn as he showered fervent kisses over her face, her throat, her hands, and held her still tighter! The strength of his hold, the oaken vise of his arms clamped about her, even the bite of his fingers on her upper arms—they all confirmed that she was *alive*—feeling, aching, trembling, but *alive!*—and, dear Lord, she had come so very, very close to being killed!

She closed her eyes and buried her face against Roarke's chest, unable to blot out the awful sensation of having solid walls give way before her, remembering time and time again the absolute futility of her reaching, trying desperately to grab on to something, then the horror of realizing there was nothing—nothing!—left to grab, and that she would fall and be smashed like a dropped egg on the flagstones way below.

"Did ye seek t' take your own life? Was that it, ye damned wee fool?" Roarke demanded. His gray eyes were ignited with fury as he held her at arm's length. Remembering their quarrel, her upset when he left her the night before, it was the first explanation that occurred to him, now that she was safe. "God's Blood, if ye did, I'll flay the flesh from yer back mysel', woman!" he threatened through clenched jaws.

"Nay!" she denied indignantly, her composure returning somewhat. "I wouldna risk my soul for what passed between us!"

"Then what happened?" he ground out.

"Truly, my laird, I . . . I dinna ken," she whispered, her green eyes still huge with terror, lashes spiked with tears. "I sat here in my favored spot as I've always done—ye know, t' watch ye at your drilling?"

"Aye," he acknowledged.

"I m-meant to watch the Maypole dancing, but when I sat down the stone—the stone moved! And when it fell, I was thrown forward, over the edge!"

Her expression was so sincere, her words so innocent of guile, he believed her, and nodded in relief. "Then 'twas an accident, pure and simple. But if not for this lad, accident or nay, ye'd now be dead! We have Hal here t' thank for your life! He caught your skirts when ye toppled—held ye back until I could get t' ye, thank God!"

Roarke's wind-browned face was little less pale

than her own as he slipped his arm about her. 'Twas as if having come so close to losing her, he feared to let her go again! He turned to Hal, who'd stood quietly watching the exchange, his normally sallow face even yellower now.

"We owe ye a debt we can never repay, laddie," Roarke said gravely and with no attempt to conceal his emotion. Reaching out, he gripped the lad's shoulder and clasped his hand. "My thanks, a thousand times o'er! I'll see ye well rewarded for yer part in this," he vowed. Shaking his head ruefully, he added, "But first, 'tis clear all else must wait until my master mason can inspect these crumbling walls. Where one block has come loose, there could be more that will follow 'ere long."

Others had followed Roarke up and were now clustered in a half-circle about the trio, their expressions both relieved and curious. Tavish and Graeme were among them, as were the lady Fionna and her woman, Flora, who was agog at the McNair slut's dice with death.

"I'll see t' it straightway, my laird," Tavish said soberly, obviously shaken. He left to seek out the mason without further ado.

"My puir, puir chick!" Fionna clucked, coming forward now and throwing her arms about Catriona's shoulders. "I'll no' forget till the day I die how it felt t' look up and see ye there, and know I could do naught!" She crossed herself with a shudder, and wrapped the girl in a fierce bear hug again.

"Master?" Hal murmured, tugging at Roarke's sleeve.

"Aye, lad?"

Hal beckoned the laird away from the nervously chattering group to the embrasure. The crowd paid them no heed. All seemed to be babbling at once now and jostling to get close to Catriona. Squatting

337

on his haunches, Hal bade the chieftain, "Look 'e here, master."

Crouching down, Roarke saw what the youth had wanted to show him—a small pile of mortar dust directly below the gaping hole in the wall. It resembled a mouth with a missing tooth where the massive block had been anchored.

"Aye, lad, I see it. Wear and tear and weather hae worn the mortar down, ye ken," he explained simply so that the lad could comprehend. "And, when enough o' it had fallen loose so did the stone break free."

With a sly look in his eyes, Hal vehemently shook his head. He drew something from within his grubby jerkin and handed it to the towering laird. "Hal found this he did, right before the lady fell. 'Twere right there!"

Looking down at what the lad had placed in his hand, then to the corner some distance away where Hal claimed to have found it, Roarke's brows creased in a frown. The rusty, broken point of a knife lay in his palm, its blunted tip white with what appeared to be mortar dust. "Ye'd have me believe the block was pried loose? That someone meant for this to happen and wanted the lady t' fall?" His gray eyes were piercing as he searched the boy's face. Roarke saw him squirm uncomfortably under his penetrating scrutiny, then give a shrug.

"Hal thinks so, aye, master," Hal admitted with a crafty gleam in his eyes. "And 'tis not the first time they ha'e tried—nay, not likely! The auld hound, master—ye remember? 'Twas poisoned it were!"

"Whist! What the devil are ye saying, laddie?" Roarke asked softly, his expression mirroring his incredulity.

"That he's tried before!" Hal hissed, casting a frightened look about him. "T' kill her, I mean!"

338

"If 'twas so, then this stripling fool bungled the deed himsel'—as he did this time, praise God, did ye no', flea?" Graeme cut in with a stern growl.

Unnoticed by either of them, the master-of-horse had come to stand alongside Roarke and Hal, and must have witnessed much of their exchange. He stood there, a towering flaxen-haired young giant with his boots braced apart and knotted fists planted on his hips. His handsome face was ugly with hatred and contempt as he looked down at the cringing lad.

"For my part, I've never trusted this sniveling little worm, sir—not since the day me and Tavish fished him oot o' Erskine's well!" he said thoughtfully.

Of a sudden, Graeme's hand came out, gripped Hal's ear and yanked it, almost jerking the boy to his feet. "I'm no' the Gilchrist, laddie, t' let Christian compassion stand in the way o' justice!" he jeered. "Tell the truth, maggot, and quick about it! What were ye doing up here in the first place, when ye had no business here? Did ye mean harm t' the lady, eh? Did ye follow her up here? Was it ye who pried the stone loose? Speak, damme ye, boy, or half-wit or nay, I'll tear the cursed ears from yer cursed head and feed them t' the corbies, piece by piece! And after, I'll prick out your eyes wi' ma dirk!"

Still holding the terrified boy by the earlobe, he shook him like a hound worrying a dead ferret, his handsome face a terrifying mask, his throat mottled red with anger. By contrast, his blue eyes were frigid as an ice-bound loch.

"Let gooo!" Hal wailed, trying vainly to tear the master-of-horse's fingers from their cruel grip on his ear. Tears of pain streamed down his face as he shrieked, "Let meee goooo!"

In answer, Graeme released him momentarily, only to scoop the boy up again by the scruff of his neck with a meaty fist knotted in his jerkin. Before

339

Roarke had realized his intent and could react, he'd swept Hal over the edge of the embrasure. He held the scrawny lad there by the neck so that he dangled perilously in midair, like a spider suspended from a web.

"The truth, laddie, or I'll let ye go—just as ye asked me!" Graeme threatened with an evil grin. His blue eyes glittered.

"Stop it!" Catriona cried. She had seen what was going on from over Fionna's shoulder, and pulled free of her embrace to run to Graeme. She plucked at his sleeve, imploring, "For the love of God, sir, don't, I beg ye! He is but a lad—and innocent! Let him be!"

"Aye, that's enough, Graeme laddie," Roarke commanded quietly, striding to Graeme's side. He placed a hand on his friend's shoulder and felt the muscles standing out in rigid cables there: noted how the sinews below Graeme's jaw were strung tight with fury. "I ken ye mean well by it, friend, but if the lad had any part o' this, he would have spilled his gorge by now—from sheer fright, if naught else! And besides, 'tis unlikely he'd be so eager t' show me how 'twas done, hmmm? With his lack o' wits, such cunning is unlikely, I fancy! Bring him in, Graeme!"

For an instant, the blankness in Graeme's glazed eyes gave Roarke an uneasy premonition that his companion would refuse to comply: that he'd release the lad to fall to his death in the inner ward below. Or mayhap Graeme's fury was so great, he simply hadna heard him? Whatever the cause, he continued to stand there for several moments after Roarke had spoken, leaning out over the embrasure with his chest heaving while the boy—grown silent now from utter fright—dangled from his fist like a harvest mannekin.

"Do it, mon!" Roarke barked.

Time seemed suspended for those few moments. The world receded. Existence narrowed to Graeme and himself and the terrified, whey-faced boy, who was moaning low in his throat now like a wounded cat. Roarke could also hear Graeme's raspy, labored breathing . . . the cawing of the keep's ravens . . . the sudden, high-pitched giggle of a frightened wench, all sounds heightened to an exquisite clarity by the import of the moment. Roarke swallowed, his jaw tightening. He couldna tear his eyes from Graeme's fist! His companion's hairy blond knuckles were clenched so tight in the boy's jerkin, their flesh was bleached bone-white, but with one false move on his part, those fingers could open and release their burden . . .

And then, when Roarke had all but decided he would have to try and force his friend to release the lad, despite the risks, Graeme blinked. His shoulders slumped. He turned his head and his eyes met Roarke's, a question in their depths. "What?" he whispered hoarsely.

"Enough, laddie," the chieftain commanded softly, urgently. "Enough!"

Without further ado, Graeme nodded. He roughly hauled the lad back over the broken ledge. He flung him to the ground at his feet before wiping his hand on his breeks with a contemptuous smile as Hal scrambled to his feet and fled the battlements like a terrified hare.

"Forgive me, sir," the master-of-horse said thickly. He managed to summon up a sheepish, engaging smile that transformed his face to its former, comely self. " 'Twould seem I — er — forgot myself for a wee while, did I no'? But — Jesu and Mary, Roarke — when I think of how very close your dear lady came t' death . . . ! Why, 'twas as if I'd gone mad! I couldna think o' aught but punishing the rogue

341

who'd dare t' harm her, whether by intent or negligence!"

"Aye," Roarke agreed, and with feeling, giving Graeme an intent look. "Nor I. However, the lady Catriona is—by the grace of God—unharmed, and I dinna believe the lad responsible for her scare."

In a louder voice, he declared, "Hear me now, good people of Corbin! The excitement is past, the drama played out, the maiden plucked from the jaws o' death! I fancy 'twould benefit us all to go down t' the hall, and forget our fears in a wee dram o' *uisqe beatha* before we resume the May Day revels. Come, all o' ye! Down t' th' hall!"

Despite his hearty urgings, Roarke hung back as everyone else filed down from the battlements, holding Catriona by the elbow so that she would not follow the others. When they were alone, he straightway took her in his arms.

"So? Are ye recovered, ma sweet?" he asked, concern in his smoke-gray eyes as they searched her face. The breeze stirred fragile tendrils of inky hair about her cheeks. The color that had fled her face was gradually returning, rose seeping into the creamy ivory of her complexion. She had never appeared more delicate, more lovely—more dear to him!—than she did in that moment.

"For the greater part, aye, my laird, I trust I am—tho' ma puir belly doesna agree!" she answered ruefully, a trace of her former spirit returning to add the suspicion of a sparkle to her eyes. But she looked quickly away when she was done speaking. Belatedly, she'd remembered their bitter quarrel and the harsh words they'd exchanged before their last parting, forgotten in the excitement. She wondered at Roarke's gentle manner now, coming so soon on the heels of his angry demand to know if she'd tried to kill herself, but—Jesu! She needed the security of his arms

342

about her too badly to question the source of his warmth and tenderness! What did their quarrel matter now, when she had felt the breath of Death against her cheek? Accordingly, she sighed and melted against him.

He guessed in what directions her thoughts lay, for she'd tensed in his embrace for a moment before softening and leaning heavily against him.

"Aye, lassie, our differences dinna seem of import now, do they?" he murmured, caressing her cheek with a calloused palm and turning her head up to look at him. Gazing deep into her emerald eyes, he continued. "God's Blood, I could ha'e murdered ye last night, lass — aye, and done so cheerfully, I was sae cursed jealous! But when I heard ye scream, and looked up t' see ye swimming on air — ! Blessed Christ! I couldna begin t' think why it was we'd quarreled! Only that I had t' save ye!"

"Nor I," she confessed, tears filling her eyes. "When I fell, it flashed through my mind that my time had come — and I could think of naught but that I'd never see ye again!" She ventured a little smile of chagrin. "I suppose there is naught to compare wi' the kiss o' death for making one realize how fragile life is, or what matters and what does no' . . . ?"

". . . or to learn who it is we cherish in this life, and that we must swallow our anger — or jealousy — t' say what's truly in our hearts, while our loved one is there t' hear the words. After they're gone t' the grave, 'tis far too late," Roarke added huskily.

There was such tenderness in his eyes, she felt as if she were melting inside. Bone and gristle and substance dissolved. She became all molten honey instead as he added softly in his musical Gaelic, "Before God, I love thee, Catriona McNair."

"And before God, I love thee, too!" she cried in

answer, her tears ones of happiness now. "With all my heart and soul, I belong t' ye, Roarke Mac Gilchrist!"

He swept her up into his arms and carried her below to her bower.

Fear, combined with their declarations of love, added a new fervency to their lovemaking that morn.

Straightway, Roarke lowered her to the pallet without so much as a word passing between them. Before she could catch her breath, he had removed her garments and stood beside the bed, looking down at her, naked, as he took off his own.

"But moments ago, ye cheated death, ma wee wren," he murmured, joining her, and his eyes were lambent fires that singed her with their heat. " 'Tis only fitting that now, we should celebrate life!"

His mouth and hands were everywhere upon her that morn. He lay beside her, his dark head dipping to suckle and draw upon one breast while he cupped its twin with his large hands, pressed it high, and rolled the aching nipple to rosy tightness between his thumb and fingers. When he was done, his damp mouth traced patterns of molten fire across her abdomen, while he stroked the sweet curve of her hips and the long, slim length of her ivory thighs.

Biting her lower lip to hold back her gasps of wonder and pleasure she thought, *His every touch is an agony of delight!* He lapped at the tiny well of her navel, then trailed his mouth down over the fleecy mound of her mons to nuzzle the softness of each inner thigh in turn, branding her skin with the fiery kisses of his most intimate possession. He found a welcome there, between her thighs, for she became all moistness and heat beneath his mouth and searching fingers, giving forth a secret cache of honey whose nectared sweetness was for him alone to savor. And savor it he did, his senses reeling as he kissed her netherlips and played upon the pearl of her passion with mouth and hand. Soon, her eyes grew clouded over with rapture. Her slender body tensed, arched. As the pulsing began deep within her, her cries became a skylark's trilling as it soared to the clouds.

When he took her that morn, came into her softness and claimed her as his own, he was no gentle master, but a swarthy, black-haired devil; a devil hell-bent to leave his demon's mark upon her!

Braced on his knees between her thighs, he lifted her legs wide and high over his shoulders, before plunging deep and thrusting hard. He buried himself to the very hilt within her pulsing heat and tightness, before withdrawing and plunging anew.

She gasped. She clung to him, twisting beneath him to press her lips to his throat, his chest. Her mouth was sweetly savage in her passion, her lips nipping his shoulders, her teeth grazing his flat male nipples. She moved her body wildly to the rhythm of his thrusts, arching and pressing herself to his lunging flanks. Her nails gauged his back as she gripped him to her. Her slender legs embraced him as she gave herself with the sweet, wild passion he had always known she possessed. And this time, she denied him nothing, withheld naught from him! She loved him with a free, sensual joy he had but dreamed of.

She is mine! he thought. The knowledge pulsed within him like a song whose melody has at last been found and captured. Aye, this time she was truly his in every way, her body, her heart, her soul, his for eternity!

The end came for him with an explosion like a summer storm. The seed left him as a fork of lightning, leaping from his loins to pour deep into her womb. Breathing heavily, he fell to her side and took her in his arms.

"In the summer, ye shall be my bride," he murmured against her ear. "And, next Candlemas, God willing, ye'll hold our bairn in your arms—the son we've made this morn, ma love!"

Catriona smiled and tenderly caressed his swarthy cheek, her green eyes dreamy with love and spent passion. Yet even now, she couldna trust him deeply enough t' tell him his bairn had already found life in her belly . . .

There'd be time in the days to come to tell him, she comforted herself as she drifted into sleep upon his chest.

Chapter Twenty-five

"My thanks, Donald," Catriona murmured in a conspiratorial whisper. "Here's a mite for your trouble. There'll be another for ye when I return—*if* ye swear ye'll tell no one I've left the keep?"

"I willna, lady. I swears it, cross my heart an' hope t' die!" ten-year-old Donald vowed solemnly.

Smiling, she tossed the stableboy the small coins she'd promised in payment for saddling her mare, then pulled the full hood of her mantle up, over her hair. With a nod to Donald, she wound the reins about her fist and accepted the clasped hands he held cupped, ready to assist her in mounting. With a boost from him, she rose gracefully into the saddle, then arranged her skirts comfortably about her. Donald handed her up the hound pup Roarke had given her, and she evaded Lyra's swiping pink tongue long enough to tuck the wriggling beastie within her mantle, along with the wee casket containing her father's and their kinsmen's ashes.

Looking down at the stableboy from her horse's back, she cautioned him in a parting whisper, "Now, remember, Donald. If anyone should ask, ye dinna ken where I am. Can ye do that, laddie?"

"Aye, lady," he promised with an adoring grin, shoving back a stray cowlick of flaxen hair that flopped across his brow. " 'Course I can! 'Tis easy as winking, my lady!" He scuffed the hard ground with his toe. His eyes never met hers but for a brief, furtive flickering, and she saw that his cheeks were flushed bright pink with embarrassment at her praise.

"Perfect! Ye're a canny fellow, and I'll no' forget your help!" Catriona vowed, and the boy squirmed in pleasure at her praise. "Stand back now!"

Donald stepped back as Catriona laid her riding whip smartly across her palfrey's rump. The startled beast careened forward at a run, the bit firmly between its teeth. Before the drum of its hooves could alert poor Hugh, the gatekeeper—who'd swung the wooden gates wide to allow Corbin's priest, Father Augustine, to enter on his ambling donkey—Catriona was through them and gone, galloping wildly down the hill toward the banks of the Tweed quite deaf to Hugh's frantic cries for her to come back.

Graeme, Corbin's master-of-horse, stepped from the heavy shadow of the stables to stand beside little Donald, who was shading his eyes as he watched the lovely lady ride away. He planted a weighty palm on the boy's shoulder, making Donald jump and squeal with alarm.

"Tsk, lad, 'tis only mysel'," Graeme soothed, "no' a cursed Norman! Ye dinna need t' startle so! I was but wondering if ye'd saddled the lady's mare with the saddle I bade ye use?"

"Aye, sir, I did!" Donald confirmed, puffing up with pride. "Just as ye said."

"Guid lad!" Graeme praised, grinning down at the boy. "And 'twas proper o' ye t' tell me the McNair lady was minded t' leave the keep. After all, the lady is verra dear t' our laird's heart. We wouldna want aught t' happen to her on account o' our neglect, now would we?"

348

"Och, nay, sir, we wouldna indeed!" Donald confirmed solemnly. He tried to console himself with the knowledge that he'd only followed the laird's orders in telling the master-of-horse the lady Catriona had asked for a horse to be saddled and intended leaving Corbin to go riding. But nevertheless, there was a gnawing pang of guilt in his breast as he remembered the pretty lady's trusting smile when she'd sworn him to silence, a pang that quite dulled the shiny newness of the mite tucked in his fist.

Catriona rode swiftly from Corbin, heading her mare around the banks of Loch Tully. They passed a few fisherman there, bobbing about in their small, round curroughs of skins, but they were so intent on their fishing, they paid her little mind. She didn't slacken her pace until she'd reached the banks of the Tweed and was certain she hadn't been pursued. When she was, she slowed the mare to a leisurely trot to consider her impetuous decision to escape the keep for a wee while. And, throwing back her head so that her hair escaped the hood of her mantle and flapped wild and free about her, she laughed merrily at her cleverness.

Since soon after dawn that morning, when she'd woken alone in her bed to hear the chapel bell tolling Prime, the first prayers of the day, she'd chafed to visit the windswept headland where Roarke had taken her that other time and scatter the ashes of her dead clansmen upon the sea.

In the month since Roarke had declared his love and asked her to wed him, she'd felt a great need to put her unhappy past behind her and start completely afresh. The scattering of their ashes would break her last ties with yesterday. 'Twas the last duty she could perform for her father and brothers on this earth, before going forward into the promise of a happier tomorrow. Summer was in, and at Lammastide in the month of August, she would be Roarke's bride. Already the lady Fionna and her women were hard at work, sewing her bridal gown, an exquisite creation fashioned from a bolt of the sheer, silky apple-green cloth that Roarke had purchased at the May Day fair outside Kelso for just that purpose. Next month, the banns would be called three times from the wee parish kirk in the hamlet, and she would be well on her way to becoming the Gilchrist's bride, she thought happily. If only she'd been able to tell Roarke she carried his child, her happiness would have been absolute!

It had looked to be a fine day for her purpose when she peered from her bow slit. The sun had been rising over the purple mountains, hemming the charcoal night clouds with scallops of creamy gold and pure, glowing saffron. The birds had been singing their wee hearts out, and the green and growing wildflower scents of balmy June had filled her nostrils like a love potion.

Her inclination to evade her caretakers for a wee while — with the solemn task she had to do as an excuse for it — had only been strengthened by spying Roarke and a handful of his men leaving the donjon's walls — just as she was about to go below and ask him if he might be free to accompany her! *Drat it!* she'd thought, disappointed and, if truth were known, a mite put out. Obviously, Roarke had had business of some import to attend to this morn, business away from Corbin that he'd seen fit to say nothing of to her. Well, then, she would escape this velvet prison for a while, and Laird Roarke Mac Gilchrist could run along and play at soldier wi' his men — *she* had other plans! Surely if she followed the river and the tang o' the salt wind to the sea, she couldn't lose her path, so what harm could it do? By the Terce bells, at latest, she'd be back at Corbin, and none the wiser, she'd decided, and put her plan into action without further ado.

Hal, the half-wit lad, had fled Corbin on May Day after saving her life, and had never returned. Nor had Roarke's men been able to find him, despite Roarke's commands that they search for the lad. Accordingly, in Hal's absence she'd collared the youngest of Roarke's stableboys, wee Donald, to help her. She'd played upon his obvious infatuation with her to persuade him to secretly saddle her mount and have it ready and waiting for her in the inner ward when she came below. Donald had readily agreed, and so, here she was!

In places, she saw as she rode along, the river-banks were low and marshy, fringed with reeds and bullrushes with the Tweed waters lapping but a few inches below their muddy, weed-snaggled edges. Ducks dabbed there, tails up, and there were wild geese honking, too, now returned from wintering in far-off warmer lands. In other places, flat ground gave way to steep hills, and the banks and the dirt path she rode followed red-stone cliffs that reared high above the rushing waters between them.

She'd been right! It *was* a bonnie day for a ride! The wind blew briskly, but was without the misera-ble dampness to it of winter and early spring months. The sun shone at intervals when it wearied o' playing hide-and-go-seek with the scudding clouds, the sky was robin-egg blue, and everywhere was fresh and green, clad in the mantle of summer. The purple heather made a haze of ling-blue over the rolling moors, and the bright yellow of gorse and broom showered the turf with gold and added their pungent scent to the air. Scattered across the distant hills were the dun-colored masses of Corbin sheep, with the smaller, whiter shapes of the lambs frisking beside their ewes. The oats and barley were standing tall and green in their fields, and the harvest two months hence promised to be a rich one. The air had a sharp, clean scent to it; the smell of grass and growing things — and the faint, unmistakable salt tang of the sea . . .

All at once, her horse shied. The unexpectedness of it almost unseated Catriona, for Kelpie was such a placid, predictable creature usually — one that didna startle easily! She let out a gasp of alarm as she scrabbled to regain the reins, visions of the dangers Fionna and Roarke had warned her of over and over again sharp in her mind. Swallowing guiltily, she darted a nervous glance about her, half expecting to see a fyrd of mounted Normans charging down the hill upon her, their shield bosses sparkling, their broadswords glinting in the sun, their arrows showering all about her. But then, she realized what had *really* happened, and shook her head at her foolishness. The mare's hooves had thudded dangerously close to a skylark's nest, woven upon the flat ground between two tussocks of grass. The startled mother bird had flown up, uttering a trilling song of panic as it soared skyward right under her mount's nose!

Poor little one, Catriona thought, pitying the brave little bird. The skylark perceived her a threat to its young, and was frantically trying to draw her away from its nest of eggs, hidden in the grass! 'Twas small wonder poor Kelpie had shied, she realized! Leaning over, she pressed her cheek to Kelpie's neck and stroked the mare's head, crooning soothing nonsense words to calm her.

She felt wee Lyra, the Irish wolfhound pup given her by Roarke, scrabbling wildly before her, jealous for her attentions. The pup worked its head free of the folds of Catriona's mantle and yapped furiously,

352

for it had spied the skylark now and was bent on escaping its confinement and investigating the fluttering, feathered twittering thing that swooped and hovered so temptingly about its mistress's horse.

"Dinna fret, birdie!" Catriona sang out, laughing at the wildly flapping bird and the squirming pup's antics. "I'll no' harm your bairns — and nor will this wee, growling beastie here, no matter how fierce she may sound! Hush, Lyra! Cease your clamor, do, ye wee lummox!" she scolded the pup as she rode on.

About a league from Corbin, she came upon a wherryman, hunched over in the doorway of his *broch,* a beehive-shaped hut beside the river that was as old as the hills themselves. Beyond the ancient hut, a sturdy, flat-bottomed ferry rode at her moorings. Before it, two fine, plump salmon were skewered over a small peat fire, which sent lazy curls of blue smoke raveling into the air. An evil-looking black mastiff cur bounded out from somewhere to bark at her, and the wherryman rose stiffly and ambled out to silence and chain the brute, his hand raised to her in greeting.

The ferryman's beard and hair were long, wild and matted, much like the ancient Pictish warriors of these parts had once looked, she thought. His ragged mantle was mildewed about the hems, and flapped in the wind as he hobbled out to meet her horse. She saw that he wore the colored cross-gaiters so favored by the norsemen of the Danelaw to the southeast laced over the threadbare legs of his breeks. Uncomfortably she wondered at the identity of his fares. Any man who'd ferry the hated Norsemen across the Tweed in return for such a gift would surely grant the Norman dogs equally safe crossing without batting an eye, would he no'? She must remember t' tell Roarke of her suspicions when she returned. It might mean nothing, but on the other hand . . . ! Who knew?

"What price your fare, Master Ferryman?" she asked, reining in her mare.

He grinned up at her toothily.

"Och, good mistress, true beauty pays no fare!" he gallantly tossed back with a wheezy chuckle. There was a crafty gleam in his brown eyes. "Surely ye ken that?"

She grinned in return and inclined her head, recognizing him at once for a merry wit and a lover of riddles not unlike Roarke's steward, Tavish. Her suspicions abated. Clearly the lonely old soul intended to bandy words wi' her t' break the monotony of his duties! On further inspection, he seemed quite harmless.

"Ye say so, do ye, wherryman?" she asked innocently, and frowned as if seriously considering his comment. "But . . . if 'true beauty' may cross the river without charge, when those less comely cannot 'less they pay, then true beauty isna true at all—but false! And, being false, must also pay!"

He nodded sagely, enjoying her lively, clever retort to his teasing compliment. "Well answered, my lady, well answered! 'Tis clear ye are a lady o' learnin' t' rival the Greathead's good Queen Ingisborg, God bless her. May I ask from whence ye come, and whither ye go, m'lady?"

"Ye may ask, aye," she acknowledged, an impish sparkle in her green eyes, "But I willna tell ye! Pray, ferry me across, auld fellow, before morning is sped and my leisure squandered in bandying words wi' ye!"

She tossed him a silver penny, which he caught in midair with surprising deftness considering the stiffness of his gait. Then, chuckling wheezily, he took her reins and led her mare down to the river and onto his ferry.

They made a smooth crossing and were soon on the opposite bank, having left the rascally ferryman behind. Moments later found them cantering on between flat fields of still more barley, oats, and rye, toward the fishing village of St. Abb's that she remembered, clinging tenaciously to the steeply sloping shore like a limpet to a rock.

Gulls and sea birds were wheeling over the Head, screaming defiance at the sun. The reek of fresh herring was pungent on the wind here. Along with it, she caught the smell of oak cakes and porridge from the fires of the fisherfolk. The aromas reminded her that she hadna dawdled to break her fast in the great hall that morning, and her belly grumbled its hunger. Shading her eyes to look below as her mare trotted up the narrow, dangerous path to the headland, she could see the fishwives in their bright kerchiefs, gutting their menfolk's catch on the little stone quay below. The sunshine glinted off their baskets of silvery-scaled fish and their sharp gutting knives, and made the whitecaps of the rough gray waters of the Firth of Forth beyond them bright as silver, too.

The last time she'd been here, there'd been snow on the ground, and Roarke had shared the warmth of his mantle with her, offering her along with it warmth of a different kind; one that fires and furs couldna give. The warmth of a kindred spirit, one that understood the loneliness and lack of acceptance she'd suffered at her father's hands, for he had known the stigma and scorn, the loneliness of a bastard's birth himself. Aye, she thought fondly, back then there'd been snow on the ground, and the wind had cut like a blade, but she hadna felt the cold wi' him beside her. Now, the tiny pink flowers of the hardy milkwort bloomed in ragged ribbons from the sandy soil, and the pastel mauve sprigs of the sea-lavender made a haze of delicate color on either side — and everything had changed. The tender feelings that had budded between her and Roarke that wintry day, ripe with all the mystery and promise of full-flowering love in their fragile uncurlings, had bloomed. And now, even as the wind blew warmer, her heart was also filled to overflowing with warmth and love.

Dismounting, she tethered her reins beneath a rock and set Lyra down to gambol and stretch her legs. Taking the wee casket, she walked slowly to the edge of the cliff. Standing on the very rim of the cliffs with the wild surf booming against the rocks below and the wind threatening to steal her breath away, she unfastened the lid of the casket and held it up to the wind, then tossed the silver reliquary to the rocks below. Tears dampened her cheeks as the blustery wind took the ashes, swirled them like a gust of smoke. In an instant, they were gone.

"Farewell, my laird father!" she whispered. "Farewell, my brothers! Fergus, Gil, and you, young Bran — I would ha'e loved ye all, and well, had ye but let me! But . . . 'twas not to be. Ah, well. What's done is done. Rest in peace, my kinsmen!"

When she could cry no more, she hugged herself about the arms and began to sing as she'd once done to comfort herself as a small, lonely child, giving herself up to an orgy of grief that was peculiarly cathartic. In a husky voice, she sang a mournful ballad of love betrayed and lost that seemed suited to her mood. Her lament rose and was whipped away on the salty wind even as the ashes had been borne away. Her song sounded like that of the sirens who lured seafaring men to their doom upon the jagged rocks below.

For never more

356

The heathered glens
Will I walk wi'
My true love!
And never more his bonnie
Lips shall kiss.
His heart was mine,
But is na'e more—
What bitter draft
Is this—!

Love. Was it truly love she felt for Roarke? Was that—that melting tenderness that filled her heart indeed love—or had she but convinced herself she loved him because she had no one else to turn to?

True, a cold weight settled anew in her breast whenever she thought of him whispering the same lilting endearments in Maggie's ears that he whispered in hers. In those moments, she was certain that, given opportunity and a sharp dirk, she could cheerfully murder the wench without a shred o' remorse! But, hot on the heels of her bloodthirsty, jealous thoughts came niggling doubts. Did she really love him? And did he truly love her—or but covet the mighty keep of Erskine over which she was now chatelaine? She bit her lip in doubt, and felt tears prickle behind her eyelids all over again. *Ye great, daft porridge head!* she upbraided herself, *'tis only your cursed McNair pride and your unhappy upbringing, the manner in which ye met, that hae made ye doubt the puir mon, and mistrust your own feelings for him—that, and the doubts common to all women when they are breeding! Trust him, lassie, and this once, trust your heart, too! They willna play ye false!* her conscience urged.

Make haste, Catriona! an inner voice urged her. *Remember what Roarke said, that time in the woodland bower when ye lay together? That if ye fled him, he wouldna take ye back? Ride home t' Corbin, and swiftly, before he returns and finds ye gone, and fears ye've run off from him! Be there t' welcome him home t' his keep with fond smiles and loving words! If ye make haste, there's still time . . .*

Aye, but there was no time left t' dither! She heeded the voice of her conscience, ran to Kelpie, and remounted her mare.

Somewhere between the headland and the ferry, she took a wrong fork in the path along the Tweed's banks, finding herself on an unfamiliar track she didna recall riding either with Roarke nor on her way t' the coast, for it drew her inland, away from the now-familiar riverbanks. Still, after she'd followed the strange track for close to a league, she was relieved to discover that, once again, it looped back to follow the banks of the Tweed as it had done before. Soon, she'd be home at Corbin, she thought happily, and with no little relief. She'd bathe and dress in her prettiest kirtle and watch Roarke's eyes soften to the misty gray she loved as he came to her and took her in his arms. Still, she must hasten! Time had vanished, and if the hollow feeling in her belly was aught to go by, it was already close to Terce . . .

Yet moments later, to her dismay she found her easy path along the rolling banks of the Tweed abruptly ended once again. It was replaced by more difficult terrain that required all of her attention.

Ahead of her, dense undergrowth grew all the way down to the water's edge. The white-rose briars and spindly willows and brambles there were too overgrown, too tangled, to permit a horse to pass between them. Instead, a stony little path veered upward, turned and disappeared from her view between some trees.

As she sat, quite still, pondering which path to take, Kelpie tossed her head and nickered in greeting

358

as if to another horse. Rising in her stirrups, Catriona wetted her lips and looked about her apprehensively for another rider. Belatedly, she remembered the accounts she'd heard of rough bands of cattle thieves who swept down from the lowlands and crossed the borders into Northumbria to steal cattle from the English. They were reputed to be ruthless, lawless fellows, men little better than animals who'd deal most cruelly with a lass alone and unarmed as was she. Sure enough, she thought she caught a glimpse of something dark at her back—something that quickly disappeared between some trees when she turned to look that way! Had it been a rider?

Though reluctant to follow the unfamiliar path and in so doing mayhap become lost again and waste still more precious time she had little choice but to go on now. If she tarried, whoever she'd glimpsed might swiftly overtake her! Heart pounding, she clicked to Kelpie and urged her on down the path which, she soon discovered, led deep into a forest bordering the Tweed.

The forest was dark after the bright daylight outside it, deep-emerald shadows everywhere. For a moment, Catriona was struck blind as a mole, forced to let Kelpie pick their way until her eyes had adjusted and she could see well enough to guide the mare through the deep-green gloom herself.

The tall pines grew thick here, no more than a man's arm-length apart. Their towering height made her shiver, for 'twas as if great giants pressed close all about her, rank upon creaking rank of them. When the wind tousled their boughs, groans sounded that were like the groans of souls in torment. She could easily imagine the wee folk at their mischief here, too, weaving glamours by which t' deceive poor mortal folk, and her heart was in her mouth. She crossed herself as she looked apprehensively about her, half convinced she would spy an elfin head peering at her around a tree trunk, or a goblin leering down at her from the fork of a pine — or the shadowy figure she'd glimpsed! So strong was the impression that *someone* or *something* was spying upon her, she had to pinch herself to banish her fears, for she could see nothing unusual at all.

"Ye're naught but a haggis-headed ninny!" she muttered. " 'Tis but a forest o' trees! There're no goblins and beasties lurking here, 'less ye count a badger or two — or mayhap a wee pup!" With a nervous laugh, she drew aside the folds of her mantle and looked down at Lyra, now deeply asleep in her lap with her huge paws twitching as she dreamed. The pup's heaviness and warmth against her was reassuring, but in that moment, Catriona would have given her little finger to have Lyra's huge sire, faithful Castor, loping beside her, instead.

The narrow bridle path wound between the tree-giants. It was probably used by Corbin's foresters as they searched the woods for poachers who set unlawful snares for their laird's game, she decided, or by woodcutters as they went to and from their woodcutting. She could hear the woodwind call of a cuckoo fluting on the gloom, and it gladdened her beyond measure to hear it. In truth, it was sae blessed hushed amongst the trees, any sound of life was welcome! She didna care for this eerie, gloomy hush on which she could hear her own heart beating . . .

"Catriii-ona!"

Startled, she hauled hard on Kelpie's reins and looked fearfully about her, wondering from what direction the call had come — or if she had in fact heard that eerie voice at all! Had she? Had she really? Or was her imagination playing tricks on her, making the cuckoo's silly notes sound like her own name, or the wind soughing through the pines resemble a ghostly voice?

"Catriii-ona! We can seeee yeeee!"

Prickles clawed down her spine on icy talons. The hackles at her nape rose in shivery waves. Blessed Jesu, nay! She hadna imagined it!

Sitting quite still, she bit her lip to smother a frightened cry and forced her hands to remain firm on the reins of her horse instead of flying to clutch her pounding heart. She wouldna give in t' the panic bursting inside her, nay, she wouldna, she was a McNair! But it was terrible hard not to, for she was quite alone — and those who would gladly have lifted a hand t' protect didna ken where she was!

"Roarke? My laird? Is that you?" she tried to demand in a clear, ringing voice. But her words came out timidly, sounding as hoarse as the croaks of a frog, she was so very frightened.

"Ha! Ha! Ha!"

"Roarke? Please, whoever ye are, show yourself!"

"Catriiii-ona!"

"Catriiiiona — !"

"Catriiii-ona! Catriiiona — !"

"Catriiiiona!"

Holy Mother o' God! The voices seemed to be coming from everywhere at once now!

"Roarke? Is that you? Oh, please, whoever ye are, I dinna like this game ye play! Ye're frightening me! I beg ye, show yersel'!"

"Ah, but it's no' your laird Roarke, Catriona! Do ye not ken who we are, then, lassie?"

She jerked her head wildly to left, then right, but she could not see the owner of that terrifying, taunting voice between the dense pines that choked off her vision in every direction.

"Nay, I don't know ye! Perhaps. . . . perhaps if ye showed yersel'?"

"Och, nay. We canna do that, lassie!"

361

"W-Why n-not?" she blurted.

"Because, lass. Just . . . because."

Her bosom heaved with her terror. Her heart threatened to leap from her very mouth. Jesu, she cried silently, why had she ridden out here alone, *why?* The prudent thing to do now was to flee; t' ride for safety with all possible haste! But . . . how did she decide which way to go? Did they—whoever "they" were—lie ahead or behind her? To left, or to right? She tried to think what she should do, but it was hard to be logical or calm when she was so terrified! If she lashed her mare into a gallop and tried to flee for the safety of Corbin, she'd lief as not ride straight into their arms, and they'd have her! Should she turn her mare back, the way they'd come, instead? Ride east? West?

"We're coming for ye now, Catriona!" the voice taunted silkily. *"Coming t' silence ye, as we should ha'e done the last time! Are ye still afeared o'us, Catriona? Are ye, lovie?"*

"My God!" she whispered, her complexion gray as ashes. "Oh, my God! On, Kelpie, on!"

Rank terror at last galvanized her into action. She slashed her crop across poor Kelpie's head, dug her heels into the mare's flanks, not caring where they went, only that they get away—and swiftly!

With a pained scream, Kelpie threw herself forward, careening blindly for the trees and, by the Grace of God, Corbin beyond.

It was a wild, nightmare ride! The pines loomed up, flew close enough t' see the roughness of their trunks, the needles on their boughs, then were gone in a grayish-green blur as Kelpie veered violently sideways and thundered on.

Faster and faster they rode, with Kelpie's hooves drumming on the iron-hard ground as she wove and twisted back and forth between the endless forest of giants. Catriona's labored, panting breaths were hardly less loud! Och, sweet Jesu, surely the woods must thin out soon? she thought desperately, Give way t' open moors and heaths? Or . . . were they galloping madly in circles? Trapped like a mouse which tumbles t' the bottom of a well and canna climb out?

Froth flew in ragged strings from Kelpie's mouth now, but the terrified mare was still no less frightened than her mistress, and didna intend to slacken its pace. It thundered on, ears laid back, the whites of its eyes exposed as they barreled down a long, curving stretch of path bordered on either side by pines and still more pines, laced together with vines.

Then, as they rounded that long, blind curve, Catriona saw something ahead in the path of her horse's hooves that froze the blood in her veins. Her belly churned, for 'twas no poor, startled skylark up ahead this time! A fallen tree trunk lay across their path, the victim of some winter gale — and 'twas too late to rein Kelpie in! The mare was bolting — they were going too fast to go round it! They'd have t' jump — and trust to God they didna perish in the doing!

"Fly, dearling! Fly like the wee, braw spirit ye are!" she begged the mare. She wound the reins about her fists and anchored her fingers in her mount's rough mane, gripping Kelpie tightly with her knees and thighs as she hunched forward over her arched neck.

As if time had slowed, she felt the mare's muscles bunch beneath her as they drew closer, closer. The horse was preparing to leap the obstacle, straining, reaching for it! She felt the massive, vital power of the animal gather, its front hooves lifting, reaching, clearing, its rump rising in perfect form. A wild elation filled her, driving out terror for the moment., Damme them, whoever they might be! They were going t' clear it, she and Kelpie! Clear it — and ride

363

free!

As they soared over the fallen pine, she screamed the clan McNair's war cry, her wild challenge pealing on the forest's hush as the horse became airborne, a Pegasus of horses:

"Never yield, but t' Death!"

Catriona saw the ground ahead and below rushing up to meet her; glimpsed a flash of winter-browned bushes with a gaudy yellow flower pinned at their heart. Gritting her teeth, she steeled herself for the jolt of Kelpie's landing . . .

And then, just a heartbeat from landing safe on the far side, she felt something give beneath her. And, in her deepest heart, she knew that this time, she was truly doomed!

Her saddle had twisted sideways. It slipped around and under Kelpie's belly as the girth strap snapped, jerking her with it. Her hands windmilled for purchase, but it was no use. The reins were torn from her grip, her seat lost as the saddle fell. She was tossed from her valiant mare's back, sent tumbling head over heels through the air to land on the iron-hard ground with a sickening thud.

A shower of stars filled her vision. Mocking laughter echoed in her ears, coupled with Lyra's frightened yelps that sounded, somehow, like the squealing of a piglet . . .

"Never yield!" she tried to whisper, but no sound would come. "Never yield, but t' Death . . ."

Oblivion.

Chapter Twenty-six

She came to only moments later to find Lyra licking her face and whining piteously. Moaning, she pushed the pup away and tried to move her arm, but found she could not. She'd taken the brunt of the fall on her left shoulder, which now ached so sorely, tears stung her eyes. Her mind seemed remarkably clear, tho', under the circumstances, for escape from the owners of those eerie voices was yet uppermost in her mind. Fear did much to keep her from wasting precious time by wallowing in self-pity or giving way to her hurt! Straightway, she struggled to sit up, perspiration pouring off her brow as she braced herself on her palm to do so. The pain that shot clear up her arm to her shoulder made her sick to her stomach, but she gritted her teeth and bore it. She had to get back on her feet and hide — run! — do *something!* She couldna just lay here and wait for them to come and find her and finish her off, like a lamb trussed for the slaughter!

With supreme effort, she managed to sit up, then kneel, then finally to haul herself upright with the aid of a sturdy bush. Tucking a squirming Lyra snugly under her arm like a wee oat sack, she stood groggily and looked about her for Kelpie. Och, nay!

Oh, dear God, nay! Her poor, sweet mare was down, lying on her side some distance from where she had tumbled herself. To Catriona's dismay, she saw that a man crouched at her head: a blond giant of a man with a dirk brandished in his fist!

As Catriona watched, too stunned to move for fear she'd give herself away, the fair man pressed the blade to the mare's throat, then drew his fist sharply across it, jerking backward to avoid the bright splash of blood that spouted as he slit the mare's throat.

"Nay!" Catriona cried involuntarily, horror-struck. "Ye've killed ma mare, ye heartless devil!" Too late to silence her cry, she belatedly remembered what had brought her to this pass once before, and could have kicked herself for being so stupid and impulsive. It was far too late for misgivings, however! Determined to flee, however painful it might prove, she started forward, but as she did so, the man turned to face her, still squatting on his heels.

"Och! Blessed Mary, 'tis but you!" she cried in relief, her legs trembling in reaction now. The blond man was only Graeme, Roarke's master-of-the-horse.

With a relieved sigh, she allowed herself to sink back down to the ground, a muffled sob betraying the agony in her shoulder.

Roarke's equerry gave her a curt nod, then wiped his bloodied blade in the grass before standing and striding across the sward towards her. Even in the gloom, his blue eyes seemed cold, his expression tight with displeasure, as he towered over where she huddled.

"Aye, Lady Catriona, 'tis I. Ye were unconscious when I came along, but ye seemed unharmed otherwise, while your mare's forelegs were broken in the fall. I thought it best t' see t' her first, since I couldna let her suffer needlessly," he added accusingly, indicating the dirk in his fist. "What about yersel', Mistress McNair? Was I wrong? Are ye injured, or but winded?"

For a moment, her temper flared and self-pity filled her. What did he care! She was sorely tempted to ask him if his laird would approve of him seeing to the needs of a horse before the welfare of his chieftain's lady! But then, she thought better of it and bit back her indignant, selfish question. Graeme was Roarke's master-of-horse. His first concern would naturally be for her mount's well-being, once he'd assured himself there was little needed doing for her. And, judging by his tight-lipped expression, he obviously felt her carelessness had cost him a valuable mount entrusted to his care — and rightly so. A mount, moreover, that she had taken out and ridden far from Corbin despite Roarke's stern orders to the contrary! That would explain why Master Graeme's expression seemed angry, rather than concerned, she thought, in an agony of guilt that her stupidity had caused the beautiful mare's death.

"Only my shoulder," she answered him timidly. " 'Tis badly bruised, and swollen too greatly t' move, but it isna broken."

Graeme nodded, his handsome face still wreathed in a scowl. He brushed a lock of flaxen hair from his eyes and strode towards her, the dirk still angled in his fist. "I'll see t' that, mistress. Never fear," he promised gruffly, his Adam's apple bobbing as he swallowed.

He crouched beside her, and with his free hand unfastened the wild-rose badge of the McNair clan that held her mantle at the shoulder. A quick glance and he'd tossed it into the grass with a snort of contempt. Pulling the mantle down from her shoulder, he brought the point of his dirk close to her

367

breast—so very close it snagged the cloth of her kirtle.

She shrank back, away from him, with a tremulous, "Jesu! What are ye aboot, sir?" as their eyes met. Risking a downward glance for a fleeting instant, she saw that the point of his blade was but a hairbreadth from the curve of her bosom!

His expression changed. His fair brows rose. "What? This frightens ye?" He looked at the blade, then back at her horrified green eyes, and grinned. "Why, my lady, I meant only t' cut away the cloth o' your kirtle at the shoulder here so that I might bathe your wound wi' water from the burn. For the love o' Mary, what did ye think I planned, my lady?"

She grimaced and looked down at her lap, embarrassed now by her foolish notions. What had she thought, indeed! In a small voice, she implored him, "Och, dinna pay any heed t' me, Master Graeme, for I fear the fall has addled my wits! I'm verra glad ye happened along when ye did, for ye see, some—men—were following me as I rode through the forest!"

"Robbers, were they? Poachers, mayhap? Or perchance they were rievers after 'strayed' English cattle, headed over the border? Why, 'tis rumored even King Malcolm Great Head himsel' isna above raiding fer English cattle on a moonlit night!" he told her, rocking back on his heels.

"Nay, I dinna think 'twas any of them. Ye see, whoever they were, they knew my *name*—they meant t' kill me!"

"Surely ye but imagined it, lassie? 'Twas a trick o' the light and shadows, coupled wi' the wind soughing in the trees, mayhap? Ye see, mistress, I saw no one—and I—er—was following ye until I lost ye a league or so back—have been since ye left Corbin," he confessed, shamefaced. "Young Donald told me ye'd seen fit t' go riding, and with Roarke awa' from his keep—well, I knew he'd want me to see t' yer safety."

"But you must have seen them! I was trying t' escape them when Kelpie jumped the fallen log and the saddle-girth broke, but then . . ."

"Mistress, I saw no one as I came through the woods," Graeme insisted, "not until I happened upon ye, lying there by the log. The rest, ye—"

They both looked up, startled, at the jingle of harness on the bridle track behind them. Catriona stiffened, her fears fresh in her mind, fully prepared to spring to her feet and run if need be. She only relaxed marginally when she saw that the first rider appearing between the trees was none other than Roarke, for his expression was far from comforting. The tall, dark laird sat his towering dark horse before a backdrop of somber pines, as if the pair o' them were sculpted from a brooding storm cloud. Beneath the black slashes of his brows, his eyes were a cold, merciless gray that found her, devoured her—and filled her with foreboding. His mouth did little more to reassure her, set in a thin, hard line, with no hint of softness to it.

"A guilty pair, if I ha'e ever seen one," Roarke said softly, bitterly.

Belatedly, Catriona realized how it must look to the Gilchrist and his men, coming upon her sitting in this grassy spot with her hair tumbling free and disheveled as if tousled by a lover's hand, her mantle in a heap about her waist, and Graeme leaning over her in what must seem an intimate fashion to casual eyes.

"Ye think so? Ah, but ye'd be wrong, my laird," Graeme said, equally softly but with marked firm-

369

ness. He stood and turned to face Roarke, meeting him eye-to-eye. "Your lady's horse took a fall. I happened along, and found them. I put the mare out of its misery, and would have tended to the lady's hurts, too, had ye no' come along. There's no guilt in that, sir—nor in us."

For a moment, Graeme's blue eyes warred silently with Roarke's steely gray. Catriona held her breath, wondering if they would draw arms, praying they wouldna shed blood on her account, for they had ever seemed boon companions, to her eye, and she had no desire to be the cause of that friendship ending.

"It isna your attentiveness t' the lady that concerns me, equerry." Roarke dismissed the matter harshly, though all watching suspected from his tone that his denial was only half truth. "But rather, what it is ye're doing here, so far from the crofts where I sent ye this morn? Word came during the night that Hamish o' Glenmuir's keep was overrun yester' even' shortly after twilight, whilst the Frazier and his sons were gone t' court at Edwin's Burgh. He found full half of his people slain when he returned—just as the McNairs were slaughtered! The Frazier and his sons and kinsmen followed the track of the murderers' horses in the direction o' Corbin. They lost them when the tracks crossed the Tweed Waters and vanished. Ye have no business o' mine t' tend to here, do ye, laddie?"

"Nay," Graeme admitted.

"Then ye have no business in these woods!"

Graeme's fair complexion darkened. "Nay."

"Then what do ye here, damme ye?" Roarke rasped.

Graeme tightened his jaw, before finally murmuring defiantly, "All right, my laird, I'll tell ye! I . . . I

370

met wi' a lassie this morning, instead o' schooling the crofters in their marksmanship as ye bade me, sir — but 'twas no' the McNair's daughter I met with, I swear it!"

"Nay? Why, then ye'll have no reason t' protect the lucky lass! Tell me your sweetheart's name?"

"Och, dinna ask me that, my laird, for I willna say. A mon wi' honor doesna kiss an' tell what lassies he's tumbled," Graeme hedged evasively.

"He does, should he wish t' live t' tumble another!" Roarke threatened icily, asking in a voice of deadly softness, "I ask again, Graeme Gilchrist. *Who is she?*"

Tavish glanced from one man to the other, discomforted by the dark expressions on their faces, while the clansmen held their breaths and waited for Graeme to respond.

"I dinna ken why ye're doing this, Roarke! Ye and I ha'e been friends since we were lads! Ye know full well I'd never betray ye! Can ye no' accept my explanation as one friend who gi'es his word t' another?"

"Ordinarily, aye, without question or thought," Roarke admitted. "Lately, however, I'm nae longer certain who my true friends are." He said this in a voice so deeply saddened, it all but moved Catriona to tears, for she knew he included her in those he doubted.

Graeme's face contorted, as if in agony. "God's Blood, Roarke, ye dinna have to twist a knife in ma vitals t' make me prove ma loyalty! Damme ye, sir, if ye must have the lassie's name, then I must surely gi'e it, for 'tis clear naught else will convince ye I speak truly. My tryst was wi'—"

"Nay, sir, dinna speak!" Catriona cried, scrambling to her feet. "Ye dinna have t' tell another lie on my behalf! This good man didna tryst wi' a lassie! He seeks t' protect me from your anger! Master Graeme

371

is here only because I disobeyed ye and left Corbin. He followed me t' keep me safe from harm, ye see."

"Is this so?" Roarke demanded.

"Aye, my laird, it is," Graeme admitted uncomfortably.

"I see. And why was it ye saw fit t' leave Corbin, despite my orders?" he gritted, his eyes shriveling her as he turned back to face her.

"My kinsmen's ashes. I felt 'twas time I saw them scattered," she murmured, "and the past laid to rest. And so, I persuaded wee Donald, the stableboy, t' saddle ma horse, and I . . . I rode to St. Abb's," she ended lamely.

"And ye couldna postpone this—pressing—business until I could go wi' ye?"

She shrugged. "At the time, my laird, it seemed I couldna, nay."

Without further words, he nodded curtly. Turning from her, he strode to his horse, swept back his mantle, and lodged his booted foot in the stirrup leather. Swinging his leg over the stallion's back, he commanded his men, "Mount up, my laddies! The day is wasting, and we've yet many leagues t' cover 'twixt here and Frazier lands if we would clear our guid name and restore the *enach,* the honor of our clan!"

"My laird, I would ride wi' ye?" Graeme demanded of him, though uncertainly.

"Ye would, mon?" Roarke asked in a stern voice. "Then what are ye dithering for? T' horse wi' ye, and hasten yersel'! Ogden?"

"Aye, my laird?" The burly man-at-arms kneed his horse forward.

"Take my lady up on your saddle before ye. Ye will ride wi' us till we reach the fork in the road. From there, I charge ye t' escort the lady Catriona to

Corbin. See her taken straightway to her chamber, and set a trustworthy guard or two at her door t' keep her there. And Ogden—warn the puir devils ye choose that she's a canny wee lass, as slippery as an eel—and that I'll have their heads should she escape their care. And yours, too, should ye fail me. Ye ken?"

"Aye, I ken, my laird," Ogden said gruffly, obviously disgruntled to be charged with guarding a mere woman—and a hated McNair one, at that.

"Guid mon!" Roarke turned back to Catriona. Sitting his horse, he looked down at her from his great height and demanded, "And you, madam? Did ye hear my orders? And did ye ken what ye heard? Ye'll be returned t' Corbin under guard. Ye'll remain there, still under guard, and await my pleasure. When I return from our search, we will—discuss—at greater length yer reasons for leaving Corbin on this very day."

"Aye, I understand ye—but I willna submit t' your orders!" she insisted hotly. "Ye're not my laird father, sir, t' send me to ma bower and bid me remain there like a wee bairn! Nay, my laird! I willna do your bidding!"

"Och, but ye shall, woman, for ye see, *I* have spoken. Ogden, see t' the lady."

So cold were Roarke's gray eyes, so ominous his expression, that some still-defiant portion of her spirit quailed and shriveled up. Instead of gainsaying him again, instead of protesting loud and long that she would not obey him, she remained stonily silent. Her body throbbed all over from the fall she'd taken. Her spirit was little less bruised. *Curse him, that black hearted Border brute!* she seethed silently. *I dinna care if he doesna trust me! And nor will I humble mysel' and beg him t' hear me out! Nor, for that matter, will I stay meekly*

373

"Owch! Ye dinna have t' hold me sae blessed tight, ye lout!" Catriona snapped irritably, wincing as she rubbed her painful shoulder. "Whist, be still, Lyra, do!" The hound pup Ogden had sourly thrust into her arms was proving difficult to handle with only one good arm.

"The chieftain gave orders ye're no' t' escape," Ogden responded gruffly. "And I'll no' lose ma head for a McNair, my lady." He took no pains to hide the contempt in his tone, but spat into the grass as they rode.

"Laird Roarke wouldna do such a thing!" she declared, her tone scathing with disbelief.

"Och, 'tis wrong ye are there, my lady. He would, an' wi'out blinking, neither! I ha'e seen him lop the head from a traitor's shoulders mysel' after a battle, wi'out so much as a flicker of an eye!"

The incident was true, although somewhat exaggerated in the telling, but Ogden spoke with such an air of conviction, a flutter of fear rose and hovered, mothlike, in the pit of Catriona's belly. She swallowed, feeling sick at the thought of Flora's Ogden minus his head, and all on her account. It wouldna be a pretty sight, an' no mistake. Ogden wasna pretty t' begin with!

"Och, very well, then. Since I wouldna have the loss o' your cursed life on my head, I'll give ye my word I'll no' escape — if ye'll but loosen yer hold a wee bit?" she wheedled. "Jesu, Master Ogden, my shoulder pains me cruelly!"

To her relief, Ogden grunted assent. He slackened his grip ever so slightly, and she was a little more comfortable when they rode back along the path the way she'd come earlier.

When they reached the ferry she had missed somehow before entering the forest, she avoided the wherryman's curious eyes and instead gazed steadfastly into the waters of the Tweed, rushing by as if in a hurry to reach the sea. Or else she sighted upon the misty purple mountains, as if the answer to all wisdom lay within their craggy peaks. She looked anywhere rather than at Roarke!

Graeme and two others crossed over first with their horses, then moments later, it was their turn, and she was standing on the flat-bottomed deck of the huge ferry as she'd done but a few hours before, only this time with Ogden gripping her wrist like a vise in his beefy fist.

The wherryman was plying his pole against the muddy river bottom with laborious grunts and vulgar straining sounds, while Roarke and his men stood silently with their heads facing into the wind, their hair blowing about and their legs braced against the choppy motion of the craft.

She dared a glance at him from beneath her disheveled mane of hair and saw that he still appeared vexed and deeply troubled. His jaw was tight, his eyes narrowed, but whether to avoid the bright afternoon sunlight or from the weighty turmoil of his thoughts, she could not fathom—and moreover told herself she cared not a whit. Hateful mon! He could lay wi' her, kiss her, fondle her, claim her, vow he loved her and ask her to be his bride. He could turn his back and sleep the night away beside her wi'out fear of her slipping a dirk in his back, and yet of a sudden, in broad daylight, he couldna trust her motives for leaving his keep? Och, the mon was a riddle wi' no understanding at all!

With a sigh, she contemplated her toes, encased in

boots of supple suede—the green ones she'd thrown at the looking glass so long, long ago in an effort t' banish Roarke's image. Between chinks in the ferry's rough-hewn planks, she could see water lapping up between them, darkening the worn suede in places, making it blotched and ugly. It seeped through to soak her stockinged feet, and she gasped at the wetness of it, then gasped again as the ferry's side bumped heavily against the opposite riverbank. She was forced to stagger to maintain her balance.

"Right ye are, my lady, here we be. Come along wi' ye," Ogden urged sullenly, trying to sound stern and in control. He succeeded only in looking huge and foolish with little Lyra wedged under his beefy arm, wriggling furiously to escape while swiping at his bearded chin with her pink tongue!

Ogden took her good hand. He stepped gingerly ashore, and turned to lift her after him. But all at once, there came a curious, high-pitched humming sound, a rush of air that kissed her cheek and ended in a meaty thud.

Catriona's head jerked about to discover the sound's source just as Ogden abruptly released her, lost the pup, threw up his arms, and toppled into the water. He floated there, facedown, a red stain billowing out on the water all about him.

Only then did she spy the feathered shaft spitting the far side of his throat, before the racing flow swept him away and she found voice to scream . . .

"Ambush! Take cover, laddies!" Roarke bellowed, drawing his claymore from its sheath.

Looking wildly about her, uncertain of which way to run to avoid other arrows, she saw Roarke racing towards her at a bent-over sprint, his sword at the ready.

The world grew strangely still. It narrowed to the

short span of marshy grass between them. All sound was blotted out, save for the roaring of her own blood in her ears.

Her thoughts raced, wild horses out of control in those fleeting seconds. With one part of her mind, she couldna believe Roarke meant to harm her. He loved her, would take her for his bride! With the other part, she was convinced with a horrible, sickening certainty that Roarke's love for her had been naught but a sham from the first, a clever ruse to lull her into trusting him, while offering her no trust in return! Now, at first sign of conflict, he was showing his true colors. She had disobeyed him, and now he was done playing games, done forever with pretending she was not his hostage. At heart, he'd always considered her the daughter of his enemy, and an enemy prisoner in her own right. Nothing had changed! He'd felt no love, no tenderness for her, as she'd once foolishly imagined. It was Erskine he'd always wanted . . . and now it had come to this! He meant to kill her, to slay the last survivor of his hated enemy clan—but she could not flee! 'Twas as if her feet were frozen to the edges of the ferry, her toes curled over the planks within her sodden boots like talons, her arms outstretched on either side for balance as the ferry lurched with the flow.

Green eyes wide with horror, she watched Roarke draw closer, stride by measured stride, his expression grim, determined. She began shaking her head from side to side, silently entreating him not to hurt her, nor cut her with his double-edged blade, while knowing she could do naught to stop him if he came on . . .

Tavish apparently feared the same as she. With a wild shout, he erupted from the screen of some brambles where he'd taken cover. He hared toward

377

the riverbank, his own weapon drawn.

"Nay, my laird, ye canna do it! I willna let ye slay her!" he roared.

Roarke heard him and straightened up, turning to face him with a look of incredulous fury. "Get down, ye damned fool. I dinna mean t'—"

Catriona screamed a second time as she saw the golden streak of a second arrow that sang past her to bury itself in Roarke's chest—fully exposed to their ambushers when he'd turned to meet Tavish.

"Nay!" Tavish howled in anguish. He sprang to catch his laird, to break his fall as he toppled, but was too late. Roarke groaned. A look of astonishment crossed his features, then he fell.

Other clansmen hastened to aid Tavish. They ran to their fallen chieftain's side, some lifting him from the dew-sodden turf onto a shield, while others protected him with still more raised like a wall about him. They bore him swiftly to the concealment of some leafy bushes, while those remaining in hiding covered their companions' retreat with longbow and arrows.

When the cowardly dogs at last erupted from their weasels' lair to show themselves, they didna last long! Graeme dispatched one with the side of his trusty claymore, while Tavish—plagued with guilt—fought like a man possessed, skewering another with his sword, and another with his dirk slipped up between the man's ribs, before turning with a howl to repel yet another attacker. The remaining men-at-arms took care of the rest—and with true Border relish, hacking from side to side with wild battle yells of, "For Corbin, and honor!" and bloodcurdling cries that were akin to the skirl of the *pibroch,* the bagpipes. Their fringed tartan *breacans* flapped about them as they battled, their colors as bright as the blood that soon puddled the riverbanks, their shields and weapons flashing in the sunlight.

A short while later, sweaty, muddied, some streaked with blood, but all grimly victorious, the clansmen Gilchrist rallied around their fallen leader, looking expectantly now to Tavish to don the mantle of leadership in his stead.

"They're all dead, 'else fled, curse their souls," growled young, freckle-faced Andrew, the piper of Corbin. He spat in the reeds fringing the banks. "Eight have gone t' hell, sir, and the rest been put soundly t' rout. How . . . how fares our laird, sir?" Andrew nodded anxiously at Roarke, who lay still and silent on the shield. His tunic and breacan were stained with gore at the chest, and he was deathly pale.

"Not good, I fear," Tavish said grimly at length. "We must get him home with all possible haste! You, Douglas, cut branches for a litter, mon! Andrew, choose another and bring up our mounts. Graeme, I charge ye t' bring our laird's bride!"

His tone was sure and firm, yet his eyes were agonized as he gave the orders. Blessed Jesu, what had he done? He had sworn fealty t' Roarke, sworn t' defend his life with his own—and all for the sake of a lassie's bonnie face, he'd betrayed him. Aye, without a doubt, he'd caused Roarke's wounding—a wounding that gave every appearance of being grave—perhaps mortal. He'd never forgive himself should his chieftain die!

"The lass, sir? But . . . he canna bring her, sir. She's gone!" cried Andrew, pointing. "Vanished!"

Chapter Twenty-seven

Never had she known such terror!

As she'd stood, trembling, on the very edge of the rocking ferry, watching in horror as Roarke fell with an arrow spitting his chest and blood pouring from his wound, someone had sprung at her from the reeds fringing the riverbank.

She'd whirled about, but glimpsed only a blur of color before a cloth came out of nowhere and was thrown over her head. Cruel, bruising hands had grabbed her, anchoring around her waist and lifting her clear off her feet. She'd been tossed over someone's shoulder and abducted at a steady lope, while the shouts, clashes, and other sounds of the bloody battle raging all about her gradually faded with distance, and her muffled screams went unheard.

Now, she was lying on the hard bed of some cart or other that was lurching at speed down a rutted track to God knew where. The ragged, smelly mantle her abductor had used to blindfold her was still fastened over her head, held in place by a rope around her throat. More scratchy ropes had been used to lash her wrists and ankles. The reeking woolen confines of the makeshift hood made her panicky from lack of air, and her bonds bit into her flesh. The hard wooden planking bruised her body with every jolting revolution of the cart's wheels. Her injured shoulder was afire. But worse — far, far worse than any of her physical discomforts — was the terror of her imaginings!

Who had abducted her, and why? she fretted. Were her abductors the same butchers who'd killed her clansmen that Yuletide eve, bent on silencing her forever as they'd intended from the first? Or enemies of the Gilchrist, clansmen who'd kidnaped her for their own dark purposes to further a blood feud? Either way, her future looked bleak . . .

It seemed forever that the cart barreled on. She tried demanding of her captors who they were, and where they were taking her, but if they heard her, she received no answer. Finally, she gave up, and against all odds, either fell asleep or passed into blissful oblivion.

The cessation of motion woke her, combined with the cold and the gnawing ache in her shoulder. Although she could not see through her blindfold, she knew by the chill air on her arms and bare legs where her skirts had become rucked up that it must already be nightfall. That, combined with hundreds of crickets' reedy trilling and the occasional, mournful "Tu-whit! Tu-whit!" of a tawny owl as it hunted somewhere close by. She'd slept for several hours.

She heard someone hawk and spit, and then the cart lurched as the driver lumbered to his feet and clambered down.

"Ho, my laddie! Over here! I would ha'e words wi' ye!"

"No one enters these gates after nightfall, stranger. What is it ye want?" demanded a younger, arrogant male voice. A guard, Catriona guessed.

"But tell his lairdship that Siward be here, and

381

that he has summat he's been lookin' fer, young sir! 'T gates'll be opened right smartly then, I warrant!" came a wheezy voice.

Catriona stiffened, ears straining. She'd heard that thick, phlegmy voice before—but where? In a matter of seconds, a face came to her. Her abductor was none other than the ferryman with the colored cross-gaiters—one Siward, by name, 'less her ears deceived her! But to what laird was he referring, she wondered apprehensively? She had not a clue—unless the wily rogue meant to return her to Roarke in exchange for some reward or favor? With all her heart, she prayed it was so . . .

Several moments passed, and then she heard the sounds of a gate being raised, felt the cart sway as the driver resumed his perch, and then rumble forward again. It stopped soon after. She whimpered anew with pain as Siward climbed down and came around the back of the wagon, hefting her up. His bony fingers gripped her again as, for the second time that day, he tossed her over his shoulder. A long interval followed, in which a wheezing Siward carried her down endless passageways, her body flopping over his back. Despite the pain in her arm, the smell of food infiltrated her blindfold, and her belly growled loudly in hunger. Still, her discomfort was as nothing compared to her foreboding. Would she soon be killed, she wondered? Ravished? Horribly tortured? All things were possible in these troubled times, when human life was cheap and clan enmities fierce and bloody, she knew all too well! Hostages taken from one clan and held prisoner by their enemies often suffered horrible fates, be they male or female. She'd heard gruesome tales of some hapless victims who'd lost their heads following a besieging of Durham Town. Those bloody trophies had then been impaled, all neatly washed, combed and shaven, on spikes about their murderers' walls! She gulped. Her belly lurched. What similar dreadful fate would be hers? And could she meet it with the courage and fortitude her brave name and her father's thegn's blood demanded? Biting back a scream of agony as Siward's back slammed against her injured shoulder, she doubted very much that she could . . .

"Put her down, oaf."

"Where, sir?" came Siward's response.

"Anywhere, mon, anywhere! My laird will be down shortly."

"Right ye are, Master Brand."

Catriona was hoisted from Siward's shoulder and dumped with little ceremony onto a floor strewn with dirty rushes, judging by the rank odor. She groaned, biting her lips to staunch the pain, but could not move to cradle her hurt, for she was still bound.

"Untie her, dolt! Whist, she is but a slip o' a lass! Were ye so afeared she'd flee ye, ye had to truss her like a Yuletide goose?" the one named Master Brand sneered.

"Slip o' a girl she might be, aye, master—but she's clever, for all that," Siward grumbled. She sensed him looming over her, heard his heavy breathing, then felt his knife sawing at her bonds. She winced as the blood flowed back into her numbed hands and feet as Siward added, " 'Tis the clever ones ye have t'watch, I say!"

"Silence, oaf! My laird comes," hissed Brand. "Off wi' the blindfold, then awa' wi' ye t' the kitchen. Tell the serving sluts t' find ye some supper."

To her enormous relief, Siward uncovered her head at last and shuffled away. Blinking owlishly against the blaze of torchlight, she found she'd been brought to the great hall of some manor or other, though it was in a sorry condition compared to Corbin's great hall. The rushes were soiled and littered with bones and food droppings, the walls black with soot from the fires, the trestles scarred and dirty. The remnants of a meal strewn across the table appeared greasy and ill-prepared, either charred black, or half cooked and yet bleeding. The bread trenchers were rimmed with greenish mold. Despite her hunger, those sorry scraps didna cause her mouth to water, she noted queasily. But then, all thought of food was forgotten as she looked up and saw the laird of the manor enter through a curtained doorway . . .

"Alan?" she queried, incredulous. Her eyes widened. *"Alan!"* With a whoop, she sped across the rushes to fling herself into his arms, laughing and crying all at once, she was so relieved to see him. "Och, Alan, my laird, it *is* you! I canna believe it!"

He recovered from his surprise, and swung her high into the air, a glad cry escaping him as he twirled her about. "Nor I you, dearest heart," he declared, his eyes feasting upon her face as if he couldna believe she was real. "Why, at first, I feared ye dead wi' your clansmen, and I grieved sorely for ye! And then, I heard ye werena dead, after all, but had been taken hostage by the bloody Gilchrist, who'd sworn t' make ye his bride and claim Erskine for himsel'. And somehow, that was far, far worse than fearin' ye gone t' heaven! Cat, my love—my own betrothed, my sweetest, dearest heart! I never thought t' see your face again! But, thank God, my prayers have been answered. Ye're here with me at last—and safe once more!"

He smiled fondly at her, drew her hand to his lips and kissed it tenderly. His mouth erased the smart of the angry chafing at her wrist where the ropes had dug in; dulled the pain of her bruised shoulder; eradicated her most terrifying fears. In that moment, when but a heartbeat ago she had expected to suffer the worst of fates at some evil laird's hands, the cornflower blue of Alan's eyes seemed like a tiny scrap of heaven. The wavy, wheat-blond of his hair was just as she remembered, too, as were his snub nose, the wee nubbin of his dimpled chin. And if the lines about his eyes and mouth were more numerous, more deeply etched than she remembered, and if he seemed far older to her than he'd done before — och, what did it matter? He was every bit the bonnie man she'd sworn to take as husband!

"Did ye . . . did ye send Siward — the ferryman — to bring me t' ye?" she asked breathlessly, her green eyes searching his face.

"Och, Catriona, I've had men risking their very lives by trespassing on Corbin lands since I first learned from auld Morag that ye hadna perished in the tragedy that claimed your kin!" Alan confirmed, leading her up the steps of the lord's dais to seat her at the table there. "And alas, some of those puir loyal fellows lost their lives today at the hands o' the clan Gilchrist! Fortunately, Master Siward had the presence of mind t' act alone, and steal ye from beneath their very noses in the hurly-burly of battle, and then deliver ye to me — a mite roughly so, 'twould seem, that fool!"

He clapped his hands imperiously, and when a serving man came running at his signal, commanded, "Bring victuals for the lady Catriona straightway, and see this slop removed." Turning back to her, he continued. "Until this very morn, my men's reports were always the same. There had been no sign of you beyond Corbin's walls. Oh, my sweet, the fears that filled my head! I imagined ye tortured,

385

ravished—suffering all manner of dreadful fates. But . . . ye seem well, as lovely as ever t' my starved eyes!" There was the hint of a question in his tone.

"Aye, I am well enough, sir. The . . . the Gilchrist, for all his reputation, is not a man t' torture or slay helpless women, I discovered these past months, be they his enemy's daughters or nay. All things considered, he is a man with his own code of honor, and I was well treated while at Corbin." Peculiarly, she'd felt a twinge of disloyalty on hearing Alan speak ill of Roarke. Just as she'd once defended Alan to the Gilchrist, now she jumped to defend the Gilchrist to Alan!

"Aye, but happily, Black Roarke will be of no further trouble to either of us in the future," Alan said confidently, and with every evidence of relish. "I have it on good authority that in the midst of the skirmish this morn, the Gilchrist took an arrow in his chest. He appeared mortally wounded when they bore him away. Was it so?"

He could not hide the eagerness in his tone, and though she could not fault him for wishing Roarke dead, it pained her nonetheless to hear it.

Catriona averted her eyes and nodded. "Aye," she whispered. "He was sorely wounded."

"The man who had your clansmen slain shouldna suffer so easy a death!" Alan gritted.

"Nay! It wasna his doing!" she protested.

"Then ye saw them?" he asked eagerly. "You know who they were? God's Blood, my love! But utter their names, and I will see that the king himself is told of it, and their murderers brought to justice!"

"I—canna."

"And why not, pray?"

"For a time after that night, I remembered nothing—not even my own name! I had suffered a blow

386

t' ma head, ye ken, and somehow, my past no longer existed! As time passed, my memories have returned — save for those of that fateful day."

"Then how can ye be certain the clan Gilchrist is innocent?"

"Because the Gilchrist is no coward!" she denied hotly. "Because I know he would never slaughter unarmed men, as my kinsmen were brutally slaughtered! Because he doesna have it in him t' murder innocent women and bairns!"

"What's this, ma dove?" He tilted her chin up, gently forcing her to face him. "Thought of his guilt pains ye?"

"Aye, my laird," she confessed, swallowing tears. "Perhaps it shouldna, but it does, no less! I . . . I canna explain it."

His expression softened. "Och, never fear, lass. Your misgivings will pass. I have heard 'tis not uncommon for a prisoner t' form a warped loyalty t' his gaoler," he confided with an expansive wave of his heavily beringed left hand. " 'Tis a strange malady of misplaced affection, they say, and who knows why it happens? Take heart, my love! Your gentle illusions that the Gilchrist is anything other than the rapacious wolf I know him for will fade, 'ere long. Then ye will see him as he truly is!"

She forced herself to nod at his reassurances. He squeezed her hand. The gesture was warm and easy, filled with the fondness he'd always shown her.

"Ye were ever an understanding mon, Alan Mac Quinlann — quite unlike my father and brothers, whose thoughts were only of war. I love ye well for your gentleness in all things," she told him softly.

"Ah! Ha!" He grinned. "Then dare I hope that your feelings for me havena changed?" His fair brows rose in inquiry.

387

"Alas, sir, my feelings are too raveled to untangle at this time! Ye see, I am—I am no longer the maid I was!" she blurted out, her cheeks scarlet with mortification. She lowered her head, shame filling her. "The Gilchrist was strangely kind, even after he learned my identity. And yet for all that, he is still but a man, and—and he—he . . ."

". . . lusted after ye?"

". . . desired me. I . . . I was the Gilchrist's leman, my laird. I am no longer the innocent girl ye hoped to wed. I have no right t' hold ye t' the contract made between us!"

"Ma puir wee lassie," Alan soothed, clucking comfortingly as he drew her against his chest and stroked her hair. "Ye have suffered so cursed much! Were I a warring, vengeful man o' the sword, I would slay the Gilchrist for ravishing ye, and dance upon his corpse! Alas, I amna such a fellow, as well ye know, but a far different sort of man. I know full well the sin lay not in you. He took ye by force, did he not? But maid or no', I love ye still, Catriona lassie. I have loved ye forever, it seems! I would wed ye as we've always planned, and the loss of your innocence be damned—if ye'll but say the word?"

She hesitated, before answering slowly, "Your very kindness touches my troubled heart, my laird. But it wouldna be fair t' answer ye in haste. I have so much to ponder—and more t' forget! If ye would grant me the time to do so, I will give ye my answer anon?"

"Of course, of course! We will speak no more on the matter this even', but celebrate your escape and our reunion in ways that please us well. Brand, have Jeannie prepare a bower for the lady Catriona, and rouse my slothful bard from his pallet! Bid him tune up his harp, and come here straightway. Oh, and Brand—?"

"Aye, mi'laird?"

"See the ferryman well taken care of for his trouble, would ye, mon?"

"It is already done, sir," Brand promised with a bow, wearing a mysterious smile that was peculiarly catlike on his long, cadaverous features.

"Now, come, Catriona, enough o' that melancholy face! Here are the victuals I ordered for ye, d' ye see, lassie? Ye may sup while we talk. Och, 'tis sae blessed glad I am t' have ye here at Rowanlee, my love!"

"And I t' be here, sir," she murmured politely by rote, but there was a hefty pang of guilt in her breast even as she said the words, which had the bitter taste of lies about them.

Was she truly as glad as she should have been, to have escaped her "enemy"? And what—*what!*—she wondered, had happened to Roarke? Was he even now dead, or slowly dying, as Alan hoped? She bit her lip and closed her eyes as a shudder of horror moved through her. Remembering his face, the way his smoke-gray eyes would dance when he teased her, the warm, earthy maleness of his touch, she found she was unable to bear the thought that he was either . . .

Chapter Twenty-eight

In her first sevennight at Rowanlee, it quickly became apparent to Catriona that her expectations of a pretty manor to match a pretty laird had been but wishful thinking on her part, a maiden's idle fantasies! Oh, the manor was a fine place, sturdily built of wood and stone upon a steeply sloping hill that gave a view of the surrounding countryside: a patchwork of moors, oat and barley fields, green hills and valleys, distant mountains and dark-green forests, with here and there the silvery glint of a burn or a small loch. It had a high-raftered hall that boasted columns of English oak and a stout gabled roof of gray slate, prettily softened by weather and age, and numerous spacious chambers that could have been made gracious and attractive, with a chatelaine's discerning eye and firm instruction given to serving lads and wenches to keep it so.

Alas, Rowanlee had received neither a thorough cleaning nor any serious attempt to make it appealing to the eye in many, many years that Catriona could see. The manor, like the servants, had an unhappy air of slovenliness and neglect that saddened her.

She was below in the hall one morning, trying to

quell the unpleasant queasiness that still plagued her upon rising from her bed by running her fingertip over the narrow stone ledge of a wind-eye. She was still grimacing at the thick layer of dust and grime that clung to it when Alan appeared. He was sumptuously dressed for traveling in a fine black shirt and breeks topped by a knee-length surcoat of gray. It was belted with a silver chain fashioned of broad, oval links. Borders of fur trimmed the hems of his yellow mantle. She had never seen him look more bonnie than he did today, with his black bonnet set at a jaunty angle atop his wheat-gold hair. A feather trailed from it, pinned with a silver badge showing Alan's crest, the rowan bud.

"Is something amiss, my dove?" he inquired, catching her expression before she could turn aside to hide her dismay.

"Aye. Ye need a chatelaine, my laird," she said bluntly and without thinking. "Someone t' see your fine manor restored to its former grace and beauty. 'Else ye must plant oats upon the sills, and reap a fine crop come harvest!" she teased him.

"Aye, I must indeed," Alan agreed, blue eyes twinkling as he turned her hand over and inspected the grimy fingertip. He frowned, as if pondering the matter. "D' ye have a lassie in mind for the task?"

She blushed, but made no answer to his playful question. Instead she suggested, "If ye would permit me, I would take pride in seeing your manor set to rights mysel'? I would need very little, save some soap and water, pails, a broom and rags, and the aid of a serving wench or two."

"So few? Why, ye may have a dozen o' my lazy sluts t' scrub and scour should ye need them, sweet Cat!" he promised. "But tell me, when did ye become so wifely in your ways, my wild wee lassie? I dinna remember ye so?"

Giving a shrug, she answered evasively, "Whist, I was never given leave to test my wings at Erskine, if ye recall, my laird? Nor to discover what talents I owned in such matters, so when I came by them, I canna rightly say." It was no lie, not really—or at least, not one that counted as a sin, surely? Before Corbin, there had been no one to teach her the womanly skills of running a household that Roarke's mother had been so eager to teach her over the past months, but she didna believe Alan would want to hear that! "But if ye'll permit me, I should like to try?"

His smile was fond and indulgent. "Go ahead then, my dear. After all, you'll be chatelaine here one fine day, if I have my way! Since my lady mother relinquished the running of this household, well, it hasna been easy t' see things done properly. Ye ken how men are about such things." He grinned sheepishly, and seeing her smile and nod he added, "I'll inform Brand that you are to be given free rein in my absence, and all the servants you require to aid ye."

"Absence?"

"Aye. Alas, I am summoned t' court at Edwin's Burgh. A messenger from the king arrived in the wee hours. I must leave for the fortress without delay. Malcolm has granted Edgar the Atheling and several of his English nobles sanctuary here in Scotland to evade imprisonment at Norman hands. I warrant he wishes to discuss with me how they can be brought safely north in secret. 'Twill be a cursed bore, no doubt, and no small hardship t' part wi' ye again so soon, my dear, but what could I say? It is the price we who have the trust of the Great Head must pay. The king himself has sent for me, and I canna refuse," he apologized.

"Och, nay, sir, ye mustna," she agreed readily, for a summons from the king was no small thing. "I wish ye Godspeed and send with ye my fondest hope that ye will fare well in your duties. I . . . I would also have ye tell His Majesty on my behalf that he is in my prayers nightly — as is the welfare of our beloved land in these troubled days."

He nodded. "I will tell him. Now. If ye want for anything more whilst I am gone but tell Brand and he will see to it, my dear."

"I shall, my laird. But fresh garments are all that I require for now, sir. If ye recall, I asked ye last even' at supper . . . ?" she prompted.

"Of course, of course, forgive me. I'd quite forgotten in my haste to depart, but 'tis as good as done. Jeannie, one of the serving women, is to attend ye. I instructed her to bring a chest of garments from the storerooms to your chamber. Perchance ye will find something suitable in it, until I can see ye gowned as befits the Mac Quinlann's lady . . ." He placed a palm on each of her shoulders and dropped a chaste kiss upon her brow. "*Adieu,* my bonnie. I will return t' ye as swiftly as may be!"

"Farewell, my laird. Godspeed!"

Having bade Alan farewell, Catriona wasted little time in rising to the challenge Rowanlee's sorry state presented. She took advantage of Alan's indulgence, and enlisted the services of a dozen wenches, rather than the two she'd asked for.

Chamber by chamber, they moved through the manor like a miniature whirlwind, leaving each nook and cranny spotless in their wake. And, basking in Catriona's generous praises and seeing the enormous change their labors had created, the increased comfort and beauty of their surroundings, the formerly idle, careless wenches toiled with increased enthusiasm and took pride in their tasks, however mundane. The hall rang to the sound of girlish song, feminine laughter, and high spirits, Catriona's loud among them.

Brooms were employed to banish sticky cobwebs and fat spiders festooning rafters and gloomy nooks. Old rushes were swept out and burned, and lads sent to gather new withies along the marshes to replace them. Rusted sconces were replaced with sturdy new ones, and fresh torches, dipped in pitch, made to fill them. The seal-oil lamps were cleaned and supplied with fresh oil and wicks. Tapestries were taken down from the walls and beaten to remove the clouds of dust that dulled the beauty of their colors. Flagstones were scrubbed with water and brooms, allowed to dry, then strewn with fresh rushes, dried flowers, and herbs whose sweet fragrance permeated the manor. Pallets were emptied, and restuffed with fresh straw or down as the case might be. Trestles were scrubbed with sand to remove all traces of crusted food, and then their surfaces were oiled to protect them from further damage, and polished with beeswax. When they were done, Rowanlee shone like a jewel.

"Blessed Mary, I ha'e never see the like!" Jeannie — the feisty, outspoken little carrot-haired woman Alan had appointed to serve her as personal maid — declared at the end of the third day of their labors. "Himsel' willna believe 'tis the same manor when he returns, an' no mistake!"

Catriona answered her with a weary but satisfied grin, brushing the sticky gray remnants of a stray cobweb from her cheek. Her condition seemed to leave her with less energy than she'd had before. She was exhausted, but still, she'd enjoyed seeing Rowanlee come alive once more, and the sense of accomplishment from knowing both her direction and her own labors had gone far to make it so.

"I believe you're right," she agreed a mite smugly, sinking down onto a small stool in her chamber and kneading her aching back. "If his lordship isna impresssed—whist, then he should be! I mean to start on the herb and spice gardens on the morrow," she added thoughtfully. "They are choked with weeds!"

Jeannie nodded. "Aye, lassie, we'll get to it soon enough, but for now, rest yersel' for a wee spell. A lass needs her rest at such a time."

Catriona looked up sharply. She met Jeannie's shrewd gray eyes with her own startled green ones. "I dinna ken what ye mean!" she insisted with little conviction. Jeannie's expression was too piercing for lies to do much good.

"Och, ye wee lummox," Jeannie murmured fondly and with none of the respect a serving woman should properly show her lord's guest. "I amna blind, nor foolish—and I ha'e seen many lassies breeding in my time! Did ye think I wouldna guess?" She grinned. "Besides, I've seen ye turn green every morn when faced wi' the prospect o' breaking your fast! And, tho' I'll grant ye our cook isna the best t' be found, he isna the worst, either! Whose bairn is it, love?" Jeannie asked matter-of-factly, though with great gentleness. "The Gilchrist's?"

Catriona hesitated, then nodded, close to tears.

"And does he ken ye're breeding?"

"Nay. I couldna bring mysel' to tell him of it!"

"Praise be!" Jeannie crossed herself, then added by way of explanation, "For a moment, I was afeared we'd have the clan Gilchrist battering at our gates wi' their claymores t' recover ye and the Gilchrist's babe!

But then, there's every chance himsel' will come searching for ye anyway, so I shallna rest easy just yet!"

"Why ever would he do such a thing?" Catriona asked with a bitter edge to her tone.

"Why? T' take ye back, o' course, lovie! A bonnie lass like yersel'. Och, I dinna doubt the mon was enamored o' ye t' distraction!"

Catriona pursed her lips. "Hmm. But enough of the Gilchrist's doings! We have much left to do on the morrow," she changed the subject. "For now, I want only t' soak mysel' in hot water, and change my clothes for some that arena stained with dirt." Inspecting her soiled kirtle, she wrinkled her nose. "Did ye have someone fetch up the chest from the storerooms? The one Laird Alan spoke of?"

Jeannie nodded and indicated an enormous, battered chest with a chipped crest of rowan buds and thistles that sat in a corner, unnoticed by Catriona till now. With a sniff of distaste, she said, "Aye, I did. There it be, m'lady, just as ye instructed. But if there be summat t' moths havena chewed within it, why, then I'll . . . I'll kiss that miserable auld Brand's scrawny backside, that I will!" She puckered up her lips and fluttered her lashes.

Catriona giggled at fiery-haired Jeannie's outrageous threat and hilariously coy expression. "Och, Jeannie, be careful, do! Ye shouldna make promises ye dinna mean t' keep. Happen the Fates will conspire t' make ye wish ye'd swallowed your words!"

"Humph! There's no fear o' them ferlie sort o' doings here at Rowanlee, mistress," Jeannie predicted dourly with a snort of contempt. "Believe me, what hasna been chewed by moths has been nibbled by mice or rats, and that's the truth, Fate or no Fate!"

"Was Rowanlee always this way?" she asked, remembering Alan's vivid and glowing descriptions of his manor when she was growing up. It had sounded a veritable Promised Land to her, the way he'd spoken of it; a fairy-tale kingdom where they would rule with wisdom, justice, and gentleness as its prince and princess. Long winter nights they'd while away gathered cozily about blazing hearths, while bards sang ballads of the great deeds of heroes and their peerless ladies, and the snow drifted down about their manor like feathers spilled from a pallet. The lazy, golden afternoons of summer they'd planned to spend idly drifting in a currough upon some tranquil loch where dragonflies dipped and flashed their brilliant wings, while Alan composed poems and songs for her pleasure alone, and she plucked at her harp. An idyllic existence where battle and hatred and enmity played no part, she wondered — or had it been a lassie's foolish dream, as Roarke had so harshly insisted?

"Indeed it was this way," Jeannie was saying, "leastways, long as I can recall, save on those few occasions when King Malcolm Great Head and his retinue have honored us with their presence. *Then* the Mac Quinlann flies into a fury, and bids the lassies scour from dawn t' dusk for days t' set the place t' rights before their arrival. And woe betide the ones who dinna work hard enough t' please himsel'!" Jeannie rolled her eyes. "Well, my lady, enough said. Let's just see what we have here, shall we?" she suggested, kneeling before the chest and wrestling with the brass catch to open it.

True to Jeannie's expectations, the garments within the chest were outdated, yellowed with age, motheaten or mildewed, for the greater part. Tugging out one damaged item after another, Jeannie would click her teeth in dismay, mutter, then toss it aside, before inspecting another.

"Who did the clothes belong to?" Catriona asked, curious, coming to watch her.

"Why, the laird's lady mother, love! She has no use for them now, alas, poor woman."

"Dead?"

"Och, nay, though 'twould be a blessing if she were, I say!" Jeannie confided, shaking her head.

"Ah, then the old dame lives elsewhere?" She didna recall Alan ever mentioning his mother before this morn, and then had done so only in passing. Perhaps she kept residence in a dower cottage somewhere on his lands?

"Why nay, bless ye! She has a chamber below the hall with all she requires, and a woman t' attend her. And as for being old — why, at three score and ten years, she is yet more nimble than most, in body, at least, and blessed with good health!"

Below the hall? His own lady mother lives *there?*"

"Aye, 'tis so. Ye see, puir Lady Shona hasna been — well — for many a year. Started off forgetful, she did, as I recall, some days not knowing her own name, or what day or month or year it might be, or by what path t' return home when she'd wandered from the manor. She grew stranger with every passing day. Sometimes, we'd waken t' find her meandering in the inner ward, every bit as naked as Adam, and her not knowing how she'd come t' be there, or what had happened t' her gown and wimple!" Jeannie confided in a whisper. "And once, I woke and she were out on the parapet beyond this bower, determined she could fly from it like a bird, and laughing fit t' raise the hackles on yer neck!"

"Then this was her chamber?" Catriona asked, glancing at the parapet Jeannie had mentioned. It led off the chamber through an arched doorway, open now to let in the sunshine and fresh air. The breeze bore the summer-scent of hay drying in the fields this morn.

"It was. And it took four braw lads to bring the lady back to her bed, that time," Jeannie recalled. "Now, she but wanders about below Rowanlee, muttering of things in the past. She canna feed hersel', or clean hersel', much less dress hersel', and so her serving woman keeps her in night-kirtles, and ties the strings at neck and wrists sae cleverly, the puir soul canna remove them! She is little different to a bairn."

"Then Alan had her cloistered below for her safety," Catriona concluded, relieved, for she'd foolishly wondered for a moment if the poor old dame had not been locked away in the dungeons by her own son!

"Either that, or t' hide her from curious eyes! Her ravings offend him, ye see? A great one for appearances is our Mac Quinlann!"

Jeannie selected a periwinkle blue kirtle that seemed less damaged than most. She tossed it to the opposite side of the chest — the side she'd designated for useful items. The pile there was markedly smaller than the other one.

"Well, I'll be! How in heaven's name did these find their way in here?" the woman clucked, holding up two long green strings, which she immediately discarded with an impatient, "Tsk!" as unimportant.

"Wait! Could I see those, Jeannie?"

With a shrug, Jeannie retrieved the strings and spilled them into Catriona's outstretched hands before resuming her task.

The strings were cross-gaiters, as she'd thought, commonly crisscrossed over the legs of a man's breeks to keep them from flapping about, or to hold up his hose. Catriona fingered them, remembering seeing Siward, the ferryman, incongruously sporting just such cross-gaiters, ones dyed the Norsemen's favorite shade of green. In fact, gaiters exactly like these. Surely 'twas but a coincidence, she decided, for she couldna imagine the wily ferryman being readily parted from his gaiters—unless, of course, the price offered had been more t' his liking than cutting a fine figure!

"We'll make a start on cleaning and airing the blue kirtle, I believe, mi'lady," Jeannie cut into her thoughts. "The skirts are a mite moth-eaten at the hems, but with you being such a wee scrap o' a lassie, 'twill stand a bit o' shortening. I believe it should serve well enough until himsel' can stir his bones t' purchase cloth t' sew ye others. Now, yer underlinens . . . Whist, will ye look at this, my lady! 'Tis all of it ruined! Well, no matter! What canna be changed must be endured, must it no'? Like as not that dratted pedlar what's come t' Rowanlee will have a length of plain goods we can use for a shift or two. Now, this yellow kirtle might—"

"Nay, Jeannie," Catriona refused with a shiver, discarding the gaiters. "I dinna care if 'tis good as new, I willna wear yellow!" Yellow had been the color *he* favored her to wear, the color of sunshine and primroses, butter and daisy-faces. Yellow had made her look like the Queen o' Elfland, *he'd* claimed, and so she wouldna wear yellow, ever again.

A dry lump formed suddenly in her throat and she turned away, tears prickling behind her eyelids as she rose and went out onto the parapet to escape Jeannie's shrewd eyes. Griping the stone edge, she gazed out at the Scottish Lowlands through a mist of tears. Somewhere beyond the purple-heathered moors to the southwest lay the Borders and Corbin. And

there, the lady Fiona, the lady Elyse, Tavish and
Graeme and Flora—all the others she'd come to
know—either tended their laird's wounds, or sat vigil
by the grave in which they'd laid him t' rest. *Oh,
Roarke!* she thought, her chest aching. *Are ye truly dead
and gone? Surely I would know in my heart if 'twas so,
somehow?*

As if in answer, she felt his babe stir in her womb
for the very first time, like the fragile beating of a
butterfly's wings.

She awoke in the wee hours, having retired early
the night before, to hear the faint, metallic chink of
harness and muffled voices. The sounds were coming
from the inner ward, she fancied drowsily, borne on
the breeze to her parapet and thence through the
door she'd left open to the sultry night. At first, she
tried to blot out the sounds and return to sleep, but
could not.

Curious—and wide awake now, besides—she flung
aside the coverlet and rose from her bed, going out
onto the parapet to discover who visited Rowanlee at
such an ungodly hour.

It was a beautiful summer's night, lit bright as day
by a full golden moon smiling down from an indigo-
blue sky. Its light flooded the tops of banked bluish
clouds. As she'd expected, Catriona could easily
make out a number of horses and riders milling in
the ward below, along with a covered cart. Even as
she watched, a figure clambered down from the rear
of it and slipped across the ward to enter Rowanlee
by the kitchen entryway. The night breeze caught the
figure's hair, lifting it. Straightway, a hand came up
to hold it down about mantled shoulders—a gesture
that was unmistakably female. Then, in the blink of

an eye, the person had gone, leaving Catriona with the impression of a flurry of mantle and skirts before she disappeared into the blackness of the manor's rear wing. In her wake, two men followed, struggling to heft a long, weighty bundle inside. A few moments later, they reappeared empty-handed, then in short order both horses and cart vanished in the direction of Rowanlee's stables.

Turning away, she frowned. It was curious that so many folk would be abroad at so late an hour, she considered as she returned to her bed, especially with folk being as superstitious as they were here in the north. Most people were afeared of the ghouls, the beasties, the witches and evil ones, that were reputed to fly abroad by night. Aye, 'twas a rare Scot who left his fire after dark could he avoid it! So what, she wondered, had been so important that those men had been abroad after nightfall, and, moreover, of such value they had carried it into the manor with such stealth?

She tried to put the tantalizing mystery aside, but tossed and turned, unable to get comfortable or to force her mind to sleep rather than wrestle with the question. Contraband o' some sort? she wondered. English gold, mayhap, sent north out o' reach of greedy King William's grasp? Or . . . had the bundle concealed one of the fugitive Saxon Edgar Aethling's men? Or better yet, the Aethling himsel'? Aye, she decided excitedly, It must be so! It made perfect sense! Had Alan not implied his important task for the Greathead was to assist in formulating a plan for the nobles' removal to safety here in Scotland? Then there was every chance he had already accomplished the dangerous mission the king had set him!

Determined that she was right — and equally determined that she must see the proof with her own eyes! — she drew a chamber robe over her night rail and slipped from her chamber.

The ground floor of the manor yielded nothing more unusual than sleeping servants and bleary-eyed sentries nodding at their posts. But as she was about to give up and return to her chamber and the prospects of a wakeful night, she saw several men appear from the head of a flight of stone stairs, ones that led down below Rowanlee. They filed past her hiding place, whispering amongst themselves. She waited until they had gone, then took the stairway they'd used herself.

Down, the spiral steps led, like a yawning mouth, so down into the darkness below the manor Catriona went. Naught but a brace of torches set in the walls held back the darkness. Their guttering light was nigh as eerie as no light at all, for by it she cast a huge shadow of herself, one that slipped along the walls beside her.

A long passageway led left and right at the foot of the stairs. With little debate, she chose left, and after a quick glance about her to make sure she hadna been followed, she slipped down it.

Here, the damp was marked. The dark walls dripped with it. The musty miasma of mildew, despair, and old terrors was marked. She shivered. Had she unwittingly chosen the dungeons of Rowanlee to prove her suspicions correct?

Looking apprehensively about her feet in the murky light, she caught the red glint of a beady eye nearby. She cried out in alarm, taking a hasty step backward. A pattering of tiny paws, a squeak, then the huge, furry water rat was gone, clearly as frightened of her as she'd been of him — if that were possible.

Beyond, in the innermost bowels of the dungeons,

down what seemed to be a long, broad passageway, a puny flicker of light illumined the walls, revealing a patch of gray stones that glistened wetly. Stepping gingerly, she headed for the light's source.

She found herself in a circular chamber where all manner of strange devices suspended from, or were bolted to, the walls. Feeling faint already with fear, her heart skipped a beat when she realized that the devices were instruments of torture! Though but fashioned of metal or leather or wood by human hands, when lit by only the puny flicker of a candle-stub someone had set in a puddle of wax atop a crude barrel-table, they seemed to radiate a pulsing life of their own. A presence that was pure, undiluted evil as she stared at them, transfixed, too fascinated to look away.

Who had suffered their hideous embraces, their spiked caresses, their blistering kisses, she wondered, dry-mouthed and sickened? How many had screamed for mercy within these walls over the centuries, and welcomed death, not as their enemy, but with open arms and a shout of joy as ally in their flight from pain? Turning away, she could not help the shudder or revulsion that shook her to the core, an emotion that made the babe in her womb stir fitfully, as if the puir mite sensed its mother's distress.

She was about to leave this loathsome place—and quickly!—when she spied a rough wooden bunk suspended by chains from the far wall. Something bulky lay upon it, covered over with what appeared to be a mantle of dark homespun. Was this the contraband, then? Or the fugitive Aethling, sleeping off the rigors of his horrendous journey? Whatever the men had been carrying lay on the bunk before her, she was certain of it. What could it be? Her chance to find out was here. 'Twas now—or never!

Now! she decided quickly. She skittered across the chamber to the candle, and pried the stub loose from its puddle of wax. Melted tallow scalded her fingers, but she swallowed her whimper of pain and returned to the bunk with the stub held aloft. Standing before it, she drew a shaky breath, grasped the edge of the covering, and pulled it aside . . .

Chapter Twenty-nine

Tingles of horror crawled down her spine like freshets of ice water as she gaped down — not at contraband nor at fugitive heirs to the throne of England, but into Siward the ferryman's bearded and undeniably dead face!

His head lay at a twisted, unnatural angle, as if his neck had been broken. His flesh was curiously dark, his glassy eyes wide open and staring — mayhap even bulging a little from their sockets. His tongue-tip protruded from between misshapen yellow teeth. His bluish lips were drawn back from gray gums in the leering grin of rigor mortis. About his throat rode a necklace of purple welts . . .

"Nay!" she moaned, shaking her head from side to side. "Oh, Jesu, Sweet Jesu, nay!"

The candle slipped from her suddenly numbed fingers and fell to the floor with a hiss, wax splashing her hems as it left her in inky darkness. Sobbing now, she picked up her skirts and whirled about, running blind from the evil chamber and its horrid occupant.

So absorbed was she in escaping to somewhere there was blessed light and air and normalcy, she didna notice the man with the torch advancing from the other direction until she'd barreled clear into him!

Her shrill scream as she slammed against his chest rent the dripping silence asunder! As arms came out to keep her from falling on the damp, lichened flagstones, she flailed at them, sobbing and shrieking curses and pleas for the man to let her go.

"Cease this madness, ye cursed lunatic!" an angry voice hissed. "I mean ye no harm. Take hold o' yer wits, and be calm, wench! 'Tis only Brand, the Mac Quinlann's man, ye ken!"

Looking up into Brand's cadaverous face was scant comfort in such poor light and in such nightmarish surroundings. She had never liked the man from the first! Nevertheless, she managed to calm herself enough for speech.

"B-back there! A dead man!" she blurted out.

"Ah," Brand acknowledged calmly, "so that explains it! Ye stumbled upon poor Siward in yer nosy pryings and wanderings aboot where ye didna belong, did ye, my lady?" he sneered, thrusting the torch close to her face to see her better.

"Aye, alas. I suppose I did," she admitted shakily. "But . . . but what—?"

"What happened to him?"

"Aye."

Brand chuckled. "Master Siward, greedy fellow that he was, God rest his soul, decided to tarry overlong wi' us here at Rowanlee. He took advantage of my laird's generosity for finding ye and bringing ye here, and outstayed his welcome. Tonight, at supper, he again wolfed down his victuals like a starving animal, as was his uncouth habit," Brand sniffed, "and unhappily fell victim to a choking spell. One that no one, alas, was able to revive him from. Perhaps a fishbone caught in his throat? Or a bite o' bread and cheese lodged in his gullet?" He shrugged. "Who knows? In but moments, the gluttonous oaf was no more! I had men carry him below to await burial."

"And the marks about his throat?"

"Marks? I saw no marks, lady?"

"But there were welts about his neck! I saw them."

"Ye did? Why, then they must have been the scars of old wounds, received long before his passing, damosel," Brand soothed glibly. "Nothing at all for ye t' concern yersel' with. Come now, I'll escort ye back to the staircase that leads above, and return ye safe to your chamber. Your hand, my lady, if ye'd be so kind?" There was the barest hint of a threat to his tone now. A warning she'd best comply, or regret it later.

Timidly, Catriona placed her hand in the bony paw he held out, and let him lead her back to the foot of the stairs. The torch, he held aloft to light their path.

"I would caution ye, mistress," he warned her upon reaching the foot of the stairs, "to keep close t' your chamber after dusk. Unfortunate accidents occur when the light is poor and one's surroundings — unfamiliar — shall we say?"

"Unfortunate accidents such as that which claimed poor Siward?" she whispered, her green eyes meeting his in the guttering torchlight.

"Aye, just so," he murmured. "Poor Siward spoke truly the night he brought ye here, as I recall. Ye *are* a dangerously canny lass!" And with that, he smiled, skull-like.

In her chamber once again, she flung herself down upon her bed and pulled the coverlet up over her head, willing the image of Siward's face t' leave her. Fugitive Aethling, indeed! What a romantic fool she'd been, t' think she'd find a prince in hiding within the dungeons of Rowanlee! Instead, she'd received a severe fright for her nosiness, uncovering instead the body of a puir gluttonous auld ferryman, were that Brand to be believed. Uncomfortably, she didna think he was . . .

Her last thought before she drifted into a fitful sleep was that she'd ask Jeannie who the riders had been and the identity of the woman accompanying them. Yet when sleep claimed her, it wasna deep and sweet as she prayed, but plagued with frightening dreams she'd thought buried forever.

She was dreaming the same dream, the one in which she was back in the narrow, cell-like tower at Erskine she'd once called her own — or so she thought.

It *seemed* to be her chamber, and yet at the same time, it was strangely different. The walls soared far, far above her, like the sides of a deep well that had its source in Hades. Only a narrow slit for a windeye let in the light of the moon. The light seemed to crawl down the walls, spreading a ghostly glimmer over the gray stones as it crept, like a sip of wine spilled on a slice of fresh bread is sopped up, crumb by crumb.

She swallowed and looked furtively about her, fear clawing at her throat. She must escape the invading light, for 'twas like the flickering phosphorescence of the corpse lights — those seen bobbing over the peat bogs on a moon-dark night!

Yet, all silvery-slithering, the light oozed down the walls towards her, inch by inch, until its unearthly glow surrounded her in a sickly haze.

"Get awa'!" she whimpered, shaking her ebony

head from side to side. "Whatever ye be, dinna come near me! Dinna!"

A cold draught came from somewhere, its breath the icy blast from the mouth of a stone-cold tomb. Her arms were bare, and as she shivered, gooseflesh rose down their length.

"The Lord is my shepherd . . . I shall not want . . . Yea, though I walk through the . . . Oh, God— *nay!*"

Before her eyes, she saw her father appear, a nightmare woven from the light of the eerie moon. Angus McNair called to her, his hands held out in supplication.

"Find them, daughter!" he entreated, his gray lips moving like that of a drowning man, gasping for breath. *"My soul cries for justice, that it may rest in peace. Find them!"*

The apparition raised his head, as if craning to look up at the windeye far above. With horror-filled eyes, Catriona saw the crimson gash that encircled his throat like a second mouth; a mouth that grinned from right to left with a mirthless glee. Blood began to pour from the slit in great, ruby rivers.

Hysteria claimed her then. Her hands flew up to tear at her hair. She ripped strands of it from her scalp, but felt no pain in her anguish. She heard a low, animal moaning coming from somewhere nearby, and the hoarse screams of a woman gone mad—and for a moment, did not know them for her own.

"Enough o' yer weeping, my bairn!" came Auld Morag's stern voice, yet it sounded in her mind, rather than in her ears. She could see no one when she dared open her eyes. *" 'Tis a McNair ye are! The blood of himself runs in yer veins, and in that o' your bairn, along wi' the Gilchrist's royal blood. For all that Angus was a*

410

devil, he was no coward—not t' his dying breath. No more must ye be afeared! I ha'e left my bairn t' guard ye, Catriona. Ye arena alone. My canny Badger-boy will keep ye safe from harm! Be strong. Be brave, for with courage, ye will triumph! Only then can what is prophecied come to be!!"

With Morag's words, she felt new courage course through her veins. The thready throb of her pulse strengthened. She rose to her feet, her fists clenched in the folds of her night rail.

"Nay!" she whispered fiercely. "Your murderers will pay, father—they will! Justice will prevail! Right will triumph—or I amna the McNair o' Erskine!"

She came bolt upright in her bed, fully awake, her fervent oaths yet pouring from her mouth.

Her heart was pounding, her cheeks wet with tears. The movement of the bairn in her womb was a desperate fluttering. Her child! She must think of the child, for through it, her clan would live on! The bairn's safety and well-being must be uppermost in her mind henceforth! Splaying her fingers across her belly, she softly crooned a lullaby in a shaky voice that steadied as she sang on. Yet it was some time before the wild thrum of her heart had slowed and the bairn's movements stilled.

A nightmare. It had only been a nightmare—no different from all the others she had dreamed when she'd first gone to Corbin. The only difference was that now there was no gentle, heathery voice to soothe her pounding heart. No strong yet tender arms to enfold her and hold the terror at bay. No Roarke of the mist-gray eyes to banish her tears and make her forget the faceless dangers that menaced her in her dreams.

She clutched the pillow to her bosom and cried herself to sleep.

411

Chapter Thirty

"Jeannie? Is that you?"

"Aye, mi'lady?" came Jeannie's muffled voice through the door.

"Thank God! Do ye come in straightway!"

She slipped the rusted bolt to fling open her chamber door, taking Jeannie by the hand and all but yanking her inside the room.

"What is it, lass? Ha'e ye taken leave o' your wits?" Jeannie exclaimed, wide-eyed as Catriona carefully closed and bolted the door behind her.

"Nay, Jean. Rather, I have come *to* them!" she said grimly. "Tell me, did ye hear anything unusual last night?"

"Unusual?" Jeannie asked, frowning absently as she inspected the periwinkle-blue kirtle she'd salvaged from the chest the day before. Sponged and shortened, the threadbare hems trimmed with a border of tablet-braiding that sly rogue of a pedlar had discovered in the bottom of his pack, then spread over a bush in the sunshine to dry and air out, it was far more presentable now . . . But to her dismay Catriona gave an impatient snort and tugged it from her hands, tossing it carelessly aside as she demanded, "Answer me, Jeannie, and t' the devil wi' the dratted kirtle for now!"

"Unusual in what way?"

"Like visitors to Rowanlee?" Catriona persisted. "Ones that arrived after moonrise?"

"Visitors after moonrise? T' my ken, we had none!" the carrot-haired woman insisted with a frown. Then her brow cleared and she smiled in sudden understanding. "Och, love, ye must ha'e heard the Mac Quinlann! Returned home in the wee hours from Edwin's Burgh, he did. If ye heard people aboot after dark, it must ha'e been himsel'!"

"I did more than hear folk aboot," Catriona declared. "I left my chamber, and went below t' spy on them!"

"Ye did *what?*" Jeannie exclaimed, aghast.

"I followed them! Och, I ken it sounds daft, but ye see, I knew that Mac Quinlann's undertaking for the king was to find a way the Saxon Aethling and his nobles might be brought t' safety here in Scotland t' evade King William and his men. Well, last night, when I heard noises and went t' look down from the parapet, I spied a cart drawn up t' the kitchens. A woman got down from it and went inside, and after her came a brace of burly louts, hefting a bundle between them. And, thinking 'twas the Aethling they were after smuggling into Rowanlee, I decided to go down and see for mysel' what it was they'd carried."

Jeannie crossed herself, pale with alarm. "Whist, ye foolish ninny! Ye empty-headed goose! The babe has addled yer wits, sure! I thought ye had more sense than t' go prying aboot in what doesna concern ye at dead o' night! Whatever were ye thinkin' of?" she demanded crossly, color riding high in her cheeks.

"Of satisfying my curiosity, what else?" Catriona declared airily, brazening out Jeannie's reproachful

413

glare, for she knew at heart her actions had been impossibly impulsive and foolhardy. Her bravado didna last overlong, however, for Jeannie's expressions remained implacable. "Och, very well then! I admit, 'twas foolish o' me. I know that now full well, for I stumbled on things I would lief have gone without knowing!" She grimaced.

So mysterious was her tone that, despite her annoyance, Jeannie couldna resist asking, "What? What was it ye saw?"

"Siward!" Catriona said hoarsely, closing her eyes as she remembered . . .

"The auld ferryman?" Jeannie said with a disappointed wrinkling of her nose. "A small wonder, indeed, t' have ye so breathless and flummoxed!" She sniffed, and crossed her arms over her bosom.

"Aye, but not Siward as we knew him! Dead, he was—and horribly so, his corpse hidden in the dungeons themselves. He was strangled elsewhere, and his body brought back t' Rowanlee for some reason, else I'm mistaken! And yet when Brand surprised me down there and I asked him what had befallen the man, he lied. Swore he'd choked on a fishbone and expired in Rowanlee's kitchens, of all tales!"

"But Siward hasna been here since the night he brought ye here!" Jeannie exclaimed. "Certainly he didna die here, 'else I would surely ha'e heard of it."

"Aye! So I suspected. So ye see, that nasty Brand's a-lying, for some purpose!" Catriona vowed with an air of triumph, like a delicate wee hound on the scent of game. "He's up to no good, and I fancy the Mac Quinlann'd best be told of it, right soon!"

"Ye'd tell himsel'?" Jeannie began doubtfully, "for all that the pair o' them are thick as thieves, wi' few secrets left unshared between them? Whist, lassie, 'tis best ye say naught, I fancy, 'less ye open up a bellyful o' worms best left untouched!"

"Ye think that Alan is privy t' Brand's doings, then?" Catriona cried. "Och, I canna believe it, Jean! I would have him told that that awful man threatened me, at very least! Surely he would not condone that?"

"He threatened ye!"

"Aye — oh, most guardedly, t' be sure, but threatened nonetheless. Cautioned me t' keep t' ma chamber of a night, he did, for fear o' 'unhappy accidents' such as befell auld Siward!"

"Then ye would be wise t' heed him, my lass," Jeannie cautioned with a shudder. "Or risk your neck! Now, enough of this matter. Do ye dress yersel', and swiftly, for the Mac Quinlann is t' home, and already asking after ye t' join him."

"He has returned so soon?" It was Catriona's turn to frown now.

"Aye."

"And the woman that rode in with him?" she inquired casually. "Who is she?"

"Woman? Tsk, ye must ha'e been dreaming after all, lassie! He took with him but two o' his guard for escort! And there was no woman with them when they returned," Jeannie asserted, the knowing twinkle in her eyes hinting that she thought Catriona jealous now.

"You're certain?"

Jeannie bustled about, filling a basin with water from a pitcher, laying out hose and underchemise, and setting combs and veil in readiness for Catriona's morning toilette as she spoke. "Aye, lass, I'm sure. Now, up wi' ye, Mistress Slugabed, and let me see t' ye," Jeannie urged.

Catriona wrinkled her nose with displeasure as she took her seat upon a stool. She washed and dried her face and hands, then sat very still so that Jeannie could brush the tangles from her long black hair and dress it.

"A bonnie lass like yersel'! Ye should ha'e had a husband long since, and a brace o' bairns at your breast by now," Jeannie clucked.

"I would sooner the pox than a spouse!" Catriona vowed with fervor.

"And why is that, pray?" Working deftly as they talked, the woman braided her hair into two thick plaits. These she wound in rosettes on either side of her head and fastened in place with hairpins.

"Because I've observed that most husbands are a curse, rather than the blessing a maid would wish them t' be!" Her lovely face screwed up in a grimace. "Husbands are much like fathers, forever wearing a thunderous scowl and bossing everyone about—and I dinna care to be bossed about, nor have a husband who'd force his demands on me. Nay, I dinna care to answer to anyone for my doings, Jeannie, as a woman must, once she is wed. In truth, I had more than enough o' being some man's chattel in my father's keep!"

"Aye, but marriage isna the only state in which a woman has responsibilities and duties she must tend to, like it or not, lovie," Jeannie reminded her in motherly fashion. She settled the veil over her hair, then placed a simple circlet of braided silks about her brow to hold it in place. "That bairn ye're carrying, for example. 'Twill demand much o' ye. Ye canna come an' go sae easily, when ye are two instead o' one, nay, indeed! The bairn must be fed when hungry, his breeks changed, his wee belly rubbed t' rid it o' wind, his tears comforted. When he's poorly, ye must sit up wi' him of a night and soothe his pain and dinna think t' find your own bed, no matter how

416

weary ye be. And when he toddles, ye canna take yer eyes from him for a moment, lest he fall, or drown, or hurt his wee self. If that isna burdensome, I dinna ken what is!"

"But that's different!" Catriona insisted. "When ye love someone, ye dinna care what lengths ye must go to t' care for them or keep them from harm. So will I love this bairn and care for it. 'Tis different from being ordered about!"

"Aye," Jeannie agreed, grinning. "Mayhap. But mark my words, ye wouldna mind pleasing a husband and tending t' his needs overmuch, however bossy he might seem — not if ye *loved* him! Nay, ye'd find a way t' appear to obey him — and go yer own way, as do all clever lassies! Now, enough chatter. Hurry below t' the hall. The master's waiting t' break fast wi' ye."

Catriona rose and crossed the chamber. In the doorway, she paused and turned back to Jeannie, who was busy gathering up the toilette articles. Like a wee robin redbreast, she never seemed to stand still, but was always hopping about from task to task, chirruping merrily. Catriona had already grown fond of her, and knew the woman felt the same. She would be honest if asked a straightforward question and not mince words.

"Jeannie?"

"Aye, aye, what is it now?" Jeannie demanded wearily, pretending to be vexed.

"Can I ask ye something?"

"Aye." Jeannie sighed and rolled her eyes.

"D' ye — d' ye like the Mac Quinlann?"

"Himsel'? Why, lassie, 'tis not for me t' like or dislike him, only t' do his bidding. Freedwoman or nay, I must yet earn ma keep."

"Come. Ye dinna have t' fear t' speak plainly,

Jean, not with me! I'll no' tell tales on ye! D' ye think he'd make me a good husband? Truly, I would welcome your opinion, for he has already asked me t' wed him, and but awaits my answer."

Jeannie paused before speaking, and her hesitation supplied the answer to Catriona's question as effectively as her words. "Nay, lass," she said slowly. "If ye want an honest answer, I agree wi' yer lord father, God rest his soul. I dinna think he's the mon for ye. God knows, your bairn will need a father and ye a husband, but not him, love. Not him!"

"And why not?"

Jeannie shrugged. "Ye can call me a silly goose if ye will, but I put great store in the manner in which a mon treats others—his servants, even his horses and hounds—indeed, all those of lesser station in life than himsel'. The way I've seen it, the noblest of men deal kindly and courteously with all who serve them, from the grandest chamberlain to the lowliest serf. For mysel', I dinna care for the MacQuinlann's ways, for he fawns on those wi' power to do him guid, but vents his spite on those he canna use t' his vantage. And that, mi' lady Catriona, is all I have t' say on the matter. Indeed, my tongue has run away wi' me—and so must you run on!"

Her green eyes pensive, Catriona nodded and made to go, but this time, 'twas Jeannie who spoke again.

"Lassie?"

"Aye?"

"I think ye ha'e found the mon ye could love and be wife to, if ye'd but be honest wi' yersel'. I have seen such a look in yer eyes a time or two!"

"When I—when I spoke o' the Gilchrist?"

"Aye, himsel'. 'Tis plain as the nose on your face, the way ye yearn for him. Flee Rowanlee, and go

418

back t' him, lass. Humble yersel'. Tell him ye love him. Bastard born or nay, I have heard Laird Roarke's an honorable fellow. One who takes care o' his own and is fair wi' all, be they laird or serf. If ye want him, swallow your pride, and go back."

"Jesu, would that I could," she whispered, swallowing the knot of tears that rose up her throat. "But he told me once that if ever I should leave him for the Mac Quinlann's keep, he would never take me back."

"Whist! Words spoken in anger and jealousy mean naught!" Jeannie insisted.

"Nay, Jean. They werena empty threats. I grew to know him well, and I believe he'd grown fond of me, too, but he meant what he said. He . . . he might ha'e forgiven me anything—except my being here. He hates your laird wi' a passion!"

"But ye didna choose t' be brought here, love!"

"Nay, I didna. But Roarke would never believe that," she said sadly.

Alan was already seated at table when she entered the hall. His eyes lit up when he saw her. He came at once to his feet and hastened to meet her.

"Good morrow, Catriona!" he exclaimed. "I trust ye slept well?"

"Quite well, thank ye kindly, my laird. But what a pleasant surprise, t' find ye so swiftly returned t' us! Welcome home! We didna expect ye back sooner than a fourteennight."

"Nor did I expect my business for the king t' be concluded so swiftly. Suffice it to say it was, and I am more than happy t' be home wi' ye again."

He drew her hand to his lips. Having kissed it, he lowered his fair head to her dark one, obviously intending to kiss her on the lips as well. Why, she knew not, but the thought of him kissing her was suddenly abhorrent. Some shadowy memory flick-

419

ered in her mind like a guttering candle, but was as swiftly gone. In the moment before his mouth would have claimed hers, she turned her head aside so that his lips brushed only her cheek.

"Whist! I have a raging appetite this morn!" she declared shakily, and forced a brilliant smile as she moved away from him to the trestle, spread with the morning fare. "Shall we break our fast, sir?"

Snatching up a bowl, she took up the ladle that stuck out from the black kettle of porridge set before them, and served him a hefty amount of it.

"There's naught t'compare wi' a fine hot bowl o' porridge t' break one's fast," she babbled on. "Some prefer broken meats, and others frumenty and such, but I—"

"Does the thought o' my kisses cause ye t' babble, Cat?" he drawled amusedly, leaning back in his chair to regard her with his blue eyes twinkling.

" 'Twas not that!" she denied.

"Then what was it?"

"Just that I was—am!—famished."

"Starving? Hardly starving, my dearling! I fancy ye've bloomed in the wee while ye've been here with us. Look how full and rosy yer cheeks are, and how pleasingly—rounded—your figure." He placed his hand upon her thigh, and squeezed it.

Incensed, she sprang to her feet, flinging him off. "Why, 'tis bold ye've become, my laird, to put yer hand upon my person so insolently! Ye would never have made so free before!"

"Bold, Cat? Insolent, sweet Cat? Is that what ye told the Gilchrist when he 'put his hand' upon ye and stole yer maidenhead, curse ye?" he demanded spitefully. "Or do ye only cry 'nay!' when 'tis I—who has waited a lifetime t' claim ye as my honored bride!— would caress ye? Jesu, Cat! Ma sweet, bonnie Cat, yield t' me your all! I've been so verra patient all these years, and ha'e missed ye right sorely!"

His hand came out to grip her chin and turn her head about. Still gripping it, he held her fast for his hateful kisses. She almost gagged as his lips smeared across hers, forcing them to part. All too soon, she felt the sharp graze of his teeth as he forced her mouth to open beneath his, the wet thrust of his tongue striking within it, and was almost sick.

As he ground his mouth against hers, he cupped her breast above her kirtle and squeezed, then toyed cruelly with her nipple as if she were not flesh and blood, but beef t' be pounded t' tenderness. Incensed, she shoved her palms against his chest, trying to push him from her, but he wouldna release her until he'd had his fill. In the end, she made herself endure the onslaught of his mouth in silence, suffer his hurtful touch. Going limp, she prayed he would soon be done if she didna resist him.

When he finally drew back to draw breath, red roses bloomed in her cheeks. Her green eyes crackled. She brought back her hand and soundly boxed his ear, hissing, "Take that, 'ye lecherous knave—and dinna think t' kiss me again—ever!—ma betrothed or nay! If 'tis kisses ye crave anon, no doubt the long-haired wench ye brought home by dead o' night will prove willing!"

"Wench?" he exclaimed, rubbing his stinging ear with a livid expression.

"Aye! And dinna deny it!" she declared, "for I saw her, slipping in by the kitchens last night!"

"There was no wench!" he ground out.

"Damme ye, dinna play me for a fool, Alan Mac Quinlann! I saw her—a lass wi' long dark hair. She rode in the cart."

"A wench with long dark hair who—? Och, ma

421

puir, jealous Cat, now I have it! So that's why ye didna welcome ma kisses! 'Tis jealous you are! Ye must have spied Mistress Goodfellow and thought the worst!" So saying, Alan threw back his head and roared with laughter.

"Saw who? I regret, sir, I dinna ken your hussy's name," she said pertly, furious that he would laugh at her.

"My puir lass! The 'hussy', as ye put it, isna a hussy at all, but the kindly soul who cares for my lady mother!" he told her. "For many years, the lady of Rowanlee has been unwell. Often, her mind wanders. Truth to tell, till Mistress Goodfellow came t' us, I didna ken what t' do for her, and was at wits' end. My puir mother has no sense of peril left her, alas, ye see. She has oft put herself in jeopardy when chambered in high places. For her safety, she's been given a small chamber below Rownalee, where the 'hussy' ye speak of tends her night and day. Mistress Goodfellow took a rare day for hersel' to go home an' visit her sickly father. We passed her upon the road on our return last night, and my man took her up in the cart t' ride the rest o' the way in comfort. I will take ye t' meet with her anon—and with my lady mother, too, of course, should ye care to. Ye shall see, Cat. I speak only the truth. There is no woman for me but yersel'."

"Oh!" Catriona said in a small voice. "Your pardon, sir. 'Twould seem I was mistaken. I didna mean t' imply—"

"Shush, lassie. Ye've no need t' beg my pardon, none at all. Ye see, I know only too well how it feels t' be jealous t' distraction o' one ye love," he added pointedly. He took up a spoon, dipped it in his oatmeal, and nodded to her to do likewise. "Come, lass. We shall eat our porridge and converse of small matters, and start this morning afresh. We'll pretend no cross words passed between us, aye, my dove?"

"Aye, and gladly," she agreed. She devoted her attention to the bowl of steaming oatmeal before her, praying his intentions to 'start afresh' would not include another sampling of his hateful kisses at some later date. She frowned. He had not mentioned Siward's death, or made any reference, however veiled, to the fact that Brand had caught her nosing about down below. Brand must have been reluctant to tell him, so clearly Alan knew naught of the body that had been brought into his keep, along with his mysterious Mistress Goodfellow. Jeannie had been wrong, she decided. Whatever the cadaverous Brand might be up to, he'd engineered it alone, and without his laird's knowledge. There were some secrets they didna share.

"Ye sent for me, my lai— God's Blood, sir! Ye shouldna be oot o'bed!"

Tavish hurried across the chamber to where Roarke, hanging over a chairback for support, was trying with little success to shrug himself into his blouse.

White strips of linen crisscrossed his chest and left shoulder, the bandage bright against the dark gold of his flesh. His black hair was disheveled, his swarthy face stubbled with several days' growth of black beard. His expression was the sour one of a vigorous, active man forced to play invalid for far too long.

"Dinna use that tone w' me, Tavish Gilchrist!" he growled. "I amna a bairn, so dinna treat me like one. A full month has passed, and I am healed, I say!" So saying, he nevertheless gritted his teeth.

Groaning, he pressed a fist to his wound before sinking onto his pallet, his face now the color of old vellum. "Mother of God!" he muttered, and uttered a stream of less dainty oaths.

As he had on many occasions since that day by the ford, Tavish felt guilt fill him, although Roarke had wholeheartedly sworn he'd forgiven him—if only after a tongue-lashing that had lasted a good hour!

"Do I seem so blessed cruel, so cursed cold and merciless, I would ha'e slain the lassie I planned t' wed?" he'd thundered that day once back at Corbin, trying to rise from his bed. Though he'd only just come to and had lost a great deal of blood, he'd thrust aside the serving wenches and his lady mother as they tried to see to his chest wound, snarling at them to wait. "I meant t' *protect* her, get her safe to cover, ye fool—not run her through wi' ma claymore! What were ye thinking of, ye damned lummox!"

"My laird, forgive me!" Tavish had implored him, little less ashen-faced than his laird. "I . . . I made a grave error which I can never undo. I saw ye—the frightened way she looked at ye! And all I could recall was the day ye swore she'd killed her father, and the hatred in your eyes then, sir! I . . . I dinna ken what came over me! I believed ye meant t'kill her—and I *knew* she was innocent and that I couldna let ye do it!"

"Och, Tavish, enough," Roarke had said wearily at last. "I know ye, mon, through and through. And I know ye meant well. In truth, I forgive ye all. Christ's Staff, even should I *die* o' this dratted woman's probings, I will yet forgive ye!" he'd gritted, casting a jaundiced eye upon his mother, which she studiously ignored as she cut him to remove the arrowhead. "But for now, be gone, laddie! Bother me nae more, lest I change my mind and decide t' have ye hung, drawn, and quartered. Yer jabberings have given me a pounding head, confound ye!"

To Tavish's relief, he'd fainted away seconds after, and the lady Fionna had seen the arrowhead cut from her son's chest at the point below his collarbone before he recovered. But Tavish's relief had been short-lived, for a few days later, despite Fionna's every precaution, the wound had grown red and swollen and a fever had raged through Roarke. A virulent infection had set into the wound, and a battle for his life had been enjoined.

Hot herb poultices had had little effect. Roarke's fever had risen and stayed dangerously high for many days. In those troubled times, Tavish had relieved the lady Fionna and taken turns at sitting by his bedside, flinching as Roarke tossed and turned and raved in the throes of delirium, alternately cursing the lass Catriona for a deceitful baggage, a damned McNair bitch who couldna be trusted, and in swearing his boundless love for her in turn and imploring her to return to him. In the end, Fionna had grimly decided she had no choice but to cauterize the wound with the heated point of a blade and drain it of pus, else forfeit his life. This she had done.

He and Graeme had together held Roarke down, one pinioning either arm, while Ian, his reeve, had managed to drip a goodly measure of whiskey between his lips. Still, it had not been enough to dull the pain completely. When Fionna had pressed the glowing red dirk to the festering wound, he had roared with agony, and lifted himself clear off the pallet. It had taken both their considerable strengths to hold him fast, and when Fionna was done, both Tavish's and Graeme's eyes were moist, their expressions haggard, their bodies exhausted.

"Catriona, ma wee wren! Where are ye flown, ma lovie?" Roarke had inquired a little drunkenly once it was over and his wounds had been bound.

"Damme her!" Graeme had muttered, his blue eyes blazing as he staggered from the chamber with its reek of sickness and medicaments. "Damme the McNair bitch, and all of her bloody ilk! Aye — and damn ye, too, my friend, for what the pair o' ye have done t' my laird!"

Tavish, steeped in guilt at the time, had been unable to voice an answer, much less defend himself. And so, with a withering, accusing glare, Graeme had stomped away. He'd not returned to sit with his laird since, unable — Tavish believed — to bear seeing his lifelong companion laid so low. Or, more likely, to stand by and hear him call so lovingly upon a McNair wench he had every reason to hate, seeing her clan had destroyed his family . . .

"Proper broody this morn, are ye no'?" Roarke inquired sourly, snapping Tavish smartly back to the present. "My lady mother had a favorite hen once who looked much akin t' ye when she was about to lay!"

"I was but . . . pondering," Tavish said evasively, ignoring the insult.

"On what?" Roarke asked, gesturing with impatience to the steward to help him on with his clothing.

"Erskine."

"Ah. And how fares the flower of the Borders since I gave the keep's administration into your trusty hands?" his laird asked eagerly, sitting down to lace his breeks. King Malcolm had officially appointed Roarke as guardian of the McNair estates, since he'd been betrothed to the lady Catriona before her disappearance, and Tavish had reluctantly agreed to administer them.

"She fares well, sir, if I do say so mysel'," Tavish said with pride. "The crops have been planted, however late in the season for it. And although the barley and oats will be tardy in harvesting, they promise to be plentiful. The McNair flocks are some of the finest I've ever seen, and should—"

"Damme ye, Tavish, ye know what I want—and it isna an accounting, damme ye! Has she been seen there? Have ye any word of her at all?"

Tavish's eyes skewed away from Roarke's hopeful ones. "None, sir. She hasna come to Erskine as we expected, alas."

"Sweet Jesu! 'Tis as she always feared, then. The men she saw murder her clansmen have taken her. T' silence her!"

He tightened his jaw, fighting down the image of his lovely Catriona, afraid and oh, so very vulnerable, with a knife at her throat, pleading with a pack of murderous ruffians to spare her life. The image of her at their hands nigh drove him to madness . . .

"Taken her, sir? Then ye dinna think, as Graeme believes, that she went willingly with those who attacked us at the ford?"

"Nay, I dinna. She might have left me wi'out a backward glance," he said ruefully, "but never her wee pup!" He nodded his head towards the corner of his bower where Lyra curled in a shaggy ball, fast asleep. He whistled softly, and the pup—much grown now—pricked its ears, uncurled, and bounded across to him to have her ears scratched. "Nay, dog, yer mistress was fond o' ye, was she no'?" Roarke said thoughtfully, petting the beast. "She would have taken ye with her, given the chance." Taking a small wooden ball from the secretary before him, he rolled it across the rushes. The pup gamboled after it and brought it back, dropping it hopefully at Tavish's feet this time and whining and eyeing him expectantly. The steward ignored the animal.

"Och, I fear for her, Tavish," Roarke said hoarsely, and his gray eyes were dark with foreboding. "There's small hope she was able t' convince her captors she remembers naught of what she saw that night, or that they'll believe she couldna identify them even had she wished to."

"Nay, sir," Tavish agreed, swallowing. "But we have tried, time and time again, to solve the riddle of the clan McNair's murderers, without success!"

"Then we must try again. As long as there's the least chance she is yet alive, we mustna give up!"

"There was something that occurred to me, sir," Tavish said thoughtfully.

"Aye?"

"Well, sir, 'tis the—the moon, sir. I was pondering on the best time for planting at Erskine, ye ken? As the farmers and I had our heads together over the moon calendars, I remembered the night Erskine was overrun, sir, and the night Castle Glenmuir was attacked. 'Twas full sir, on both occasions. And I got t' thinking, happen our 'friends' prefer a clear, bright night for their foul deeds, think ye no'? Happen if they should strike again, it could well be wi' the next full moon, not three nights hence?"

"Why, 'tis a worthy thought, friend, and one I'd not considered!" Roarke admitted, casting his steward an admiring glance. " 'T be forewarned is to have the vantage, is it no'? I'll send word to our sister keeps, and advise them to be vigilant for the next sevennight. And for ourselves, I shall see more guards posted on the walls, and all newcomers t' Corbin treated with utmost suspicion from this very day. Good thinking, mon!"

428

"Thank ye, sir," Tavish said with a flush of pleasure rising in his freckled cheeks. "And while we're on the subject of newcomers, I've been thinking about that, too. The McNair was no fool, was he, Roarke?"

"Nay, he was not. What are ye getting at?"

"Given his caution, who would a canny chieftain such as the McNair himsel' allow t' enter his keep in midwinter, with a blizzard howling, food in short supply, and the threat o' Norman attacks on everyone's lips?"

"Someone he would have no reason to mistrust, clearly?" Roarke suggested, warming to the guessing game. He drew a chair up to a small table and waved Tavish into it, pouring them both a generous measure of whiskey to aid their thoughts. "A priest, mayhap?" he suggested. "A band o' murderous nuns, wi' dirks beneath their habits?" He shook his head and laughed at the idiocy of his suggestion. "Och, laddie, who knows!"

"Now, come, sir, dinna mock the thought, for of a certainty, we are on the right track! Aye, ye may laugh, but it must have been someone—or rather, *many* someones—similarly beyond reproach as your party of holy sisters, or Angus wouldna have flung his gates wide, would he? Think again!"

Roarke's smile fled. Seriously he said, "Very well, then. Someone he knew, mayhap? Friends he'd mistakenly trusted? Allies turned sour?"

"Possible. More than possible—indeed, most likely!"

"Hmm. But if that be so, I canna help wondering why the McNair's body wasna with the others. Why he was *alone* in his chambers when death took him? The answer points to a wench having killed him, Tavish, the left-handed bitch o' my puir Cat's nightmares. One he'd taken to his chamber to sport

429

with—or mayhap she enticed him there, for her own dark purpose. The comb and the strands of hair snagged in its teeth do bolster my certainty that him, she slew hersel'."

"Very well then. We have the scene. The keep, half-hidden by the swirling snow, and the McNairs at their supper, confident both foul weather and late hour bring no threat from without, either from Normans or enemy clansmen. A band of people—on some pretext unknown to us—arrive at Erskine's gates. They clamor for admittance, and the gatekeeper grants them entry—tho' only after seeking his lord's permission, which for reasons also unknown to us, is readily given. One—a wench—the laird finds pleasing, and takes to his bed. She murders him, while her mysterious companions slay the others."

"And when they flee in t' the blizzard, not a clue do they leave behind them t' betray their identity."

Lyra had given off her woeful staring at Tavish's face in the hopes that he would play with her. She worried at his boot, instead, growling threateningly. "Och, awa' wi' ye, ye worrisome wee bitchling! Give over," he laughed, but the pup wouldna let up. Reaching down, Tavish retrieved the wooden ball from under his stool. Originally painted red, time and wear had made its bright finish patchy and dull. He was about to throw it for the hound to fetch when he hesitated, turning it over in his palm.

"And where did this come from?" he asked curiously.

"Hamish found several like it, scattered on the rushes at Glenmuir after his people were attacked. I gave it t' the pup in lieu of her gnawing on my boots," Roarke said with a shrug.

Tavish grew very still. His face paled. "What is this?" he whispered.

430

" 'Twas found at Glenmuir, the morn we were attacked by the ford. As I said, I had it off Hamish. He thought it curious, since the bairns of his keep owned no such plaything, but it meant no more t' me than it did t' him. I had forgot about it, what with ma wounding."

"Sweet God in heaven!" Tavish exclaimed. "I have seen such as this before—at Erskine. D' ye not recall, my laird? When we were meeting with the Border lairds in the month of April, I remarked on how it had made me shudder t' see such innocent playthings amidst such butchery?"

"Aye, I remember something of that like, now that ye mention it," his laird acknowledged. "But are ye certain? There were no such baubles at Erskine when I took Catriona there t' see her kinsmen shriven. I examined everything most carefully that day, laddie. There were no wooden balls such as ye described, I would stake my life on it."

Tavish wetted his lips. "But there must have been! They were there when Graeme and I went there. Ye . . . ye must be mistaken, sir. For if not—" He let the thought go unvoiced, for 'twas one too terrible to speak aloud.

"For if not," Roarke finished for him, "someone saw fit to remove them before I went there. Someone, moreover who knew what they signified—knew that they could tell how entry was gained to a canny man's snowbound keep—and was determined to keep that means a secret!"

"Then that someone works from within Corbin, Roarke," Tavish murmured in a voice so low and filled with dread, it was barely above a whisper. "God help us, that someone is in league wi' the murderers, and one o' us, t' boot!"

"Aye," Roarke breathed, his gray eyes narrowed

431

and filled with a brooding fury that made his steward flinch. "The same treacherous 'someone' that the lad Hal warned me of—the one he claimed sought t' take my lady's life not once, but thrice. Jesu, Tavish, what a blind, damned fool I've been! We have harbored a serpent in our breasts this past sevenmonth!"

For several long moments, silence reigned between them as both men pondered the knotty riddle. And then, of a sudden, Tavish sprang to his feet, slamming fist into the palm of his other hand. "By God, Roarke, I fancy I have it! I know in what guise entry t' Erskine and Glenmuir was gained—and how, if I am right, they will seek t' gain entry t' Corbin!"

Roarke stood and strode across to the windeye, moving stiffly with his wound so newly healed. Gazing out at the green and purple moors and glens, he urged his steward quietly, "Tell me, then, my riddling friend. Tell me how 'twas done."

"Our murderers were *players*, my laird, my life on it! Traveling players, who wander from keep to keep. Are they not granted entry at any gate without question or thought, on account o' the merry diversions they bring! Singing. Tumbling. Feats of magic." He drew a breath before adding, "And *juggling*, Roarke. Juggling!"

"The wooden balls. Aye, laddie, ye must be right!" Roarke agreed heavily. "It all fits!"

"But ye dinna seem pleased, sir," Tavish complained. "Do ye not see? Knowing this, we shall be forewarned, do they come here!"

"Aye, laddie. Ye've done well. Dinna mistake my mood. I am pleased beyond measure that ye have untangled the riddle."

"But the traitor in our midst—ye would know who he or she might be?"

"Aye, lad. Aye. I willna rest easy, not until he—or

432

she—reveals themsel'. They would know, ye ken, Tavish? They could tell what happened to ma bonnie lass that morn . . ."

His eyes were damp as he turned to face Tavish, filled with anguish—and foreboding.

Chapter Thirty-one

A full month passed following Alan's return from court. A full month in which he ignored her, to all intents and purposes. Nay, ignoring was not exactly the word for it. Rather, his attitude seemed changed. Rather than pressing his attentions on her or harrying her to accept his suit and name a wedding day, he kept his distance and seemed to be brooding. Ofttimes, she'd glance up from the harp she was strumming to find him watching her, staring at her belly with an unfathomable expression in his eyes. She suspected he had guessed her condition and was seething with jealousy, but it was only a guess, for he never voiced his thoughts. Indeed, so silent had he grown over the past week, she could think of nothing but what she would say when he demanded outright if she was with child or nay. Accordingly, Day found her distracted, irritable, and flighty as a grasshopper, while Night found her sleepless, however exhausted, unable to sleep for her troubled thoughts regarding Alan.

As Alan had promised, he'd taken her below Rowanlee's hall to meet his mother and the woman, Mistress Goodfellow, who tended her, in the first week of that month, seeming almost fawningly eager to satisfy her suspicions regarding the woman. Although she'd already visited the dungeons of Rowanlee on that other, memorable occasion, she'd been amazed by the damp-riddled storerooms catacombing the ground beneath the manor, though the one in which the lady Shona was housed was quite comfortably appointed, considering.

Catriona had properly greeted the tiny, pathetic little woman in her voluminous white nightgown, hiding her amazement that the lady Shona was quite bald, save for a few wisps of stringy white hair that dangled from her pink pate, and had not a single tooth left in her mouth.

"Good day, my lady," she had volunteered courteously, sweeping her a curtsey that Fionna would have been proud of. "I am honored t' meet w' ye at last."

The lady Shona had toddled barefoot to her side, nimble for one of her years. She'd peered up into Catriona's face, her eyes bright as any magpie's with their cunning, avaricious gleam. "Who be this wench?" she'd demanded of Alan. "Eh? Eh?"

"'Tis the lady Catriona, Mother," Alan had supplied. "D' ye recall—the McNair maid I was to wed?"

"Catriona? Did ye say Catriona, eh?"

"Aye, Mother. Ye have it."

Seeming satisfied, the old woman had shuffled off, ferreting about in her caskets and chests and crooning to herself as if she'd forgotten her son and Catriona's existence. Then, of a sudden, she'd looked up, as if startled. Her face had registered terror when her gaze came to rest upon Catriona. She'd pointed a bony finger at the girl and screeched, "Green eyes bring bad fortune! Who is she, this green-eyed wench, sae bonnie and fair? A changeling brat, I warrant, aye, that's it! What else, as fair and fey as she? Be gone, and take your evil hence, ye witchling! Be gone, I say! We hate ye here, ye ken? All o' us hate ye!"

She advanced on Catriona, who gasped in shock and took a hurried step backward. But before the little woman could do aught more, her nurse had enveloped her in her plump arms and, crooning platitudes, had winked over the old woman's shoulder as she turned her aside with an apologetic, "My pardon, lady. Ma puir mistress isna hersel' this morn', I fear."

In faith, she need not have said so! 'Twas transparently clear to Catriona that the lady Shona understood very little anymore, and lived in a world of her own making. However, she had warmed to the buxom country wench's warmth and good humor, and her obvious fondness for her charge, and had nodded that she understood.

As Alan escorted her back above stairs, she had made polite conversation with him, expressing her pity for the old woman whose wits had fled — while saying nothing of her certainty that the flaxen-haired dumpling who tended her wasna the woman she'd spied the night Alan returned from Edwin's Burgh!

Two things had been transparently clear following that day. Either Alan, for some reason, was lying to her, and wished to keep the mystery woman's identity secret — or else he knew nothing more of the dark-haired wench who came and went about his keep by night than she did? Which was it? she'd pondered many times since, while growing no closer to an answer.

The days passed. The moon waxed full again. And, as they had with the last full of the moon, the sounds she'd heard before awoke her. The muffled blowing of horses, the jingle of harness, the murmur of muted voices, carried on the breeze.

Going out onto the parapet with a dark mantle thrown over her night rail to conceal its whiteness, she saw the now-familiar cart, with riders milling about it, in the inner ward below. 'Twas again drawn up to the kitchen entryway. For a second time, she saw the long-haired woman clamber down—from the driver's seat, this time—her skirts bunched up about her thighs.

"So, lassie, ye dinna sleep here," she told herself thoughtfully, cradling her chin in the cup of her palm. "D' ye share Master Brand's bed, then? Are ye Auld Skullface's paramour? Does that explain yer nighttime visits to this manor—and Alan's conviction that ye dinna exist, save in my dreams, or as his Mistress Goodfellow?"

Her craving to know the truth was nigh unbearable! 'Twas said that curiosity killed the cat—but 'twas satisfaction brought it back, was it no'? she told herself, for—ever impulsive, to her peril, despite the scare she'd had the last time!—she was determined to discover the strange woman's identity. Or at very least, her true purpose for visiting the subterranean chambers of Rowanlee at this ungodly hour.

Throwing a dark kirtle over her gown, she lit a taper from the ashes of the fire and went to her chamber door. Pressing her ear to the wood, she listened. Praise God! She could hear no sounds from beyond it. Surely everyone was already fast asleep for the night?

Tiptoeing out into the passageway, her candle held aloft to light her steps, she made her way down the stairs to the great hall. Many sleeping figures were sprawled about on the rushes there, some snoring, others muttering in their sleep. One of the gaunt-flanked hounds that crowded the hearth even on such a sultry night as this, stirred and uttered a warning growl. It made no move to bark an alarm, to her relief, obviously recognizing her scent as familiar to it. Since coming to Rowanlee, she had missed her dear wee Lyra and the pup's clumsy affection. And, in her loneliness, she'd taken a few moments each day to feed tidbits to the scrawny curs that huddled about Rowanlee's hearth. She was thankful now that she had.

From the great hall, she took the small stairway down to the passage that led off the kitchens. Pausing at the foot of them, she wondered if she'd somehow missed the woman, for she could see or hear no sign of her.

She was standing there in plain view, the taper held above her, trying to decide what to do, when a puddle of light suddenly flooded the flagstones at her feet! In its wake, the monstrous shadow of a woman shimmied up the stone walls before her.

Hastily pinching out the candle, she felt frantically behind her for a hiding place. To her relief, she encountered a narrow recess in one of the walls, naught but three handspans deep, yet completely hidden in blessedly deep shadows.

She ducked back into it in the nick of time, pressing her spine against the dripping walls and almost holding her breath as the woman drew closer. Her footsteps made a scuffing sound that grew louder and louder. And then, in an agony of breath holding and enforced silence, Catriona heard her very breathing, smelled the woman's perfume, as she drew level with her nook — and halted!

The torch carried in the woman's left hand, cast a giantess's shadow on the stone walls, which were greenish, mildewed, and oozing damp to the touch. The moisture glistened like spittle in the puny light. The woman paused for an instant, her profile hidden

438

by her long, straight mane of inky hair as she looked about her briefly. 'Twas as if she were taking her bearings — or listening to see if she'd been followed, before — thank God! — she passed on, just a handspan from Catriona's hiding place.

She continued to hold her breath until the woman had moved all the way down the passage. Then, when she'd taken the spiral staircase down to the chambers below, Catriona drew a shaky breath, stepped into the passage, and followed her down.

The woman walked quickly. Her feet were hidden by her long skirts, giving the eerie impression in the guttering torchlight that she was gliding *over* the flagstones, rather than walking upon them, as Catriona slipped down the passageway after her.

Up ahead, the woman abruptly veered off in a new direction. She lost sight of her momentarily, being so far behind. So far, that when Catriona turned the corner, she'd vanished! Panic made her heart hammer for, long and winding, the gloomy passage yawned ahead of her like a narrow tunnel — or the deep, dark well of her dreams! It was made threatening as a trap about to be sprung with shadows everywhere, like the passageways of nightmares that seem to reach forever into unknown, hostile wastes, with all manner of dangers lurking in the darkness, but waiting to spring!

Then, she caught a glimpse of the woman's skirts as she rounded the bend in the passage and vanished from view, and knew that her fears had been grounded. The mysterious woman had passed by the lady Shona's sorry quarters. Clearly she had no innocent purpose in mind!

Picking up her trailing skirts, Catriona flew down the passageway, all attempts at subtlety or concealment tossed to the winds now. Like a tenacious wee terrier worrying at a rat, learning the truth was everything to her now!

As she'd expected, on rounding the bend in the passage she saw no one, though she'd heard the rusty groan of hinges as a door thudded shut in the woman's wake. She moved down the passage, gliding from shadow to shadow. So many doors! Common sense dictated she must have gone inside one of these cells, for she couldna have disappeared into thin air, but—which one?

She tiptoed down the passage, pressing her ear to each of the closed doors, her excitement mounting. Yet she heard no sound from within save for the squeak and scurry of rats.

The heady scent of the woman's perfume had grown stronger with every step she took, she noted suddenly. Before one door, it was nigh overpowering. Here, Catriona halted, certain beyond all question that she stood in the very spot the woman had paused but seconds before!

"Since ye arena a will-o'-the wisp, t' vanish at will, ye must ha've gone inside, my lady," she muttered under her breath, and pressed her ear to the wood.

"How bonnie ye are, damosel! Surely a lass sae fair should grace a Norman donjon?" she heard. Why, 'twas Alan's voice, she thought indignantly. The wench must be his paramour after all, that lying knave!

"Och, my laird!" she heard the woman answer. " 'Tis too flattering ye are, to be sure!"

The words, delivered in a husky, seductive voice, also came from behind that door, and ended in a trill of smoky laughter. Catriona clamped her jaw, for 'twas the way a woman might speak as she prettied herself for her lover's bed!

Without hesitation, Catriona grasped the iron ring

and flung the door wide open, all but falling inside the cell in her eagerness to accost the mystery woman and demand to know her identity and purpose.

"Who are ye?" she panted, breathing heavily as she stood on the threshold. "Where's the Mac Quinlann, and what do ye here by dark of night, when none may — may — when none — ?"

She fell silent, of a sudden, her accusations frozen on her lips as she looked about her in sudden bewilderment. She flicked her head, but it did nothing to clear the roaring that had begun in her ears; a roaring that she couldna drown out as the past rushed up to meet the present, and were forged as one . . .

It was again that wintry Yule night, with the blizzard howling about Erskine, but — everything was subtly changed. The cell was empty but for the woman, who stood with her back to the doorway. Her long, straight black hair streamed down over her shoulders as she admired her reflection in a looking glass. She held a comb in her left hand — the devil's hand, Catriona thought vaguely, swallowing, though she could not move, could not speak, could scarce draw breath. More damning yet, that comb was carved of rowan wood, patterned with thistles and rowan buds — the very twin of the one that Tavish had found gripped in her dead father's hand! The one with the lady Shona Mac Quinlann's badge carved upon it . . .

The truth scalded her throat like acid, loosening her tongue.

"Damme ye!" she hissed, her eyes green shards that glittered in the light. "Ye've been found out, at last! I ken what tricks ye play on innocents, ye murdering bitch! What ha'e ye done wi' the Mac

441

Quinlann? Did ye slit his throat yet, as ye once slit my father's? Is he even now dead, in a pool o' his own blood?"

The woman made no answer. She merely stood there, uncannily still. She gave no indication that she was even aware that Catriona was behind her, let alone had spoken. Her very stillness radiated a charged expectancy, to Catriona's thinking.

Striding across the cell, Catriona grasped the woman's shoulder and spun her around. All fear of her was forgotten as she ground out, "Answer me, damme yer soul! I remember it all — everything! — Ye canna lie! Tell me, *Where is Alan?*"

"Och, dinna fear, my dear Lady Catriona. Your bonnie Alan's in no danger, I promise ye!" a lisping voice declared.

And, as Catriona gaped, openmouthed — as the brutal truth struck home! — the missing fragments of her memory returned with a sickening jolt that slammed the breath from her belly with the force of a fist. Her thoughts reeled, as if the world had been tilted on its axis, for the elusive, snub-nosed face of her nightmares was no longer elusive, no longer shadowy! It was all terrifyingly real, terrifyingly clear, as the woman lifted her face to meet Catriona's accusing eyes . . .

Her father's murderer looked back at her from amidst the long black tresses of a wig. Its rouged lips parted in a sneering smile as it bobbed her a clumsy curtsey and simpered:

"Surprised, are ye, m' Lady Cat?"

Chapter Thirty-two

"Blessed Mary, 'twas *you!*" she cried, her face ashen, her green eyes dilated with shock and betrayal. "I saw ye! 'Twas you who killed m-my father in this—this guise!"

Involuntarily, she shrank back, taking one, then another, step, until she was flattened against the wall.

"Aye, Catriona, 'twas I!" Alan sneered, turning from the looking glass in which he'd been preening himself, and impatiently casting the comb aside. "And all this time, ye never once suspected, did ye, ye gullible fool!"

His face was grotesque in the rushlight, a parody of a woman's face with its powdered cheeks and painted lips intended to disguise the sparse, peachy down on his cheeks and jaw. He minced towards her on dainty feet, his skirts lifted to clear the flagstones, aping a woman's light-footed gait with nightmarish ease. His head tilted coquettishly to one side, he laughed as he watched her face change, enjoying the revulsion that filled it as he asked, "Why, m' lovie, whatever renders ye sae pale? D' ye not care for your betrothed now? D' ye not think he makes a comely wench?" He fluttered his lashes and pursed his lips, pirouetting once, twice, to show off his disguise, before adding coyly over his shoulder, "Yer lusting father thought so, damn his soul!"

Bile rose up to scald her throat. Her belly squeezed. "God's Blood, ye disgust me, ye monster! Ye sicken me! Ye killed them all, did ye no', ye damned, bloody butcher!" she choked out. "Ma family. Ma puir Gordie . . . And blind Auld Ranulf . . . My . . . my clansmen! Ye slaughtered them all! But why, Blessed Jesu? What had they ever done t' ye?"

"They stood between me and Erskine, Catriona. That was reason enough!" he snarled.

"You and Erskine! But . . . there was never any hope o' ye having Erskine!"

"Nay, there wasna—not sae long as your kinsmen lived and I yet remained an outsider t' your family. But as your *husband*—och, I could have been laird o' the strongest keep o' the Borders! *If,* by some unhappy fate, your kinsmen should chance t' die . . ." He smiled thinly. "And I intended t' make *certain* that they perished—once I was yer husband."

"I see. So all this time—all these years!—ye were only waiting, biding yer time?" she whispered. Her lower lip trembled as the enormity of his betrayal, the depths of his monstrosity, struck home. "The things ye said—the plans ye made—the love ye swore for me all those years—'twas all but lies?"

"All? Nay, not quite all, dearling," he chuckled. "Ye're a comely morsel, after all, and I oft used t' imagine ye snug in ma bed. Aye, manys the time I took pleasure in imagining mysel' taming the McNair's proud bitch o' a daughter t' my every whim!" He shrugged. "What mon wouldna lust t'

444

tame such a wild, spirited beauty as ye for himsel'? Aye, Catriona, ye were t' be the gilding on my lily, lass! The jewel in the crown that was Erskine! And so, I bided my time, as ye said. I waited patiently for ye t' become a woman, believing once ye'd seen your first blood, your cursed father must name our wedding day. Ten years I waited, Catriona — *ten* cursed, long years after your damned Gilchrist took Corbin from me! We might ha'e been happy together, too, after a fashion, had my ambitions been fulfilled . . ."

"But ye grew tired of waiting — was that it?" she demanded bitterly.

"Nay, lassie. I had patience aplenty! 'Twas your fool of a father tipped my hand, by riding into Rowanlee one winter's morn, his trio of devil's spawn wi' him," Alan remembered, a flicker of distaste and contempt crossing his face. "That mannerless oaf, that — that barbaric swine! — swaggered about *my* hall, drinking *my* mead, filling his fat belly on *my* meats. He and your brothers had the spleen t' mock me! He sat in my chieftain's chair, his boots propped on my trestle, and drew a parchment from his surcoat. He slashed it in two wi' his dirk before he flung the pieces in my face! 'Your betrothal t' ma lassie is nae more, my laird Quinlann!' he jeered. 'I'd sooner die than wed my Moira's lass to a foppish weakling!' *Weakling!* He had the gall t' call me that!" he gritted, his face turning purple with remembered fury under its clownish layers of paint. "And then my fury knew no bounds, for he told me he intended to wed ye t' the — "

"The Gilchrist!"

"Aye."

"And you — ?" she asked breathlessly, her fists

445

clenched within the folds of her kirtle.

"And I?" Alan smiled thinly. "Well, I knew then that Angus McNair had t' die, and that his whelps and clansmen must die with him, did I no'? There was no alternative worth considering, no longer any reason t' delay. What had I t' lose now by killing them? Angus had already seen t' it that you were beyond ma reach! And so, I decided t' take Erskine by force. But . . . since I couldna hope t' hold on to her should the Normans invade our lands, as all signs point—I needed help. Strong allies who would guarantee that Erskine remained mine." He smiled, smugly. "Fortunately, a plan was not long in coming to me.

"In the deep snows o' November, I crossed the Tweed and rode south t' York, where William's armies were quartered for the winter. There, I made a bargain wi' a man dear t' King William. His name was de Rocher, Gervaise de Rocher. My friend Gervaise is an ambitious fellow, Catriona. The third son of a Norman earl wi' a raging thirst for power and land—but scant likelihood o' inheriting either from his father, with two hale and hearty older brothers before him. I was able t' speak with de Rocher, and outlined my plan to him. De Rocher liked what I said. 'Give me the Border keeps upon a platter, *mon ami,*' he demanded, 'and ye can rest easy. Ally yourself with me, and King William's armies will fight t' uphold your chosen cause.' I knew then that Dame Fortune had smiled upon me, and I plotted the downfall of Erskine, Glenmuir, Corbin, and the others. As well ye ken, my clever plot succeeded!" He hummed softly, watching as recognition dawned on her face with the familiar, lively tune.

"Oh, Jesu," she breathed. " 'Twas the players!"

446

"Aye, quite so, ma canny lassie," he acknowledged, chuckling at his cleverness. "The gates o' your father's keep were flung wide t' welcome the traveling players in t' Erskine that bitter night. And, once inside, my men and mysel' made short work o' your trusting kinsmen. For the greater part, they were unarmed. Those that wore their dirks lost them to the clever magician's sleight of hand! All were unsuspecting. I' faith, the night's work was child's play!"

" 'Twas infamy!" she hissed.

"I was encouraged t' employ the same clever ruse t' gain entry t' the other keeps. After all," he added with a wolfish grin. "I believed there were none left t' tell how it was done . . . until ye surprised me in yer father's chamber. I knew unless I silenced ye, ye'd talk, and I had no hope o' overpowering the other clans by any means but stealth and guile. My clansmen are too few.

"I bade ye halt, but ye ran, dearling! And so, I sent my men after ye into the blizzard, but—they bungled the job o' silencing ye! 'Twas a stroke o' fortune for me that ye didna recall what happened that night, for I was sorely troubled t' learn from Auld Morag that Gilchrist had found ye. A loyal assassin," he smiled, "was appointed t' finish ye off. But, like a wee cat, it seemed ye had nine lives and wouldna die! Thrice he tried, and thrice he failed! But all will yet turn out as planned. This even', my merry troupe will enter Corbin t' entertain the Gilchrists one last time! And come dawn, de Rocher will have the keeps he charged me t' take, and I, the lasting friendship of the Normans—and the king who'll rule o'er Scotland 'ere long!"

"Sweet Jesu, 'tis a traitor ye are, Mac Quinlann—aye, and a madman, too!" she cried. "The Gilchrist willna stand by and meekly watch his clan destroyed. Nor Scotland's neck crushed beneath the Norman heel! Roarke's a canny mon. He willna fall fer your ruse, as did the others. He'll send the mummers packing from his gates!" Throwing back her ebony mane, her green eyes glittering with conviction, she challenged, "Think again, my laird, for ye willna triumph in this! Roarke willna let ye!"

"Think ye no'?" Alan gave a smirk. He chuckled. "I beg t' disagree, fair lady, for ye see, your canny Black Roarke willna be there t' bar the gates when my mummers come t' his hall. And nor will he be there t' hear the pretty melodies of the flute, the tabor and mandolin, that will, in truth, prove the death song o' his clan!"

"What? And why will he no'?" she whispered, stricken. In the rushlight, her complexion was the color of tallow.

"Because even as we speak, dear heart, your Roarke leaves Corbin's gates. He rides forth in the company of one he trusts—one whose true loyalty is pledged t' me alone! And, all unsuspecting, 'tis this one who'll slay him!"

"A false hope, my laird! 'Tis already full dark," she protested bravely, though her knees trembled. "The Gilchrist would never leave his keep sae late, after what befell the clans o' Glenmuir and—and Erskine—at nightfall!"

"Nay?" he purred. "Och, but I beg t' insist you're wrong, Cat," Alan countered, a little smile twitching at his lips as if he found great mirth in the thought. "Ye see, dearling, he believes he rides t' meet with *you!* A bonnie jest, is it no', that ye'll be the instrument o' his ruin?" He threw back his wigged head, and laughed.

His laughter froze the blood in her veins. For a moment, she couldna move, couldna think or react. Her hesitation cost her dearly. When, belatedly, she found strength and sense to whirl away from him, to flee the cell and run back down the passage to the stairs, she found her escape route blocked. Alan's men were coming down them, two by two, all decked out in the parti-colored costumes of tumblers and jugglers!

"Good even', s-sirs," she stammered, looking wildly about her. "I beg ye, step aside! I am in haste!"

It almost worked. Almost! Like a miracle Mac Quinlann's men politely stepped aside to let her pass through their number. With a thundering heart, she took the stairs up, two at a time, almost gaining the level above.

But then, Alan's voice rang out. "Stop her, laddies!"

Catriona looked frantically about for a way between his men, around them—something!—but it was no use. Immediately, they closed ranks around her. Cruel fingers gripped her, dragged her back down the stairs to the passageway, with one burly Mac Quinlann guard holding fast to either arm. She was securely pinned. No matter how violently she struggled and kicked, bit or scratched to break free, her slender strength was no match for their steely fingers and beefy arms . . .

"Bind her and toss her into the cart, lads," Mac Quinlann commanded, chucking her beneath the chin as they jostled her past him.

"Damme ye t' hell, ye traitor! Ye murderer!" she screamed. "Ye'll no' win! Ye willna!" Then her cries were muffled as they dragged her away.

449

Chapter Thirty-three

As Catriona had once been abducted in the ferry-man Siward's cart, now she found herself trussed in the back of another, this one driven by the Mac Quinlann in his monstrous disguise.

Lying there, her arms bound, her head thudding against the boards with every jolt of the cart, she could see little. Her view was limited by the wooden hoop that held the cart's covering in place; inky sky, shot through with twinkly stars, and a full harvest moon, glimpsed between black, leafy treetops. She grimaced. Why was she even bothering to look out? It didna matter what she saw, for she had no need to look for landmarks. She knew where they were bound.

Corbin, Alan had said. There'd been excitement in his voice, in his cornflower eyes. They were bound for Corbin! And once there, they would halt below the wooden palisades that surrounded the keep, and call out to Hugh in the gatehouse. They'd beg him to let a humble troupe of players pass through his gate. With winning jests and smiles, they'd offer bored, sleepy Hugh a tempting sample of their antics — mayhap finding a silver penny in his ear, or whisking a silken kerchief from beneath his cap. When he was duly amazed, they'd promise t' entertain the clan Gilchrist in like fashion, in return for their supper and warm beds for the night. And, she feared, their insidious plan would work perfectly — *if* Alan could be believed, and *if* her normally wary Roarke had indeed been enticed from his keep by some traitor he trusted!

That someone couldna be Tavish, please God! Nay, Tavish — dear, trusting, Tavish! — was too akin to the man her father's reeve, Gordie, had been, with his love of magic and riddles, music and song, to betray anyone. He was so loyal and trusting, he would suspect nothing. Left in command of Corbin by his laird, he'd innocently grant permission for Hugh to fling wide the gates and let the players in — little knowing 'twas Death he granted entry that night!

She shivered at the thought of finding the Gilchrists as she'd found her clansmen that dread winter night. And, remembering, she could almost smell the reek of blood in her nostrils, the sour tang of spilled wine, the stench of slaughter. Could remember now with crystal clarity the two men who'd ridden her down in the snow. And Brand, with his claymore brandished aloft, smiling as he cracked her across the skull, then his laughter as they rode away, leaving her for dead . . .

Blessed Jesu, she had to get free, *had* to! If she could only loosen her ties, she'd spring down from the cart and run until she dropped. Run as hard and as fast as she could, across country. There was every chance she could outpace the cart and riders. They were forced to follow the well-worn track up hill and down vale, else risk breaking an axle or a wheel, while she could fly in the straight path of a crow. She needna fear to lose her way in darkness, either. Her path would be lit by the midsummer moon that was as round and full as a pumpkin, bright as any lanthorn. Aye, she'd warn them, and the clan would be ready and waiting when Alan and his tricksters came. And Roarke? She bit her lip. Roarke would give her as loving, as tender a welcome as any she'd ever imagined, if she sounded the alarm that saved his clan. He'd tell her how dearly he'd missed her. That he understood she'd not gone willingly to Rowanlee . . . or Alan's arms.

Straining against the ropes, she tried wriggling her fingers and toes in an effort to loosen them, mouthing a foul oath when her efforts served only to exhaust her. Useless! That hateful Brand had taken spite in fastening the ties so tightly, there was no hope of her wriggling free. Another way, then. She fumbled about, only her fingers able to move at all, in search of something sharp on which she might saw through her bonds. But she discovered nothing sharp anywhere, save for the splinters of wood poking into her back.

There were other objects in the cart-bed, however. She could feel just enough of the bulky items to be able to tell what they were. Masks! Players' masks! One felt like a stag's head: another, she thought was a wolf or a fox — it certainly had fur and fangs aplenty! There were also costumes, and something in wicker baskets — wooden balls? Skittles? Hoops? Aye, she thought so. For a fleeting moment, she considered trying to dislodge the baskets. She was almost certain she could push them from the cart, but what purpose would spilling them serve? Alan might hear, and halt the cart. Certainly he'd be angry. He might even react by having her strangled, as Brand had delighted in telling her he'd slain Siward. The ferryman had, apparently, planned to doublecross his master. He'd made rash threats t' tell the Gilchrist where she might be found, if Mac Quinlann wouldna give him more gold t' keep his mouth shut. His double-dealing had cost him his life. Nay. Best leave well enough alone. She would welcome any delay, but not at the cost of her own life!

Frustrated, she stared up at the night sky until she was almost mesmerized by its starry beauty. The breeze was warm, fragrant with the summer scents of hay and sun-warmed earth sprinkled with dew. 'Twas a night for lovers, a sky for wooing and ballads, a sultry night for kisses and caresses, not murder, she thought, tears choking her throat.

She was still sniffling when she heard a thud on the canvas covering. She stiffened. Fallen leaves? A shower of early nuts that the playful breeze had loosened? Then an upside-down face and a pair of dangling arms appeared below the rim of the hoop, and nuts and leaves were forgotten as a scarecrow figure pressed a finger across its upside-down mouth, obviously warning her to keep silent!

A moment more, and a boy had somersaulted over the hoop and landed lightly inside the cart. He scrambled to her side on all fours, and inwardly she groaned with disappointment. 'Twas Hal, the halfwit. A simpleton, while she needed someone with *all* their wits about them this night!

"We've nae time t' dither, mistress," Hal whispered crisply. To her astonishment, he sounded no more tetched than she did — mayhap less! Drawing a dirk from his belt, he added urgently and with perfect sense, "Ye must ride t' Corbin and warn the Gilchrist that they come!"

"Ride?" she squeaked. "Upon what, dolt? Ma broomstick?"

"There's a nag tethered at the crossroads back there, beneath the hanging tree. Ye'll find it. Now, awa' wi' ye, mi'lady!"

She had no time to argue or question, for without further ado, he all but dragged her to her feet. Chivvying her to the rear of the wagon, he helped her to swing her numbed legs over the edge. He even gave her a parting shove between the shoulderblades to get her started in the right direction as the cart slowed to navigate a curve.

She landed on both feet in the rutted road, gritted her teeth at the impact, then was off and running for the hanging tree and the promised horse.

Hal took a moment to fashion a lifesized mannekin t' replace the lassie in the cart-bed. He lumped skittles and masks beneath the worn mantle to approximate her body-shape, before he crawled inside the reed basket he'd emptied, and pulled the lid over his bowed head.

"Where was it ye said the lady Catriona was to meet with us?" Roarke asked, reining in his horse.

In the bright moonlight that silvered the grass and leaves, Graeme turned in the saddle. " 'Tis but a short distance more, sir. There, where the woods begin."

Roarke grunted.

They rode on, side by side, in the companionable silence of friends who'd known each other too long to need idle chatter to fill the void.

True to his word, not much later Graeme halted

454

his horse at the edge of the forest, the same place where Roarke had surprised him with Catriona. He dismounted.

" 'Twas here, the lady's servant said."

"Ye call her 'lady,' lad? The McNair's daughter?" He chuckled. "Why, I didna think ye sae fond o' her, the dour looks ye always sent her way!" Roarke grinned, swung his leg over the saddle and likewise dismounted. The horses cropped the lush grass while their riders waited.

Graeme wetted his lips, seeming uncomfortable. "Well, ye were fond of her, Roarke. We all knew that! And then, ye made plans t' wed the lass, and had the banns read. For your sake, I couldna treat her discourteously, now could I, McNair or nay?"

"Why not? God knows, ye've more reason t' hate her than most, laddie!" Roarke said softly. "Your father, your three brothers—!"

Graeme's head jerked around. His jaw hardened. "Time heals, does it no'—or so ye've always said. I am recovered o' my grief, and the need for vengeance!" he insisted.

"Are ye Graeme? Are ye truly?" Roarke spoke so low, Graeme had to strain to hear him against the reedy chirrupping of the crickets.

"Aye, sir! That I am!"

"Then where is she, lad? And why, pray, did she send word t' you that she would meet me here, at moonrise? Why not have her messenger deal wi' me directly?"

Graeme laughed. It had a harsh, breathless quality. "Och, mon, who knows what goes on in a lassie's head? She'll be here, never fear—ye'll see!"

"Nay," Roarke said heavily. "She'll not."

He strode slowly across the grass towards Graeme.

455

There was a look in his gray eyes that bleached the other man's face as he halted two tailor's lengths from him.

"Roarke?" Graeme whispered, almost beseeching. A nerve danced at his temple as he stepped back apace. "Roarke!"

"Aye, laddie?"

"Dinna come any closer! Jesu, mon, your eyes! Dinna look at me that way, I beg ye!"

"Why? What is it ye see in ma eyes, laddie?"

"Sadness," Graeme whispered. "Och, a terrible, terrible sadness."

"Aye, I greave," Roarke confirmed. "Aye, I sorrow. Ye've read it right, my friend."

"For the lass? That she left ye?"

"Nay, lad. For you! That *ye've* left me."

"But I am here, and with ye! How can ye say that?"

"No, Graeme. Ye arena. Not anymore. Not in yer heart, where it counts. You're against me now. I can see it in yer face, mon! Ye canna deny it. I know, ye see. I came here wi' ye, knowing."

"How . . . how did I betray mysel'?" Graeme asked hoarsely.

"Och, in small ways that might ha'e gone unnoticed, had I known ye less well. I first suspected ye were up t' something when ye pretended a terrible anger at the half-wit lad that May Day morn, and dangled him over the battlements. Ye claimed 'twas because ye believed he'd tried t' kill the lady Catriona, and wished t' force him t' admit his guilt. That ye cared at all what happened t' a McNair, male or female, wasna the way o' the Graeme I knew, you—who'd always hated their clan! And, coupled with what the lad had been trying t' tell me

456

when ye grabbed him by the scruff, 'twas doubly suspicious . . .

"So, Tavish and I put our heads together. We began sifting through all that had happened. Each time, ye were the missing factor in the puzzle. The night o' the blizzard, you alone were awa' from our keep—wenching, ye claimed, and snowbound in your sweetheart's croft. Or were ye instead at Erskine, laddie, t' the elbows in your enemy's blood? And the morning after I had word that Glenmuir had been attacked, and many of the Fraziers slain, ye were here. Ye were t' meet wi' yer master in the woods that day, were ye no'? That's why ye were here, where ye had no business being, when we stumbled upon ye. Ye meant t' slay the McNair's daughter and silence her once and for all. Ye didna follow her t' keep her from harm!"

"I had no choice!" came Graeme's anguished protest. "He . . . he demanded it of me—it was his price!"

"No matter. We all have choices, lad."

"But h—he swore t' tell ye o' my part in the McNairs murders, should I refuse his commands!"

"And like a puppet, he jerked the strings and ye danced to his tune!" Roarke thundered, his fists balled into knots at his thighs. "His name, laddie. I would hear it from your lips. Who is it ye serve?"

"Do what ye must. I canna say," Graeme growled, wetting his lips. He looked much akin to an animal with its foot caught in a snare.

"Then mayhap I can help ye oot?" Roarke offered grimly. "Does Rowanlee strike a bell—Rowanlee, whose crest is the rowan bud and the thistle? The same crest that was carved upon the comb we found, clutched in the McNair's fist? And does the name

Mac Quinlannn mean aught t' ye? Damme ye, Graeme Gilchrist, why? Ye had my love, my trust — and ye spat upon them both! Betrayed me for the coin o' that bastard fop!"

"Never for coin!" Graeme spat, his expression enraged. "Nay! Never! Ye wrong me, my laird. I was no Judas, t' sell ye for silver! Never you, Roarke!"

"Nay? I say ye lie!"

With a cry like a wounded animal, Graeme drew a dirk from his boot and sprang at Roarke. The impetus of his spring slammed the chieftain down onto his back in the dew-soaked grass, with Graeme sprawled atop him.

Roarke's arm snaked out. Muscles bulged in his upper arms as his fingers clamped over Graeme's in a desperate bid to wrest the weapon from his grip, before the man could plunge it in his heart . . .

"Halloo, gatekeeper! Stir yer bones!"

The strident jangling of the bell set alongside the gate cut through the hush of night.

"Eh? Who goes there?" came Hugh's grumbling voice.

"Who?" There was a chuckle. "Why, naught but a troupe of humble players, good sir!" Brand minced. "And our purpose on begging entry to your fair keep is but to delight all within its walls! What did ye fear, good sir? Normans?"

"Normans be buggered! Come oot, where I can see ye better!"

With a gracious inclining of his head, Brand handed the reins to the black-haired lass beside him and clambered down from the cart. He wore a fool's cap with jingling bells, and was dressed in red tunic

458

and red-and-yellow parti-colored hose. Drawing wooden balls from the pouch at his waist, he juggled them in the moonlight as he strolled to the gate-house. Standing below it, he made a deep bow to Hugh, craning from the gatetower, and caught the balls without missing a one. "Your servant, gate-keeper!" he declared. "Lads! Come forth. Show your-selves as humble players all!"

One by one, his men came forward, all similarly dressed. Some approached turning somersaults or cartwheels across the greensward, while another set up a lively tune upon a set of pan-pipes.

The suspicion on Hugh's face vanished, replaced by a delighted and eager grin. "Players, are ye? Then I'll send word t' the steward that ye're here, master?"

"Goodfellow!" Brand said with a disarming smile. "Master Goodfellow, and his goodwife, Mistress Goodfellow."

"Yer servant, mistress," Hugh mumbled, tugging his forelock and nodding in the direction of the bon-nie wench yet seated in the cart.

The wench simpered. She giggled behind her hand, lisping, "And yours, Master Gatekeeper."

"A moment, sir," Hugh said hurriedly, and disap-peared from view.

"The girl?" Master Goodfellow inquired out of the corner of his mouth while they waited. The "wench" glanced over her shoulder, into the rear of the cart, where a slender figure was huddled beneath a cloak. "Fear not, good Brand, she is yet there. Both secure, and blessedly silent, thanks t' the wee love pat ye gave her! When next she wakens, 'twill be t' relive the nightmare o' her clansmen's deaths!"

When the gatekeeper returned soon after, he was grinning broadly. Straightway, he hastened to unbar the gates and with the help of his lad, they flung them wide.

"Master Tavish, Corbin's steward, bids ye and yer company welcome in our laird and lady's absence, sir. Come in! Come in! 'Tis many a long year since we've had players at Corbin!"

"Aye, t' be sure. But t' night, ye're in for a rare treat, friend! One that willna be soon forgot, I warrant!"

Brand strode through the gates. The wench on the cart clicked to their horse, snapped the reins, and the vehicle followed him in. Behind them came a dozen others, all wearing masks or animal heads, all skipping and jumping about in the merry fashion of traveling players. No one noticed as yet another masked player slipped from the rear of the cart and followed the players inside as the huge, wooden gates creaked shut in their wake.

Hearing the excited murmur of chatter and the rowdy cheers of welcome that went up as they entered the great hall, the wench driving the cart looked across at "Master Goodfellow" and winked. Brand smiled thinly in return. For all his jolly costume, 'twas the grin of a death's head . . .

Chapter Thirty-four

Roarke pulled himself free of Graeme's weight and staggered to his feet, breathing heavily as he hung over the man, rocking on his heels.

He didna feel any sense of victory over this man who'd betrayed Corbin and his clan. Could not bring himself to feel anything more than a keen sense of regret for what might have been and for the loss of a good man turned sour, for he hadna slain Graeme in fair battle. As they'd grappled for control of the knife, Graeme had turned the dirk upon himself, and had fallen on the blade.

Even as Roarke knelt and turned him over, the laird could tell that the dagger had pierced a vital organ, though there was little blood as yet. The blade prevented the wound from bleeding.

His expression dark and sorrowful, he reached to draw out the dirk that protruded from Graeme's belly. Removing it would hasten the end of his life-long companion. In a rush of blood, 'twould all be over, and long moments of agony spared him. 'Twas the kindest thing to do, and more than he deserved.

"Nay, dinna touch ma dirk. Let it lie, I beg ye. 'Tis as well I die slowly," Graeme whispered, painfully turning his head to look at Roarke, "for I must speak wi' ye, and there is little time left me."

The light had already begun t' dwindle from his bright blue eyes, Roarke saw. Death called to him.

"Ye must know, I couldna ha'e slain ye, my laird, not for any price!" he began. "Ye must believe me! I thought . . . I thought I could bear anything, rather than the look o' disgust in yer eyes when ye learned I'd betrayed ye and Scotland both. Aye, even if it meant I must slay ye t' keep ye from finding out! But when it came down to it — when I had to choose — I couldna do it, though my life depended on it! We were as brothers, we three. You, the eldest, and Tavish and mysel'. Nay. 'Twas the McNair wench I was after all along — the last of his hated seed. She had t' die, Roarke! Ye ken why, do ye no'?" he pleaded, reaching up to grip Roarke's surcoat in his trembling fist.

"Your father and brothers," Roarke said heavily, gently untangling his hand. "For what her father and her clansmen did to them."

"Aye, Roarke, aye! It had t' be done," he insisted, his eyes glittering feverishly. "They couldna rest, ye see? Their spirits still wandered, even after all these years, unable t' find peace or enter heaven's gates. When the wind was right, I could hear them calling t' me, Roarke — imploring me t' bring their murderers to justice and take vengeance on their clan. Ye were too merciful, my laird," he reproached Roarke. "Far too merciful! The McNairs deserved no better end than that they'd given others!"

"Ye saw what befell your kinsmen that day, did ye no'?" Roarke asked. He had often wondered why the child Graeme had been back then had asked no questions about the deaths of his father and brothers, nor shed so much as a single tear on hearing they'd been slain. He'd long suspected the reason was the lad had witnessed the McNairs' cowardly ambush of his huntsmen and their bloody deaths, but had shrunk from asking him outright.

"I saw. I saw it all! I was angered that morn, for Father had told me I was too young to go hunting wi' he and my brothers. I went anyway, followed them on my pony. I saw the McNairs ambush them, slay them all! They gave no quarter, but hacked to left and right, like reapers scything through a cornfield with their claymores, though the corn they reaped that day was the bodies of Gilchrist men," he described bitterly.

"I saw my brothers cut down, skewered on their blades, and then . . . ! Jesu, then 'twas my father's turn! I knew I should try t' do something, but—but I was afraid, and couldna move! I was too much of a coward to do anything t' help them," he whispered. "And so, they died. All of them! After, I watched from my hiding place as they mutilated the bodies, laughing all the while—and still I did nothing." A tear coursed down his face.

"How could ye, laddie? Ye were little more than a bairn!"

"No matter. I'm t' blame. I should have tried. God knows, I should have tried! But it doesna matter now. It took too long for the McNairs t' pay, but 'tis done at last, and done well. I dinna hear their voices in the wind anymore, Roarke. They've forgiven me!"

"Aye, lad, no doubt they have. Sleep now," he urged with infinite gentleness, placing his hand on Graeme's brow. "Ye will be with them anon. 'Tis over, laddie."

"I did what had t' be done. Mac Quinlann

463

planned it all—the players, everything. He meant t' curry favor wi' the Normans, and gain Erskine for himsel'. Aye, he planned it well—except for this. Ye were meant t' die this night, my laird. He demanded it, swore he would reveal my part in the McNairs' deaths if I refused. But I couldna betray ye, Roarke. You are my laird, my friend. Ye know that, do ye not?"

With those words and a rattling sigh, Graeme breathed his last. But there was no time to ponder his death. Roarke unpinned the *breacan* at Graeme's shoulder, and pulled it up to cover his body, the tartan he had betrayed in life lending him dignity in death. This done, he ran to his stallion, and vaulted onto its back.

"On wi' ye, Roth! We must ride like the wind!" he urged the beast.

"Och, 'tis such a bonnie mon ye are, t' be sure, Master—Tavish, was it?" the black-haired lass purred archly. She touched the steward's shoulder, and trailed her left fingertip down his arm. His flesh crawled beneath his sleeve, but of course she didna see it.

The redheaded steward blushed furiously, resisted the urge to pull away, and gulped. "Aye, mistress. Tavish is my name. And yours, pray?"

The snub-nosed wench turned cornflower-blue eyes up to his, and with a flirt of her lashes murmured, "Ye may call me Alanna, if ye wish. *Do* ye wish, ma braw Master Tavish?"

He nodded.

With a chuckle of smoky laughter, the wench leaned against him and rested her head upon his arm. Standing side by side, their bodies touching, for a while they watched the antics of the players, who were tumbling about on the rushes, or juggling, or performing sleights of hand, drawing cheers of approval from the gathering. All the players, that was, save for one short fellow wearing a fox's head for a mask, who stood apart from the others and only watched the goings-on.

The wench yawned hugely. Turning to her, Tavish inquired, "Are ye weary, mistress—er—Alanna?"

"Weary? Och, nay, sir! I am but bored and . . . restless." She side-eyed him, and made a saucy wink beneath the curtain of her straight black hair.

"Restless, is it, now? Er . . . happen I could—er—think of something t' rid ye o' your . . . restlessness?" he offered, turning crimson. He hesitated, then with a look of resignation he slipped his arm about her waist and tugged her to him.

"Och, ye young rogue!" The wench giggled, trying to squirm free. "Is it but a rough and ready tumble ye're after, then? D' ye think Alanna some easy slattern because she roams wi' the players?"

"Nay, nay, Mistress Alanna, how could I think such a thing? 'Twould be unworthy of me!" Tavish denied with ardor burning in his eyes. "I fancy ye're the bonniest creature these Borders ha'e ever seen—and if I dinna have ye . . . ! Whist, I'll die o' longing!" He made as if to draw her into his arms and kiss her, but she evaded his arms and pushed him back.

"My lusty laird, for shame! Not here!" she chided under her breath. "Not where all can see! I amna a tart, t' be tumbled by one, then passed about from man to man!"

"Forgive me," Tavish groaned. "But already, ma

blood runs hot for ye! We Border cocks are lusty lads, ye ken, sweetheart? Men o' hot blood and passion who know little of patience! When we want a lassie, och, sweet Jesu, we canna—willna!—wait for aught, but must have 'er, and be done!" His blue eyes burned with fervor, and seeing the light in them, the wench smiled.

"Then take me from here, and straightway, ye handsome devil!" she purred, twining her arm through his. "Chapel or chamber, meadow or nook, I care not, ye have me that wild for ye! I care only that we be alone t'gether!"

"T' the chapel, then," Tavish suggested, licking his lips. "None will disturb our sport there." His brows rose in inquiry, and she nodded eagerly. Taking her hand, he led her from the hall.

But before they left, Tavish saw Master Ian, Roarke's reeve, glancing his way. Over the wench's head, he gave a barely perceptible nod, which the reeve returned before vanishing between the players.

As the musicians began to pluck their mandolins, pipe their flutes, and play their tabors, Tavish led the wench out into the sultry night.

And, as silently as a shadow, the player in the fox's mask slipped out behind them to the kirk.

"Wait! Did ye hear a cry just then?" Tavish exclaimed, standing stock-still just inside the chapel doorway.

" 'Tis naught but the nighthawk, lover," Alanna purred, drawing him inside the kirk and pushing the door shut behind them. "Like me, she calls t' her mate."

Tavish gave a nervous laugh which echoed on the

hushed silence. "Sweet Christ! 'Twas a mistake t' come here, I fancy," he declared. "Thought o' sinning in the house o' God has soundly doused my ardor!"

"Och, but I will stoke its embers, never fear," she promised wickedly, her eyes glinting like chips of hard blue glass in the moonlight streaming through the stained-glass windows. "Come along wi' Alanna, lovie. She'll see ye set t' rights, and teach ye what fun's t' be had by sinning!"

Like a man led to the gallows, he let her lead him across the nave to the tiny west transept.

"Here's a fine place for us. Won't ye spread yer mantle over the cold stone, sweetheart—and un-buckle yer claymore, laddie! I wouldna have ye prick me—leastways, not wi' that!" She winked.

Casting her a long, measuring look, Tavish gave a curt nod and unpinned his tartan *braecan* at the right shoulder. His back to her, he grasped the mantle and made to do as she'd bidden.

The movement he'd been anticipating, waiting for with bated breath, was instantaneous! The moment he offered her his back, she lunged! 'Twas only in the nick of time he twisted sideways to evade the blade she'd drawn from her bodice and now brandished aloft in her fist. Tavish's arm snaked out, and he locked his fingers about her wrist and squeezed, grinding bone against joint.

"My pardon, *Alanna!*" Tavish ground out, his nor-mally gentle voice laced with scorn. "But I learned long ago never t' turn my back on a wench—not even a wench wi' the makings o' a beard!"

A torrent of enraged curses spewed from the crea-ture's mouth as, with his free hand, Tavish tore the wig from Alan Mac Quinlann's head and flung it aside with a foul oath of his own. He used the lever of his grip on the slighter man's wrist to slam him back against the wall and pin his dagger hand above his head. 'Twas the left hand with which he'd drawn steel, he noted grimly, the devil's hand. Roarke had been right on all counts!

The man's face would have been comical, were it not so sinister. Reddened lips, reddened cheeks, powdered brow and chin—a layer of paint coated a face drawn up in a rictus of loathing as the steward's grip tightened and tightened. Och, the sight o' him in the patchy light made the gorge rise up his throat!

"Drop the blade!" Tavish commanded, his face thrust into Mac Quinlann's. "Drop it, else I'll break yer cursed wrist!"

The dirk clattered to the stone, and for a heartbeat, Tavish relaxed his grip in response. It was enough!

Alan smiled, and as Tavish began to frown in puzzlement, the man brought his knee up hard between his splayed legs, slamming it full into his groin. He chuckled as the steward doubled over and reeled away, clutching his middle. His face was white with agony, his mouth opened in a soundless scream.

"A whore's trick, good sir!" Mac Quinlann jeered, springing for the fallen dirk and scooping it up by the point of the blade. "Did ye not learn that one long ago, eh, *Master* Tavish, love?"

He raised the dirk above his head, and drew back his arm to throw it. Tavish raised his head, and saw the light flash off the blade the second it left Mac Quinlann's fist!

He threw himself clear, and staggered upright, drawing his sword in the selfsame moment—only to see Alan Mac Quinlann standing stock-still, as if frozen in place. Then he suddenly jerked sideways,

468

like a puppet yanked by a string, and thudded heavily to the ground.

His fair head was slumped to one side. His blue eyes were wide and staring up at the stained-glass window, and beyond. The light of the single candle left burning on the altar was reflected twice over in their glassy depths. There was no doubt in Tavish's mind that he was dead.

Tavish went and stood over the body, looking down at it in bewilderment. "How the devil—?"

"Och, 'twas no devil, sir," corrected a calm voice at his back. "Just this—and ma strong right arm! He's dead, 'else I missed ma mark. Turn him over. Ye'll see."

Tavish swung around. He looked up to see a short, slight fellow standing above him in the chapel gallery. He was wearing a fox's mask, and a leather slingshot dangled from his fingers. With a shrug, Tavish did as the speaker had suggested, and nudged Mac Quinlann's head to one side. A neat, round hole leaked blood at his right temple. The stone had embedded itself within it causing death instantly.

Tavish looked quickly back towards the masked youth, perhaps wondering if he would be next? As the steward glanced upward, the fellow took off the mask and stood there, a grin wreathing his narrow, foxy face.

"Hal?"

"Aye, sir. 'Tis Hal."

"Well, Hal, 'twould seem I have ye t' thank for my life!" Tavish said bemusedly.

"Aye, sir, happen ye do," Hal agreed without conceit. "But I didna do it for ye. 'Twas for Mother I slew this one. 'Twas by his orders she were killed, ye ken? His turn t' die for his infamy was long overdue!"

"Mother?"

"Aye, Mother—or so I called her. She was known t' ye as Auld Morag."

"The witchwoman! Then she is dead, also?"

"Aye, sir, alas, long since, thanks t' him!" He nodded at the body sprawled on the cold stone floor. "But she were no witch! She was naught but old, and a woman—and there's no sin t' being either, that I know of!"

"Indeed not," Tavish said gravely. "Forgive me."

Truth was, he felt a little dismayed to be having such a conversation with a youth he'd always believed tetched in the head, and who'd proved he was far from it this night! "What say we go inside, laddie, and add your skill wi' the sling and my strong right arm t' those of the Gilchrist's men?"

With a nod, Hal disappeared from the gallery in his mercurial fashion; one moment there, the next gone, and both accomplished with the grace and speed of a cat. Drawing the claymore he'd returned to his belt, Tavish followed suit and left the kirk at a run.

At the sound of a horse traveling at speed, he swung about, sword at the ready, to see a lathered black stallion careening into the bailey. Its glistening sides heaved in the moonlight. Its eyes were rolling wildly as its rider reined it in then slithered from its back in almost the same move.

"Thank God, my laird!" Tavish shouted, relieved to see his chieftain unharmed.

As suddenly as he'd disappeared, Hal was there beside them, grinning broadly.

"Aye, laddie, none other," Roarke agreed, eying the unlikely pair. "Come on wi' ye, men. Time's awasting, an' we've work t' do this night!"

Drawing his claymore, he headed into the keep with Tavish and Hal at his side.

Chapter Thirty-five

"The Gilchrist's dead by now, I warrant," Flora said, still with her head bent dutifully to her mending with a bovine devotion to her task that infuriated anxious, restless Catriona, who jumped with every clash of arms and loud cry that carried to the bower from the keep below. "Must be, else he would ha'e returned," she added. "Mark my words, there'll be Normans strutting about this keep come All Saints!"

"He canna be dead, damme ye! I carry his child!" she blurted out in an effort to silence the woman.

"Aye, so I'd heard," Flora said spitefully with a sniff and a dismissing shrug, as if the matter were old news and of scant interest now. She hadna forgiven the McNair bitch for her bonnie Ogden's death, not likely. All her fault, it'd been. His men had told her as much. And, although Ogden had seemed to look for his pleasures elsewhere before he met his end, she just knew she could have won him back from that Saxon slut, Betty, had he lived—perhaps even talked him into wedding her—if not for *her* doings . . .

"You . . . heard?" Catriona exclaimed, frowning. "But I told no one!"

"Why, mistress, 'tis no great secret. Everyone at Corbin has known ye were breeding since soon after ye . . . left!" Flora said slyly. "From Master Tavish down t' the lowliest spit-boy. I overheard the lady Fionna telling the Gilchrist mysel'. He laughed, he did, and asked who the bairn's father might be."

"What!" Catriona cried, wounded to the core. "Ye lie! He wouldna have said such a heartless thing, he wouldna! 'Tis your cruel words ye put in his mouth!"

"Well, indeed, now! So it's 'liar' ye call me, do ye? Whist, if that's all the thanks I get for telling ye naught but the blessed truth, Mistress McNair, I'll keep ma mouth shut henceforth!"

For several moments, Flora continued with her darning, the violent stabbing sound as her needle jabbed into the heavy cloth the only sound in the chamber. Her lips were tightly pursed, her movements jerky with indignation. She volunteered nothing further than the occasional incensed sniff.

"Did he—did he truly say that?" Catriona coaxed in a despairing tone, knowing she'd get no more from the malicious drudge unless she wheedled it from her. "Please, Flora, I must know!"

"Aye, he said it, right enough," Flora insisted with another sniff. " 'Twas after he returned from a visit wi' his Mags up on the crofts, as I recall." Her brows rose in inquiry as she asked, "Ye *did* ken he took up wi' that slut again, the minute ye ran off wi' the Mac Quinlann, o' course? He told Master Tavish 'twas all for the best ye'd vanished, for he'd wearied o' ye."

Catriona didna bother to contradict the hateful woman, knowing the futility of it. But her jaw tightened, and a sick, heavy feeling spread through her belly. Tears smarted behind her eyes, forcing her to blink rapidly to dispel them. Flora's revelation that

473

Roarke had turned to his comely widow the very moment he was recovered stung too sorely for speech, coming in the wake of hearing about his cruel comments. She clenched her fists, bitterly reminding herself 'twas only what she should have expected; no more, and not a dram less. Her own father hadna harbored a whit o' fondness for her in his body—why should the Gilchrist ha'e proved any less false? Unable to speak for trembling so violently, she only swallowed and nodded. "Go on, pray."

"Well, the lady Fionna said she must speak wi' himsel' privily, and drew him into her bower t' do so. I was in the anteroom, see, laying out the clothes the lady would take with her t' visit laird Hamish o' Glenmuir, and I couldna help but hear. I thought to mysel' 'twas a cold-blooded, heartless thing fer a mon t' say, but . . . ! Well, who am I t'—?"

She cocked her head to one side, her eyes suddenly bright as a jackdaw's, lighting on some shiny bauble. "Whist, now, will ye listen to that, my lady? 'Tis the skirl o' the pipes! That lovely laddie, young Andy's just a-playin' his wee heart out, t' be sure. Listen, mistress, d' ye hear? 'Tis the victory song o' the Gilchrists he's after piping! God be praised, I do believe the Gilchrist's returned and the battle won!"

Flora dropped her mending and ran to the door, craning her head through it to see into the hall below. "Aye, mi'lady, I was right! It's the Gilchrist himsel' and looking just as bonnie as they come! And . . . well, I never! The half-wit lad—that sly weasel, Hal? He do be down there, too! My lady? Why, where are ye off to, lady? Shall I dress your hair, mistress, 'ere ye go below? Do ye hear me? Lady Catriona . . . ?"

But Catriona thrust past her and was gone, the

squared set of her shoulders betraying her mood.

Flora turned about to hide her expression. A slow, malicious smile spread across her homely face. Her plan had worked! The McNair witch had swallowed her lies as easily as a salmon devoured a fly! If she wasna mistaken, there'd be no McNair at Corbin, queening it over the Gilchrists, in the near future! And happen there'd be no Mistress Flora, either—not if her plans for her bonnie cattle thief, the riever, she'd met at the May Day fair, bore fruit . . .

Corbin's great hall showed every sign of having been the scene of a rousing battle when the three men rushed inside, claymores at the ready.

Clansmen with bruised and bloodied faces nursed their hurts with tots of whiskey, sprawling amidst trestles that had been overturned, flagons that had been upset, and tapestries that had been torn to the ground. A dozen bodies littered the rushes—but not a one belonged t' the clan Gilchrist, Roarke saw with relief.

"Ian?" he roared, sheathing his sword and casting about him for his reeve.

"Never fear, sir, 'tis over. Our plan worked, sir, smooth as honey! When they turned on us in the midst o' their revelry, we were ready for them, by God! In truth, my laird," shy Ian added with a rare grin, "I fancy their surprise was so great, by the time they knew what was afoot, 'twas over and done!"

"Were any o' our laddies wounded?"

"One took a scratch on the cheek. Another broke his fist on a hard Quinlann head. Other than that, we escaped unscathed."

"Praise God!" Tavish said fervently, crossing himself.

"Amen!" murmured Catriona, coming forward. "Ye dinna ken what went through ma head whilst I waited for Flora t' tell me 'twas over!"

"Nay, but I can well imagine, my lady," Tavish murmured with sincerity.

Aye, he could remember all too well the pitiful sight she'd been when she'd ridden through Corbin's gates earlier the eve before, arriving not a quarter hour ahead of the players. Leaves and twigs had been snarled in her hair, which had been a wild black witch's mane flying all about her. A scratch had drawn blood across one cheek, livid against the pallor of her lovely face. But it was her eyes he'd never forget, emerald and huge and shining brilliantly with pride and hope as he ran to lift her down from her sorry, mud-spattered beast.

"Pray God, tell me I amna come here too late?" she'd cried. "Tell me that all is yet well wi' ye?"

"Aye, mi'lady there's naught, awry, though we—"

"Praise God!" she whispered, cutting him off. "I ha'e ridden nigh three leagues in darkness, up hill and down dale, through bush and briar, ditch and bog, Master Tavish—and all the while I was afeared no matter how I pushed ma nag, 'twould be for naught! They come, Master Steward! Those butchers—the same that slew my kinsmen!—they ride on Corbin this very night. 'Tis as traveling players they will come, with the Mac Quinlann himsel' in the guise of a lass! Hurry, mon, there's no time t' waste! Call oot the garrison! And when ye have, ye must tell Roarke that I'm here—that I rode t' warn ye! Ye must make haste!" she'd begged, tugging at his sleeve for emphasis.

So frantic and insistent had been her tone, so

476

exhausted and bedraggled her appearance, he hadna the heart t' tell her they'd already solved Erskine's riddle, and watch the eagerness and newfound pride flee her shining eyes. Accordingly, he'd nodded and bidden her go above to her old chamber with the serving woman, Flora, and rest hersel'. Wearily, she'd agreed to do so. Then, but moments later, he'd heard the gatehouse bell sounding the arrival of new-comers to Corbin, and had known it was begun . . .

"It took courage for ye t' ride here by night and warn us o' their coming, after what befell your kins-men, lady," Tavish continued, casting Roarke a nod and an intent, meaningful look to signify that he should go along with him in this wee falsehood. "The clan Gilchrist will be forever in your debt, will they no', sir?" he added with a grin, turning to nudge Roarke in the ribs. The chieftain was grinning broadly at sight of his lady, as if he'd lost a copper penny and found a silver shilling in its place.

"What's this? Our debt, laddie? Och, nay, I think not!" Roarke bantered, going along with the steward, tho' in his own fashion. "Such courage was nae more than I would ha'e expected from . . . the future lady o' Corbin, and ma bonnie bride! 'Twas all for the guid of our clan, am I right, ma brave, wee Cat?" He raised his brows, and made as if to go to her, patently eager to take her in his arms; patently ex-pecting her to fall into them. But, on both counts, he was to be sorely disappointed . . .

"Hold where ye stand, sir, and dinna lay hands on me! Do ye come no closer, for I amna and never shall be mistress here," she declared frostily. "Nae more than I'll be your bride!"

"What is this?" he roared, dumbfounded. "Do ye say ye went willingly t' Mac Quinlann, then?"

"Not willingly, nay. But . . . nor am I eager t' return t' ye! 'Tis the bairn ye want, not me, I ken full well, if either o' us! And I would be loved for mysel' alone—or loved not at all! And as for marriage . . . ! Why, I dinna want to wed ye, ye great dark brute! Wouldna, were ye this last mon alive! I' faith, a McNair woman can do far better for hersel' than marry a baseborn brute wi' the taint o'bastardy t' his name!"

A shocked gasp traveled through the listeners like breeze through a field of barley stalks as Roarke's face darkened with anger. His gray eyes crackled, but before he could retort, she'd spun about and fled the hall with a flurry of mud-spattered skirts. His pride forbade that he should call her back, or plead or beg, after what she'd said! That, and jealousy.

"Will ye let her go sae blessed easily, ma laird?" Tavish exclaimed, astounded at the pair of them. They were acting like bairns—nay, worse! "Go after her, sir! Ply her wi' kisses and vows o' love! Tell her ye want no lassie but her, and she'll return straightway, I promise ye!"

"Never! Ye heard her, did ye no'?" Roarke snarled. "She wouldna wed one as *baseborn* as mysel'! And I . . . ! Whist, mon, I must ha've been moon-struck t' ever think o' marrying a cursed McNair!"

And with that, he turned on his heel and strode off in the opposite direction.

She was running blind when Hal caught up with her. Running as hard and as fast as she could t' get away from Corbin and *him*. No power on earth could make her stay, not after what he'd dared to say, not after he'd said he doubted the child she carried was

478

his! There were tears rolling down her face when Hal, breathing heavily, caught hold of her elbow and swung her around to face him. He alone had had the common sense to follow her from the hall and, spying her haring through the gates of Corbin as if the devil's hounds nipped at her heels, had hastened to follow her.

"Why d' ye flee himsel', mistress?" he demanded, his narrow face querulous. "There's naught for ye t' fear, not now! The Mac Quinlann canna harm ye, for I slew him mysel' with this," he declared with grim satisfaction, drawing a leather sling from within his grubby shirt.

"Praise God!" she said fervently.

"And the master-o'-horse canna lay hands on ye again, for he took his own life, rather than slay his laird. The Gilchrist told us."

"Then 'twas Graeme Gilchrist who wanted me dead?" she cried, incredulous, her hurt and anger forgotten for the moment in her amazement.

"Aye, mistress—but he couldna do the deed, not wi' Hal t' watch over ye!" He grinned slyly. "Thrice he tried, and thrice he failed! Mother would be right pleased wi' her Hal, for he has done all she asked. So, lady—why d' ye flee, when ye could be the Gilchrist's bride?" he bluntly demanded again.

"I go because I willna stay where I amna wanted for mysel'," she choked out. Bringing her head up in a show of spirit and pride, she tossed her hair and told the lad, " 'Tis the McNair I am now, and 'tis t' my keep at Erskine I shall go, for 'tis there I do properly belong. I dinna need the Gilchrist, nor his cold charity, nor any o' his damned ilk!"

"T' Erskine?" Hal shook his head dubiously. "But my lady, Erskine is also under the Gilchrist's hand.

479

Has been, by the king's command, since ye disappeared that day from the ford! Master Tavish sees t' the running o' the keep now, on the Great Head's orders!"

"Tavish?" she echoed, startled.

"Aye, he's seen t' everything, Our Lady bless him! Erskine's serfs were given seed from Corbin's stores, and her fields were planted at his direction. 'Twill be a late harvest this year. There'll be no new loaves baked for good fortune come Lammas Day, but 'twill be a fine crop, nonetheless. Enough that Erskine's serfs and crofters willna go hungry this winter," he added approvingly. "Already Master Tavish has made arrangements for the sheep-shearing next full of the moon. And then, when autumn comes, he will see t' the culling and slaughter of the flocks and herds and the salting of their meat for food next winter. Erskine thrives, my lady. Her heart beats once more. She lives again, ye'll see."

"Nay, I willna, for I canna go back there," she argued fervently. "Not so long as my demesne is under the cursed Gilchrist's hand! I shall petition the king t' have my father's keep returned to me, but until then . . . !" She bit her lip and looked away, blinking rapidly. "In faith, until then, I . . . I have nowhere t' go."

"Mother bade me look out for ye," Hal told her slowly and with reluctance.

"Mother?"

"Aye—the one ye knew as Auld Morag. Her what delivered yer lady mother o' ye. She is gone, now, alas."

"Dead? Och, nay!"

" 'Tis so, but I'll tell ye more on that anon. Ye're welcome t' lodge wi' me, if it please ye, mistress? I

480

know a place — a hidden place, where few folks come. 'Tis but a poor shelter — far beneath yersel' — but 'twould be my honor t' serve ye there for as long as ye need me?"

With but a moment's hesitation, she nodded. Where else could she go? And Hal, at least, had made the offer of shelter, strange lad that he was, on his own behalf, offering her welcome without other motives for his kindness.

"Very well. I accept, and gladly. Lead on, pray, good Hal."

Chapter Thirty-six

Hal's "secret place" proved to be the woodland cave where the witchwoman and midwife, Auld Morag, had once lived. The same simple dwelling where Catriona had gone to visit Morag that wintry day two years past, to learn the rhymes to conjure up her true love's face on St. Agnes's Eve.

Tucked snugly in the lee of a hill where the ling heather grew wild and free and purpled the slopes, the cave had been carved from the earth by the short, dark folk who'd lived in these parts long ago; the ones, it was whispered, who'd possessed the gifts of magic and bewitchment, and who could still be heard singing and chanting on certain nights of the year. It was also where Auld Morag had raised Hal, Catriona learned in the following weeks, the "Mother" whose snippets of wisdom he had quoted with such irritating frequency from the first moment they'd met!

Long grasses and summer wildflowers bloomed all about the crude opening to the cave; the white briar-rose, the cowslips, the buttercups and daisies all nodding sleepy heads in the breeze wafting through the rough door of wooden planks. A cairn of stones rose from the grassy banks alongside a small, burbling spring nearby, marking the place where Hal had buried Auld Morag.

Sometimes they would return from a day spent abroad, gathering herbs and berries or tickling for trout in some burn or other in companionable silence, to find an offering had been left there by the country folk whom Morag had helped in her lifetime; a crock of butter, mayhap, or a wedge of cheese or some oatcakes, and once, a wee skin of *uisge beatha,* fiery whiskey, which Hal, with a shifty glance to see if she'd noticed, took for himself.

"She were good, she were," Hal observed one day, nodding his head towards the cairn. He was unusually talkative, she guessed, on account of the sips of whiskey he'd been sneaking all day! "Some folk thought she were a witch, but I dinna believe it. Her skills were in the healing arts, an' in the making o' simples an' tending t' sick folk and animals, and such. No witchcraft in that, eh, mi'lady? 'Tis but sense ye need, and knowledge."

His tone was gruff with sorrow, and pity stirred in her. Squeezing his shoulder, she murmured matter-of-factly, "Ye loved her."

He sniffed noisily, but wiped the snot away on grubby knuckles, refusing to give way to tears. "She were all the mother I knew since the day they brought me to her. Been left, I had. Naught but a few months old, a bairn yet, and I'd been tossed in the woods to starve! Left out like an unwanted kitten that nobody had the kindness t' drown and put oot o' its misery. A female badger had mothered me, Morag told me when I were old enough to ken what she meant, and the miracle of it. Suckled me, she did, along wi' her young. Her milk kept me alive. I lived wi' the badgers in their burrow until men came. They dug the badgers out for their barrel-sport—ye ken, my lady, how they place the badgers in a barrel, and bait the puir beasties wi' dogs set to pull them oot?"

"Aye, I ken," she acknowledged with a shudder, for 'twas a cruel, bloody sport, and the badgers had but little chance of surviving it.

"That's when the men found me. I were that wild and savage by then, I was more animal than boy. They brought me t' the wise one.

"She oft used t' talk o' the days when the lady Moira o' Erskine yet lived, and she were summoned t' the keep t' deliver her firstborn. Loved your mother somethin' fierce she did, and you, too, my lady, when ye were born. Aye, and your lady mother loved her, too! 'My dearest Queen Mab,' she used to call her sae fondly, and Morag thought 'twas a merry jest t' be named for the Queen o' the Fairies!" His foxy smile faded. "But too soon the lady died, birthing her second, young Master Bran, and Morag could do naught t' stanch the bleeding and save her, though she tried wi' all her heart. Your laird father forbade Morag ever t' enter Erskine's gates, after that.

"She never forgot ye, though—lived for your visits, she did! She sensed the danger coming that Yuletide—knew it somehow in her bones!—but she were too late t' do aught to halt it. He killed her, did ye know? The skull-faced one! The man called Brand—him what served as that devil, Mac Quinlann's familiar? He fastened a cord about her throat, and drew it tight before he left her for dead.

"The light was already leaving her eyes when I came home and found her. But with her last breath, she told me what to do. 'See t' ma puir wee Cat!' she implored me. 'Ye must make haste! She be all alone in the world now, and that dark rogue, the Gilchrist,

484

holds her hostage at Corbin keep, while his men ride even now t' Erskine! He will be angered, for their slaughter will be laid at his feet. Ye must guard her well, laddie, for there are those who want her dead!'

"She couldna tell me more, for there was no time left her. After she'd breathed her last, I ran as fast and as hard as I could t' Erskine and hid in the well there."

"But why?"

"I knew the Gilchrist would be wary o' strangers, once he heard what had befallen the McNairs, for he's canny, is the Gilchrist. I thought—hoped!—if 'twere t' seem I'd been brought *unwillingly* t' his keep, he wouldna run me off wi' a boot t' ma rump. Aye, and it worked, an' all! I played the simpleton and came t' Corbin to watch over ye, as Mother had said. It were a braw guise, too, for folk dinna fear t' talk freely before a stupid half-wit lad," he added with a sly grin. "So, I listened, and I heard much. I observed, and I discovered more! 'Twas Graeme Gilchrist took the platter of victuals from me that eve—the one that lazy slut, Flora, pestered me t' bring up t' ye, that she might dally wi' that donkey, Ogden. I suspected he meant no good by it, even then, for what master-of-horse would willingly play the serving lad—and to a McNair woman he had every reason t' hate, at that? I meant to toss the victuals on the fire, but when I reached your chamber, I found the hound by the hearth, dead, and knew that I'd been right. Then you came in, and ye suspected me o' his mischief, mistress!" he accused, his expression wounded.

"But why didna ye speak up for yersel' and tell me what was afoot that morn in the kirk?" she cried. "Ye could ha'e warned me t' be on my guard, at least?"

"Would ye have believed the likes o' me, over the

485

word of fine, bonnie Master Graeme, his lairdship's boon companion?"

"Aye! O' course!"

"Mistress!"

"Well, nay, I suppose not," she admitted.

"I *know* not," Hal said with conviction. "Besides, I could prove naught at the time. At the very least, the Gilchrist would ha'e booted me from Corbin's gates for accusing his companion o' murder. And what good could I ha'e done ye then, lady?"

"What good, indeed!" She pondered all he'd told her for a moment or two, then asked him, "But what about after ye fled Corbin? How did ye know what the Mac Quinlann was about if ye werena at Rowanlee?"

"Och, but I was!" he crowed, his eyes twinkling. "Leastways, enough times t' know how ye fared—and that bonnie Mistress Jeannie clucked over ye like a hen wi' a favorite chick—and when it was t' the minute that Mac Quinlann grew soured towards ye! There can be no secrets, my lady, in a manor filled with gossippy wenches—lassies who'll tell their all for a pedlar's amulet o' herbs for a love charm, or as an aid t' beauty! And, when I wasna filling my ears and belly in Rowanlee's kitchens, I was watching the manor from wi'out!"

"The pedlar was you?"

Hal only grinned in reply.

Some understanding seemed to have been reached in the days following Hal's loquacious account of himself and his actions. Although his talkative bent ran out at approximately the same time as the whiskey, by then she'd gained a deeper insight into his character. While she found him no less fey and

486

flighty than she ever had, and though he still had the
woeful habit of sneaking up behind her on soundless
feet and scaring her half to death, they managed to
get along well enough, all things considered, for two
so different.

As they had once done in Morag's time, the wild
things came to their door of an evening, some to
drink at the spring, others to take tidbits from Catriona's hands, and still others to have their hurts seen
to. There were red and gray bushy-tailed squirrels
and shy, lovely deer, stalking through the long grass
on elegant legs to water's edge. Long-eared hares,
grinning foxes and their gamboling cubs came too,
and once, Hal's brothers, the badgers, in their
striped white-and-gray robes, came ambling out of
the woods with the gloaming to beg for morsels of
meat and roll around in the moonlight like pups.
Hal hunted for their pot, of course, but he never set
his snares or used his sling within a league of their
cave-home, and the wild things came to trust them
as they'd once trusted Morag.

Catriona learned much from Hal in those months.
Little by little, she grew as familiar in the lore of
herbs as was he, and knew what would heal, and
what could kill, and the right amounts to accomplish
either. And, as her belly swelled, and the burgeoning
life in her womb could be readily glimpsed in the
vigorous kicking movements beneath her shabby kirtle, she sensed a new gentleness and concern in Hal's
manner.

More and more often, he suggested they rest when
their treks in search of some elusive herb or other
took them far afield. And, when he didna think she
knew it, he would stare at her face and then at her
swollen belly with eyes made muddy with worry, and
shake his head.

487

"What is it, laddie?" she asked him one day when he seemed even more silent than was his wont. Leaning back against a thick tussock of grass, with a straw wisp jutting from her mouth to chew upon, she gazed up at the deep blue sky above and awaited his answer.

"The bairn!" he blurted out. "When will it come?"

She laughed, though in truth she was far more nervous about the impending birth that she let him see. "Whist, is that why ye seem so afeared t' day? Dinna fret, laddie, I'm no' about t' birth this very moment! This wee dumpling has a bit o' growing yet t' do!" she declared, patting her belly. "The autumn will see him born. Not before."

"But I know naught o' birthing babies!" he said hoarsely. "Who will help ye? Ye could bleed t' death like your lady mother, mistress, and I could do naught t' help ye!"

Biting her lip, she forced a breezy smile. "But I have no ambition t' die, Hal. And since 'tis said that only the very good die young—I fancy I shallna perish for quite some time yet. Dinna worry yersel'. When the time comes, all will go well."

"But ye canna be certain, mistress! Things . . . things can go awry, no matter what charms ye wear against them! Say ye'll let me summon the lady Fionna when yer time comes?" he pleaded. "Kind she is, and wise in such matters."

"Nay!" she hissed, her expression hardening. She spat the straw from her mouth and hauled herself clumsily to her feet, wearing a scowl. I forbid ye t' summon her, d' ye hear me, Hal—or anyone else from Corbin, for that matter! Swear ye willna, no matter how things go? Swear it on Auld Morag's grave!"

"Nay!" Hal refused for once, his jaw jutting obstinately. "There are some things ye canna force me t' swear to, lady, and this be one o' them!"

"Ye must, laddie," she commanded imperiously, drawing herself up to her full height and trying to look queenly, though her big belly rendered her more comical than regal, had she but known it. "I am the McNair!"

He snorted and spat in the grass. "McNair or nay, ye dinna own me!" he growled, and stomped off towards home, leaving a dumbfounded Catriona to humble herself and waddle after him like an ungainly duck.

Summer came and passed in a golden haze of broom and gorse, sunshine and fair winds. The shearing had ended long since up on the moors. The harvest had been gathered in, and the harvest feasting was over. Autumn came in with a snap!

Night brought the mists. Day, a damp chill in the air that found one's bones and gnawed upon them. The leaves turned overnight it seemed, and between the pines, which modestly declined to shed their robes as other trees did, the hard ground was ablaze with drifts of colored leaves, red, russet, and yellow, that crunched underfoot. There were fallen acorns and nuts, and the green prickle-balls of the horse-chestnut. There were also pinecones to be gathered for winter kindling, hundreds of them, large and small, scattered amongst the leaves.

One morn in November, Catriona labored at the task of pine-cone gathering with more energy than she could recall having in many months, while Hal went off on his own somewhere, wearing a secretive smile.

He returned much later with a brace of plump hares dangling from his fist, to find her leaning against a tree and clutching her belly, her sack of pinecones fallen at her feet. The ground beneath her was wet, the leaves sodden.

"Did ye hurt yersel', lady?"

She shook her head.

"The bairn?"

"Aye. 'Tis coming, I think. The waters have burst!"

With Hal's help, she reached the cave, and by then, the pains had begun. He made her comfortable on the willow couch, strewn with furs, that he'd made ready and as if to give her encouragement — or perhaps to reassure himself! — he showed her what it was he'd been acting so secretively about.

"Here, my lady," he mumbled, handing her a large basket woven so beautifully of withies, it could have held water. "I wove it mysel'. 'Tis for the bairn's bed."

His unexpected kindness moved her to tears.

"Nay, lady, I beg ye, dinna do that!" he cried. "Dinna weep! I'll take it away — burn it, if ye will! I didna mean for it t' sadden ye!"

"Och, Hal, don't! That's no' why I'm crying, ye lummox! I weep because . . . because 'tis the most beautiful basket I've ever seen!"

And so, Hal's basket sat in readiness alongside the fire in the smoky cave, lined with the soft furs of young animals Hal had hunted for the purpose. But although her pains came with amazing regularity all that day, and increased in severity and length that evening, there was still no babe to fill the basket by the next morn.

Hal's face registered his shock when she stumbled outside the following morning, and the cold autumn light showed him her face. She was exhausted, her green eyes ringed with shadows, her complexion pale as whey. And the pains, which had ceased for a short while during the night, had clearly returned full force.

490

"Ye must eat something, mistress," Hal fussed. "Ye need your strength! Come, will ye no' drink a sip o' this barley bree I've brewed for ye?"

"Och, I canna! I will spew it up, I know I will!"

He was about to insist, when a pain so violent gripped her, she was unable to stifle a scream. She doubled over, and would have fallen had Hal not caught her up and carried her inside to the willow pallet.

"I swear by Our Lady Moon, mistress, ye canna go on this way, 'else ye and the babe will surely die! Let me run t' Corbin and fetch help!" he pleaded.

"Nay!" she ground out, the flesh about her mouth bleached white from pain. "Nay! I forbid ye!"

"And I told ye long ago, I wouldna swear, my lady!" Hal growled, grimly taking up his staff of ash in readiness to leave.

"If ye go, I willna have ye back!" she threatened, desperate now. "I willna!"

"I shall worry aboot that 'ere I return!"

Chapter Thirty-seven

"Get out!" she hissed. "The lad shouldna have sent for ye! I dinna want ye near me!"

"Aye, I ken, but I willna leave," Roarke said bluntly. Unfastening his woolen mantle, he spread it over the sorry pallet of willow boughs to soften them. "The bairn is coming, and ye need help, my lady. There's only we two lads to give it ye, and give it ye we will, like it or nay. I've never been one t' dance t' yer tune, mistress, if ye recall. I stay!"

She could not retort as she wished, nor consign him to Hades, for another pang was hard upon her. It robbed her of breath, drove thought from her mind. Leaning against the damp earthen wall of the cave to brace herself, she bit down on her lip as her belly rose, hard and high, beneath her splayed fingers.

The pain was like a tidal wave, rising higher and higher. Just when it seemed she could bear it no longer wi'out letting loose a scream, the wave broke. It crashed upon the shore and ebbed as suddenly as it had come. The next pang came hard on the last. This time, the pain was so intense, she ground her teeth together and screamed while it lasted, unable to swallow the cry. Her face was mottled red with the pressure, her exertions so great that sweat streamed from her brow. She was alternately panting then shivering with exhaustion when the pain ended. Closing her eyes, she slumped against the wall, licking dry lips.

"How long ha'e ye been this way?" he asked, hiding his fear beneath a stern tone.

"What's it t' ye? Be gone wi' ye, I said! I dinna need ye, Gilchrist. Not here, not now, not ever!" she muttered. "Moreover, ma bairn doesna need ye. 'Tis a father he needs, his name, his love. He'll get none o' those from a heartless rogue who'd deny he fathered him!"

"Deny he fathered . . . ? Sweet Christ, what is this nonsense ye're speaking? I would never—never!—deny your bairn as my get, ye wee lummox! Visit upon my bairn the same anguish my royal sire visited on me? I couldna be sae cruel—do ye not know me better than that! Who filled ye up wi' this fairytale? Who was it told ye this falsehood?" he demanded in a voice so low and soft it was murderous. "For by God and all the saints, I'll have their tongue for it!"

" 'Twas Flora!" she tossed at him. "Flora told me, the night the Mac Quinlann was slain. She said . . . she said ye'd taken up with yer Mags again, straightway ye'd recovered from your wounding. And she swore that when the lady Fionna told ye she suspected I was wi' bairn that ye laughed, and asked her if she knew the name of the babe's father!"

"And ye believed her?" he thundered. "You ran from me, t' live in this damp, filthy hovel, because ye chose t' believe the word o' a jealous slattern, rather than ask me for myself? God in heaven, I should

493

wring yer wee neck fer yer low opinion o' me, ye lummox! Aye, happen I'll yet tan yer wee rump fer it, after ye've delivered."

"Then ye'd have me believe that Flora lied?"

"Aye. And royally!"

"Then prove it!"

"Nay, Catriona, I can prove nothing, for Flora isna at Corbin t' admit her lies. On All Saints Eve, she ran off t' her native Highlands wi' a riever she'd taken up wi'. So ye see, 'tis my word ye must take on this, else believe what ye will! However, whether ye believe me or nay, my bairn shall yet have his father's name, by God!" Roarke promised grimly, adding, "Whether or not his lady mother do welcome a husband!"

Turning to Hal, who hung back in the shadows wringing his hands with fear, he ordered crisply, "Lad, take my horse. Ride wi' all haste to Corbin, and bring Father Augustine here straightway! And Hal . . ." he cautioned, "dinna ask nor beg him. Say it is by my *command* he is sent for, and that I'll see him gone t' the devil himsel' should he tarry!"

Hal needed no second urging. He nodded and was gone in the blink of an eye. Moments later, Roarke heard the drum of hooves as he rode away.

He gave Catriona a speculative glance, but she appeared to be resting quietly between her pains. There was nothing more he could do for her for the moment. Instead, he looked about the cave where Morag had once concocted her potions and simples. He found some stubs of tallow candle amidst the cobwebs and grime, gathering dust upon crude shelves that still held her herbs and powders, pestle and mortar. He set them close at hand in readiness for lighting, and went outside with a large crock to

494

draw water from the icy burn.

Daylight was fast fading outside the cave, he saw. Soon, the purple gloaming would come creeping through the glens, 'twould be difficult to see. He had no wish to watch Catriona endure what promised to be a difficult birth in darkness, he thought with a twinge of foreboding. God, nay! He had little enough knowledge of such female things in broad daylight, save for the lambing of ewes!

Nevertheless, it was almost full dark when Hal returned with the priest. Her birth pains were still coming hard and fast, and lasting longer with each one.

The barrel-bellied, tonsured cleric waddled in to the cave. His rubicund face was oily with sweat in the candle's light, for all that the autumn eve was growing chill and damp with mist. His cheeks were round and shiny as red apples, betraying his fondness for rich victuals and strong drink.

"You sent for me, my lord?" the priest simpered.

"Why else would ye be here, dimwit?" Roarke snapped, giving him a sharp look. "I would have ye marry the lady and mysel', wi'out delay. The bairn's birth is imminent. There's no time for dilly-dallying, if he's t' be born on the right side o' the blanket!"

"I quite understand, my lord," Father Augustine said pompously, steepling his fingers atop his ample belly. "However, I am required by my office t' ask ye first if there is any impediment that would prevent this marriage from taking place? Have ye a betrothal contract, signed by her father and duly witness—"

"God's *Blood!*" Roarke gritted, knotting his fists and scowling fiercely. "How does the 'impediment' that the bridegroom is a murderer of bumbling *priests* strike ye?" he insinuated in a voice loaded with menace. "For I swear 'twill be so, Father, if ye dinna commence straightway!"

Augustine primly pursed his lips, his expression reproachful. "Now, come, come, sir, there is no need for such harshness. As a servant of God, I demand ye show me the respect I'm due!"

"Respect is earned, not owed, Priest," Roarke seethed. Gripping Father Augustine by the cowl of his habit, he lifted him clear off the ground with one huge fist and slammed him against the wall of the cave. His sandals fell off. The hems of his frayed, grubby habit rose, revealing plump white buttocks, dimpled knees, pudgy pink legs and dirty feet, all windmilling frantically on air.

"Now, say the words, damme ye, before I lose my temper in earnest!" Roarke rasped, his face a mask so very dark and stern as he thrust it into the priest's, the man's teeth chattered. He was visibly paler when Roarke released him to slide back down the wall.

"D' ye, Catriona — er — Catriona . . . ?"

"Moira!" Roarke roared. "Catriona Moira McNair!"

"Catriona — Moira," the priest babbled, "take this — this — man — Roarke, laird o' the clan Gilchrist, to husband? Will ye —"

"Enough blathering, damme ye! Get t' the heart o' it, by God, else rue the day ye took yer priestly vows!" Roarke bellowed, striding back and forth like a man possessed. "The babe is but a pang from being born!" It was no lie. The last stage of birth was imminent, for Catriona had taken to the pallet and was grunting and straining alarmingly, the urge to bear down and deliver the infant overwhelmingly strong upon her.

Augustine gulped. "Do — ye — take — this — mon — for — husband?" he mumbled so rapidly, the words sounded like turkey gobbles.

"Aye, curse him. For the bairn's sake, I must!" Catriona gritted, casting Roarke a look that was pure and undiluted venom between panting breaths.

"And do ye, Roarke, take this maiden — er — woman — lady — as your bride? Do ye vow t —"

"Aye, aye, ye ken full well I do! I vow all of it, ye dolt!"

"Then before God, ye are wed!" Augustine declared rapidly. He made the sign of the Cross over them and, feeling a little braver now it was done, he beamed benevolently like a smug little cherub, steepled his fingers upon his belly once again, and declared, "Ye may kiss your bride, mi'laird!"

"Later," Roarke said rudely, waving him away and thrusting past him to the pallet. "My bairn is anxious t' be born. T' Corbin wi' ye, and ha'e yer scribe scribble the marriage contracts. Catriona, dearling, hold fast t' my hands," he commanded, kneeling behind her with his arms extended. "When the next pain comes, ye must push!"

"Ye haggis-headed moron!" she ground out, screwing up her face and taking puffing breaths. "I dinna need *ye* t' tell me that, ye great lummox! I can think o' naught — ah! — naught else but . . . but — aah! — the accursed puuuushiiing! Aaaagh!! Aaaah!"

But, nevertheless, she took his hands in hers, clung fast and bore down. Her face contorted. Their fingers, laced together, were locked. Where she gripped Roarke's hands, her nails cut his palms like talons. They gouged so deep into his flesh with her efforts to push the babe into the world, that blood was drawn. But Roarke didna so much as flinch. He

497

braced himself against her straining, so that he could help her bring the bairn forth before exhaustion claimed her strength and it died within her, and she with it . . .

"There's my brave, wee lassie!" he crooned, his eyes tender as they rested on her weary face in the wake of her pain. "Another push, and 'twill be over, Cat. Just another. One more, and ye'll hold our bairn in yer arms. Come, my love, ye can do it, for 'tis a braw wee lass ye are, my heart, my own!"

"I canna, Roarke! I have tried, but it has been so long. I'm sae weary!" she wailed piteously. "My strength and will are spent!"

Her words wrung his heart. Living in this sorry, musty hovel, she had carried his child, she and the badger-boy struggling to live off the land without anyone to protect or provide for them. Guiltily, he considered that he could have seen that she had soft pallets of goosedown to sleep upon each night, fine platters to dine off, with only the choicest morsels to tempt her appetite. But . . . she had been too proud to ask for his help, and he had been far too proud, in his jealousy and hurt, that she had called him baseborn and bastard, to offer it. Well, enough of pride. Pride was for fools! And devil take jealousy! He would have no more of either, now that he saw what damage his pride—and jealousy—could do! He swallowed, remembering suddenly that her lady mother had died in childbirth. His gray eyes darkened with fear. If his pig-headed stupidity had cost him his bride and his bairn both, he would never forgive himsel'. He couldna live without her! The past few months had proved as much . . .

"Weary or nay, ye will do it, Catriona," he told her sternly, "for I willna let ye die and leave me alone! I command ye to push, and push ye will!"

"What?" she cried, her green eyes wide with questions—and no little indignation. "Ye think t' order me aboot in this, too, ye bossy lout!"

"You heard me, lass! I willna end up a miserable, lonely auld battlehorse like yer father, who was too embittered, too filled with pride and hate, t' cherish his little daughter after his woman died! I love ye, ma feisty wee dragon, ma wren, ma Queen o' Elfland! And I willna let ye die! Marry, I forbid it! Hold fast t' me, hold fast! I swear if ye do, I'll never let ye go! Draw strength from my strength, heart o' my heart, and bring our bairn forth. Come. Obey me this once, bossy or nay. Push, my dearling, *push!*"

His words, his fierce expression, his obvious sincerity, unlocked the chains of wounded pride that had imprisoned her heart. All the bitterness she had erected like battlement walls about her came tumbling down. He had called her heart of his heart. He had vowed he loved her and would never let her go! Said that he couldna bear t' live without her. Oh, it was enough, and more.

"And I—I—love—ye, even if ye are a great, bossy dark brute, Roarke Mac Gilchrist! And I didna mean what I said! Ye must believe, I dinna care if ye were baseborn, or fatherless, truly I dinna—!"

Her vows were cut short as another pain engulfed her. Her eyes locked to his, she gripped his arms, clung fiercely to him as if she were drowning, and he, a passing spar. "Roarke! Oh, Roarke, *help me!*"

Her face contorted. She tucked her chin down against her chest. Her shoulders hunched as she bore down, and then, blessed miracle, a burning pain seared through her like the touch of a red-hot iron. But she was no longer alone in her travail. His arms were there to brace upon. His eyes were filled with love and encouragement, and with one last push, she did it!

Glad little cries of relief escaped her as the babe's head and shoulders slithered free of her passage.

Exhausted, she sank back on the pallet. With a glad shout, Roarke knelt to support the infant's dark, bloodied head; to wait while the rest of its perfect wee body was born. His expression was rapt with wonder as he stroked the inky curls plastered to its little head. And, as if in protest, the babe — although still not fully born — hiccuped and gave a protesting wail at its father's caress. The sound was more wondrous to Roarke's ears than an angel's song! He threw back his head, and laughed aloud with sheer joy.

"His mother's hair, by God! Aye — and her lungs!"

Another surge, another pulse of her body, and the child was fully born. It slipped free into its father's arms like a fine red salmon swimming upstream, linked to its mother only by the birth cord now. The babe lay cradled in its father's two large hands, red as the sandstone cliffs of the Tweed and wriggling and squirming as lustily as a hound pup.

"A girl?" Catriona prompted, for Roarke said nothing more. She wondered if he'd forgotten her part in this, now that it was over. He simply knelt there, candlelight gleaming in his lustrous black hair as he gazed down at his babe. There was such gentleness in his expression, such wonder, it brought tears to her throat.

"A son," he murmured, shaking his head. " 'Tis a bonnie heir ye've given me, Cat, a wee braw laddie who's perfect in every way — and I thank ye heartily, dearling! Mary Madonna, will ye look at the size o' him! What a chieftain he'll make, ma wee laddie, wi' his father's teachin'!"

Moving with utmost care, he took up the sharpened dirk and the cords he'd made ready. He severed and tied the birth cord. Taking up his own tartan *breacan*, he bundled his son warmly, then proudly placed him in his mother's arms. There'd be time enough to bathe him later, when the afterbirth was delivered. A lifetime, in faith!

For now, the sight of that wee dark head, so tiny against his Catriona's pale face amidst the tartan bundlings, touched his heart as naught had ever done before. Love for the child, love for its mother — his willful, wild Catriona — welled up and overflowed his heart.

Huskily, he told her, "Already he wears the tartan *breacan* of his clan, as befits my heir and namesake. Roarke Camden Mac Gilchrist the Second will never know the shame and sorrow of having his father deny him, as I once did. Nor will he ever feel the anguish that his mother felt, to bear her father's name, but never know his love. Our bairn will be raised with his father's name, and with our love surrounding him, Catriona. And, in its warmth, he'll grow strong and tall t' manhood."

Roarke Camden Gilchrist. Aye. She liked it well. 'Twas a fine, strong name for a fine, strong bairn to grow into. She smiled as she looked up at Roarke, and reached out to clasp his hand and press it to her cheek. He took it in his, and kissed it, and love filled her. How sorely she'd missed him! How she'd longed for him these lonely months! And now, at last, he was here, the bairn safely born, and never had she felt such sweet contentment as she did now! She was exhausted, but both pain and weariness would soon pass into memory, she knew. What would remain was the recollection of the moment when he'd looked into her eyes and held her tightly, and sworn he'd love her always, for she'd known he meant it with all his heart.

There would be other babes to join wee Roarke—she knew it as surely as day followed night. She and Roarke would create them, would share a passion so sweet, their children would be the heroes—and heroines—of whom Scottish legends were told . . .

"When ye're rested a wee bit, we'll go home t' Corbin, wife. Hal bade Hugh bring a cart and follow him here, so the pair o' ye may ride the way in comfort." He grinned. "My lady mother should be returned from Glenmuir by then—and in a fine spate that she missed her first grandbairn's birth, *if* she can wrest her thoughts from her handsome Hamish Frazier!"

He knelt down, and kissed her lips, brushing damp strands of inky hair away from her face.

"There'll be other babes, I fancy," she said, smiling. She blushed and looked quickly away, embarrassed by her boldness so soon after delivering this babe.

"Aye, my bride. There'll be others," he agreed, and added wickedly, "Wee, fiery dragons and small 'dark brutes' aplenty! Master Longstaff will see t' that, never fear!"

There was a roguish twinkle in his mist-gray eyes as he chucked her beneath the chin. A lusty twinkle that promised endless tomorrows yet to be shared. Days in which to love, to live, to dream—and nights to spend in breathless passion . . .

Epilogue

'Twas a day in the season of spring, the Year of Our Lord 1069, when the Norman fyrds began their invasion of the Scottish Borders. Under cover of darkness, they recklessly ferried or swam their massive destriers across the foaming rush of the Tweed waters at full spate, gaining the opposite banks shortly before sunrise both wet and exhausted, and shivering in the early-morning chill. The taking of Corbin—reputed to be the most impregnable of the mighty Border keeps—was to be their first target.

Foregoing the lighting of cooking fires for fear the Scots would see the smoke and suspect an attack was imminent, they congregated on the river's bank to break the night's fast on cold broken meats, cheese, and hunks of dry bread, all washed down with the finest Norse mead and Saxon ale. Their bellies full, their bodies warming, their pulses beginning to race a little now with the excitement of a battle soon to be fought that day, the Norman knights tamped their high spirits and knelt on the greenward before their bishop. They grew hushed to a man while he offered prayers to God for a swift and honorable victory over the Scots. Then all was hurly-burly as the *écuyers,* the squires, hurried to armor their lord-knights, while the pages brought up their mounts.

Sir Gervaise de Rocher leaned against a tree, awaiting his squire's attentions. He was in foul temper, having learned from the spy he'd sent across the Borders, deep into Scotland, some days before that that cursed Scottish fop, Mac Quinlann, had failed him utterly. So much for a barbaric northerner's empty promises, de Rocher pondered disgustedly, his upper lip curling with contempt. Not one of the powerful keeps he'd promised to deliver the greedy Norman on a platter had he managed to win — not one! Moreover, 'twould appear Mac Quinlann had himself been slain some months before, and so de Rocher would not have even the brief pleasure of teaching the dolt with the point of his sword the cost of making false promises . . .

"Your armor, my lord de Rocher," his squire murmured, speaking softly. He knew de Rocher to be in bad humor, and had no eagerness to feel the weight of his hand or boot this morn.

"A moment more, squire," de Rocher began irritably, turning to face the lad with a disgruntled scowl wreathing his dark face. But as he did so, his eyes narrowed. His attention caught elsewhere, he looked beyond the youth, rather than at him, to a spot high on the craggy red cliffs looming above the Tweed waters. A spot where he thought he'd spied the bright wink of polished metal, glinting between the early-morning mist rising in thick drifts above the cliffs.

"Turn about, squire," he commanded, "and say me true. Do you see a brightness up yonder — the rising sun glinting off a shield boss, mayhap?"

The squire squinted. He looked where the knight

had ordered, but could see nothing. Whatever had been there, if anything, had now gone. "I see naught amiss, my lord," he said earnestly. "There is nothing there."

De Rocher watched the spot for a few moments more, then shrugged. Mayhap he'd been mistaken. Whatever it had been, it was gone now.

"Ready me then, young Guy!" he bellowed. "By the grace of God and my strong right arm, I'll be a landed knight 'ere sunset!"

"It has come! After all this time, sir, it has come!" Tavish declared, gaining the notice of all who sat at the trestles in the hall, breaking the night's fast. His eyes were dancing with excitement, his freckled face flushed with high color.

Roarke sprang to his feet and strode to meet his steward. "The signal, mon?" he demanded, his expression intent, eager.

"Aye, mi'laird! The guard we set on the cliffs signaled but a few moments past. The Normans are coming, sir!"

"And has the signal been passed on? To Dunroth in the west? And east, t' Glenmuir?"

"Aye, sir. 'Tis all as ye ordered. Hugh saw to it, even as he sent his lad t' bring word to me."

"Guid mon. And the garrison?"

"I've roused the garrison, sir. Even now they are turned out in the bailey, ready to depart on your lairdship's command. Their mounts stand waiting beside them."

Roarke grinned. " 'Twould seem those weary months o' drilling paid off, eh, laddie?" he vowed, clapping Tavish across the back and eliciting a broad

505

grin of agreement from the red-haired steward. "See t' my armor, laddie, and we'll be awa'!"

Tavish nodded and took off at a run, while Roarke returned to his bride.

"You should ha'e been a mon, lassie!" he said fondly. "Your notion worked just grand!"

In the days following the Mac Quinlann's death, it had been apparent to Roarke that, when wind conditions were fierce, the methods the Border lairds had agreed upon that long ago April morn for signaling an imminent attack using signal fires or chapel bells, were rendered useless. Both smoke and the sound of tolling bells were swept away. Catriona, anxious to be rid of the hateful mirror that had figured so prominently in an unhappy segment of her past, had suggested to Roarke that her looking glass be cut down into several small pieces of polished metal, and a portion be given to each of the lookouts on the cliffs and keep walls up and down the Borders for signaling. Liking her idea, Roarke had readily agreed and seen it done. For her part, Catriona had secretly prayed her idea would never have to be put into action! Alas, it had, and the day she'd dreaded had come at last . . .

"The Normans?" she whispered, growing paler than she'd been for many months.

"Aye."

"Oh, Roarke, nay!"

"Dinna fear, lassie. They come expecting sheep t' shear, but will find only wolves!" he swore with a wicked grin of relish. "Hamish? Yer honeymoon wi' my lady mother is over, mon! Ye'd best hie home t' Glenmuir, and wi' all haste, lest ye find your castle in ruins 'ere ye bring your lady home!"

"I go, damme ye, Gilchrist, all in guid time!"

Hamish agreed with a scowl. "If my twa braw laddies canna deal wi' a few cursed Normans until I return, then they arena their father's sons! I'll see ye well awa' before we take our leave."

Roarke nodded. He turned then to the womenfolk, who were eying him anxiously. "Jeannie, lass, ye'll see the bairn and my lady safely hidden above, all doors bolted behind ye?"

"Ye dinna need t' fret, my laird," Jeannie promised calmly. "I'll see the lassie obeys ye in this, if she doesna in aught else! I havena found a lady it pleases me t' serve, only to lose her to those Norman leeches!"

Roarke nodded. He'd grown to like the feisty little woman's spirit more and more since Catriona'd asked him to have her brought from Rowanlee as nurse t' their bairn. "Guid lass! You, Hal! Stay wi' the womenfolk. Keep them safe for me, 'ere I return, will ye no', laddie?"

"Aye, master. Ye can count on me!" Hal promised, his scrawny frame puffed up with pride at the confidence Roarke had shown in him.

Roarke nodded in satisfaction. "Then all is seen to. I must make ready."

It seemed but moments later that Roarke was armored. He cut a braw figure with his black hair furling in the breeze, mounted proudly on his snorting battlehorse, which he sat at the head of his clansmen.

Leaning forward in the saddle, Roarke looked across the bailey at his mother—the new Lady of Glenmuir since her wedding to Hamish the Yule before. She stood with her auburn head resting

507

against her husband's burly chest. The Frazier had one arm curled fondly about her waist, Roarke noted, betraying his love for Fionna as true. He need have no fears for her future with the laird o' Glenmuir as her man. That he loved her was plain!

He turned then and looked fondly down at his wife and their sleeping bairn, cradled in her arms. Seeing that he was about to take his leave, capable Jeannie came and took wee Roarke from her so that Catriona might go to her laird's stirrup and give him her kiss of blessing and good fortune, and a favor to take into battle with him.

He leaned down from his saddle and caught her up, pressing his lips to hers in a long and fervent kiss; a kiss she eagerly returned with a soft sigh of regret and yearning at its ending.

"God be wi' ye, my laird!" she whispered, fighting tears as she tucked a strip of the yellow kirtle Roarke loved so well into the chain mail covering his chest. There it would be closest to his heart. "I love ye!" she added fervently. "Never forget it, never doubt it, not for a moment! I'll be here, waiting, when ye return!"

"And I will return—never doubt that, either, my love!" Roarke vowed softly. "I have too much t' live for now t' fail!"

"Nay, my laird Roarke, ye willna be defeated, not in this. Ye canna, for such is the prophecy given t' Auld Morag long since," Hal reassured him with confidence, stepping forward. " 'But for her fairest, brightest blossom,' Mother said, 'the clan McNair will wither and fade,' " he quoted for all to hear. " 'Then will the raven's standard fly high over the Tweed waters, and he that was bastard-born be laird above all!' " The badger-boy chanted the words exactly as Auld Morag had once chanted them to him;

in the singsong tone in which her voices spoke through her. "D'ye see, my laird? The omens favor ye! Ye *canna* fail!"

With a broad grin that made his gray eyes dance, Roarke nodded, laughed, and took the sparkling helm Tavish held out to him.

"Shall we awa', ma friend?" he queried the steward jauntily. "I've a mind t' see these Normans put t' rout right swiftly!"

"Aye, my laird! No more than I! Let's awa'!"

The two men lifted their heavy helms over their heads and gathered their horses' reins in gauntleted fists. With a nod to the ladies, Roarke raised his arm in salute and they rode through the gates of Corbin, into the early-morning mist, to engage the enemy.

Their men marched or rode after them three abreast, clad in their proud clan *breacans*. Andy, the piper, strode along in the van, playing a stirring call t' battle on the *pibroch*, the bagpipes; a lusty skirling that sent a thrill down each man's spine, and fired their thirst for battle.

As if in omen, the wind rose as the clan Gilchrist marched t' war, loudly snapping the pennants that flew from the battlements of Corbin. As one, the little gathering in the bailey below, and those left behind to guard the keep, looked up. They saw the proud raven standards of the laird of Corbin streaming triumphantly on the wind. And as one, they threw off their bonnets or caps and cheered.

Catriona smiled as she took the bairn from Jeannie. Lifting him high, she showed him how his father's standards blew wild and proud o'er the keep. Over the Tweed Waters that embraced the Scottish Borders.

"Look, my dearling!" she whispered. "Will ye look!

509

Auld Morag spoke truly, my bonnie! Your father will yet be laird above all — even as he's laird o' my heart!"